FORGED BY HEART AND CLAWS

FORGED BY HEART AND CLAWS

JEN L. GREY

ANYA

Anya
An Imprint of Meredith Wild LLC

Cover Design by Covers By Juan

Paperback ISBN: 979-8-88953-203-3

CHAPTER ONE

The floor of the sanctuary-like hall shook so hard that my teeth rattled, despite Vad's arms and dark, leathery wings surrounding me. My stomach roiled, and my pulse hammered.

You don't know what you've done. The words my many-greats-grandfather had spoken moments ago rang in my ears, along with the screams of the guests who had joined us for Vad's coronation and our wedding.

What had I done? He'd never told me why I couldn't marry Vad and become his Shadow Queen, so what the fuck did that even mean?

A rumbling crack rocked my body, and I placed my hands on Vad's chest and pushed back from him to get a better look.

Briar, no, Vad linked through our new fated-mate bond, trying to pull me to his chest once more, though I fought him, the strange added weight of the crown atop my head pressing down hard. Blood trickled down my cheek from where the sharp tips of the crown had dug into my scalp just moments before the earthquake happened.

The discomfort vanished when I saw why he'd said that.

The palace was falling apart. Shattered glass and slick oil streaked the floor. Some of the guests were flying away through a massive hole that had formed in the ceiling. Other people were trying and failing to use magic against the fire that had broken out where the massive chandelier had fallen. Their panic increased as their magic continued not to work.

What was this? Why had it happened when Vad placed the crown on my head?

As if Fate had a wicked sense of humor, the earthquake stopped as quickly as it had started, and the fires extinguished for no apparent reason. Thick coils of smoke rose from the singed red carpet and charred benches.

My lungs ached, and Vad's worry and distress pulsed through our bond, adding to my own panic.

Eerie silence settled over the room, and my wolf nudged for my attention. Something silver glimmered out of the corner of my eye, and I turned toward the dais where the wedding and coronation were supposed to take place and looked up. On the back wall above it, a shining silver stag shone on a black banner with the black shadow-furred wolf banner below it.

I inhaled, and Vad followed my gaze.

For a moment, everything seemed to still.

The stag gleamed as if lit from behind the banner. A lump formed in my throat. Were my eyes playing tricks on me?

Its multi-pronged antlers shifted, and the woven silver lines lifted off the fabric like thread becoming flesh. My breath caught, and nerves prickled down my arm. Something about it called to me.

My right hand tingled, and I tore my gaze from the stag to the fiery butterfly tattoo on top of my hand and wrist. It pulsed and flared, the wings fluttering within my flesh, their gentle rhythm rippling despite my body feeling weighted down. "Vad," I gasped and pulled my hand closer to me.

His arms flexed, keeping me tight against him, but when he saw my hand, his body somehow became more rigid.

Something sharp pricked against my lower back and the nape of my neck where his hands sat.

The stag's hooves struck the marble floor of the wrecked hall with a resounding echo. Its black eyes focused on me, and it walked in our direction, its hooves clicking as the air thickened until it was hard to breathe.

Its silver form radiated soft light, and my wolf stirred, hackles rising in caution. She wasn't sure what to make of this creature any more than I was, but she wasn't hunkering down or surging forward like it was an actual threat... at least, not yet.

The hoofbeats resonated through me as it approached, the stag's eyes glistening like liquid night as it stared into my soul. Vad's arms remained around me, but I pulled out of his grip, taking a step toward the stag.

What the feck, Briar? That's the Guardian Beast of the Aurelines. Be careful. It could destroy you. Vad stepped in front of me and spread his wings, cutting off my view of the animal.

Don't fight it unless it gives us a reason to, I linked with Vad. *It feels as if it's calling me.*

Vad's wings extended a little farther, and he inhaled. *I won't allow anyone or anything to harm you again.*

I need you to trust me. It's coming toward us anyway.

For a moment, he remained in position, but when I touched his back, he lowered his wings.

The stag was ten feet away.

My heart pounded, and Vad's hands clenched at his sides as the massive stag stepped in front of me. I tipped my head to meet its gaze, and my stomach clenched. This magical animal had to be at least twenty feet tall.

It lowered its head toward me, and my entire body tightened.

Vad flinched and raised his clawed hands with a deep, threatening growl.

The stag pressed its muzzle against my head, the touch soft as velvet. Every nerve within me seemed to ignite at once.

Wait, I linked as the warmth of its breath swept over my face and the spot where my pulse raced in my throat.

Huffing, Vad didn't strike but kept his stance ready to attack.

A cold jolt of energy pierced my skull, ran down my spine and into my limbs, and spiraled back until it focused in my wrist. The blood in my veins surged hotter, and yet my wrist remained chilled. My heart pounded as rage flowed through the bond from Vad.

"Stop now." Vad swiped at the stag's throat, but his hand went through it as if it were a ghost. The stag's ears flicked back, but it didn't look at him.

Vad lurched back as if an unseen hand had thrust him away. He lunged for me, but something pulled him farther back until he was about twelve feet away. When it released him, he lurched forward but stopped short as if he'd hit an invisible wall. His steel gray eyes flashed as he snarled, but no sound left his mouth either.

I wanted to help him, but I couldn't. My hand ached, and I jerked my gaze downward and found that the butterfly had stopped moving. A greasy sensation sloshed in my stomach, and a sharp, icy scent like mint and junipers filled my lungs. A pained cry rose within me, but my voice locked in my throat.

Vad pounded against the invisible barrier, screaming at the stag. His cold fear rushed through the warm spot that connected us, shrinking and mixing with my pain.

I tried pulling away from the stag, but I couldn't. My legs refused to move, my feet seeming glued in place with the stag still towering over me. Vad's rage and fear coursed through me, bellowing inwardly.

I'm all right. Even though this entire encounter was

uncomfortable, a part of me knew that it didn't need to end.

It hurt you! I will kill it for that. Vad narrowed his eyes and breathed heavily.

The stag huffed and stomped one glowing hoof as if in warning.

The magic continued to swirl inside me, but I had to calm Vad down. I couldn't bear feeling how scared and upset he was.

I tugged on the warm spot in my chest where Vad and I were linked, and pushed soothing calm toward him.

Some of his tension ebbed, and the stag's velvety nose brushed my forehead again, its soft fur tickling me. The stiffness in my wrist intensified, and I shut down my connection to Vad enough that he wouldn't feel my emotions so clearly.

Another blast of warm air struck my head and chilled before the stag drew back.

My chest heaved, and I pressed my other hand to my wrist, fingertips brushing the butterfly mark, which had gone still.

The ink was locked in place, and my skin crawled. I'd gotten used to the way the tattoo moved, and now it felt like I'd lost something.

Pressure built. The air tasted harsh and sharp, as if lightning was about to strike. My breath frosted, and every hair on my body stood on end.

Are you all right? The link between Vad and me was calmer now, but his words were clear. His posture remained tense.

The room darkened, and the air dulled, reinforcing that the stag and its magic had vanished. But the discomfort running through me hadn't. I did find relief that there wasn't so much pressure on my body.

My wolf-shifter eyes adjusted to the darkness, and I turned to Vad. *Yes.* I paused as my throat tightened. How had I not noticed this before? *Your shadows are gone. Are you hiding them?* My stomach clenched, and the discomfort echoed within me, as if it were trying to get me to focus on something.

"Run!" His expression twisted into agony, and his wings flared. He lunged upward and flew over me, then dropped.

I spun around and saw an orange-haired man running toward me. "You stole our magic, you bitch!" His words, shrill with rage, cut through the silence.

I searched for a weapon as he removed a dagger and jumped. Vad spread his wings to shield me and reached for the attacker.

"No!" I exclaimed as the dagger cut through his wing. His pain exploded through me, and blood hit my face and body as I pivoted around him and jumped on the fae's back.

The attacker stumbled forward and fell into Vad. Vad stumbled back, and something clanked to the ground. The bloody dagger slid a few feet away from where it had fallen from Vad's wing. But before I could do anything, the fae dropped to the floor and rolled on top of me, closer to the dagger. His weight compressed my lungs, and before I could fight back, something sharp struck the side of my stomach.

Then his body lifted from mine, and I sucked in a large breath and reached for my side, where the fucking prick had stabbed me. Thankfully, my dress with all its layers had partly protected me. I grabbed the handle of the dagger and pulled it out of the fabric.

"No one harms Briar." Vad bared his teeth, his fangs longer than I'd ever seen them. He held the man by the throat. "Now you must die."

Blood spurted from Vad's wing, but he didn't seem to notice. His claws cut into the man's flesh, puncturing and crushing the attacker's throat. Then Vad slammed our attacker's body to the floor with a sickening crunch.

"Are you okay?" Vad rushed over to me, the man's blood covering his hands.

I looked at the wound. It hurt, but I'd had worse. Still, blood trickled from my side. "I'm fine. What about you?" My attention went to his wing.

"Also fine. But we need to get you out of here. Go through the door on the groom's side of the dais. Back to the left. Use the dagger for protection." Vad pushed me in that direction.

"Traitor prince!" One of the Shadow Fae guards lunged forward with a halberd pointed at Vad's chest.

"Stand down." Vad thrust an arm out to keep me back as he seized the halberd with the other hand and wrenched it to one side, sending the black armored guard staggering as the spiked blade slammed into one of the dark wood benches.

The guard's armor clinked and creaked as he struggled to regain his balance. "You both deserve death. This is your fault! You let your kingdom down for a human."

Vad snarled and jammed the halberd deeper into the wood.

I ducked around Vad and stabbed the guard in the throat where the black plate armor ended at his chest and the helmet started. Blood spurted from the wound, and he gurgled, lurching back. The dagger came free with a sickening squelch.

Madness and chaos exploded within the shattered hall. Most people were trying to escape, and terrified screams came from all directions.

On the dais, Shadow Council leader Vyraetos tried in vain to call for order, hands lifted. "Everyone, please, calm down. We will sort through this. Return to your seats until we light torches for those without shadow sight." His voice boomed out yet failed to carry far over the roar of panic and violence.

"The traitors are moving!" one of the Shadow Council members shouted, pulling her hood lower over her face. "They're taking over the palace!"

"Vad and the beast are the real traitors! They've destroyed the vestment!" another Shadow Council member screamed.

"All loyal to the true Shadow Fae, capture the false prince and his whore prisoner!"

"Or kill them!" another shrill voice screeched.

"Defend the king and queen!" A large Shadow warrior, who had been near the dais, lifted his sword. His wings snapped out in a defensive posture. A few of the black-winged guards snapped forward, halberds pointed at the crowd, though they looked about with uneasy glances.

Briar, run! Vad's voice crashed through my skull like thunder. *Get into that room and close the door. I'll be right behind you.*

Not without you. We aren't getting separated again! I adjusted my grip on the dagger. More blood dripped down my iridescent gown, soaking the layers of beautiful pastel fabric and delicate butterfly patterns while the panicked outcry continued.

Another Shadow Fae lunged at Vad, this one a woman in a dark-pink gown with long, artificial claw-tip nails. Vad punched her in the chest and knocked her back. She staggered away but caught her balance enough to lunge again and slash at his face. She caught air, momentum swinging her sideways. He closed the distance and slashed her throat with his claws.

It happened so quickly that I hadn't been able to help. Yet my entire body tensed from him being attacked once more.

Vad took my hand and dragged me toward the door. *We need to leave as quickly as possible,* he linked.

Deep cracks had formed in the floor throughout the hall. The towering double doors had twisted and splintered, and a large piece of stone had pinned one shut. A heavy pounding sounded on the far side of the door as someone tried to get in. Most of the guests were still trying to flee—some on foot, some flying. Those who I assumed had no night vision fumbled around with their hands out, staggering and groping their way through the dark. Most everyone's faces were marred with scars and blemishes that seemed to have just appeared now that their glamour had failed, their appearances ragged.

I cast a look around the hall for my friends to see what state they were in.

Princess Elara, Vad's sister, lay on the dais, one pale hand lifted, Vad's friend Silus supporting her head. Her glamour had fallen away, and her black wings had collapsed, the right one twitching. Vyraetos knelt beside her with his palm pressed to her head and his other hand guiding Silus's hand over hers. He whispered something to Silus, and Silus shook his head, his gaze fixed on Elara's face as he blinked rapidly as if straining to see.

Most of the Aureline Council members had vanished, along with many of the Shadow Council members. Bride candidate Calla Lily had disappeared as well, but Kaylen stood near the door between two non-winged Aureline guards who were arguing with two of the Shadow guards.

The remaining Shadow Fae guards sparred and fought one another as some shouted to protect the king and others shouted to kill us. A black-armored Shadow Fae without a helmet and encircled by four other guards held up his sword. "Enough!" he shouted. "Remember your loyalties. Get to the king and queen!"

Most didn't respond, and it wasn't hard to see where the lines were falling. We were outnumbered.

"Briar! Run!" Many-Greats shouted as he groped his way between benches toward me. "Don't let them near you! Don't trust anyone. Especially not the Aurelines!"

My heart twisted, and bitterness filled my mouth. He had the fucking nerve to tell me not to trust the Aurelines? No kidding! I'd learned that in prison.

Finally, I spotted my bride-candidate friends behind him, feeling their way through the benches toward the aisle.

Guards entered through the gaps in the twisted door, one

at a time, each armed and carrying a torch. Shouts and bellows from beyond the doors confirmed more were coming. Most of the Aurelines had vanished.

"Rhielle! Girls!" I shouted as Vad continued dragging me toward the door. "Follow my voice!" There was no way I was leaving any of them behind. Other than Rhielle, who was Shadow Fae, none of them could see in the darkness.

Another guard charged and swung his spear toward my chest, with another following hot behind him. I grabbed the spear and shoved it to the side as hard as I could, causing him to stagger forward and jam the point into the bench to the left of me.

Vad drove his palm into the guard's face with a sickening crunch that made my stomach roil. Pain shot through our connection, and I moved closer to his side as blood poured from the guard's nose. When Vad removed his hand, I saw a deep gash from where the man's helmet had cut into his palm.

Vad didn't pause; he plunged his claws through the guard's eye sockets. "Do not touch her!"

The second guard raced toward Vad, club raised. I jumped and jammed the dagger into the guard's armpit as he swung for Vad's shoulders.

The guard groaned and missed Vad by inches. Vad spun around, his eyes darker than a stormy night. He caught the club, just as a blur of dark purple to my left caught my eye.

I spun around as a tall Shadow Fae in an ornate purple surcoat leapt at me, teeth bared and hands reaching for my throat. Several scars seared his left cheek, and a long scar cut across one eyebrow, ugly and red. "Filthy beast!" he spat. "You've destroyed everything!"

I shifted my weight to my back foot, pretended to move to the left, and positioned the dagger at my chest, ready to strike. His eyes widened, and he tried to shift back as he lifted his arm, but I'd already jabbed toward his neck. I clipped his right hand and forearm, cutting into silk and flesh.

He lunged again, screaming like a wild animal, eyes blazing.

I dodged out of his way, spun, and kicked him in the backside. He crashed into the floor and sprawled out, and a sickening thwap rang in my ears as blood spilled from his head.

A sour taste filled my mouth. The scent of blood sat heavy on my tongue.

We weren't even close to being safe.

I scanned the room and found more guards running toward us from the back of the chamber as the pounding on the splintered door got louder and the twisted wood started to fracture as people fought to break it in. I suspected they weren't going to be on Vad's side.

Vad snapped the neck of another guard and used the man's corpse as a shield. Another winged guard attacked, his sword striking the corpse's armor and sliding off. But Vad's gaze snapped to me and the noble who'd come at me.

His steel gray bloodshot eyes glittered with rage as he bared his teeth, fangs fully revealed. The dark purple marks beneath his eyes indicated he hadn't slept in days. Growling, he slammed the corpse into the next guard, knocking his sword aside, then grabbed the guard's helmet at the neck and twisted.

For now, we were safe. But for how long?

I can't leave without my friends, I linked as I searched for them again.

I located Rhielle as she was grabbing her lover Veralt's arm and saying something. He gave a curt nod and jumped up on the nearest bench, then leaped into the middle of the aisle closest to the doors and charged forward.

"I can't see anything, and my magic won't work even a little!" Velessa called out. Still cradling her wounded arm in the sling, she bumped into Yuki as she tried to find her way along the benches. Yuki steadied her and said something I couldn't catch.

Rhielle shoved past Many-Greats, grabbed Velessa by her good arm, and dragged her through the narrow space. As she passed Yuki, Rhielle grabbed her with her other hand.

Vad whistled two high notes, three lower notes, and one high note. Silus lifted his head, his expression grim. Vad's other—and in my opinion, better—trusted friend Thalen jerked toward us. He had one hand gripped tight around Myantha's wrists, and she was pleading with him, tears streaking her cheeks. He then adjusted his grip, knelt, fumbled around, and snatched up the green-dipped blade that had fallen out of Myantha's dress. He tugged her forward, shaking his head and saying something I couldn't catch. She pulled back and dug her heels into the rumpled red carpet.

A flash of concern cut through me at the sight of that dagger. It looked like the ones the assassins had used in the third trial. Why did Myantha have one?

Quen shrieked as she tried again and again to make fire. Only two small sparks and a bit of smoke trickled from her palms. "Whatever happened, I'm blaming Kaylen!"

Holding her hands out, Thalira tried to make her way forward in the darkness toward my voice. Her long blue skirt trailed along the floor, and she stumbled over a bump in the red rug that ran down the center. "Briar!" she called out. "Briar, what happened?" She froze, lifting her hands defensively as Veralt charged forward with heavy steps. Quen spun in their direction as well, grasping at Thalira but missing.

Scowling, Thalira held out her arms at Veralt and commanded, "Whoa! Stand back, whoever you are, or I will cut you!"

Veralt caught hold of Thalira's arm and replied, "If you cut me, you'll die. I'd prefer you just follow. This way, ladies." He grabbed Quen, too, and pulled both forward.

Rhielle forced her way past two fleeing guests, her wings brushing the walls as she dragged Yuki and Velessa with her. Their stumbling steps scraped on stone, their bodies colliding as they tried to keep up.

Two guards pushed through a gap in the door, the wood splintering around them. They carried torches that cast eerie light into the hall. "The magic is gone! All of the magic is gone! The portals have died."

Thalen broke into a run as soon as the weak torchlight filled the room, his grip still locked around Myantha's wrist. She stumbled after him, heels dragging over the carpet. His other hand clutched the green-dipped blade, his expression like carved stone.

"Treason!" someone shouted from farther away. More screams echoed off the cracked stone walls.

Guards continued to push through the opening in the door, the heavy tramping of booted feet on the other side announcing that there were even more to come.

Many-Greats raced toward me. I adjusted my grip on the dagger, half tempted to lash out at him. But now wasn't the time or place. I needed answers. No more riddles.

Silus heaved Elara into his arms. Her head sagged against his shoulder, her lips pale, her breath shuddering in short gasps. Vyraetos moved with him, one hand pressed to her side, his jaw locked tight as he whispered something. They darted through the doorway on the left. Rhielle was close behind as Vad shoved me forward. Veralt passed us, pulling Quen and Thalira forward. Thalen had nearly caught up to us as well.

His wings flaring out, Vad seized my arm and shoved me ahead of him. "Move! Now!"

I stumbled forward, feeling his hand at the small of my back as we raced toward the dais. I dared one more glance over my shoulder to see that another dozen guards had broken through, all charging down the main aisle. I glimpsed Vad's wings again as we ran. The coloration was uneven, mottled with darker patches and streaks. The talons at the ends had lengthened and curved into hooks, sharp enough to tear through flesh.

"Briar!" Velessa called out as Rhielle dragged her and Yuki through the doorway. "Faster! There are too many of them!"

Rhielle reeled her back in as Veralt charged through the doorway with Thalira and Quen in tow, and Thalen pulled Myantha in as well.

We reached the steps of the dais, and I nearly tripped on the cracked marble. Vad's hands steadied me, then pushed me forward again. "Get inside!"

I scrambled up the steps, heart hammering. The stiffness in my wrist ached now, the butterfly tattoo still frozen. Many-Greats skidded to a stop next to me and pushed me forward. "I will explain everything that I can," he said roughly.

Yeah, he would.

I bolted through the doorway and into a dimly lit chamber, blood pounding in my ears.

The iridescent fabric of my wedding gown swished around my ankles as I spun around, reaching for Vad.

He was less than three strides away, his massive wings tucked tight against his back as he charged forward, guards moving fast behind him. One of the spear holders halted and lifted his weapon.

"He's throwing the spear!" I exclaimed.

I grabbed Vad's arm to drag him in faster, and as soon as he was over the threshold, he slammed the wooden door shut with a bone-jarring boom.

A split second later, the spear punched through the wood with a sickening crunch...and agony exploded through our bond.

Chapter Two

Sharp pain shot through my left wing as something pierced it and ran through my shoulder, higher than the last wound. Hot blood poured down my chest, and I growled. I glanced down. A wooden shaft protruded from my shoulder, the spearhead sticking out about six inches in front of me. I struggled to move forward and knew what I had to do. I grabbed the shaft.

Don't rip it out yourself. You'll make the wound much worse, Briar said in my mind as her worry pulsed through the bond.

We can't stay here. I had to get Briar and Elara to safety as quickly as possible, which meant removing the spear. I yanked on the shaft, trying to pull it out, but pain burned through my wing and shoulder, and nausea roiled in my stomach.

I stumbled, and my wing flinched, adding to my agony. I groaned.

"Vad, what's wrong?" Thalen called loudly from somewhere in the crowd, not worrying about formalities.

Velessa yelped. "Don't yell next to my ear like that. You scared me."

"I'm fine." The last thing I needed was for Thalen to fly through everyone to reach me. We didn't need any additional chaos just because he couldn't see me.

"As fine as anyone with a spear stuck through his wing and shoulder could be." Verault rolled his eyes and smirked.

"What?" Elara gasped. "Vad?"

"We need to treat him—" Silus started.

"No, we're not treating me here. It's not as bad as it seems. We need to escape before all of us get injured or killed," I spat. These people were after Briar and me, and I refused to let her get more injured than she already was. I'd happily take another spear as long as she remained unhurt and standing.

Quen took a shaky breath. "Which way do we go? I can't see a damn thing."

"Just stay put. Vad can't go on like this," Rhielle answered.

Heavy thuds pounded against the other side of the door. "Open this door at once, and surrender yourselves to the custody of the Shadow Kingdom."

"I am your king," I snarled over my shoulder. Furious as I was, perhaps we could play this out and stall them. Every second was going to count. "You would dare to speak to me in this fashion?"

"You have betrayed the kingdom, sir," the guard said. "It is our duty to take you into custody with the rest of the traitors. You will be given a fair trial. If you do not surrender, we will be forced to break down this door and take you captive by force. If you or those with you die, it will be on your head. Surely you do not want more of your people's blood shed?"

Bryn moved toward us, blinking hard like he was trying to see. "Briar, the two of us need to get out of here *immediately*."

The feck she'd be going with him. The Aureline Council leader was the reason we were all in this mess. I clutched the shaft harder, getting ready to yank.

Stop that. She scowled and narrowed her eyes. *You're going to make yourself bleed more.*

I released a tight breath. *Briar, you need to--*

If you're about to tell me to go on without you, stop. I refuse to leave you behind. We've been through too much, and I'm staying by your side. Briar touched my arm, her concern spilling into my chest. "I won't go anywhere without everyone here."

As if Fate wanted to emphasize the horrifying nightmare I'd put her through, flecks of blood in her wavy, copper hair caught my eye, and I noticed her green eyes were glassy with unshed tears, her gown stained in crimson. My heart contracted painfully. She'd gone through so much because of me.

"Sir, what is your answer?" the guard outside demanded, his voice cracking slightly. "Don't force us to break down this door."

I rolled my eyes, sneering. They made it sound so reasonable. "Do you truly expect me to surrender?"

Veralt rubbed his hands together and stepped up beside me.

"Let's handle this then," he grumbled, grabbing the spear's shaft behind my wings and snapping it in two.

"Fecking void!" Painful spasms vibrated through my wings. I grew weaker, but at least his removal method was faster and caused less damage than sawing through it. The tip of the spear pushed out farther in front of me, dark and slick with my blood. The metallic tang with sweet undertones filled the chamber.

My head spun. Feck, that had hurt. But I couldn't stay pinned to the door. Especially with Briar refusing to leave me.

A series of heavy thuds vibrated through the wood and rattled the hinges. It sounded like wood against wood, so they had probably grabbed a bench to use as a battering ram. We had to barricade the door and slow them down as much as possible.

"I just want it known. If we die, I'm blaming Kaylen," Quen muttered. "I feel like this is all her fault."

"Same, but I think this is beyond her powers." Velessa

massaged the wrist of the arm she had in the sling. "At least, I hope so."

Veralt grabbed a couch and shoved it in front of the door. Rhielle removed one of the decorative swords from the wall and thrust it at a diagonal angle through the door handle and the bottom loop of a lamp frame to help secure the door. Those swords weren't any good for fighting as the blade was too dull to even cut cheese, but the metal was solid. She seized the second one and put it through at the opposite angle.

Yuki hugged herself, her mouth twisting as if she'd tasted a lemon. "No one wants Kaylen to have that kind of power, but what's going on with Calla Lily? She was so friendly. I thought she was sweet. She hugged me."

Thalira cast a soft look at Yuki. "Not everyone who hugs is a friend."

These ladies should be quieter, but I knew if I demanded silence, it would make them more antsy and talkative. Besides, it wasn't as if the guards didn't know we were in here.

I decided to pretend to put them to use. "Someone, make sure that other door is locked." I gestured weakly at the door on the far side of the room.

Vyraetos checked it and returned to where Silus was holding Elara near the cluster of Briar's friends. Myantha and Thalen stood whispering together in the corner on the other side of the chairs and couch. Tears glinted on her cheeks.

Now to determine the rest of our plan, which meant I had to get this fecking thing out of me.

I drew in a ragged breath, adjusting my grip on the six inches of shaft between the spearhead and my chest. If I thought about it, I wouldn't do it, so I didn't pause. I yanked—hard.

Stinging and burning sensations rippled through the sensitive flesh, and blood gushed everywhere. Wincing inwardly, I clenched my jaw. The bleeding would stop relatively fast because the spear had missed major vessels. But feck, the pain had me wanting to lie down and rest.

That wasn't a possibility. I steadied myself and took in our surroundings, trying to formulate a better plan.

The groom's chamber was simple, with little that we could use for the next phase of our escape. A bureau and vanity with a large oblong mirror dominated the left wall, and a sitting area on the opposite side contained a small settee, ottoman, end table, and two velvet chairs. The door I stood before was opposite another door at the far end, both firmly shut. The torches had guttered out, but lighting them now would allow light to seep under the door and warn the people on the northern side, cutting off our time to escape. We had to get out of here before the guards from the Ceremonial Hall had time to warn the others and access the private hall that connected to this chamber.

We had a few minutes to make this work, and no option for failure.

"Let's get this door better barricaded." I set the spear aside and rubbed the wound across the top of my shoulder, wondering whether I needed a makeshift bandage. My wing would stop bleeding soon, but I didn't want the shoulder wound to leave a blood trail.

I clenched my teeth and ripped a thick strip of fabric from my surcoat just as another loud jolt jarred the door. Angry shouts sounded, as if more guards were gathering. Good. Let them stay focused here.

Clicking her tongue, Briar took the strip from my hands and tied off my shoulder wound proficiently. My stomach clenched. I knew so little about the woman standing before me, yet I felt as if I'd known her forever. When her fingers brushed my shirt, the jolt of our connection surged through me, even with fabric between us. It eased some of the pain.

"How does it feel?" She looked me straight in the eye.

"Perfect." I smiled and pecked her lips before crossing to the dresser and pulling it toward the door. My wounded wing screamed as I strained, and the legs grated across the stone floor.

Veralt seized the second couch and dragged it over to shore up the first one.

Moving to the opposite side, Veralt lifted with me. Together, we placed the heavy wooden dresser on the new couch, the drawers clacking as they shifted. Loud curses and bellows on the other side of the door confirmed the guards were trying to batter down the door. But that would take them a while.

Veralt grabbed another chair and balanced it on top of the pile as another heavy thud shook the door. "Come get us, fecking assholes. I'll use your corpses for torches!"

"Can't we get some lights in here so we can see?" Quen asked. "We can't do *anything.*"

"If you can find a light source, be my guest. At least until we depart," I said. "But the groom's preparation chambers aren't typically outfitted with flint or fire sources."

"Great." Quen huffed. She folded her arms over her chest and shuddered. "No problem. I love not being able to see."

Thalira fumbled about and then gripped her shoulder. "We'll get our powers back somehow, and the light too. Then we'll deal with Calla Lily."

"Maybe we can set her on fire." Quen arched a brow.

"Maybe there's another explanation. I don't believe Myantha tried to kill Briar—maybe Calla Lily was a pawn too? Someone could be forcing her hand. She gave such a good hug." Yuki shrugged. Her grip around herself tightened. "I miss my sisters."

"Calla Lily is a traitor and must not be trusted." Bryn reached out and grabbed Rhielle's arm as she passed him.

"Briar, I can—"

"She's over there." Rhielle removed his hand from her arm and stepped back. Stooping, she hefted up the ottoman and carried it to pile on top of the bureau now perched precariously on the couch.

"I'm fine, and we aren't leaving without the others." Briar crossed to him and took his hand, then turned it over to reveal tattered cloth and bloodstains. "Did someone try to stab you?" Her brow creased.

A part of me hoped they had. The bastard deserved some pain for what he'd done to us and our kingdom.

Yet, he scoffed. "Only a flesh wound. This is far more important." His auburn hair was wild and unkempt, and a scrape along his arm and a rent in his formal gray robe suggested someone had tried to stab him and mostly failed. It was less of a wound than what I wanted to inflict on him.

He said, "Briar, everything I've done, I've done to protect you. You must believe me."

"Now isn't the time." Briar's nose wrinkled. "I want to hear everything once we're safe."

Who is he? I linked to her once more, not sure what this connection between us was but grateful for it nonetheless.

He's like my great-great-great—hell, I'm not even sure how many greats—grandfather. Briar's hands rested on her waist.

He's your family? I bit back a scoff, but the truth sat hard in my stomach. She was an Aureline. Did she know what that meant? And I'd jeopardized not only my kingdom but all of Nytheria. *Are you sure we can trust him?*

I don't know for certain, especially after this. Her forehead lined, and she frowned. *But I need to know why he told me not to tell anyone that I was from his line and what me being crowned has to do with all this chaos.*

My lungs worked more easily again, but the fact that she

had hidden him from me still gave me pause. Perhaps there was more she hadn't told me or thought to tell me.

My heart stung a little at the betrayal, but I pushed it away. Even with everything, I would've made the same decision. She was meant to rule by my side. *We will speak of this further when we're in private.* We were going to run out of time. "Veralt, see if you can spot any movement through that exit, but don't open the door. There's a mirror in one of the drawers."

Veralt grunted an agreement and rummaged through the drawers. When he found the slim mirror, he carried it to the door. He dropped down to the floor and slid the mirror under.

The guards on the other side of the main entrance battered the door again. *BOOM!* From the shouts and yells on the other side, a decent crowd had formed. But not all of them were there, which was the problem.

I gritted my teeth. "We're moving to a safer location. If you can see in the shadows, help guide those who can't. If we get into a fight, the sightless ones need to find a wall and get down. Do not stab or strike anyone unless they're attacking you or you're certain they're your enemy." The last thing we needed was friendly stabbings.

"We don't have much time," Vyraetos said from the center of the room. He was next to Silus and Elara and had his fingers on Elara's throat as if taking her pulse, her head resting on Silus's shoulder. Briar's friends blocked my sister mostly from my sight, so all I could really see was her dark and now-thinned hair. "The princess needs to be stabilized. She requires rest and warmth."

I took Briar's hand—I refused to be separated from her—and the two of us pressed past Quen, Thalira, and Yuki. "We'll get her somewhere safer and warmer as soon as possible. Is she bleeding? Everyone, check yourself for blood or anything that needs to be tended so we don't leave a trail."

Briar sucked in a breath, and a moment later, I saw what had startled her. This was the first time I'd seen Elara up close without her glamour. She looked so frail, even bonier than I had expected, her skin paper-thin and bone white. Bruises and sores marred her hands, and likely her sleeves hid far more. Her wings twitched, the muscles so atrophied that, without a miracle, she would never fly again. What was it with the two most important people in my life keeping secrets from me?

Silus's gaze flicked in my direction, but I knew he couldn't actually see me through the darkness. His jaw was so tight, I was surprised his teeth hadn't broken, and I had no doubt that, as soon as we were safe, he'd be having a word with me. He likely blamed both Briar and me for this.

The sense of urgency to get out of here rose even more within me.

"Vad, I'm fine." Elara's voice was strained, and she slurred her words. Silus held her tighter, his cheek against the top of her head.

Briar slipped to the other side of her and placed a hand on Elara's arm. Her lips pressed into a tight line as her brow furrowed with concern. *She needs rest and treatment.*

I know. I squeezed Elara's hand gently, feeling how much more delicate her bones were. Had she withered even more since we'd last spoken?

Icy fear ripped through me. Her pulse throbbed in her throat, but it was threadier than it should be. My lack of shadows and magic coursing through my veins struck me like the spear had through my wing. No longer could I offer her my own strength. Of all that had changed, why did *that* have to be taken away? How was I going to keep my sister alive? She couldn't even draw a little shadow power, and she was fading fast.

I became aware of a stinging pang on my head as blood

rolled down my cheek. Feck, the crowns. As precious as these crowns were, running and fighting while wearing them was a hazard. "Briar, we need to put the crowns somewhere safe." I reached up and removed mine, guilt twisting inside me at the thought of leaving them behind.

Elara lifted her hands weakly. "I can hold them. Let me at least do that. Those were our parents'."

I hesitated, then nodded. With Silus carrying her, the added weight wasn't an issue. "All right. But if you must choose between your life and these crowns, remember your life is more important."

She took my crown and settled it on her chest. Then she accepted the second one from Briar. "It won't come to that."

"Which way should we go?" Veralt pressed with a gruff voice.

I shook my head, trying to clear my thoughts of all the conflicting emotions swirling in my chest.

The absence of my shadows ached throughout my body in a way similar to grief. In the absence of my glamour, I'd noticed other developments, too. My claws and fangs were longer, and my wing talons had grown as well. They gleamed in the dark. Never had they been this defined, even under the glamour. What else had changed from the loss of my magic?

"If you aren't going to tell me, I'll go my own damn way with Rhielle, and we'll leave your asses behind," Veralt growled.

Rhielle smacked his arm lightly. "We're not leaving Briar."

"We can take her with us. I'll throw her over my shoulder," Veralt said.

My gaze snapped to him, and I snarled, baring my teeth. *No one* would take my mate.

Before I could say anything, Briar stepped toward him. She arched a brow and balled her fists. "Try to take me from him, and I will rip your throat out."

"Silus, put me down so you can move faster," Elara mumbled.

"No way." Silus shook his head. "I'm carrying you the whole way."

"We need weapons." Briar bit her lip and looked around.

My attention homed in on Thalen, who was still standing with Myantha and scowling.

"Bind her. We'll interrogate her when we get to safety." Maybe we needed to gag her as well. It was risky to keep her with us, and she would probably try to alert the guards once we made our way out of this second door and toward the royal family's quarters.

"No. Please." Myantha lifted both hands and blinked despite not being able to see. "I didn't do anything. And don't leave me behind. I *swear* I didn't do it!"

Thalen's shoulders tightened, his whole body becoming tense. "She has answers." Thalen looked in my direction despite not actually being able to see me, his words fast and almost desperate. "I'll make sure she behaves and will handle it myself if she doesn't."

"Fine. Keep her close, Thalen. Don't let her near Briar."

Myantha nodded meekly. Thalen's brow tweaked, but he remained silent.

I pointed at her. "If you betray my beloved, I will destroy you without a second thought, and I will ensure you suffer." Then I looked at Thalen. "I need your dagger for Rhielle since she can see in the darkness."

Nodding, he handed it to me, and I passed it to Rhielle. Briar still had her dagger, and I had my claws. Since they insisted on being out, handling any other weapon with finesse would be challenging. Everyone who could see might as well be armed.

Another thunderous crash rocked the door, rattling the

furniture barricade. The dresser slid forward several inches, its legs scraping against the couch.

"Feck them. They're breaking through!" Rhielle darted forward, pressing her shoulder against the furniture pile. Briar joined her, bracing herself against the shifting mass and pushing one of the velvet chairs back into place.

I moved quickly to help them, ignoring the burning pain in my wing as I threw my weight against the barricade. A jagged crack appeared in an upper door panel as another impact shook the frame. The dresser wobbled precariously, threatening to topple. Angry bellows rose as someone shouted for more light.

Briar grunted beside me, her face flushed with exertion. "They're getting angrier."

"Let them waste their energy." I shoved the dresser into a more stable position. "Veralt?"

"It's clear. Far as I can see." He pushed himself up from the ground near the door, then snatched up the broken spear, still wet with my blood. "But it's time to *move*. Do you understand?"

The furniture creaked as we forced it back into place. More wood splintered, and a heavy crack suggested that someone had gotten an axe.

I shoved the couch against the door again, checked to ensure that two swords were still in place, and glanced around at everyone. "Let's go." I gave the furniture barricade one final shove, ensuring it would hold for at least a few more minutes. The door frame creaked under the pressure from the other side, another heavy blow landing.

I thrust my hand into my own pocket to retrieve the keys. When the palace had been built, sigils had been used to protect almost everything, but my own ancestors had insisted that we have traditional locks as well, in case something disrupted the magic. Fate bless them for their foresight.

I thrust the slim key into the lock of the other door and

twisted it. It clicked open, and I eased the door ajar, peering into the darkness beyond. Even with my natural Shadow Fae vision, it took effort to see. The hallway stretched out in both directions, furnished with the odd end table and several oil paintings. The air smelled of incense and smoke, no trace of blood or death. A touch of stale emptiness undercut all of it, as if to remind me that the magic of our kingdom had vanished.

We made our way out slowly, those who could see helping those who couldn't. Veralt took a position near me and strode farther down the corridor, head cocked as he listened. I drew Thalira and Quen out and guided them to the wall, whispering for them to follow it in a straight line until they reached Veralt.

Briar gripped Yuki's and her many-greats-grandfather's hands. Rhielle took hold of Thalen and Myantha, and Vyraetos guided Velessa and Silus out, walking between them while Silus carried Elara. Once they reached the narrower hall, he pressed Velessa in front and put his hand on her shoulder.

A deafening crash against the barricaded door punctuated my orders. The furniture shifted again, more violently this time. Wood splintered.

Feck.

I closed the door, locked it, then grabbed the nearest ebony end table that sat beneath the painting. This wasn't going to hold long, but every second gave us an advantage. I lay the painting on the stone floor and put it at an angle so that it would strike the wall when someone tried the door—with any luck, it would buy us a few minutes—and then I jammed the rug under the door as far as I could.

I slid to the front of the group. Other than Vyraetos, I was the only one with sight who knew the palace, and I was the only one who could see *and* knew where we were going.

The palace was full of intersecting passages, and these were at least finished. I hoped that we could make it to one of the larger halls before a fight broke out. Choke points like this were death traps.

My nostrils flared. This corridor smelled of fear and sweat, our scents mingling. The cracking and pounding against the door of the groom's chamber grew steadily softer and duller. Distant shouts confirmed that the search continued.

I took us down the next hall and up a small flight of stairs toward the older corridors. The cut marble walls were coarser here and pitted with age. It wasn't the fastest route to the royal family's quarters, but it was the least likely path our enemies would search. They'd be planning ambushes, and there would almost assuredly be one set up before the main entrance to the royal family's quarters. The locks would hold for a time, so long as the most trusted servants who had been given those keys could not be found. I had one and Elara another.

A distant crash echoed from behind us—they'd broken through the first door. My pulse quickened, and I took us through another turn in the halls. Every breath and footstep still seemed too loud.

I paused at another intersection, listening. Distant shouts echoed from the main corridors—they were organizing search parties but seemed confused about which direction we'd taken. Good. Let them waste time searching the wrong areas.

We slipped from the narrow passages nearest the outer walls to the broader halls that led to the center of the palace. The pitted black marble became sleek and smooth again. We were nearing the eastern way. Ahead lay a series of halls that went in eight directions. We'd need to be even more cautious. With the numerous walls and open paths, it'd be easier for us to be spotted or ambushed.

A voice from an upcoming side hall cut through the darkness. "Your Majesty." A soldier stepped in front of me, his hand snapping up in a salute. He bowed his head. "Come with me, Your Majesty."

I hesitated, my arm stretched out to make sure Briar stayed behind me. My instincts prickled, warning me that something was off.

He had no wings and no helmet, so he was one of the lower guards. His lighter colored studded leather rather than black-plate armor suggested he was a scout, though he did not wear an insignia. It was little wonder we hadn't heard him. His soft leather boots and lack of metal plates meant he could move silently, even without magic to mask his steps.

"Come with you where?" I asked coldly. "Who are you? Identify yourself."

The guard dipped his head forward, his sleek black hair shifting with the movement. "I am Otnel of the Second Scouting Guard. Please. Come with me. I'll get you to safety."

"Do you swear your loyalty to me?" I stared at him hard, aware of Briar edging closer. Though I could have asked for a vow, I didn't. There was something far simpler and more potent.

"Of course, Your Majesty. I mean no harm to you or your family, and I am wholly loyal to you." He bowed his head lower. "I'll get you to safety."

Briar's hand squeezed my arm. *He's lying.*

That was all I needed. I'd learned about her ability to smell lies when I'd visited her in Colm's prison, and I loved how useful it was now.

I walked alongside him. "Where are we going?"

He cast a look in both directions as he stepped into the intersection of the halls. "Left, to the north near the Night Rose Gate."

I gave a nod of assent as my mind spun through this. We were entering a smaller cross-corridor with six hallways branching off. The most likely point for an ambush was a few hundred feet more, at the northernmost passage. That was where the halls returned to their typical grandeur, the chandeliered ceilings higher and carved statues offering cover.

I held my hand up to signal the others to remain farther back and folded my wings against my spine. My wounds stung and itched with the movement. "Lead the way. We'll go single file to avoid drawing attention." *Briar, throw something to the left to distract him. Something small.*

"A wise course, Your Majesty." Otnell dipped his head forward once more, straightened, then strode forward. His boots made no sound on the slick marble as he rolled his feet. I walked half a step behind him.

Briar fell behind by two steps, and soon I heard something roll and bounce with a soft *clack-clack*. I glanced back and saw a small glass bead.

Otnell turned in the direction of the bead. Lunging forward, I seized his neck and snapped it. The sickening crunch of bones exploded in my ears. Holding his body, I dragged him to the ground and set him against the wall. Then I pointed in the opposite direction to signal our new course.

Briar nodded, her expression grim. *How much farther?*

Past this next connection point, and then to the northwestern hallway and up a staircase. So long as no one made a sound, we might avoid the ambush. I led the way with silent steps, and we ventured into the cross-corridor. The calls of searching guards echoed farther ahead. My muscles ached. I glanced back to see if we'd been followed. Nothing moved in the darkness.

Suddenly, Yuki yelped, the sound echoing off the walls. I spun around, gripping my dagger.

She clutched one hand to her chest, blood dripping from her fingers.

"Did you hear that? They must be this way!" a deep voice shouted from the far end of the northern hall, about two hundred feet away.

Chapter Three

Yuki stumbled, and I slowed to help her stay upright. We were still holding hands. My heart raced, and the scent of fresh blood filled my nostrils. She leaned back against the wall, clutching her other hand.

"We need to hurry before they escape," another guard growled, his voice carrying down the hall.

Vad's attention snapped from Yuki to the hall ahead.

From the corner of my eye, I watched as at least eleven dark forms rounded the corner about two hundred feet away. The heavy clanking suggested they all wore plate armor and carried weapons.

"Feck," Vad snarled.

Blood poured down Yuki's fingers and wrist, then dripped onto her beaded green gown. Something like green-coated metal protruded from her pocket, causing my blood to chill.

No. Please don't let this be what I fear.

More shouts and yells rang up and down the halls, indicating even more guards were heading toward us.

Thalira slipped in alongside Yuki and looked at her hand. "What happened?" Thalira whispered. When she reached out to grab Yuki's hand, she touched the top of Yuki's pocket where the metal protruded. She jerked back and looked down despite not being able to see the small cut along the top of her hand. It wasn't as deep, but it was deep enough.

Biting my lip, I carefully grabbed the handle of the green-coated dagger and lifted it from Yuki's pocket.

A sour taste filled my mouth. It looked exactly like the one that had fallen from Myantha's dress and the one the assassins had used on me, which meant the green had to be poison. *Please tell me we can access the antidote that you gave me for the poisoned weapons,* I said to Vad.

It's in the Healing Hall in the opposite direction. We need to reach the family quarters, and then we'll take a back way there. There isn't time to go directly without getting caught.

My chest tightened, and dread pooled within me. A small cap sat on the tip of this blade, likely to keep it from cutting through the fabric easily. My blood heated, and I turned to Vyraetos, who didn't have a weapon.

I held it out to him. "Be careful not to nick yourself with this. It has the green poison on it."

I kept my attention on Thalira and Yuki. "Put pressure on those cuts, and whatever you do, don't let up. We're going to need bandages." I ripped off strips of my gown and bound Yuki's hand fast. She winced at the tightness, and blood darkened the fabric almost at once. Vyraetos wrapped Thalira's with a strip he tore from his own robe.

"There they are! The traitor king is this way! Sound the alarm!" a deep voice yelled. More shouts followed as the cry rippled through the halls like poisoned water.

Their voices were like knives in my chest. Fuck them all! I squeezed Yuki's hand and cast a look around our position. It wasn't a great spot for a fight. We were in the middle of a series of hallways, which gave our pursuers multiple potential points of attack. But it also meant more avenues for escape. I linked to Vad, *Are we fighting here, or is there a more defensible place nearby?*

Vad growled. *We need to go somewhere more defensible.* His wings snapped out. "This way," he said in a low, sharp tone, and charged ahead toward what must be the northwestern hallway. *We'll set up our own ambush for them. Top of the staircase under the chandelier. Fewer access points.*

I gripped Yuki's hand tight in mine and grabbed Thalira's too, then bolted after Vad. My lungs filled as I searched the air for any trace of our attackers and anything we could use against them. One more glance over my shoulder, and I counted eleven chasing after us.

We ducked into the northwestern hall and ran as fast as we could. Our steps thundered now, echoing off the marble walls. Behind us, the sounds of pursuit grew louder. The guards' heavy boots pounded against stone as they gained on us. Alarms rippled out, heavy bells sounding down faraway halls and echoing back to us. If the whole palace hadn't known we were here, they knew now.

"Halt in the name of the true Shadow Kingdom!" one shouted.

"Surrender now, traitor king!" another called out.

The passage broadened, its walls lined with ancient oil paintings depicting Shadow Fae victories. A steep staircase with a curving banister loomed ahead, and the passage tightened as we climbed it, Vad taking the stairs two at a time.

I kept my grip firm on Yuki and Thalira, feeling their slick blood between our fingers as it soaked through the cloth. That wretched poison. Fate help us, I needed to get that antidote into their systems before they bled out. My own healing powers had been so muted that I'd scarcely survived the third test after the assassins stabbed and shot me.

On the landing, we faced four peaked archways that led

into new halls, with two smaller doors set in the nearest wall and shut tight. Small sitting areas had been set up near the southern and northern halls, complete with rugs, velvet couches, and velvet chairs. Huge oil lamp chandeliers with dangling glass prisms hung in the area, and additional oil lamps adorned the walls.

Vad pointed at the small door on the right. "That's a storeroom. In there, we'll find flint and steel in black metal boxes with the fire symbol. We'll take a stand here to clear the path."

I nodded. Turning to Vyraetos, I pressed Yuki's and Thalira's wounded hands into his. Yuki had gone deathly pale, her jaw clenched. Thalira kept her posture rigid and one hand clasped tight over the other's small, bleeding wound, her lips pressed in a tight line.

Arching a brow, I said, "Don't let up on the pressure. Girls, I'll be back." I bolted across the chamber to the storeroom, my Shadow Queen tennis shoes squeaking on the marble.

Our pursuers were getting closer, their heavy steps and loud grunts echoing up the staircase from nearby halls. How much longer before others heard and came running?

Vad's voice rose into the air. "If anyone is afraid of the fight to come and wants to leave, the best exit is the southern door. There will be guards in place to keep anyone from leaving if they follow standard protocol, so you'll have to hope they don't decide you're a threat and kill you or take you prisoner."

"Feck you, Shadow King," Veralt growled. "I run from no fight my woman desires."

"We're setting the stairs on fire. I'll crash a chandelier and spill the lamp oil when the guards are on the staircase. Gather furniture so we can throw pieces at the guards and block the landing after the fire starts," Vad said. "The wounded can rest in one of the sitting areas. Make a barricade for them."

I flung the hall closet open and stepped inside. The bins and boxes were organized on shelves with symbols and smelled like lavender, lamp oil, and cotton. I seized a cool metal box and tucked it under one arm, then tipped several bins forward until I found folded white cloth and grabbed that too.

Back on the landing, Silus had taken Elara to one of the dark velvet couches and was holding her while Vyraetos bowed his head and furrowed his brow, tending to Yuki's and Thalira's hands. Quen knelt beside them, her fists knotted in her crimson dress as she whispered something, and Velessa nodded, stroking Thalira's arm.

Many-Greats and Myantha stood a few feet away near a red-faced, quivering Thalen, who was more agitated than I'd ever seen him. Veralt carried the rug from the sitting area to the staircase while Rhielle grabbed all the paintings in reach and stacked them haphazardly in a pile a few feet from the stairs. Vad had flown up to a chandelier and was working on the fixtures with his wings spread wide for balance. The oil lamps and prisms clattered, and the oil sloshed as his weight rocked the twelve-foot frame.

A savage grin tugged at my lips. This plan could actually work.

I ran to the sitting area and set the bin of cloth next to Vyraetos. "Here. Bandages." I turned to Quen and set down the metal box.

Even without magic, the Shadow Fae were able to see in the dark, so maybe that meant, as a Fire Fae, Quen had some latent fire ability. "Quen, can you use flint and stone even without magic?"

Her dark eyes blazed. "Yes!" She held out her hands, fingers twitching. "Give it here now!"

I opened the black box and removed one set of flint and steel, then pressed it into her hands. There were small cardboard-like packets inside as well, perhaps to serve as fire starters. I knelt on the marble and pressed open the packet to reveal dry fibers as Quen positioned herself next to me.

"The tinder is here." I pressed it to her hand.

She nodded, muscles taut as she struck the flint against the steel. *Tchk*! Bright orange sparks flared, briefly illuminating the space in sharp relief. Quen turned her head back and forth as if taking in the entirety of our situation and what was available. *Tchk! Tchk!*

Thalen's head snapped up as the light flared. "Yes! Keep doing that!" Darkness re-engulfed us. More sparks flared into the air.

"Myantha, don't move," Thalen commanded and squeezed Myantha's hands before releasing her and leaping. His wings caught the air and propelled him upward until he seized the chandelier over the nearest doorway. Darkness crashed back in around us, then more sparks flared. Thalen kept working at the fixtures by touch, lips curled in a focused snarl.

Heart pounding, I ran to the wall and grabbed one of the lamps. The oil sloshed within as the curved glass cooled my hands. If we weren't afraid of being spotted anymore, light would help us fight.

Glass and metal clanked and rattled above, and the scent of lamp oil intensified. Vad flew to the next chandelier over the northern entrance. "Someone keep watch by the stairs. Shout when you see them."

"Watching," Rhielle called back. She shoved one of the small decorative tables into the pile.

Veralt finished stamping the rug into the stairwell and ran back up to the storeroom. "They're almost here!" He ducked inside and began grabbing items without care.

"Is the bleeding getting worse?" Thalira's voice shook.

Vyraetos shook his head, the lines in his face deepening.

"The wounds aren't clotting."

"You're going to have to tourniquet them." I grabbed more lamps from the wall beyond the doorway and brought them back. "Those wounds won't stop bleeding for anything. It's something in the venom. Whatever you do, don't get cut on anything else."

"I'm so cold," Yuki whispered, sagging back against the wall. Blood had soaked her arm and into the green of her dress, making a red river down the bodice and skirt. It dripped to the floor in a puddle. Thalira's hemorrhage was slower, not yet dripping through the cloth wrapped around her hand, but already the fabric was darkening.

"I'll get a fire going. You're gonna be warm, I promise." Quen's voice was tight, and her hands shook as she struck the flint and steel. "You can't die on us, all right? Neither of you. I'm not giving anyone permission to die."

Velessa stroked the hair back from Yuki's face. "It's all right. We're going to get you safe. You'll get back to your sisters." She swallowed hard, her throat bobbing and her features pale as if she didn't believe the words she'd spoken.

My heart clenched, and my blood chilled even more. Fate help us. How much time did we really have? Yuki might have an hour or so if we kept her still. Thalira would have longer, as long as the bleeding didn't worsen. Neither could be injured again.

I had to focus on the fight at hand. Saving them would be impossible if we all died out here, but we had to move fast, or their time would run out.

Quen struck the flint again and again. *Tchk-tchk-tchk!* More sparks flared. Each one flashed into existence with enough light to burn in that moment. They fell onto the small tinder pile, pale smoke curling upward.

Veralt shoved more tinder in her direction, smashed his boot through two paintings, and then thrust those at her too.

"Here, fire girl."

Grunting in acknowledgment, Quen scooped up the tinder and rearranged it on the painting before resuming her strikes with the flint and steel. *Tchk! Tchk!*

My wolf growled, her hackles lifting. Something was coming, and she inched forward in preparation.

She wanted to shift.

My skin tingled, and fur sprouted on my body as I linked to Vad, *I'm shifting.* Then my bones broke, and I found myself on all fours. My eyes widened as my heart thrummed steadily and blood flowed faster through my veins. Whatever had kept me from shifting in the Ceremonial Hall was gone here.

A strange shivering sensation trembled down my spine, and my breath caught. There was no ripped fabric around me. How was that possible? Instead of standing in the remnants of my gown and kicking off the sneakers with *Shadow Queen* written in sequins on the bottom, I had taken on my full wolf form and left behind no evidence of the outfit I'd been wearing.

That's better. They won't be able to spot you as easily, Vad replied as he continued working. *Watch out too. Crossbowmen and scouts generally wear leather armor, spearmen vary, and swordsmen typically wear metal plate armor.*

Boots pounded closer, and metal plate armor rattled, not just from the stairwell below but from the southern hall and then—I twisted my head in time to see movement in the eastern hall. A thin, dark-clad male shape crept closer, gaze fixed on Vad as the chandelier groaned and clanked on the opposite side of the room. He lifted a crossbow from his side.

Vad, southern hall! I lunged past the others, my claws clattering on the stone.

The man froze mid-step, less than twenty feet away. His lips tightened, and he whipped his crossbow down to point at me, aiming for my throat.

Too slow.

I jumped and slammed into the scout's chest hard enough to send him crashing into the wall. The impact vibrated up my jaw and stung my forelegs.

Briar? Vad linked to my mind, fear in his voice.

I've got this. They're coming through the southern hall too.

The man gasped, eyes wide, and brought the crossbow up again, the bolt aimed point-first at my muzzle. I bit down on his hands, and his bones made a sickening crunching noise.

He shrieked, and the crossbow clattered away as he clawed at my ear with his other hand. I reared back just enough to reposition my jaws around the base of his neck and bit as hard as I could.

Behind me, Rhielle screamed, "Here!"

The guard's artery pulsed hot and wet across my tongue. I released him, letting his body collapse against the wall, his head lolling and his eyes wide open in death.

Something metal groaned, then snapped. I spun in time to see one of the massive chandeliers slam into the stairwell with a thunderous crash. Glass globes shattered in a deafening cascade, shards scattering across the marble like a spray of frozen rain.

The chandelier's iron arms twisted, and the frame collapsed on impact as several guards stopped short or screamed. Oil bled across the stone, the scent rising thick and acrid in the air. "Southern hall!" Vad shouted from the chandelier over the eastern hall.

I raced back into the large room, the thick taste of copper in my mouth.

Quen struck again. *Tchk—tchk—tchk!* Sparks cascaded, bouncing and dying, until one landed in the curled threads on the painting and this time caught. A faint glow bloomed. Stronger smoke curled upward, thin and gray. Quen bent low and exhaled in careful breaths, her hair swinging forward. The threads darkened, then flared orange, small flames licking the edges of the canvas as the oil paint blackened and blistered.

The hall lit with a wavering glow, golden light granting everyone sight. Quen squealed and clapped her hands. "We've got fire!" She grabbed one of the lamps and picked up a piece of the flaming tinder to light it, not bothered by the heat as it curled around her fingertips.

Velessa's eyes widened, and she grabbed another lamp with her good hand and brought it to Quen. She took the lit one to Thalira, and then Yuki grabbed another unlit lamp.

Veralt snatched up a piece of flaming canvas and hurled it into the stairwell as Vad swept down, grabbed a couch, and shoved it toward the eastern hall.

The stairwell erupted in flames. Orange tongues leapt up the walls and licked down toward our attackers, who stumbled back in a confusion of curses and hoarse shouts. Glass popped in the heat, and the sickly sweet smell of burning paint and resin bit the back of my nose as I ran back in. Veralt picked up a couch and chucked it into the stairwell, laughing loudly as screams rose from below.

Silus settled Elara on another couch and carefully climbed to his feet. He ran to the pile of furniture Veralt and Rhielle had made and broke a leg off the coffee table, then ran to the side of the southern hallway and waited with the table leg raised as if he was ready to hit a home run with someone's head.

I raced toward the southern hall, blood thundering in my ears. Five more guards charged through the southern hall with swords and spears. I set my sights on the nearest scout, who wore leathers and wielded a short sword.

"Watch the ground!" one of the armored guards behind him screamed. "The bitch is a shadow beast now—"

Vad dropped from the ceiling straight onto the screamer.

"What did you call your queen?" He seized the guard by the helmet and yanked his head sideways, then slammed it again and again into the marble wall.

The ringing clang of the guard's head became a drumbeat for my own attack amid the chaos. The leather-clad scout swore and swung his sword at me. The blade whistled past my muzzle as my hind legs skidded on the slick marble. I twisted midair, jaws snapping at his sword arm. He managed to wrench back, but it cost him his balance. I lunged for his leg, jaws clamping below the knee. He cried out and swung again, catching my shoulder with a slice that burned through fur and skin. I ripped sideways, yanking him off his feet, and his head bounced off the floor with a *crack*.

Blood spattered the black marble. I let go long enough for him to start to crawl away, his hands scrabbling at the tile. Then I lunged again and bit through his throat with everything I had. His cartilage and windpipe collapsed under my teeth, the taste hot and metallic. I shook him once, then let his body fall to the floor twitching, blood pumping out in spurts.

Another guard charged me, spear leveled at my chest. I ducked and caught the shaft between my teeth. The man yanked back, trying to wrench it free, but my jaw locked, and the wood splintered. I whipped my head sideways until my own muscles ached, throwing him off-balance.

I'd barely knocked him over when another swordsman came at me. I darted to the side and felt his blade nick me, cold and sharp. I spun and went for his ankle, crunching bone and sending him sprawling. I leaped onto his back, slamming him to the ground. His face was a mask of terror, his scream brief as I crushed his throat.

Vad continued to slam the head of the man who'd insulted me into the wall until a chunk of helmet and skull caved in. The man's body slid down, staining the stone with a glistening dark smear.

Vad then flew toward the southern hall and landed hard on a sword wielder's back. He stomped his boot down and snapped the man's neck as Silus struck another in the face and snatched up his sword, then drove it across the helmeted skull of another attacker.

A spear wielder charged Vad, but he clamped one hand on the spear and redirected it, then seized the man by his throat and ripped through his jugular. Blood sprayed in a wide arc, hot and metallic, splattering the marble and Vad's black silks.

One of the aerial fae swept in, spear lifted high. Thalen tackled him around the middle and drove a blade he'd snagged under the neck of the man's helmet. He jammed it in deep and twisted, then let the body fall, his feet balancing on the ledge of the arch as his wings compensated for the angle. He then leaped down and tackled another plated guard, who sprawled to the floor. Myantha darted forward, seized the guard's helmet, and pulled it off. Thalen slit the guard's throat.

I shook my own dying swordsman, jaws clamped tight. His flailing blade sliced my shoulder, and I howled inwardly with pain and rage. I flung him hard, and his body smashed into the marble then sagged flat, limbs twisted.

Another soldier raised his sword high and aimed for my withers. Quen vaulted onto the man's armored back, shrieking, "Eat fire, wanker!" She jammed pieces of flaming, shredded canvas straight into his helmet's eye slit. He howled and clawed at his face, stumbled backward, and struck the half wall overlooking the floor below. Rhielle dove and grabbed him at the knee, then hefted his unwieldy frame over the edge. Black smoke billowed up as he screamed.

More and more guards raced in, most armored but wingless. Velessa and Quen had lit over a dozen lamps, and the ghostly golden light now lit the landing. Black smoke rolled up, choking those who were flying, and Silus, Rhielle, and Veralt defended the injured. Vyraetos was trying to form a better tourniquet on Yuki's hand, blood flowing from his shoulder where he'd been shot with a crossbow bolt. Vad, Thalen, and I fought to take down the guards entering through the southern hall, but I kept watch on the other halls.

A deep grating howl of pain had me snapping my head left. One of the swordsmen had caught Veralt in the side with his blade. Rhielle struck the guard with a table leg; then Veralt seized him and snapped his neck. Blood soaked Veralt's shirt, but he stayed upright, snarling.

"Get that tied off!" Rhielle dropped the table leg and seized the swordsman's weapon.

Veralt grunted, picked up a spear, and flung it at one of the other attackers. It missed its mark and clattered on the floor.

A flash of metal caught my attention. I spun just in time to see a blade arcing at me, and I flattened myself and shot forward. The tip of the blade caught my tail and raked down in a painful slice. I yelped.

Briar! Vad's words pounded in my head.

Snarling, the guard kicked me in the side. "Die, shadow beast!" His heavy metal boot connected with my ribs and drove the breath from my lungs.

I snarled, then feinted right before lunging at his exposed thigh. *I'm fine. Focus on your fight.*

My teeth scraped metal. The rotten tastes of iron, sweat, oil, and blood filtered through my mouth. Still, I managed to grab hold and lock down on the armor, the metal cutting into my gums, and I shook my head violently. The man grunted and slammed the pommel of his sword into my skull.

Light exploded behind my eyes, and blood streamed down my face. I staggered and fell.

I'm coming! Vad's voice echoed in my mind. I could barely

see him through my closing eyelids, my blood thundering in my ears. Three guards were on him now, and he wielded one of the fallen spears, his wings lashing out and his gaze furious and desperate as he looked to me.

The swordsman advanced on me and lifted his sword. My body was too heavy to move, blood streaming from my wounds.

"Leave her alone!" Velessa darted next to me with an oil lamp in her good hand. She flung the lamp like a grenade, and it exploded over him, coating his armor and setting him ablaze. He staggered back, screaming and flailing. Thalen tackled him and shoved him against the balcony.

My eyelids sagged shut, my head still exploding and my ears ringing.

Velessa crouched down in front of me, her back to the southern hall. "Come on, Briar. Come on. Let's get you—"

A dark figure of a man lunged forward, and a silver sword erupted from Velessa's chest. An armored glove clamped down on her shoulder... and he twisted the blade.

CHAPTER FOUR

A strangled gurgle escaped Velessa's throat.

She looked at the sword protruding from her chest. Her hands flew to the blade, fingers trembling as they grasped the dull sides uselessly. There would be no saving her.

The world spun, and my head throbbed, but somehow, my vision cleared. That *bastard* would pay.

The metal-plated guard ripped the sword free and shoved Velessa forward. She slumped, her face in front of mine as the light faded from her eyes.

She was dead. And I hadn't been able to protect her. But I could get revenge for her sake.

My throat tightened, and my claws scraped on the marble as I fought for traction. As the guard kicked Velessa's body with his metal boot and lifted his sword toward me, I surged. But my paws slipped in the warm pool of blood from her chest, and I slid to the left, protecting my most injured side, which continued to throb and sting.

His sword missed me by inches, and then he kicked me in the chest. I flew backward, my back slamming against the wall, and dark edges lined my vision. The ringing in my ears intensified. Velessa's blood—her death—coated my fur, and the copper scent had bile inching up my throat.

I dropped back to all fours, just as everything blurred and the floor moved under my paws.

Vad roared as his anger and fear slammed into our bond. He linked, *I... way...*"

Had my concussion impacted our bond?

I tried to leap, but the guard rushed forward and kicked my sternum. My body lifted, and he seized my throat and slammed me against the wall with even more strength than before. I couldn't breathe. My joints cracked as I clawed at his armored wrist, but my strength faded.

Horrified cries erupted throughout the chamber. Yuki shouted, "Velessa's dead!" Her words echoed in my head like a funeral bell. And worse, I might be following in Velessa's footsteps.

The guard's grip crushed my windpipe, and the edges of my vision darkened. My lungs burned, and I knew this had to be the end.

Suddenly, the guard's eyes bulged, and his grip loosened. I crumpled to the floor and gasped as he patted at the spear protruding from his neck. A dark arm struck him on the head, and he dropped with a loud *thud*.

Vad crouched beside me, his silver eyes glowing in the flickering gold lamplight and orange firelight. He lifted me into his arms. "Briar?"

I sucked in more air, and the world steadied. The burning in my lungs receded.

I linked, *I'll be fine. I just got stunned. I need a second.*

He carried me to the couch and lay me by Elara, then kissed the top of my head. "Take your time. Let me know if you need me." Then he disappeared.

Be careful, I connected as he entered another fight. The ringing spiraled through my head, adding to the churning in my stomach. Many-Greats brandished a broken chunk of wood like a club as he prepared to attack a guard, and Vyraetos continued to bind Thalira's shoulder, where a bolt protruded. Tears rolled down her cheeks.

Fuck. She'd gotten hurt again. We had to find shelter and get the antidote, or she'd bleed out. I refused to lose another person I loved.

Yuki sagged against the wall, her long skirt resting on the dark marble, and hugged her bound hand to her chest as she sobbed and stared at Velessa's body. Elara was barely conscious, her breaths slow and ragged, but she still held the crowns. The couches that had been staged to provide a rough barricade provided precious little protection.

As if Fate wanted to let me know it could get worse, more guards charged in, six from the southern hall and two from the western.

My chest tightened. How many more would come? Probably dozens. Maybe even hundreds. We'd held out so far, keeping the attacks to a trickle, but everyone had been wounded at least once. The cuts and nicks on me burned and ached, and Velessa's blood had dried in my fur.

I couldn't lie here and give up. Not after what Velessa had sacrificed for us. I had to fight, and most importantly, we needed as many hands on deck as possible, or more lives would be lost. Maybe even Vad's. My heart seized and twisted.

I tried to push myself off the couch. The room tilted sideways, and the velvet cushions, slick with my blood, dragged against my fur as I slid to the floor. Every movement sent fire up my spine. My legs trembled under my weight, and my thoughts formed thick and slow, like I was wading through fog. I braced against the cold floor, willing my body to move, but my legs buckled.

I hit the ground hard and helplessly watched chaos unfold

around me.

Quen darted from the side of one of the leather-armored swordsman, her broken flaming spear a streak of orange in the smoke. She slammed it into the gut of a soldier charging from the southern hall, the crack of impact lost beneath his scream. He swung wildly, but she ducked low, a snarl on her lips as she twisted the shaft deeper into his abdomen. He dropped, clutching his stomach. He would be gone soon enough.

Rhielle was right behind her, a blur of motion and firelight. Her stolen sword sliced clean through a guard's thigh, and the spray of blood that followed was so thick she had to have hit an artery. He dropped, trying to crawl, but she was already pivoting, purple skirts flaring around her legs as she brought the hilt of her blade crashing into another guard's helmet.

I needed to help them. There were too many guards, too many blades, and not enough of us. I pushed myself again, willing my legs to move, but they refused. They were useless and numb, like the blood loss had carved me out from the inside.

A third guard rushed Rhielle from behind.

Quen moved fast. She dropped to one knee and snatched a sword from a fallen soldier. "Behind you!" she shouted.

Veralt was already moving.

He lunged, his stolen blade flashing as it collided with the guard's spear shaft. The clang of metal cracked through the room. The guard stumbled, thrown off by the sheer force of the hit, and Veralt didn't waste a breath. He struck with the flat of his blade, slamming it into the soldier's ribs.

The guard hit the ground in a crash of metal and curses.

Veralt didn't pause.

He stepped forward and stomped his boot down on the man's head. Bone cracked beneath the pressure, and bile burned the back of my throat. The broad muscles across his back tightened as he lifted the blade high, then brutally struck the guard's neck.

My stomach twisted hard. I'd seen death before... more than my fair share. But I would never grow numb to the sound of a killing blow or the flash of hate in an enemy's eyes. They were people, after all, but they'd started the fight.

Above me, Thalen collided in midair with a winged guard. His talons, buried beneath white feathers, punched clean through armor and flesh alike. Both of them screamed as they spiraled toward the floor, locked in a struggle. The enemy's spear twisted and carved a jagged line across Thalen's wing before they crashed.

Thalen hit hard, crying out as his body jerked and he curled protectively around the mangled limb. "Scaffing void!"

Myantha bolted toward him, skirts flying behind her. She was nearly to him when another soldier surged forward, spear leveled at her chest.

"Get back!" Silus burst from behind the stairwell's half wall and grabbed her mid-stride, arm locking around her waist as he yanked her aside.

The spear grazed her shoulder, but she didn't scream. Silus slammed his club into the attacker's face. Bone cracked, blood sprayed from the guard's nose, and he stumbled backward.

Myantha shoved free of Silus and dropped to Thalen's side, looping his arm around her shoulders and dragging him up.

Silus didn't stop.

He struck again, his next blow caving in the helm until the soldier collapsed, a broken mess at his feet.

I panted hard, every breath shallow and jagged. I had to get back into the fight.

Across the chamber, Vad ripped a spear from one of the fallen soldiers and hurled it with a roar. The weapon sliced through the air, striking a guard square in the chest with enough force to lift him off his feet. The man slammed into the wall and crumpled, stunned and gasping.

Vad didn't pause.

He tore the helmet off the downed warrior and slit his throat with his claws in one brutal swipe.

Blood drenched him.

I dug deep, pulling strength from some hollow place in my chest. My paws slipped on the blood-slick marble as I rose, legs shaking beneath me. The wound in my side pulsed, sharp and burning from the blade's bite. But I clenched my jaw and forced myself upright.

Pain screamed through my muscles—and then I saw him.

A soldier rounded the corner, crossbow raised—not at me, but at Elara.

She was still slumped where I'd left her, pale and crumpled against the couch, completely exposed.

No!

Adrenaline surged. The pain dulled, not gone but erased beneath the need to protect her. I launched forward, my body trembling with every step.

When I was halfway there, he fired.

The bolt slammed into my shoulder, and fire ripped through the muscle, twisting my body mid-stride. But I didn't stop. I couldn't.

The breath left my lungs in a strangled cry, and I collided with him in a blur of fur and blood. My jaws snapped on his throat before he could reload. Flesh tore beneath my teeth, hot and wet, and his scream cut short to a gurgle.

We crashed to the floor together.

His body jerked beneath me as blood poured from the open wound, puddling on the marble and slicking down my snout. His heartbeat weakened, and he twitched once, then stilled.

"Kill the shadow beast!" another guard screamed.

I jerked back just as a spearman charged with his crossbow aimed at my chest. My paws skidded on the slick marble as I lunged sideways, narrowly dodging the bolt, which sliced past me and shattered against the stone.

Across the room, Vyraetos released Thalira's limp arm, her blood streaking his hands. His eyes snapped to the fallen spear near his feet, and he grabbed it in both fists.

He bared his teeth and twisted, slamming the spear into the wall. The soldier charging him froze, eyes wide in confusion, then terror, as Vyraetos yanked a dagger from his belt and drove it into the man's eye socket. The venom-coated blade hissed as it sank deep, and Many-Greats slammed the attacking soldier in the back of the head with his club.

The guard gurgled, his knees giving out as he lurched to the side. Vyraetos shoved the corpse aside without flinching, already scanning for the next threat as Many-Greats stepped forward and braced for his next battle.

Around us, the chamber burned.

Smoke choked the air, thick and acrid, stinging my lungs with every breath. Firelight flickered off blood-slick armor, and screams echoed all around us. Winged guards still surged from every side, steel flashing like fangs in the haze. Shadows pressed in, coiling at the edges of the battle like they were waiting for the blood to run dry before devouring what was left.

Through it all, we fought.

Every one of us was bleeding, staggering, running on fumes and anger. But none of us fell back. We held the line because there was no other choice.

But how much longer could we keep this up?

Are we going to fight until they wear us down and pick us off one at a time? I linked to Vad, breath ragged, wobbling with every step.

A guard, who had been knocked in the head by Silas,

twitched and tried to pull himself up. As he got to his knees, I lunged and clamped my jaws down on his throat. The twisted rim of his helmet scraped my gums, but the artery was there, and I didn't care. His hands clawed at my fur, then slackened.

We're leaving as soon as we have an opening. Vad turned toward the northern hall, his lips curled in a snarl.

What's back there? I linked to him as I pulled away from the corpse.

Another ambush, he answered, his anger heating our bond. *At least some of them know we'll try that route. The northern and eastern hallways both lead to the royal family's chambers, but the northern hall is the shortest way there since the eastern winds and curves. We could take the longer path to lose them, but the stretch of hall before the family rooms in either direction will be far harder to fight through. With our injured, we'll be vulnerable.*

Shit.

We needed to pull the waiting guards here so we could make our own trap. I glanced down the northern hall. It was broader, had fewer chandeliers, and had a lower, flatter ceiling. Winged fae would find flying harder. I could force the guards into the open where their numbers wouldn't matter so much. *I'll lure them in.*

Absolutely not! Vad scowled, his jaw working. He bashed a helmeted guard's skull with the bottom of his hilt, knocking him against the wall. Another guard lunged, and Vad blocked the man's spear with his sword, sending the weapon clattering to the floor.

Trust me. Get everyone ready. My claws clicked across the marble as I ran toward the northern hall with every sense raw—from the smoke, from being coated in my friend's blood, and from the sounds of my friends and the beat of my whole heart, fighting to live.

Fear slammed through our bond as Vad realized what I

intended, but I was fast.

I bolted straight into the hall, my guttural howl tearing from my raw throat. Despite my determination, my strides were uneven, but I pushed forward anyway.

Dark shapes flickered from around the next corner of the hall.

In the low light, I couldn't make out faces, but the light reflected off some armor. Others moved like shadows in leather. Then the stench of sweat, oil, and blood hit me like a wave as five guards surged forward with their blades already drawn.

"She's in beast form," one growled.

Flattening into a crouch, I pinned my ears and whimpered, letting my tongue roll from my mouth. The blood dripping from my shoulder helped sell the illusion. I made myself look weak, wounded, and frightened.

Come on, assholes. Take the bait.

"Can she hear us?" one asked.

"She isn't acting like it. Siln, shoot her," a voice hissed. "If she's running, they must've routed them."

"Briar, get back here!" Thalen shouted from far behind me. His voice cracked with alarm, but I wasn't sure if it was real or if he was playing along.

"Briar!" Vad bellowed from farther in. "Don't go that way. We're running east!"

I yipped and spun, then started racing back toward the chamber.

A sharp whistle cut through the air, and something grazed my back. Pain sliced through me as I dove between two pillars. The crossbow bolt clanged off the stone behind me, hitting hard enough to chip marble, then clanked across the floor.

I glanced back and counted the guards chasing me. Blood thundered in my ears. I linked to Vad, *I'm coming straight in. Four of the fifteen men chasing me have crossbows. The rest have swords.*

If any of them touch you, I'll shred them, he snarled through the bond. *And when we're through here, you and I will have words.*

As long as we live to have them, I linked and barreled toward the landing, the guards thundering behind me.

Vad stood with Veralt on the far side of the hall door, both ready to strike.

I slid through the arch and cut sideways at the last heartbeat, skimming the half wall that protected the stairwell. Pain flared through my battered body, adding to my torment.

Near the southern hall entrance, Silus and Thalen were battling three guards and sidestepping corpses. Quen dropped from the ceiling and landed on two men, driving daggers into their necks with ruthless precision. A wicked cut bled along her calf, but she didn't slow.

"Don't get in line of sight of the entrances," Vad shouted. "Four crossbowmen are coming from the north."

One leather-clad guard had taken up a position at the edge of the hallway's entrance as if the wall would protect him. Not a chance. My muscles bunched as I launched myself at a crossbowman taking aim at Vyraetos from across the landing. My jaws closed on his forearm, bone crunching between my teeth. He screamed, and the weapon clattered away. I shook my head, tearing muscle.

"Behind you, Briar!" Thalen shouted.

I dropped the guard and spun. A blade hissed past my ear, missing by inches. I ducked low and lunged, driving my shoulder into his gut. He doubled over, and I shredded his face and neck, tearing him down to the black marble.

"At least another twenty coming from the south," Rhielle yelled.

"Same or more from the east," Thalen said, sliding out of

the way. Bells rang deeper in the palace, a call to arms, and Thalen's face said it all. We couldn't hold them off forever. "They sound lighter and faster. The plated ones lag. So best to double that number to know what we're up against!"

"Get back!" Vad snapped. He launched himself into the chandelier above the western entrance. It cracked with a sickening snap, and the whole thing tore free and smashed onto the floor, spilling oil everywhere.

Quen seized a hanging lamp and hurled it through the smoke and ruin. It struck with a clatter, and flames erupted, eating the leaked oil.

"Thalen, take the other chandelier," Vad commanded, pointing where the west corridor opened. He flew to the chandelier above the northern arch and crouched there like a watchful god. From that height, his voice cut clearly through the noise. "Do not cross any open archways until I give the signal!"

Another leather-armored swordsman charged out of the northern entrance. I lunged at him with a snarl and clamped my jaws on his thigh. I wrenched him down, ignoring the sword that clipped my tail and biting harder.

He screamed and dropped his sword, then clawed at my ears and snout. I twisted and shook him until bones ground and snapped. He collapsed with a broken cry, and I hauled him by the leg away from the archway so another guard couldn't shoot me while I was there.

Rhielle snatched a fallen spear, launched herself across the archway, and flung it. The spearhead *thunked* into a swordsman's chest, knocking him back.

I locked my teeth in the man's throat and twisted. A sharp, burning shock seared my left shoulder, another bolt burying itself deep, and my leg spasmed.

How badly are you hurt? Vad's voice punched through the

bond.

I'm fine. At least, for now. Maybe for a few minutes more. My shifter healing fought to restore me, but the bolts embedded in my flesh stung, preventing my body from doing more than slowing the bleeding.

The sound of running boots thundered again.

Gasping, Rhielle ran out of the northern hall. A crossbow bolt whined past her, not even an inch from her cheek. "We're almost out of time!"

Face set in determination, Veralt grabbed Rhielle's arm gently but firmly. "Enough of this fight."

Silus scooped Elara into his arms. She murmured something too faint to catch, her eyelids fluttering and her breathing far too slow.

Vyraetos helped Thalira to her feet. She swayed but managed to stand. Yuki nearly collapsed as he steadied her. Many-Greats moved behind Yuki to steady her further as he said something that made her nod.

Rhielle whispered something to Veralt. He gave a curt nod and crossed to the two women.

Veralt crouched and lifted Yuki as if she weighed nothing. She winced, shivering against him, then went limp, her head falling against his shoulder and her wounded hand pressed to her chest.

He glanced at Thalira and shifted Yuki to one arm. "C'mon, water girl."

Thalira shook her head, grimacing. "Yuki's in worse shape."

"You think I can't carry you both?" He swept her into his other arm. She let out a small gasp but didn't fight him.

Vad perched high on the chandelier, his gaze slicing through the chaos as bootfalls thundered closer from either hallway. Quen crouched nearby with an oil lamp clutched tight and three more at her feet. At Vad's nod, she leaped up and slammed them into the frame behind her.

With a groan of protest, the chandelier tore free from the ceiling, bolts and glass raining down. Vad kicked off from it just before it crashed into the floor. Shards of glass exploded, and oil fanned across the stone in slick puddles.

Quen hurled her lamp. Flames exploded in a whoosh of heat.

Vad lunged onto the chandelier above the eastern entrance. "Go!"

Silus ran toward the archway with Elara in his arms. Veralt followed, carrying both women. Thalira's face twisted in pain with each jolt, but Yuki didn't move at all.

Quen grabbed two more lamps. Vyraetos seized another pair along with a small box he tucked under his arm. Many-Greats picked up a couple of fallen swords. Rhielle ripped three more canvases from the walls and tossed them into the growing blaze near the northern archway.

I hesitated.

Velessa's body lay crumpled behind us, motionless. Her eyes stared, unseeing.

My breath caught in my throat.

The pounding of boots came louder now, matching the rhythm of my cracking heart.

"Briar, come on!" Rhielle called from the eastern arch.

Briar, it wasn't your fault. Vad's voice pressed into my mind through the link, and a steadying calm slid through the bond. *But if you don't get into the eastern hall, I'm going to carry you there myself. I'm not dropping this chandelier until you're through.*

Some part of me wanted to give him a smartass response. But the words died before they could form. He was right.

I tore my gaze from Velessa and lunged forward, legs

threatening to buckle and lungs squeezing tight. Smoke burned my nostrils, and tears blurred my vision.

Thalen and Myantha ran under the archway. Thalen glanced over his shoulder, white wings twitching against his spine. "Briar!"

"Move your butt, Briar! We aren't leaving you behind," Quen shouted, hands full of lamps. The golden lamplight surrounded her, bouncing with each step as oil sloshed inside the glass bases.

"Briar," Many-Greats shouted as he started toward me. "Hurry!"

I bared my teeth at Many-Greats and forced myself forward, stumbling, shaking, but building momentum.

As soon as I cleared the arch and made it a few feet down the hall, Vad stomped down on the chandelier. It went down with a screeching groan. More glass exploded, and acrid oil splashed. He shot through the archway, and Quen darted forward, hurling one of her remaining lamps. It hit with a sharp crack and exploded, and another wall of fire and smoke rose behind us.

Surging to the front of the group, Vad linked, *If you need me to carry you, I will.*

I'm fine. The stinging aches and burns lanced along my body, but I didn't slow.

Almost to safety. Just a little farther, I told myself.

Then we'd get Yuki, Thalira, and Elara what they needed.

Down the eastern hall we ran. Tears blurred my vision as I remembered Velessa's face—the shocked tension in her expression and the life draining from her eyes. Leaving her body behind felt like its own betrayal. The knowledge that she wouldn't have wanted us to stay behind offered little comfort. The senselessness of her death hit deep, and if we didn't move fast, Yuki and Thalira would share her fate.

If Fate were kind, they wouldn't. But Fate could be such a bitch.

Vad gestured toward the left archway ahead. Vyraetos and Many-Greats kept pace in the center, holding two lamps by their handles. I ran behind Veralt and alongside Thalen and Myantha.

If Myantha wanted to kill me, this would be the perfect time. Unease twisted in my gut. I couldn't believe she would, but how many things had happened that I never would have believed could?

The scent of fresh blood thickened in the smoke. I scanned the hallways...and my blood turned to ice.

Chapter Five

BRIAR

A jolt of fear slammed through me.

Yuki's wounded hand flopped limply behind Veralt's neck. Blood trailed from it in thick, steady rivulets, soaking into his tunic and splattering the marble floor.

The bandage had come loose. Crimson streamed from her palm, each drop a warning.

Vad, how close are we? Yuki's bandages have slipped. She's bleeding bad.

I chased the others around the corner, panic pounding in my ears. We couldn't stop, and I couldn't even signal Thalira to help. I stayed close, heart galloping as we poured into a narrower hall. The smoke thinned, but my vision swam. Breathless gasps and frantic footfalls echoed off the stone around us.

We had to move faster.

The corridor narrowed again, funneling us through a hall lined with towering columns like the northern hallway. My paws hit the marble hard, claws scraping with each stride. My lungs burned, every breath tinged with the metallic tang of blood and soot.

Then—*there*—I spotted our goal. The entry to the royal family chambers.

Vad surged ahead, silver eyes locked on the heavy black doors at the end of the hall. His wings flapped once, sending a gust of stale air past us as he tore into the folds of his tattered surcoat. Keys jingled as he yanked them free.

He jammed one into the lock.

Metal scraped, and the tumblers groaned.

Shnkt!

Vad staggered. His jaw clenched in pain as he reeled back with a hoarse cry. Pain flared across the bond like a hot blade.

A bolt stuck out of his side, buried through his already shredded surcoat.

Vad! I snarled, the sound ripping from my throat as my claws skidded across the marble. My jaws snapped at the air, helpless and enraged.

"Vad!" Thalen shouted.

Cries erupted from behind us.

"There they are!" a voice rang out from farther down the corridor. "I hit the prince! I need more bolts!"

I'm fine. Vad tossed the phrase back to me. Gritting his teeth, he shoved the door open. The hinges shrieked in protest as they parted.

He grabbed Silus, who was still carrying Elara, and shoved him through.

The guard at the end of the hall fumbled with his crossbow as he tried to reload. More footsteps pounded from around the corner, closer now.

Vad braced against the doorframe, one hand pressed to his bleeding side, the other clenched around the key ring. His eyes swept over us. Veralt charged through first with Thalira and Yuki. Quen and Vyraetos followed with the lamps, their footfalls harsh and quick. Many-Greats darted in behind them with a worried glance at me, his brow furrowed. Thalen and Myantha darted after them, and I closed the distance.

Vad jerked his head at the door. *Inside.*

I lunged forward, ears pinned, fur slick with blood.

Twang.

Pain exploded in my hip. Another bolt, buried deep.

A choked yelp ripped from me, and my back legs buckled. I stumbled, the marble sliding out from under me, but I didn't stop. I dragged myself forward, each step agony. Blood dripped from the wound, trailing in vivid streaks across the floor. No way to hide it. No way to outrun what came next.

Briar?

I'm fine, I bit out through the bond, even though I wanted to collapse.

"Get inside!" Many-Greats shouted.

Vad growled low behind me. His eyes burned like silver flame as he glared down the corridor. "When we meet again," he shouted at the reloading crossbowman, "You die!"

Two more crossbowmen rounded the corner, weapons raised.

I stumbled past the threshold and into the front hall of the royal chambers, my body screaming. Vad followed me and slammed the door shut.

My legs gave out.

Thalen grabbed a narrow table from beneath a crooked painting and shoved it against the door. Rhielle ran up beside him and stabbed her sword through the handles, locking it tight.

Silus rushed to an alcove and gently laid Elara across one of the black-cushioned couches. Veralt did the same with Thalira and Yuki, his tunic now soaked in blood.

Quen set the oil lamps on the floor and slid to her knees beside me. "You all right there?" Her voice was tight. "Do I need to pull the bolts out?"

Spots swam in my vision. I dropped my head to the cool

black marble, my breath wheezing from my lungs. The pulse in my hip throbbed in time with the aches in my shoulder and side, but I managed a weak head shake. Not yet. I needed to brace myself.

Vad dropped beside me, his hand moving to my neck and muzzle to support my head. *What do you need?*

Pain flared through the bond in both directions, so sharp it left my vision spotty. *Just a few breaths.* My mind clawed for focus. *I'll shift back. It should heal me.*

I didn't tell him it could also tear me apart. Shifting wasn't safe for me in this state. Not with this many wounds. Not with three bolts buried in me like thorns. But I couldn't stay like this. I'd shifted during the last trial, when I was nearly as bad off. I could only hope my body would survive it again.

Many-Greats started forward. "We need to have her treated."

"We will. Stay back and let her focus. She'll tell me what she needs." Vad's hand swept over my head, gentle despite the tension in his jaw. *Whatever you need, my love. We've got a few minutes.*

Then his expression turned hard. "Tend to the wounded now. Stop the bleeding. We can't leave a trail." He looked to the others as Many-Greats drew back, his manner tense and cautious. "Barricade the door. Use anything you can find."

I tried to focus, but the agony was unrelenting—the bolt in my hip throbbed with each heartbeat, sharp and deep. The one in my shoulder made it hard to breathe, the muscle torn and twisted around it. My side burned as if someone had poured fire beneath my ribs. Each wound pulsed like a war drum, refusing to let me forget how broken I was.

I had no choice.

Vad, I pushed through the haze, *you need to remove all three bolts so I can shift.*

He stiffened, silver eyes snapping to mine. *All three?*

If I shift with them still in me like this, it'll shred me from the inside. I whimpered, unable to hold the noise back. *I can't heal otherwise.*

His thumb brushed under my jaw, soft even as his other hand clenched into a fist. *Briar... pulling them will make you bleed even more. You've already lost too much blood.*

If you don't... I took in a breath. *I'll die.* My head lolled against his palm. *Do it, Vad. Please.*

His jaw flexed, his silver eyes flashing with something feral. Then he looked up, voice snapping like a whip. "I need hands—now! Cloths, bandages—anything to press against the wounds the second these bolts come out!"

Rhielle and Quen were already moving. Silus tore a strip from his tunic, while Veralt ripped a tapestry off the wall. They gathered around us in a half-circle, weapons still in reach as the pounding on the door grew louder. The others remained at the door, putting more furniture against it to barricade it for as long as possible.

"Hold her steady," Vad barked. "When I pull each bolt, press down on the wound and don't let go until I say."

I'm ready, I pushed through the bond, though my body trembled.

Look at me. He cupped the side of my muzzle, forcing my gaze up to his. *Stay with me. Stay here.*

I gave the smallest nod.

He wrapped his fingers around the first bolt—the one buried in my hip—and wrenched.

Agony ripped through me like claws tearing muscle from bone. My body arched, a strangled yelp breaking from my throat as hot blood spilled over his hand. Many-Greats pressed hard with a cloth, staunching what he could.

"That's one," Vad whispered. "Two more."

"You can do this, Briar. You're strong," Many-Greats murmured, though his hands trembled a little.

My vision blurred to gray at the edges. *Hurry,* I gasped.

His hands slid to my shoulder. "This will be worse." Then he yanked.

I howled hoarsely, the sound muffled against his arm as I writhed. Blood sprayed the black marble. Rhielle shoved more fabric over the wound, her palms already slick.

"Last one," he said, voice rougher now. "Stay with me, Briar."

I barely heard him over the hammering in my skull, but I forced my eyes open. *Do it.*

His grip closed around the bolt in my hip, and he pulled.

The pain went white-hot. I nearly blacked out, jerking once before I collapsed in his lap. Everything inside me wanted to let go—to drift away into dark silence—but his voice dragged me back.

"Shift *now,*" Vad ordered, his forehead pressed to mine. "Pull the wolf back, Briar. Do it now."

I'm too weak...

I can't lose you! Imagine if I were in your place. He forced determination toward me.

Imagining him bleeding out with a potential way to save himself shook me. I dragged my wolf back, even as the pain tried to tear me apart. Bones cracked, muscles twisted, and the sound of my shift filled the hall.

Then, with a final lurch, it was over.

I lay on the cold stone, my body trembling as blood loss fogged the edges of my mind.

My wedding dress clung to me once again, the shimmering silk torn and stained, the delicate lace dark with blood. A symbol of the bond I'd been willing to fight and bleed for.

Now it was soaked in the proof that I had. Somehow, it had

survived the transition from my wolf form back to human. I'd never seen anything like it, and I was grateful to not be naked, even if I didn't understand how this was possible.

One of Vad's wings curled around me, shielding me from the others as he slid an arm under my back. "Easy," he murmured, voice rough with unleashed fury. "You're safe. Just breathe."

But beyond him, the door rattled again. This time, it buckled inward a little.

Quen hissed. "They're almost through!"

Vad's gaze flicked to mine. "Then we move with her."

He lifted me gently, like he could shield me from the worst of it with just his touch.

The pain still lingered—sharp in my hip, raw in my shoulder—but dulled enough for my vision to clear.

I lay on my back, breath sawing in and out, head cradled by Vad's arm. Then I saw the three bolts he'd removed. The bitter tang of iron clung to the back of my throat.

Vad's wing curled tighter around us. "Easy. Deep breaths."

I forced one in, slow and steady, then rasped, "You need stitches. And Yuki—her bandage came loose."

His jaw flexed. "Vyraetos is with her. What do *you* need?"

A fist pounded against the door. "Come out now!"

The next blow cracked the frame.

Veralt stormed back, dragging a heavy couch from a side room and slamming it in front of the entry. "Feck off, all of you!"

"I can move now," I said, bracing my hand against the floor. "Let's bind what we can."

Vad helped me upright, and the movement sent a fresh wave of nausea roiling through me. Blood was still pouring down his side. With a grunt of pain, he tore the bolt free. Blood gushed out. I ripped a strip from the ruined hem of my gown and tied it tight around his ribs, anchoring the fabric with shaking fingers.

Then I pushed to my feet and stumbled toward the alcove.

Thalira held Yuki's hand and rubbed it slowly.

The bandage on Thalira's shoulder had bled through completely, saturating the linen until it clung to her skin. Her dark complexion had taken on a waxy sheen, and her palms, once warm and steady, were now pale and trembling.

But it was Yuki who stole the breath from my lungs.

Her skin had gone nearly gray. Lips tinged blue. Glassy eyes half-lidded and unfocused. "Cold," she murmured, voice slurring, barely audible.

Panic clutched my throat.

How was she crashing this fast? She hadn't run. Hadn't fought. Hadn't done anything to cause this kind of blood loss.

I reached for Thalira's hands and recoiled at how cold they were. "Quen," I called over my shoulder, "bring one of the lamps. Get Thalira warm—avoid her wounds, no rubbing. Just hold the heat close."

They were both freezing.

A chill settled into my bones, a cold I knew had nothing to do with air temperature. *Do we have blankets where we're going?*

Vad plucked the bolt from his wing with a wince and slid it into the pocket of his surcoat. *We'll grab more as we go.* Concern bled through the bond, sharp and jagged when his gaze flicked to Yuki and Thalira. He didn't say what I already felt in my gut.

I turned back to them. *I'll get blankets.*

"Oh." Quen's voice softened, and her brow furrowed as she knelt beside Thalira. "Yeah, let's get you warm." She wrapped her arms around her, pressing Thalira's head to her chest. She started to rub Thalira's arms then stopped.

Thalira's lips trembled. Her gaze never left Yuki.

I grabbed Yuki's hands. There was barely any warmth left. The bandage at her wrist had stopped pulsing with fresh blood, but it wasn't enough. Her skin looked like she'd been bleeding out for hours, not mere minutes.

Her eyelashes fluttered weakly as she looked toward me, and something in her expression changed. It wasn't pain—it was *fear.*

I inched closer to adjust her position, and that's when I saw it.

Her right slipper peeked out from beneath her skirt, soaked a deep crimson that had already darkened to near-black. Droplets of blood pattered onto the stone. I lifted the skirt—and bile hit the back of my throat.

Dozens of cuts crisscrossed her calves and shins. Some were shallow, but most were deep. Shards of glass glinted in the folds of her gown like the fabric had swept them up, trapping them against her skin. Her shoes had protected her feet, but that hadn't helped while she was being carried. The glass had been pressed into her skin. She probably hadn't even felt it.

I slid my fingers into the silk and removed a sliver... then another. And then even more.

She was bleeding *everywhere.*

Vyraetos stood silently nearby, his hands folded tight. The look in his eyes shattered me.

She had minutes.

Yuki's lips parted. Her head barely turned. But her eyes... they found me for a moment. "Sorry," she breathed. "Didn't... mean to cut myself. I'm... such a mess." She inhaled a shallow breath. "Don't want to die here."

Tears burned the back of my eyes. "You have *nothing* to apologize for."

"Calla Lily," she murmured, a shiver racking her. "She hugged me..."

"Calla Lily will pay. I swear it." My voice shook as I motioned toward the lamp.

Vad brought it over and set it on the table beside us.

Rhielle placed a hand on Yuki's shoulder, fingers gently curved. "It's going to be all right, Yuki," she whispered. "Just breathe. Rest. Think about home—all right? The grasslands. The sun on your face. You and your sisters weaving baskets and carving sigils while the wind smells like wildflowers."

Yuki's eyes slid shut.

Myantha approached silently, carrying another lamp. She set it near Yuki's feet, her gaze locked on our friend's face. Silent tears slid down her cheeks.

My heart screamed, and I held Yuki tighter. Her pulse fluttered against my fingers, so damn faint. The scent of blood and bitter venom flooded my senses, curdling my stomach.

Yuki tried to smile. "My sisters..."

Her voice broke, barely more than air. Her eyelids fluttered.

Then her eyes rolled back.

Her chest lifted with one last breath—and stilled.

It didn't rise again.

Stillness spread through the room, too sudden and too final.

Quen rocked back on her heels, still holding Thalira. A small, broken sound slipped from her throat—a whimper that cracked at the end. She squeezed her eyes shut, but the tears came anyway, spilling down and soaking into the bloodstained blue fabric of Thalira's shirt.

Thalira bent forward, shoulders shaking. Her uninjured hand reached up, clutching Quen back with trembling fingers, her cheek pressed into her hair.

I couldn't move.

Couldn't breathe.

First Velessa. Now Yuki.

This couldn't be happening.

My wolf howled within me, but no sound made it past my

lips. Rage and grief twisted together until my body trembled and my eyes burned. My hands shook. My knees buckled.

This wasn't supposed to happen.

She was supposed to survive.

I pressed the heel of my palm to my chest, trying to hold myself together. But my breathing came too fast, too shallow.

Vad's presence slammed through the bond, flooding me with warmth. He dropped beside me, his hands gripping my shoulders.

It wasn't your fault.

Out loud, his voice was steel. "We need to move. If you've got wounds, finish binding them now. We can't leave a trail."

My instincts took over, even as my mind drowned in grief. Two had been lost. I couldn't lose anyone else.

I rose on shaky legs, eyes locked on Yuki's still form. I couldn't process this—two friends dead in less than an hour. My brain refused to accept it, but my body understood.

With trembling hands, I adjusted her on the couch with her hands resting on her green dress as if she were sleeping. Like she might open her eyes and smile again.

A massive thud struck the door, heavy and large. The furniture barrier jolted, wood groaning under impact.

"Briar." Vad's voice was low but urgent. His hand closed around my wrist, pulling me back from the edge of shock. "We need to move. *Now.*"

"They've got a battering ram," Thalen shouted from his position near the door. He stepped away fast. "No one leaves a trail."

We had seconds. Maybe less.

I forced my limbs to move. We needed to get Thalira to safety. She'd been hit by a bolt—*but maybe her dress hadn't caught the glass like Yuki's had.* Her skirt was shorter. Maybe. Hopefully.

Footsteps rushed around me. While I'd been focused on Yuki, someone had been gathering items. Vad handed me blankets and a box and pulled me farther down the hall and through the corresponding corridors.

The others were already in motion.

A tense silence settled over us, pierced only by the steady *thud... thud...* of the ram against the door. Each blow reverberated through my body like a countdown.

We moved deeper into the royal chambers. Dimly lit rooms blurred past. Another sitting area, a narrow archway, then another archway that brought us to what looked like a private dining area. Beyond that, a smaller room with a heavy oak door.

Vad stopped in front of a marble panel. His fingers pressed into what seemed like natural cracks and flaws in the stone.

A soft *click* echoed, and the wall opened diagonally as if seamless magic had carved the passage from stone itself.

"Go," he ordered, nodding toward the stairwell hidden behind it.

Thalen ducked in first, Myantha and Quen close behind with the lamps. The narrow stairs descended steeply into darkness, but the path was clean.

Silus went next, Elara limp in his arms, her breathing shallow but steady.

Another blow rocked the doors behind us.

This time, something cracked.

My nerves tightened, and I dug my fingers into my arm. *Do you have anything like wolves or dogs for tracking?* If so, we needed *something* to mask our scent.

Thalira and Rhielle went down next, Rhielle's arm steadying Thalira while careful not to jostle the bolt. Many-Greats brought up the rear, pausing long enough to give me a stern look like he expected me to follow him.

No. Vad responded. *Only magic. And that's not working for anyone. Once we're inside, we'll lock the door. I mussed the rug in front of my chambers and left a few other clues to lead them to a dead end.* He slid an arm around my waist.

I nodded and leaned into his warmth. He grounded me, pushing back the chill of the grief gnawing inside.

We would have our revenge on everyone who'd attacked us, and Calla Lilly would pay.

I'd find one of those venom-coated daggers and show her how much it hurt to bleed out. Then I'd bite her for good measure.

Vad guided me onto the stairs, then pulled the door shut behind us with a firm *snick*. His arm remained around my waist, anchoring me as we stepped down the narrow stairway.

The walls closed around us. Traces of quartz sparkled in the black stone, catching bits of lamplight. The rock was coarse, uneven in places, though the floor had been worn smoother from use. The staircase spiraled in four tight coils, and our breaths echoed on the walls, the sounds of our friends carrying back to us softly.

We passed several simple, sealed wooden doors, and a shiver of unease shot down my spine.

"Keep going to the gathering room," Vad called out in a low tone. "It's the most defensible point and closest to the outer passages. If we have to make a run for it, that's the best spot."

He looked down at me. Concern furrowed his brow and radiated through our bond. A jagged edge of pain soon followed, probably from his injured side.

But his determination didn't waver. *You need to rest.*

There is no rest. We have to get the medicine for Thalira and Elara, I linked back to him. My mind spun with strategies and timelines. *We'll need food, water, and shelter too.* I clutched the blankets closer.

There are underground rivers in the caverns here, he answered. *We have access to one near the gathering room, and we have some food stores. Enough for a couple of days, but the passages will help us reach the outside.*

We rounded the corner to find a single door, soft golden light spilling from the doorway. Inside, the room was lined with shelves that contained boxes, cloth, and supplies.

Rhielle knelt beside Thalira and wrapped a blanket tightly around her trembling shoulders. Quen sat beside them, whispering as she gently pushed the hair back from Thalira's clammy forehead.

Silus set Elara down on a thick, black leather mat. Her breathing was still too shallow. Vyraetos knelt beside her, fingers pressed to her pulse, his jaw tight. Thalen crouched beside her, holding out a dark waterskin, and Myantha hovered behind him, hands braced on her knees.

Many-Greats set out ointments and salves between Thalira and Elara as Vyraetos kept shaking his head.

At the far end, Veralt rifled through the boxes. "There's dried fruit and salted meat here. Not much else."

Stepping into the room, I wrapped my arms around myself. Vad squeezed my arm once more, and I managed a small nod and started toward Thalira and Elara.

A flash of movement startled me.

Before I could react, Silus lunged at Vad.

His fist connected with Vad's jaw in a sickening crunch.

CHAPTER SIX

Silus's punch echoed like a gunshot in the chamber.

My body snapped to attention.

What the actual fuck!

Vad staggered backward, slamming into the doorframe. Pain twisted his features as he struck his wounded side and fresh blood seeped through the already soaked bandage. He grunted as he shot one clawed hand out and dug into the wooden shelf beside him to keep himself from falling.

"This is all your fault," Silus spat, looming over Vad with rage burning in his eyes. "Every death. Every drop of blood. It's on your hands!" His voice cracked. "And now our magic is gone. All of it, because of *her.* I told you she was *trouble.* I bet you regret your decision now."

Vad rebounded, moving past me to get to him, but I linked, *Stop. Please. For me. He's upset, scared, and hurt. Let me handle this.*

Silus's words had cut because he was right. The loss of magic had been because Vad chose me. Maybe he did regret it, and the fated mate bond was the only reason he was being protective of me. Not by choice but a fated duty.

Vad stopped at my side and pressed a hand to his wound.

Silus pointed a trembling hand toward Elara. "If she dies because of you, I swear by everything I am, I'll spend the rest of eternity making you pay."

My blood warmed at that threat. How dare he threaten his king and my mate!

Vad's face paled, and his silver-gray eyes blazed. *If he doesn't shut up, I* will *intervene.*

"Fecking void, Silus!" Thalen jumped to his feet, his voice sharp with disbelief. "Are you trying to die?"

Myantha turned away, covering her face. Veralt raised an unimpressed brow, and Rhielle rocked back on her heels.

"Vad." The ragged whisper came from Elara, who stirred weakly on the mat.

Not moving his hand from Elara's arm, Vyraetos frowned.

My pulse raced faster. Now he was even upsetting Elara. Something had to give.

"What the hell are you attacking him for, idiot?" Quen's voice cracked like one of her fire whips.

Vad's breaths were shallow, each inhale hissing through clenched teeth. "Silus—" He ground out.

I launched myself forward, my bloodstained wedding gown tangling around my legs. My shoulder slammed into Silus's side, driving him into the wooden floor with a *thud*.

Before he could recover, my hand was at his throat, my fingers locked around the soft flesh beneath his jaw, my face inches from his with my teeth bared.

A low growl vibrated in my chest, my wolf surging beneath my skin.

How dare he lay hands on Vad! The man who'd saved all of us and led us through hell. And he called himself his friend?

If I didn't know how much Elara loved Silus....

"Touch him again," I snarled, tightening my grip just enough to restrict his movement, "and I'll rip your throat out."

Silus's eyes widened, his hands flying up to claw at my grip. His pulse hammered beneath my fingers while his breath came in strangled gasps. The acrid scent of his fear and shock filled my nostrils.

I didn't let go. "He's your king and your friend. He does *not* deserve this betrayal.

"You've made it clear you want Elara to live, which we all want as well, but right now, you're the one getting in the way." My voice dropped to a dangerous low. "You want someone to blame? Fine. Blame the people who attacked us. Blame the traitors. Blame whoever orchestrated this." I snarled. "But don't you *dare* blame the man who's been fighting beside us to keep everyone alive."

I released him and stepped back, my hands trembling at my sides.

Silus slumped against the door, coughing, rubbing his throat. His eyes flicked from me to Vad, his fire dulled but not gone.

The room had fallen silent, everyone frozen in place as they watched us.

"We've already lost Velessa and Yuki." The words felt like sandpaper against my throat. "And that was after Vad and Elara lost their father, King Merrick." My voice cracked. "So many have died."

I met each of their gazes, one by one. "If we fall apart now, we hand them *everything*. The throne. The realm. Our lives. Fighting each other only makes their job easier."

Silus bowed his head but didn't look away. A hint of something passed through his eyes. Respect? Guilt? Both?

He straightened his surcoat and lifted his chin. "As you say, Your Majesty."

Vad stepped beside me, his hand resting on my shoulder with a comforting buzz. A slow, approving thrum pulsed through our bond, deeper than words, rising above the pain and anger still roiling in him.

"The last thing we need is to turn on one another," he said, voice level but firm. His gaze locked on Silus. "After we reclaim the palace and everyone we care for is safe, if you still have grievances, we can settle them formally. Duel, if we must. But until then..." His wings flared behind him, his body still taut with pain, but he didn't flinch. "Channel your rage toward the ones *hunting* us.

"But if you ever lay a hand on Briar, even raise your voice to her, I'll end you where you stand."

Silus's upper lip curled, but he said nothing.

"I don't want you two fighting." Elara rose on shaky legs. Her fingers dug into Vyraetos's shoulder as she steadied herself and stood. "None of this is Vad's or Briar's fault. Something else is happening. Something bigger than all of us. The only way we'll have a chance to survive is if we stop acting like enemies and start fighting like a family."

Vyraetos spoke softly. "Wise words, Your Highness, but may I suggest refraining from walking until we've gotten you the proper medications? Standing will be far more feasible after you have been fully treated."

Elara's jaw clenched. Despite the pallor in her cheeks, fire flashed in her dark-blue eyes. She pressed the palm of her hand against the wall. "I'm not walking. I'm standing. And I want to know what's going on. Do we have any idea what happened up there?"

"Not fully." Vyraetos gave her arm a small tug, guiding her back with care. "But treating injuries must come first. Once everyone's stable, we'll determine our next course of action."

"I *am* stable," Elara snapped. "However, my brother was shot, and he's pretending it doesn't hurt when I know it does." She threw Vad a cutting look that dared him to argue. "Before he goes off on his next escapade, that must be dealt with."

"I agree." I nodded and raised an eyebrow at my mate as his mouth opened. "He needs to be treated before we leave for the Healing Hall."

Vad frowned, but he shook his head. "I don't need anyone to see to my injuries until yours are tended."

Turning both palms up in surrender, Vyraetos shrugged. "You see, Your Majesty? I'm outnumbered."

Vad's face hardened. "I said I don't need anyone to deal with my wounds until Briar's are tended to first."

I smirked, knowing victory was in my grasp. "Perfect. So you'll let them treat you once I'm handled?"

"That is what I said." His brow creased.

"Perfect, because I'm fine!" I spread my arms wide and rolled my shoulders. "Wolf healing. Shifting allows my wounds to heal quicker."

"Convenient," Vad scoffed. He shrugged off his blood-soaked surcoat and draped it over a shelf, then undid the remains of his black tunic, blood still slick across his ribs.

Vyraetos lifted a box marked with a staff symbol, peeled back the lid, and removed a roll of bandages and a jar of thick salve.

"Is there anything in there that will help Thalira and Elara?" I folded my arms. "Thalira needs something to stop the bleeding."

"She's stable, but not for long," Vyraetos said without looking up. "We'll do what we can here, but without the antidote..."

I nodded grimly. "Then we move quickly. It could take us hours to come back with what she needs."

Across the room, Many-Greats knelt beside Thalira, pressing a small silver flask to her lips. She drank hesitantly and grimaced. Quen joined them, checking Thalira's skin and arms for glass fragments—searching for the same signs that had marked Yuki before she died.

A tight ache cinched my chest. Grief coiled sharp and fresh in my throat, and I swallowed it back.

Myantha crossed to me and gently placed her hand over mine. Her dark brown eyes shimmered, glassy with unshed tears. "I'll help you get the medicine if you want. But you have to know—I never meant to hurt you. I would *never* hurt you, Briar. I swear it. If it weren't for you, I'd be dead."

I inhaled slowly, but not a trace of sulfur laced the air.

Trusting people had already cost me too much... but magic was gone here, so she couldn't cover up the smell.

I squeezed her hand. "I believe you."

Tears slid down her cheeks, and she ducked her head with a sniff. "I can't believe Yuki and Velessa are gone."

My throat tightened. "I know." The weight of grief pressed on my chest, and tears stung as they filled my eyes. I forced them back. Now wasn't the time. If I started crying, I wouldn't be able to stop. "We'll get through this and bring their killers to justice."

Vad cast a glance in our direction. *Does that lie-smelling ability of yours ever mislead you?*

Not this time because no one has magic. It's hard to get the spell right to cover the scent of a lie, and the fae aren't aware that I have the ability. People can manipulate it with half-truths or omissions, but Myantha isn't doing that.

Across the room, Quen growled with frustration. "So it was Calla Lily we should have been watching, not Kaylen. Figures."

"What happened to Kaylen?" Elara asked weakly. "It looked like they were dragging her away. That would suggest she wasn't involved in the decision-making, or perhaps she'd served her purpose." She hesitated. "And Calla Lily...I don't remember seeing her."

"She vanished," I said, my thoughts racing. "The Aureline guards had Kaylen though. There weren't many of them in the Ceremonial Hall, and I didn't spot Calla Lily anywhere near the fighting."

I glanced at Myantha again, pressing my fist against my chest. "How would Calla Lily have gotten the knives into everyone's pockets? And why?"

Many-Greats rummaged through the supply box Vyraetos had opened and pulled out salves and ointments. His once-elegant garb was shredded in multiple places, and blood soaked the bandage wrapped around his arm. "It fits with what Calla Lily has already done. Vad and Thalen can attest that she slipped a venom-coated blade into one of your gowns' pockets too, Briar. Initially, I believed it was to frame you, but now I wonder if perhaps it was also meant to kill you. Perhaps both. The blade matched the one used in the assassination attempt."

He straightened, face grim. "I'm still not certain how deep her involvement runs. But one thing is clear—Calla Lily is not to be trusted."

"What are you even talking about, old man?" Quen demanded as she crossed her arms. Fire blazed in her eyes. "You were the liar who stood there and announced Calla Lily as Fate's chosen. You wrapped that lie in your role as an Aureline High Council member!"

With sweat beading her forehead and her lips taking on a dull, grayish cast, Thalira lifted her head and glared at him. Beside her, Rhielle didn't speak, but disapproval radiated from her rigid posture.

Many-Greats sighed, his muscles tense. He dragged a hand through his wild auburn hair, making it even more unruly. "Briar, I realize that we must speak about what has happened, but I would prefer to have this conversation in private—"

"Tough," I cut in. "We're running out of time. Say it now,

or don't say it at all."

Pain shot through our bond, and Vad grimaced. Vyraetos had pulled one of the embedded bolts free. I flinched and caught his gaze.

I'm fine, he reassured me.

We may have to redefine what fine *means,* I shot back.

A faint smile tugged at his lips, then faded as he focused once more on Many-Greats.

"I'm leaving as soon as Vad's treated," I told him firmly. "So if you've got something to confess, now's the time."

Many-Greats clenched his jaw, a muscle ticking as he held my gaze. He exhaled and tilted his head. "When Calla Lily learned you were part of my lineage, she threatened to expose my treachery. I assumed she meant she'd inform the prince. And she was already at the threshold of Briar's room with guards less than thirty feet away. One well-placed shout would've unraveled the entire plan to get you out."

Gasps followed along with murmurs of surprise. Elara covered her mouth as Silus scowled. Thalen's shoulders slumped as if he were confused.

Many-Greats' throat bobbed as he swallowed hard. "She offered me a deal. If I went ahead with my plan to remove you from the realm, she wouldn't tell anyone or try to harm you. In turn, I had to announce that *she* was the one chosen by Fate. Publicly, with all the authority my position carried."

His mouth tightened as the weight of the betrayal settled between us like lead.

I stared at him, waiting.

I felt a shift in Vad's energy—a bristling storm just under the surface. His silence spoke louder than words. Vyraetos kept working, dabbing his wound with a glowing blue liquid, though his eyes flicked between us. He was listening to every word.

"And?" I asked when the silence dragged on too long. My

voice was cold. Flat. "You took the deal?"

Many-Greats offered a slight stiff nod. "I saw no reason not to when your life was in the balance. She told me that she had no desire to see you dead. Simply out of the way. And since you had to go home to keep the warning from Fate from coming true, it seemed a viable solution. She told me that Kaylen would make a scene, and after Kaylen's failed announcement, I had to present her. She made me vow to do so."

"And you did." Vad growled the words.

Many-Greats lifted his chin but focused on me. "I do whatever it takes to protect my family. And I had sworn to Ember that, no matter what happened, I would protect you and bring you home. That's why I made you promise not to tell anyone that you were related to me and why I never told you my name. It saved your life."

"Of course, she's Aureline, and related directly to you," Thalen snorted. "I've called her Chaos since the beginning."

Others mumbled, but no one truly reacted. We were all beaten, injured, and exhausted.

Vad's jaw flexed. I could feel the fury simmering in him, hot and sharp.

"Did Calla Lily say anything else?" I asked. Given what was on the line, it was hard to know whether Calla Lily was involved in the planning or just another pawn like Kaylen. "Did she say how she knew that Kaylen would try to claim the title?"

"She probably just knew who Kaylen was and what she was like," Quen muttered.

Many-Greats shook his head. "She left immediately after I made the vow, and she helped me get two of my men into position to retrieve Briar and send her home. That was all that was required, and I didn't push for more. I was more interested in getting Briar to safety."

Annoyance flashed through me, and I felt it mirrored in

Vad as well.

I pursed my lips. "And then what?"

"I took advantage of the confusion that followed your disappearance. The High Council, along with the joint council between the Shadow and Aureline, was in disarray. Most of the council members were too shaken by the signs to take clear action. Two council members came to me in private to ensure that Calla Lily was named officially. The collapse during the third bridal trial only deepened the confusion."

Vad shifted suddenly. "If I'd known picking Briar would cause the loss of magic—"

"You wouldn't have picked her," Many-Greats interrupted flatly.

Vad's anger flared hot. His lips curled into a snarl as he took a step forward. "Don't you dare presume I'd ever choose anything over Briar. I would give up the crown, my realm, and my magic for her. There is *no one* else for me."

The air crackled. Even Vyraetos froze, the bandage in his hands forgotten.

Many-Greats shook his head, like he didn't believe Vad.

Vad's voice dropped, low and lethal. "I would burn this realm to ash before letting her go. The fact that you thought otherwise says more about you than me."

Emotion flooded through the bond like a raw, unshakable devotion.

Some of the weight lifted from my chest. I hadn't realized I had needed to hear him say that, no matter what, he chose me. And somehow, someway, I fell even harder for him. *I love you.*

Love isn't strong enough to describe what I feel for you.

Blinking, Many-Greats cleared his throat. "I stand corrected."

Vad cleared his throat, and some of his anger eased. "Who were the council members who approached you? Was one of them about so tall—" he lifted a hand "—with light-blue eyes and freckles? Perhaps in league with someone on the Shadow Council?"

Many-Great's brow pinched, and his lip curled. "Yes. Bram. I suspected him already. He and three others had been behaving oddly, speaking in hushed circles about the instability of the current system. Some believe Fate's ways are obsolete. That it's time for a drastic change."

His voice dropped lower. "There are whispers of removing all the kings and queens and installing one single ruler for the entire realm."

Vyraetos clicked his tongue with disapproval. "I have heard similar rumors. Some of our council members were compromised as well. I suspect that this mutinous horde believes they can justify this coup by claiming Fate has allowed it and use that lie to crown themselves."

Silus stood beside Elara again. "And they knew that this union would end our magic?" His tone was clipped but calm.

"No. No one knew what Briar was except me," Many-Greats said sternly. "If they had known, they would have tried even harder to kill her. And not only them, but others as well. I did send Briar away. I had this handled." His eyes narrowed at Vad. "You vowed to send her home."

"She is the one who decided her home is with me," Vad said coldly. "I kept my vow." He stepped closer, smoothing his tunic with one hand. "You should have told us more, given the threat was that serious."

"What could or could not have been said is now irrelevant." Many-Greats narrowed his eyes, and the wrinkles in his face deepened. "I warned you as best as I could without putting lives in more danger. I would have said more at the coronation, but your purple-haired friend—"

"Don't speak ill of Velessa." Quen balled her fists. "If you hadn't been acting like a creepy old bastard trying to keep our friend from being queen, she wouldn't have had to silence you. You think we don't know that Briar and Vad are meant to be? That there wouldn't be consequences for what you did?"

Many-Greats opened his mouth, but I cut in, "That's enough. What's done is done." I turned toward him. "As far as Calla Lily goes, do we know how she got the daggers into everyone's pockets? You said she planted one in my room. Did she break into theirs too?"

Did we need to search for more? My hand slid tentatively to the pocket in my dress, even though I knew nothing was there. But if she'd gotten into everyone's room, then who knew what else she had done? The timeline mattered as well.

"We were all in my room, getting ready for the wedding," Thalira said, her voice strained. She gasped every few words. "She came in to wish us luck. Hugged Myantha, Yuki, Velessa, and me. Maybe she slipped them in then."

My stomach turned. I remembered Yuki and Velessa mentioning those hugs. It had meant something to them. Now I saw it for what it was—another layer of Calla Lily's cruelty.

"So we still don't know whether she was a vile opportunist or part of a larger plan," Rhielle muttered. She crouched beside Thalira and reached into her pocket. Her expression twisted as she removed a blade smeared with the same iridescent green substance. "Fecking void."

My shoulders tightened. A cap covered the blade's tip, keeping it from piercing anything easily, but the sides would've easily nicked skin.

Veralt swore under his breath. "Brutal bitch."

Thalen stood next to Myantha now, his hand cradling hers. They exchanged glances, and there was concern in his eyes.

"None on Quen, or you, Rhielle?" Vad reached into one of the boxes higher on the shelf and removed two sheathed daggers. He passed one to me. The smooth leather sheath had a button-on strap that allowed it to be fastened to a belt or sash.

"I don't do hugs," Quen muttered. Her brow furrowed. "I should have shoved her out the door as soon as she came in."

Rhielle shrugged. "I wasn't interested in random affection."

Thalira cut her eyes away, her eyelids shuttering. Her breaths sounded shallow and uneven.

I crouched beside her and wrapped my hands around hers. "Thalira, I give you my word that I'll do everything I can. This won't be how you die."

Her lips trembled, and tears clung to her dark lashes. She squeezed my hand with her uninjured one, but her fingers were cold as ice. "I know you will," she whispered, quiet and certain.

Those four words nearly broke me.

I forced myself to smile, squeezed her hand again, and rose. "How's the pain?" My gaze dropped to the bolt embedded in her shoulder. The bandage around it was already dark with blood. Though the wound was deep, the bolt hadn't pierced all the way through. Holding it in place was the only thing keeping her from bleeding out.

"It's manageable." Thalira pursed her lips. "Whatever Councilman Bryn gave me took the edge off."

"There's a small wood stove two doors down on the left," Vad said. "You can heat water. There isn't much wood, but it's built in such a way that the smoke is dispersed without drawing attention. At least one of the teas will help with pain. Use it for heating food and water only. No hot baths. We need to make the supply last."

Many-Greats snorted as he examined the vials and salves laid on the bench. "That tea won't work miracles. These herbs and tinctures are rudimentary. Nothing here will treat medical conditions. It'll be pain relief at best, with potentially antiseptic properties."

I narrowed my eyes at him. "We're not in the Healing Hall, and miracles aren't coming. Just do what you can. Keep the pressure on all of Thalira's wounds and check for shards of glass or small cuts."

Vyraetos gestured Vad over. The two of them slipped into a quiet conversation while Vyraetos packed away jars of salve and opened another bin.

"Don't dally while you're up there," Many-Greats warned. "This rebellion has been planned for ages, but we still don't know everyone who is involved. I have allies, but they won't know where to find me. We need to determine whether the loss to magic is beyond this palace, as I suspect, and who is leading this coup."

"How did they know that Vad choosing me would sever our magic?" I asked. "If that's what they wanted, why wait until now?"

"I don't believe that they did. We knew they were manipulating the bridal competition, and we knew a few other loyal members who were on our side. But we didn't know the extent to which the manipulation had gone."

My gut hardened.

"It has always been known that a royal must not wed an Aureline. Aurelines are neutralizers," Vyraetos explained from his position on the far side of the room with Vad. He sealed the jar of salve and set it back on the shelf in front of a bin, then pointed to another as if to show Vad.

"Please understand, Briar, I couldn't tell you that." Many-Greats wrung his hands. "If I had, you'd be dead. And once they knew about you, they wouldn't have stopped with just you. They'd have hunted down your sister as well as anyone loyal to you and killed them all."

I went still. Ice crawled down my spine. "They know about Ember? Is she in danger?"

This couldn't be happening. Not now, when we'd lost everything.

Chapter Seven

My breath caught. The room spun for just a second, but it was enough.

Ember.

My older sister was strong, brave, and an amazing leader. And if she was even remotely in danger because of *me*...

A growl rumbled deep in my chest. "Tell me she's safe. Tell me they don't know about her."

Many-Greats didn't flinch, but the seriousness in his expression twisted something in me. "If they overheard you speak of her, they know. But beyond that..." His voice was grave. "They know you are from Earth. It will not take long for them to connect the threads. The descendants of the Aureline who fled carried unusual magic. And if certain members of the Aureline Council believe those individuals or their descendants threaten their cause, they'll want that threat eliminated. She's fine for now, but this is... complicated."

My nails bit into my palms. Ember hadn't asked for this. She was just trying to get the supernatural world back in order. She didn't need yet another entity to target her.

"The portals aren't working, right?" My voice trembled. I hated the sign of weakness, but I couldn't help it. "If the magic's gone, then they wouldn't be able to use them to get to her."

I was desperate for logic to smother the panic spiraling through my chest.

The winged guards who'd dragged me to this realm in the first place hadn't seemed hindered at all. Ember and Ryker had gotten to my room as the portal was closing—they'd seen me disappear in front of their eyes.

Many-Greats shook his head, but Vyraetos answered louder and more firmly. "The magic was taken at the crowning. Fate acted through the Stag. And though our magic was taken, that interaction did not suggest judgment, but change. A transformation. Fate doesn't speak in words but through actions and symbols. This was one."

He nodded at Vad and glanced at me. "*Most* of our magic is gone. But the innate abilities like sight, speed, and senses remain. The portals may hold trace magic. Enough for travel, perhaps, but limited. Not with an army or even a team."

"But one assassin?" I rasped, my throat tight.

Many-Greats stilled as well, his arms hanging at his sides. His jaw muscle ticked.

The worst kind of threat was the one that could sneak through. That no one would see coming until it was too late.

Vyraetos cleared his throat. "I cannot say. I would assume that no more than one or two people could make it through a portal and back. Perhaps three if it were one of the older portals. In past magical disruptions, those locations retained the most remnants."

One was all it would take.

I swallowed hard as dread weighed me down.

Rhielle moved beside me and pulled me a few steps away. "You'd better come back, Briar." Her voice was gruff but steady.

She adjusted the scarf around her neck, revealing a sliver of the deep, jagged red scar beneath. The mark of survival. Of betrayal. "I don't like getting attached to people just to lose them. There's been enough of that. And I'm not about to let those bastards win another inch."

I reached out and squeezed her hands, burying my fear. "Watch over them. All of them."

Rhielle nodded once, sharp and sure.

I didn't let myself look back at Thalira. If I did, I wouldn't be able to walk away. She had too many fractures, too many wounds that hadn't healed.

"Are you ready, Briar?" Vad's voice came from behind me.

As I started to nod, Thalen interrupted, clapping his hands together as he crossed over to us. "Ready? Great. I'm going with you."

Vad shook his head. "We aren't taking a full party. This must be swift. And I won't be alone. Briar is going with me."

I smiled inwardly. He hadn't asked, he'd just known there wasn't a chance in hell or Fate's plan that I'd let him go without me.

"Like I said, you're not going alone," Thalen replied, unbothered. "You two basically count as one, and if one of you gets the bright idea to sacrifice yourself in some grand gesture, someone's got to be there to make sure you don't *both* go down." He folded his arms and flashed his crooked smile, but the weight in his tone said he meant every word.

"Won't it be hard for you to see?" I asked. Even with a little light filtering into the castle, it was dark.

"The servants will be relighting the torches and lamps in the main areas. Tradition and common sense." He lifted his hands with a smirk. "Besides, if we have to split up, you need someone else who knows the palace like the back of his hand. That's me. I'll get flint and steel to take as well in case."

Myantha placed a hand on his arm, and he brushed his fingers over hers.

Vad sighed and dragged a hand through his hair. "All right."

Veralt grunted from the center of the room, a box tucked under one thick arm and dried fruit in one hand. "Rhielle and I will come as far as the exit. We should leave—"

"We aren't leaving until this is settled." Rhielle returned to his side and swatted his forearm. Her brow lifted in a sharp arch. "I'm not leaving my girl."

Veralt lifted his shoulders in a dramatic sigh and popped a piece of fruit into his mouth. "As the light of my life commands, we wouldn't *dream* of leaving. Where do you need us?" When he glanced down at her, she gave him a subtle smile.

"Here. Protecting the injured and preparing for departure." Vad gestured around the room and toward the hall. "If the guards find this place, everyone will need to move fast and deeper into the tunnels.

"Elara and Thalira will both need to be carried. The rocks get coarser and sharper the further down you go. There won't be any light unless you're carrying it." He motioned a right turn with a hook of his hand. "Take the larder path. Use light if you need to. It's the same way we're heading initially, but once you reach the sealed door, go left. Then keep one hand on the wall and go right every time the tunnel opens again."

He waited until Rhielle and Veralt nodded before continuing, "Keep tight against the wall at all times. Eventually, you'll reach the vesting chamber. There is fresh water and only two entry points, and plenty of crevices and cracks for cover. That path will let you avoid the most dangerous sections by the river. We'll meet you there."

Veralt's eyes sharpened beneath the lazy smirk. "What about supplies?"

"Prepare bags to take if we need to run. Essentials only. Put them near the door so we can grab them if needed." Vad rubbed the bandage on his hand. "We don't know how long we'll be underground. But if something happens to us above or we don't come back, you move. Don't wait. You protect them."

Vad turned to Silus. "Set the tripwires after we leave. Start with the top of the staircase. You know where the key is, right?"

Silus nodded, expressionless. "Yes, I'll mark the larder path last. Wire set with ball bearings and cups three inches off the ground, or razor wire and no sound?"

"Razor wire at the top of the staircase, but hidden. Wire with ball bearings everywhere else. Have the razor wire prepped to put up across our escape path if needed." Vad's jaw flexed. "Gather all the weapons we've got, including whatever we brought with us. Check the smaller storerooms for supplies. Clothes, gear, anything can help. Once we retrieve the medicine, we'll make another supply run before we move out."

Rhielle rubbed her arms, and one of her hands moved to her throat. Her fingers brushed the edge of her scar. "How likely is it that the guards will find us? How certain are you that none of the servants or guards know of this place?"

Exhaling, Vad scratched the back of his neck. "My family kept this secret with great care. But you're correct; no secret is perfect. As long as no one has access to magic, the wards and sigils set in the walls and door frames will not work either for protection or location. We left a false trail in the royal quarters. That will hopefully occupy them for a while."

His gaze went to me and then Thalen, and he waved a hand. "Let's go."

Vad took the lead, slipping into the hall. Thalen fell in beside me, one hand trailing the damp wall, the other resting on my shoulder as he prepared for the darkness.

We padded past two sharp turns. The tunnel narrowed and tilted downward. The air grew damper with each step, and Vad ducked under a crumbling overhang. We followed him into a chamber with a metal door.

Vad pulled a key from his pocket and twisted it in the dust-clogged keyhole. The tumblers groaned, then shifted, and with a muted *click*, the door opened on squealing hinges.

Vad slipped through first, scanning both sides before waving us in. I ducked into the darkness with Thalen behind me. The metal door slid shut with a soft *snick*, leaving us in silence.

A tunnel stretched before us, long and low, arching wide. The corridor's chill bit through my bloody, torn dress and sank right into my bones, and the humid and stale air smelled of stone and mildew.

My wolf vision sharpened, and I could see the branching passageways, every jagged edge, every patch of slick stone, and how the floor tilted upward now. Vad's eyes glimmered with shadow sight too, but Thalen's hand squeezed my shoulder tighter. I slowed so he wouldn't trip.

"Don't worry about me, Chaos," Thalen murmured. "I can keep up."

"You better," I whispered back. I wanted to say something funny back, something normal, but nothing came to mind.

After a hundred paces, the passage leveled off. Vad led us through another set of branching passages, and I tried to remember each one in case something happened and I had to navigate back alone.

We climbed a winding staircase carved from the rough black basalt. The stairs were narrow, uneven, and slick in some spots while jagged in others.

At the top, we came to another metal door. Vad pressed his palm flat on the surface, then leaned his ear to the seam. After a moment, he pressed his hand against the small handle and eased the door open.

We emerged into what had once been a quiet seating

alcove. A black velvet sofa sat untouched beside a black stone end table topped with a small sculpture of an obsidian wolf that had to be a representation of their shadow beast. The air stank of blood and metal.

The lamps flickered sporadically, casting moving golden pools across the floor. The gaps between the pools were thick with shadow.

Those pockets of darkness had my hair standing on end, worse than if the room had been pitch black.

We kept to the wall, moving in silence.

When we reached the cross corridor, we turned left, and the destruction hit like a punch to the chest.

Shattered doors. Blood smeared across the floors and walls. Lamp oil pooled like slick shadows across the floor. Furniture overturned like someone—or something—had given chase. Sculptures lay crumbled and vases smashed.

What part of the palace is this? My pulse ticked in my throat.

One of the hosting halls, Vad linked back. *Not all members of the royal families and dignitaries attend the ceremonies for weddings and coronations, often because they're too young or ill or antisocial and would distract from the events. Those people and their attendants stay here to rest for the duration of the event. Then, later, when we have the feasts and celebrations, they participate as they are able or permitted.*

Blood had dried in thick, coppery puddles, some no bigger than the size of a palm. *Could they have started the attack during the coronation?*

If they used silencing spells, yes, Vad responded. *Something went wrong.*

I swallowed hard. *I think they were planning this the whole time.* With all the high-ranking guests attending, the timing had been too perfect. *This wasn't just an opportunity ambush.*

This was done on purpose.

We passed a doorway where a strip of pale gray fabric clung to the splintered wood. I recognized it immediately.

An Aureline guard cloak. Maybe this was where so many of the Aureline guards had been.

My stomach twisted.

It was too quiet. The sort of quiet that didn't feel like an aftermath.

It felt like a warning. Like something was still here, watching and waiting.

Unease prickled down my spine.

Vad pointed ahead. "There." His voice was barely a whisper.

A Shadow guard lay crumpled near the hallway's edge, his helmet gone and his throat slit. His fingers were still curled around his sword. Just beyond him, another body lay still. Another guard with the same wound and fate.

Vad's gaze shifted to something at the edge of the next door. A dark smear across the floor. A blood trail.

At the start of it lay a single small, delicate blue shoe.

Heart racing, I stepped forward and picked it up. It was a high heel, embroidered in blue and spattered with blood. The inside was lined with velvet, and the outside sparkled with crystals. A polished sapphire water serpent wrapped around the toe, and a carved fin crowned the heel.

Blood had dried in specks across the leather and sole. Nausea roiled in my stomach. The shoe's owner had run through blood.

"That's one of the younger Aquen princess's slippers." Thalen sighed. "They're the only ones allowed to wear sapphires like that."

I surveyed the hallway. "Is there an exit near here? Maybe she got away." It didn't seem likely, but in a room full of blood and terror, I clung to the small hope. Especially since the shoe was so small—it seemed that this princess was only a child.

"No." Vad flinched and pointed to the area where the drag marks disappeared. "That's the way to the dungeons. It looks like she tried to flee, and they caught her."

Thalen's nostrils flared. "I can't think of any reason to take one of the five Aquen princesses, unless it is a hostage situation."

"Maybe they're capturing all of the royals so they have no rivals. No one to speak against them." That was what had happened back in my world, and what Ryker and Ember were trying to recover from. "It's an illusion of peace."

A flash of red caught my eye. Two pinpricks in the dark. Almost like someone had opened their eyes.

I stiffened, but when I blinked, they were gone.

Vad's head snapped toward me. *What?*

Thalen scowled, tilting his head as he listened intently.

I thought I saw something. I bit my bottom lip. *Red eyes in the dark. Then they disappeared.*

I nodded toward the place where that flicker of scarlet had vanished. *Something feels... off.*

Vad stepped inside, hand hovering at his dagger. The lamplight glistened on his dark claws. Thalen tensed beside me, tracking every shadow.

Returning, Vad shook his head. "Nothing." But the sharp line in his jaw told a different story.

We resumed our careful progress, each step quiet.

As we rounded another corner, I glanced behind us again. My nostrils flared as I searched for any sign of danger. These halls were even creepier. The sputtering torches gave off uneven, sluggish light, as if the palace were struggling to wake up. The shadows kept shifting. Twice, they seemed to move, but each time I looked harder, there was nothing there. Maybe I was imagining it? My fingers flexed, and I curled them against my palm.

The uncomfortable sensation the stag had awakened pulsed hard in my chest, pressing through my veins like frostbite. My wolf growled in response.

Vad stopped at a small side door tucked between faded tapestries. He pressed his ear to the wood, then eased it open with a slight creak.

The air hit me like a slap, the sharp tang of blood mixed with the electric scent of medicinal herbs. But some other scent lay underneath it. A sweetness that wasn't right.

Whose scent was that? I scowled, trying to place it.

The lamps inside had all guttered out except one at the far end of the chamber. The soft yellow glow barely illuminated the nearest patient rooms, which held empty beds and scattered blankets. There were no bloodstains here; it looked as if people had fled rather than been attacked. So where was the smell coming from? My wolf bristled.

No bodies. No guards. Just a wet, sucking silence that felt too loud.

Vad stepped ahead, Thalen a pace behind him. Our footsteps made barely any sound as we edged forward. Each breath pressed tighter against my ribs.

We passed the two stone columns at the end of the hall, and Vad turned toward a circular room deeper in the Healing Hall.

The dark door was firmly shut, and he pressed it open.

A soft, glowing light came from farther back in the room, and Vad froze.

His entire body went rigid, and horror shot through our bond.

Chapter Eight

I'd seen death before. Delivered it more times than I could count. But this?

This felt personal.

I stood frozen in the doorway of Physician Morlo's medical chamber, my hand braced against the frame.

Morlo's body lay slumped over the long stone table—the same table where we'd sat just days ago, discussing the coronation and threats.

Now his skull was cracked wide at the crown, and the brown eyes that had always been half-lidded with exhaustion had been burned from their sockets. Blackened veins spidered down his face and throat, the flesh around them brittle and singed. His hands were splayed across the table like offerings, fingertips raw and nail-less, each bed caked in dried blood.

This was a warning, a message, and a punishment.

The underlying scent hit next. Cloying lavender and sharper rosemary—his signature blend—tainted with iron and something darker.

Merlinite.

Behind me, Briar gasped.

"Scaff—" Thalen started to swear but stopped. A strangled

sound followed, as if he'd swallowed the words.

I couldn't move or breathe, because I knew who had done this.

Colm.

He must have killed Morlo before the wedding and coronation. He'd been planning this from the start. His magic had been enhanced, and his powers strengthened and mutated.

And I'd handed him the object that had allowed his plan and powers to amplify. I hadn't expected the consequences to come so swiftly.

Shadow magic was difficult and demanding, and even painful for those who shouldn't channel it. But this wasn't the work of natural progression.

A memory snapped into place like a blade at my throat.

Elias.

The chained prisoner, drained for power, whom Briar had met in the Aureline dungeons and begged me to save. What if he hadn't been the only one? What if Colm had perfected a way to siphon life, not just to fuel spells but to transfer power?

It had been happening in Colm's prison. If they'd been careful, who was to say that any number of individuals hadn't also been drained? How likely was it that Colm would assist someone like Kaylen without also gaining something for himself? And why would it be limited to only those two?

I dragged a hand down my face, fury rising within me.

I'd been so desperate to get Briar back that I hadn't stopped to consider the possibility that he could be draining another's magic and essence to transform himself. I'd banked on the merlinite orb being an easy way to gain favor and navigate the situation.

The cost hadn't simply been sentimentality and my sister's ire. It had cost the life of a man who had served the royal family with unshaken loyalty for centuries. A man whose last words to me had been about his desire to celebrate my wedding and coronation.

My eyes shut, and my throat locked with hot rage.

Colm's vicious face flashed into my mind, those smirking eyes, leathery skin, and artificial claw tips. He'd tortured my beloved, and he would have destroyed her in the most cruel and painful ways imaginable.

If there were a way to ensure that his suffering would be greater than Briar's and Morlo's combined, I would do it. Colm would pay. And Morlo would be honored. He'd been a good man who'd deserved none of the suffering and indignity he'd no doubt endured in his final hours.

"Why did no one help him?" Briar whispered. The glow from the vials on the far shelves cast the room in a pale, eerie green and blue light. "How did anyone miss this happening?"

"Silencing sigils." My fingers brushed one etched into the doorframe. "When the door is closed, no sound can pass through." I'd never questioned their effectiveness, but there was no doubt of it now.

"Scaffing void." Thalen dragged a hand over his mouth. "Who did this, and how?"

"Colm Ainle," I spat.

Thalen's brows lifted as the truth slammed into him. "Feck. All right. What do we do? Colm's an even bigger problem now."

For once, our lack of magic was a good thing. "Colm can't use his new powers right now. So, we gather what we came for, get back to our allies, and regroup." I squared my shoulders. The horror still gripped me with cold fingers, but we had to focus on survival.

There were countless dead already, and Morlo wouldn't be the last. All we could do was make sure their deaths counted for something.

I moved to one of the cabinets and removed a stiff black

leather satchel that Physician Morlo had often used. He'd always brought it on his night visits to my father and Elara. It was already stocked with most of the medications, teas, poultices, and treatments Elara needed. Vyraetos had told me what to look for to stop Thalira's bleeding and other medicines used to treat wounds.

I set the satchel on the small round table near the largest cabinet. "Gather anything that might be useful. Morlo labeled everything. I'll get the treatments for Elara and Thalira."

Morlo had been meticulous in both his record-keeping and his labels. Even though Briar wouldn't be as familiar with the names, she'd be able to determine general categories and find tools.

She went to one of the narrow cabinets and began removing bandages and suture kits, stacking them carefully into the bag.

Thalen began gathering jars of herbs and salts for wounds and poisons, along with several glowing, viscous solutions.

I found the specific antidotes Vyraetos had described and tucked them into the satchel. I also snatched extras of the clotting tincture, in case we encountered more of those venom-coated weapons. We couldn't be caught unprepared again.

When I finished, I turned my attention to the vials lining the shelf wall. Some of the containers held mushrooms, their bioluminescence the brightest of the bunch of what I assumed were either tinctures or failed experiments. Others contained stones pulsing with dim, fluctuating light. I gathered a few to serve as light sources in case we ran out of oil.

But as I stooped to retrieve a vial holding a black-capped mushroom, something else caught my attention. A thin line of light leaked from a narrow seam behind the shelves. I stepped closer and opened the narrow wooden cabinet.

Inside, several additional vials had been hidden away. Two in particular made my breath hitch.

They sat beside a venom-coated dagger just like the ones used to murder one of Briar's friends and to wound Briar. The vials held a pale-blue liquid with hair suspended inside.

In one, Rhielle's magenta hair floated gently with no glow.

In the second, Kaylen's blonde hair drifted like silk, but three of the eight strands glowed, while the other five did not.

That was concerning.

I wrapped both vials in clean bandages and placed them in the bag. Perhaps Vyraetos or Bryn would know what the difference in hairs signified. Morlo had mentioned that exposing stolen magic could be more time-consuming if the victim had taken steps to mask it. That could explain why some hairs glowed and the rest did not.

But unease twisted my gut. Something felt *off*.

Briar's hand slid over mine, her touch grounding me. "Vad," she whispered, her eyes wide with concern. "Where's Elias? You said he was rescued and brought somewhere safe, but what if Colm found him and killed him or took him prisoner? We need to get him if we can."

Good point. I should've already thought of that.

My thumb stroked the back of her hand. "You're right. He might be able to tell us more about who is involved."

Of course, I knew Briar's concern stemmed from compassion for Elias.

Mine stemmed from strategy.

But it didn't matter. She was right either way. And the way she thought of others, even now—it stirred something warm in my chest.

I pressed a kiss to her temple, then pulled one of the glowing vials from the bag and wrapped a clean bandage loosely around it to dull the glow enough to offer light without making us a beacon in the dark. "We're going to get Elias."

Thalen frowned. "Would they have already taken him—"

"Not if Physician Morlo kept his secrets," I cut in, voice firm. "And I believe he did. Until the end." I stepped toward the door, still gripping the wrapped vial. "Come on. We need to hurry."

Thalen stepped into the corridor first, the stiff black leather bag clutched in one hand. Briar hesitated, glancing back at Morlo's body. Grief shimmered in her eyes, raw and quiet, even though she'd barely known him.

I followed but paused in the doorway, unable to tear my gaze from the man who had been the royal family's most trusted physician. A man who had brought me poultices and lectures in equal measure. A man who deserved so much more than this.

A man I'd avenge.

I swallowed hard, anger and guilt warring inside me. There was nothing we could do for him now.

Thalen's hand rested on the heavy, dark oak door. He met my gaze with grim understanding. I gave a single nod, and he closed the door. The sound echoed, a final punctuation to a life of service.

The hallway pressed in, the air thick with the scent of blood and loss.

A familiar and suffocating weight settled over me. The weight of loss—of my father, my mother, and all those we'd lose if we failed now. There wasn't time for grief.

Vad? Briar's voice brushed my mind, tentative but steady. She slid a hand over my arm. *I'm here. I'm with you.*

I closed my eyes and let the sensation of her presence anchor me, her strength and the way she held my hand, allowing the buzz to jolt between us. *We'll mourn him and all the others. But not tonight. Right now, we survive. We get everyone out. Then we make them pay.*

I forced my legs to move, quickening my steps as I led Briar and Thalen into the shadows.

Behind us, the door to Morlo's chamber stayed shut. But in my mind, it burned like a promise. His death would not go unanswered.

We paused only long enough to grab a few more items, including warm blankets, spare clothing, and rations, before slipping out a side door and deeper into the quiet corridors. The hallways were thick with shadow. Every door we passed was closed and silent as a crypt.

I kept Briar close, my hand hovering protectively just above her back, needing to know she was there and safe. The faint light from the vial Thalen carried lit our path in a low amber shimmer.

I counted our steps: six to the ornamental archway, and three more to the carved panel embedded in the stone.

I pressed my palm to the panel, fingers seeking the pressure-point switch hidden in the spiral pattern.

Click.

The seam opened with a muted pop, and a whisper of cool air rushed out to greet us, thick with the scents of healing herbs, lavender, cedarwood, and faint traces of lamp oil.

"Quickly," I murmured, ushering Briar through first, then Thalen.

The narrow passageway curved slightly and then descended. Silence curled around us like a second skin. Most of the rooms we passed were shrouded in darkness, abandoned and untouched, except one.

A faint strip of light spilled from beneath the farthest door.

Someone was here.

I passed Thalen the vial, moved closer to the door, and pressed my hand against it to open it on silent hinges.

Every instinct in me screamed to fight. No one should be in here. No one but Morlo, my father, and me.

The small chamber held a bed, a table, a narrow cabinet,

and a glowing oil lamp.

And in the bed lay a figure tangled in rumpled blankets.

A Terran fae, broad-shouldered, shaggy-haired, and staring blankly at the ceiling with unblinking eyes. His fingers were curled tight in the fabric beneath him, as if he were bracing for pain. Bandages wrapped his torso, shoulders, and arms, leaving only one bear-claw tattoo exposed.

His gaze snapped to the door.

"Elias?" Briar whispered, pressing in beside me as I opened the door the rest of the way.

He struggled to sit up, eyes bleary but wide. "Briar?" Relief flooded his features, and he clapped one hand over his mouth, choking on a ragged sob.

She held a finger to her lips and darted to his side. "Can you walk, Elias? Some of the Aurelines have attacked and taken over the palace. We've got to get you out of here before they find you and finish what they started." She explained the situation to him quickly, then asked, "Are you willing to come with us? We need to learn everything you know about your captors."

"I'll help you any way I can, and I'd rather risk walking than end up back in those monsters' hands." He shoved the blankets aside and eased out of the bed. His scarred, bruised legs wobbled, and he planted a hand on the wall to steady himself. He wore soft blue trousers and a loose tunic.

Briar slid in beside him. "Do you need help walking?"

"Maybe—maybe just a little," he admitted, obvious affection and gratitude shining in his eyes.

A low growl rose in my throat as he slipped an arm around her shoulders. The urge to snap him in half seared through me, suddenly and irrationally. Of course he felt indebted to her. She was the only reason he was still alive. But that didn't mean he had to *touch* her.

Thalen bumped my ribs on the uninjured side, shooting

me a look edged in amusement. I scowled when I caught the teasing grin he didn't bother to hide.

Bastard.

Yes, I knew I was being ridiculous. But I didn't need him pointing it out.

With a wide, crooked smile, Thalen nudged past me and slid into position on the other side of Elias. "You help Vad, Chaos. I've got our new friend. Come along then, Badger Claw. Let's get you somewhere safe."

"They're *bear* claws," Elias said, wincing slightly as he transferred his weight to Thalen's arm.

"Really? Fascinating. Never would have guessed," Thalen deadpanned. "Now let's stay quiet so we don't draw any extra attention. I feel like we can all agree that one fight tonight was enough." He looped an arm around Elias's bony torso to better support him.

I reached for Briar, guiding her into the hall.

Then something rustled in the dark.

I stepped out fast, my wings flaring wide as I scanned the corridor.

Nothing.

No movement. No sound. The hall was closed off. Nothing could get in here. There was no way in or out besides the passage behind us. The attendants who brought food and medicine wore enchanted pendants that wiped their memories the moment they left. Morlo had overseen every detail.

Besides, that hadn't sounded like fae footfalls or the brush of fabric.

It had sounded like *claws*.

Something *was* here.

Something wrong.

The air shifted, sharper now, like the storm before a strike. No magic hung in it, but danger clung to every breath.

Briar's concern blended with mine. She linked, *I feel it too.* She stepped beside me, surveying the room. *Do we check the rooms?*

No, I linked back. *There isn't time. Let's get back to the others.*

As we hurried silently down the halls, hugging the wall to make our way back, not one person crossed our path.

Not a servant.

Not a guard.

No one.

The silence crept under my skin like a sickness. The palace was massive, but it wasn't big enough that *everyone* could have disappeared.

We'd reached the last cross corridor before the secret door when a sudden string of bloodcurdling screams pierced the air, echoing in every direction.

I froze, listening to the noise and determining its location. "Sounds like it's coming from the halls that lead to the barracks."

"Could it be from the battle in the Ceremonial Hall?" Thalen's voice wavered.

"It doesn't sound like a battle." Briar's nostrils flared as she scented the air and then frowned.

She was right. There was no clash of weapons, no shouts, and no commands. Just fear and pain...and then it ended. As if someone had just snapped a neck or crushed a windpipe.

Elias shuddered.

We wasted no more time.

Down we went into the passage, my head scraping the low ceiling more than once. Every six or so steps, I cast a look behind us. The walls felt like they were closing in on us, as if the stone itself expected violence. Briar's hand twitched in mine, her pulse quickening. Her unease filtered through our bond, confirming she felt the discomfort too.

Halfway down the first spiral, she stopped.

I halted, every sense on edge. Thalen and Elias paused behind us.

"What is *that*?" Thalen whispered. His grip stayed firm around Elias's waist. A faint golden glow pulsed from the vial in his other hand.

"What did you see?" I asked, voice low.

Briar shook her head, jaw clenched. "I thought I saw—" Her brow pinched. "Never mind."

But it *wasn't* nothing.

Fear spiked through our bond, sharp and fast, like glass buried in my ribs.

I scanned the darkness and, for a split second, I caught it. Red eyes watching from the curve of the stairwell. Gone before I could track them. A shadow beast?

I inhaled deeply, checking the air for blood, for rot, for anything familiar.

Nothing.

Just cold, humid air and the steady echo of my own pulse in my ears. "Come on. Let's move."

We needed to get back to the others, *now*.

The narrow passage spat us out into the onyx cellar. This was the worst of the corridors. Every footstep echoed off the arched ceiling, and the only light came from what we carried. I didn't need to press a hand to the cold stone wall, but I did it anyway. My nerves remained on alert.

I motioned for everyone to halt, then pointed to the thin tripwire and the cup of ball bearings balanced on the lintel.

"Don't break the wire." I stepped over it and held out my hand to Briar. She didn't need it, but I offered it anyway. My blood thrummed as her fingers curled into mine. Her long, wild copper curls bounced as she hopped over the wire.

Thalen and Elias followed.

A few more seconds, and the door was locked behind us. We were safe...for now.

We made it back to the gathering room within minutes.

Silus was sitting against a wall, Elara's head resting on his thigh, his arm curled protectively around her. Myantha and Rhielle were sorting bags, and Veralt was checking supplies. Vyraetos was crushing something bitter in a mortar, grinding it one-handed with a pestle clenched in the other.

Thalira looked half asleep, her posture drooping as Quen held a lamp over her to warm her hands.

"Praise Fate!" Vyraetos breathed, grabbing the leather bag from me and taking it to Elara. Silus straightened and cradled her head, and her long lashes stirred. Her breaths came slow but steady.

When Quen spotted us, her face lit up, and Thalira gasped. Hope and fear flashed through her dark eyes as she reached for Quen. Her skin had gone waxy, and beads of sweat clung to her forehead. The bolt lodged in her shoulder hadn't budged. "You found it?" she rasped.

Briar beamed. "We got it. You're going to be all right." She crossed over to them.

Thalira reached out with her healed hand and pulled Briar down into a tight hug. "Thank you," she whispered.

"You'd have done the same for me." Briar hugged her back. Through our bond, relief surged so hard that emotion pricked within me.

Briar had adopted these women's fates like they were her own. And now that I *felt* her loyalty to them, I finally understood. Words had never been enough.

"I told you, you aren't going to die." Briar sighed.

"No dying." Thalira agreed with a weak laugh. "Except for Kaylen, Calla Lily, and whoever caused all this." She grimaced.

Briar helped her sit up and tucked the blanket around

her. "Are you still in pain?" She placed her hands on Thalira's shoulders, taking care not to touch the bolt embedded in her flesh.

"I can manage. It'll get better now." Each of Thalira's breaths came shorter than the last.

I gestured for Briar to return to the mat.

Even to someone with no medical knowledge, it was obvious Thalira's life wasn't safe yet.

"We brought back everything." I turned to Vyraetos. "Pain relievers. Blood restoratives. And several types of medicine." I refocused on Thalira. "Some of the medicine will help with the pain as well as blood restoration." I set the last satchel down near her feet. "Vyraetos will take care of you. Is there boiling water?"

One of Morlo's staple remedies had been red tea infused with a hazelnut base and whatever additional ingredients and elements he'd deemed necessary for his patient.

"Water has been boiled, and everyone had some tea. More is heating now," Myantha said, appearing on the other side of Briar. Her gaze flicked to Thalen and then back to us. "Do you need help with anything?" Briar shook her head as Myantha flung her arms around Thalen. "I was so worried about you." Her voice was muffled by his shoulder.

Thalen parted his lips like he wanted to say something witty, but no words came. He hugged her back, nuzzling his face against her neck.

Elias bumped into a shelf and swayed, as if he didn't know what to do with himself. His hands slid against his trousers, searching for pockets that weren't there.

Quen's eyes flashed, and she went to him. "Come on. You're with me." She didn't wait for an answer, just gripped his hand and guided him to sit near Thalira. "What do you need? Food? Water? Rest? Heat?"

"I—" He blinked and stared at her, wide-eyed, as she crouched and pressed her palm just beneath his jaw.

Quen tilted her head. "You're cold, and your pulse is thready. My other patient is in better hands now, so you're all mine."

He leaned back against the wall, but his expression flickered between alarm and confusion... and something else. "Oh?"

I left them to it and checked on Elara as Vyraetos prepared the medication. Silus had curled his big frame around my sister.

Elara propped herself on one elbow as Silus steadied her with one hand. "I'm feeling better." Her voice was weak, but the fire in her eyes burned bright. She reached for my hand.

I took it and rubbed my thumb over her icy knuckles.

She was lying. We both knew it. But sometimes we needed the lie more than the truth. She would be fine in time, and I'd buy her that time as long as I could. I'd lost more than enough. She wouldn't be counted among the dead.

Forcing a smile, I nodded. "Good. When the time comes, I want you there with me so we can spill these traitors' blood together."

Her brow furrowed as she squeezed my hand tighter. "When it's time to kill them, I *will* be there. I will take their lives for Father's. I want to feel the heat of their blood on my hands and see it spill across the stones."

Silus's hand splayed on her shoulder. Pride flashed in his dark eyes, along with protectiveness.

"Father will be avenged. All who have fallen will be avenged," I vowed, and then turned to Silus. We might have clashed before, but I knew he'd hold the line. "Any warning signs while we were gone?"

Silus shook his head. "Nothing serious. Except..." His brow pinched.

"What?" I pressed.

He scowled. Elara gave him a small nod, urging him on.

His jaw clenched. "When I was checking the eastern side of the onyx cellar, down near the stone door, I heard screams. Faint but clear. Someone pleaded with them not to put her in there. She said she was the Sylvan princess and offered a deal, but they laughed at her."

"The old dungeons." I scowled. My father had had them sealed for a reason. Those pits were worse than Firellan's Spine. "We found a young Aquen princess's shoes. It looked as if she'd been dragged away." I held his gaze. "We need to get out of here, find allies, and form a strategy."

"They'll be watching the main entrances and exits." Silus pursed his lips. "We should assume they'll cover the roads as well."

My plan took shape. We would leave through the tunnels and climb into the mountains. But first, we had to stabilize the injured enough to survive the journey. The timing would be tight. The river beneath the palace held fresh water but also connected to a brackish river along the sea. At this time of year, tides could make the lower tunnels deadly. Elara and Thalira had little chance of survival right now, but come morning, things might be different. "Right now, everyone needs rest and food. If you haven't eaten, do it."

Morning would be for decisions. Assessing our wounded, our resources, and our chances.

After settling on watch shifts and confirming that the run bags would be finished, I snagged a few handfuls of dried meat and assessed everyone. Thalira and Elara were sipping their medicinal teas. Rhielle and Veralt had settled in one of the corners of the room. Quen was chatting with Elias, and Myantha and Thalen had disappeared, but they'd be back soon enough. Vyraetos was just returning with a steaming bowl of broth in his hands. Its only real virtue was that it was hot.

Briar stood near the center of the low-ceilinged room, brow furrowed and thumb rubbing her bicep.

Concern flared through our bond.

"What's wrong, beloved?" I went to her at once.

Worry etched her face. "Where's Many-Greats? My grandfather? He's gone." She fidgeted with the neckline of her wedding gown.

A cold spasm cut through me. Bryn was gone?

Had the old man betrayed us?

CHAPTER NINE

I gripped the torn silk of my wedding gown with bloodstained fingers and turned in a slow circle. The flickering lanterns cast warped shadows across the walls, and the air reeked of mushroom broth and scorched herbs—bitter, earthy, suffocating. My stomach churned.

Many-Greats had disappeared *again*.

He'd pulled the rug from under my feet repeatedly. Why had I hoped he'd stay around and help clean up this mess? I should've expected this, but once again, I'd hoped he'd do better. A hollow sensation expanded within my chest, and I pressed my hand over my heart.

Vad crossed the room to me, slow and steady. When he reached me, he touched my cheek gently as a tremor rippled through our bond. His brow furrowed, the lines in his forehead deepening. "Gone?"

"I've looked everywhere." My stomach knotted. "Could he have gotten into any of the locked rooms?" Something wasn't right. I exhaled and scanned more of the dimly lit area.

There was no trace of him.

Vad crossed his arms, tension rolling off him. "Bryn wouldn't vanish without a reason." His tone held a biting edge of suspicion. "If he's gone, he has a plan or a price."

Anger flared through the bond, and I raised my hands. "Wait. Hold on. He wouldn't betray us." My voice cracked with conviction. "He's done everything possible to protect my sister and me. He's weird and secretive, but that doesn't mean he's a traitor."

Even as I defended him, that hollow place in my chest ached harder. Because...I wasn't sure. "I didn't even know he existed until a few months ago. He started appearing in Ember's and my bedrooms through some portal, talking about stuff I didn't even know existed. He never told us everything or stayed long. But he cared. He made sure Ember knew I was alive. He helped me survive, though his actions were misdirected." My voice softened. "Even when he tried to send me home, I think it was because he believed it was the only way to protect me. Not because he didn't care."

When I mentioned the portals, Vad's expression shifted. His eyes narrowed. A dark look flashed across his face, gone before I could decipher it.

He turned and stalked down the hall, checking door after door, tension bunching in his shoulders. "You didn't tell me. Not that he was on the Aureline High Council. Not that you were an Aureline."

Pain struck me like a blade between the ribs, fast and unforgiving. "Because I didn't know." I wrapped my arms around my waist. "I didn't know he was on the council until I was in that prison. Even then, he didn't explain what that meant. I didn't know I was Aureline. Not really."

The words tumbled out, each one faster than the last.

"*This* isn't where I was raised, Vad. I didn't grow up with talks of curses and magic warnings. I didn't know what being Aureline would mean, or anything about the fae." I blinked hard, my throat tightening. "I was dropped into a competition where everyone wanted me dead, and the one person who seemed to have answers made me promise not to tell anyone I knew him."

Vad stopped in front of a door but didn't open it. He tensed, his wings flicking behind him as he stared at the wood like it might open on its own.

Something in his expression softened, and he sighed. "These past days haven't been easy for any of us."

"I know." My fingers fidgeted with the bodice of my gown. "I never meant for *any* of this to happen. I didn't know me being crowned would strip power from everyone. It's not just hard on you. I'm in a horrible position too."

His gaze dropped to my hands, and for a moment, it looked like he was going to reach for me again. Instead, he stepped aside, resting his hand on the door beside us.

"That was one of the doors I couldn't get in." I eyed the door.

"He's not in there." A faint smile tugged at Vad's mouth. He looked amused, but then I realized he didn't want me looking inside.

I lifted a brow. "What don't you want me to see in there?"

He shrugged one shoulder, though the emotion pouring through our bond told another story. He cycled through anger, grim satisfaction, and faint disgust, but not at me. "Because to find out that you were taken to Firellan's Spine, Thalen tracked down one of the guards involved, and we...spoke with him."

A beat passed.

Then the meaning hit. "So there's a dead body in there?" I crossed my arms.

He shrugged. "Thalen ran out of time to remove the body without drawing attention. And you don't need to see what happened to him."

Warmth spread through my chest. Not because of the body,

but because he had done that for me. For what I'd suffered. I swallowed. "I don't condone torture. But I won't lie and say I'm sorry he's dead."

"I don't regret it." With a rough exhale, he pulled me hard against him.

My cheek pressed to his chest, and the steady thud of his heart grounded me. Wrapped in safety, I breathed in his smoky scent.

His arms tightened around me, and his chin dropped to the top of my head. "He was among those who hurt you, and I swore they would all pay. And they will. But if we open that door, the stench will ruin what little peace we have."

A smile tugged at my lips. "Well, we're trapped beneath a palace mid-rebellion. I agree that we can skip the smell of a corpse."

He chuckled with his warm breath brushing my hair. "Your grandfather is not here. And unless he's foolish enough to turn on us, there's nothing more we can do tonight."

"He won't betray us," I said firmly, even though I didn't entirely believe it. "I'm angry with him—no, anger isn't strong enough. I'm *furious* with him, but I don't think he's capable of turning against us."

Vad pulled back just enough to meet my eyes. "And I meant what I said earlier. I don't blame you for any of this."

"I truly am sorry. I never dreamed this would happen. I would've told you *everything if* I'd known. I can't blame you if you regret being with me."

His expression hardened. "Regret it?" Our bond blazed with anger. "I have *no* regrets about being with you, Briar. Even if I had known everything at the beginning, I'd still have chosen you. You are *mine,* and I am yours. Don't ever question that. I wasn't just saying that to Silus when he was running his mouth."

The fierceness of his response rocked me, chasing every ounce of my concern away. His wings flared as he pressed me into the wall, fitting his body perfectly to mine. He dropped his mouth to my ear and growled, "The only regret I have is that I didn't realize who you were to me from the start. All those wasted nights. All that time I could've had you in my arms and in my bed."

He paused, eyes flicking toward the dark hallway and then back to me, blazing with hunger. "We could wait before we rejoin the others. Veralt has the watch. No one's expecting us for a little while."

I arched a brow. "So you want to... what? Hold hands and share our feelings?"

He huffed a laugh, his thumb brushing my jaw with maddening tenderness. "Not exactly."

He grew hard against my stomach, and the spicy scent of desire infused the air. He was utterly focused on me, and I wanted him too, more than anything. It wasn't the safest place, but it seemed safe enough. And Fate help me, I needed this. Needed *him*. "We're spending time together now."

His mouth curved into a half-smile that made my stomach flip, his fingers sliding to my waist. "Yes, but there are different kinds of 'time together.'" His voice became lower, rougher. "And I'd rather not have an audience for the kind I'm thinking of."

Heat knotted my stomach.

The bond between us vibrated, sharp and hungry.

"Traditionally," he murmured, his mouth brushing my ear, "brides and grooms consummate their marriage within an hour or two of the ceremony. We're behind schedule."

I snorted, even as my pulse kicked. "We were a little busy."

His grip on my waist was anything but playful. "I think it's time we caught up."

My fingers traced the hard planes of his chest, his heart

thundering beneath my right palm. "You sure you want to rush into sex right now? Maybe we should wait and make sure we're really ready for it."

He growled, the sound vibrating straight through me, then kissed the tip of my nose. "Yes. I want to have sex now. If you'll have me."

I stood on my toes and pressed my lips to his. The kiss was soft at first, but then it wasn't.

His arms crushed me to him, one hand tangled in my hair, the other gripping my waist like he couldn't bear to let go. The world fell away—nothing existed except his scent, his heat, and the bond tightening between us, until I couldn't tell where his need ended and mine began.

He swept an arm around my back and started to lift me, then winced.

I broke the kiss and studied the bloodied bandages on his side and shoulder. "Vad..." The wounds in the fleshy membranes of his wings had mostly healed, though they still had dark, scabbed edges.

"I'm fine." His voice was rough, wounded, wanting. "Not injured enough to stop."

He pulled me in again, kissing me like a man possessed.

Without breaking away, he guided me backward down the hall. My shoulder brushed the cold stone wall, and then he pressed open a narrow wooden door I hadn't noticed before. I glimpsed dust and old wood as he tugged me inside and kicked the door shut behind us.

The room was barely wider than his wingspan and lined with crates and barrels. Lips never leaving mine, Vad set me on a crate and stepped between my legs with his hands braced around my hips.

I fisted the front of his shirt, pulling him closer. His body pressed firm and hot between my thighs. He pressed his forehead to mine.

"Does it hurt?" I murmured, brushing his shoulder.

He caught my lower lip between his teeth, then answered against my mouth. "Only when I'm not touching you."

My breath hitched, and I grew dizzy. "Do whatever you wish, my beloved. Take what you need. I'm yours."

His fingers dug harder into my skin, and I wrapped my legs around his waist, careful of his injuries, and pulled him to me. The silk of my wedding gown bunched between us, lifting as he slid his hands beneath it, over my hips and between my thighs.

Our tongues danced together hard and hungry. The claws of one hand found the edge of my panties while the other hand went to my breast.

He kissed me, hard, hungry, desperate. As if I were the only thing left in his world that mattered.

I tangled my fingers in his hair, tugging him closer as his hands roamed over me, my mouth just as hungry and demanding as his. Our bond thrummed with shared desire, each sensation echoing between us. His lips trailed fire down my neck, and I gasped as he nipped at the sensitive spot below my ear.

"You like that?" he purred as he braced me against the wall.

I whimpered, feeling as if I might implode.

"Good. Keep making those sweet noises." He nibbled, then nipped a line down my neck as his claws gently pressed against my core. "I don't have my shadows to help tend to you this time, so I suppose you'll have to settle for me."

A sharp gasp escaped before I could stop it, and I clamped a hand over my mouth.

A feral grin spread across his face, one that screamed *possessive* and *primal.*

He kissed me again, swallowing every whimper as his

fingers dipped lower, gliding over my wet folds. His touch was slow, teasing, precise, and playful, even with the claws on his fingertips, dragging over me in strokes that made me arch and my pulse gallop. I rocked against his hand, desperate for more, but he held me right on the edge, denying me the friction I needed.

Groaning, he pressed harder, but still not enough, before his mouth returned to mine in a kiss that stole my breath.

I gave him every gasp and moan.

His hands mapped every inch of me like he was memorizing each contour and tremor. As if tonight might be our last, he hooked a claw in my panties and yanked them down in one smooth motion, letting them fall to the floor.

Cool air kissed my skin.

I trembled, staring at him through half-lidded eyes. He was my mate. He was mine.

His thumb brushed my cheek. Then he caught my chin and tipped my face up, his gaze burning through me. "I love you more than life itself," he rasped. "My magic, my kingdom, none of it matters next to you."

Then his lips crashed over mine again. He tasted of smoke and salt. Like everything I shouldn't want, and everything I could never live without.

My wolf surged forward, needing the connection just as much as I did. The pulse in his neck called to me, and I didn't hold back.

I bit him hard, right above the collarbone.

He shuddered as blood welled under my tongue, hot and metallic. I licked it slowly, relishing the way his body responded to me.

His growl vibrated deep in his chest. Then his hand shot up to the nape of my neck. His claws grazed my skin as he tugged firmly to remind me who he was.

That I belonged to him.

"My...*wolf*," he said, the word unnatural on his tongue and yet so beautiful. "My claws and fangs don't scare you?" His thumb brushed my cheek.

My breath caught, and heat coiled in my core. I tilted my head and grinned. "Your claws are magnificent, but your fangs? Are they really big enough to be called fangs?"

His eyes darkened, and a low growl rumbled. "*Every* part of me is more than big enough to satisfy you, and I know how to use all of it."

His fangs nipped at the base of my shoulder, and my wolf whimpered. Even though our connection was complete, the act of sharing blood was so personal. His teeth sank into the soft place where neck met shoulder, and I gasped. His palm slid over my mouth, muffling the needy sound.

His tongue swept over the bite, and pleasure spiked through me like lightning. My legs locked around his hips, and he tugged the bodice of my gown down to my waist in one sharp jerk, baring my breasts.

The silk pooled at my ribs, but I barely noticed. All I could feel was *him*.

His mouth trailed down my chest, lips parting over the swell of my breast. He sucked a bruise into the flesh, bit down hard enough to sting, then soft enough to make me moan. My hands fumbled at his shirt, desperate for skin to skin. "Fuck!"

He chuckled. "Feck."

I grinned, even as my breath caught. "That's such a stupid word."

With a wicked glint in his eyes, his tongue swept into my mouth just as his fingers slid inside me.

I jolted as pleasure crashed through me.

Hold still, he commanded. Curling his hand in just the right way, he made me *feel* the careful caress of his claws with every movement. His mouth pressed to the hollow of my throat, his tongue licking a line to my jaw as his hands devastated me.

He leaned back just enough to look down at me. His eyes blazed molten silver, pupils blown wide. "Perfection. You are pure perfection."

My pulse pounded, and I gave him a hungry little smile and hooked my fingers into his belt. His hard length pressed against my core, and I groaned.

"This is so unfair." I cupped his hardness. "I'm practically naked, and you're still dressed."

He arched a brow. "Not for long."

Stripping the gown the rest of the way off my body, he flung it aside.

I growled and struck his shoulder lightly. "Get your clothes off before I *take* what's mine."

His grin turned feral. "Come claim me, *my beloved*."

His shirt vanished, tossed somewhere behind us, and I took in his blood-smeared skin and bandaged wounds. I reached for the edge of the wrapping, intending to smooth it down, but he caught my wrist and pressed a kiss to the inside. "Later. I need you."

And his mouth was back on me, licking one of my nipples. He alternated between sucking, licking, and biting, every stroke more possessive. I whimpered as his hand slid up my thigh again, driving me to the edge.

He plunged his fingers inside me, slow and sure, and my body clenched around them. I couldn't get enough of him. His claws scraped gently, drawing out another whimper.

"You're loud," he murmured, his voice thick with pride. "Do you want them to hear you?"

I shuddered. "Yes," I gasped, then bit my lip. "No. Maybe. I don't care."

I tried to choke back my moans. I didn't *want* an audience, but everyone probably knew what we were doing. "You're still wearing your pants."

"Not for long," he repeated.

The catch in his voice sent a shockwave through me. He stepped back half a pace and reached for his belt. The buckle gave with a low *clink*, and his pants slid over his hips. Leaning forward, I tugged them farther down, scraping my nails over the hard lines of his thighs.

He was magnificent—every inch of him. All muscle and power. All *mine.*

With a low growl, he pulled me flush against him, hips grinding against my inner thighs and the thick ridge of him rubbing against me, hard and hot.

"Easy, my sweet bride." His fingers worked me open again. His thumb circled, stroked, and flicked. The friction continued to build until I could barely think. Then the head of his dick nudged against my folds.

I clutched his shoulders and gasped as his hips bucked. *Harder.*

He laughed roughly. "Patience, my love."

"Never."

My head dropped back against the wall as he pushed deeper, stretching me until I was full.

Then he moved.

Slowly at first, going deep and at a steady pace. He pressed me against the wall, and the crate beneath me groaned in protest. Every time I clenched around him, he let out a ragged breath and murmured my name.

Everything we felt for each other exploded through our bond, and his body tensed each time I drew close to my own release.

His mouth found my throat, and his teeth and tongue grazed the mark he'd made, then lowered until his lips traveled even lower, closing around my nipple. He sucked and bit repeatedly until pleasure and pain blended together.

It was all too much, yet not enough.

He snarled and slammed me harder against the wall. The crate shook under me, and the whole room trembled with every brutal thrust. His wings flared behind him, shuddering with each movement.

One arm wrapped around my back, bending me into a perfect arch, while the other slid up my throat, his thumb pinning my jaw. His eyes locked with mine. "Look," he rasped. "You're all I see. All I want."

He devoured me like we were the last two alive. Like I was his salvation and his ruin. Like he could never get close enough, deep enough, hard enough to satisfy the ache. And I felt the same for him.

I wrapped my legs tighter around his waist, heels digging into the muscles of his back. I met every thrust with a desperate need. Our pleasure started blending together until I wasn't sure what was his and what was mine. The bond between us crackled.

He drove into me with his jaw clenched and his fangs bared. "You're mine," he growled.

"You *are* mine." I could barely form the words. My entire body was tightening, the heat in my belly nearly too much. "Always."

His hand slipped between us, his thumb stroking my clit. My body shattered as an orgasm crashed through me. I bit back a scream, and he slammed in deep. His whole body quivered as his ecstasy mixed with mine.

My vision whited, then blurred back. The euphoria between us strengthened as we both fell farther than ever before. His head dropped to mine, both of us breathing hard, our bodies locked together. I felt every pulse inside me, every shudder that passed from him into me.

I cupped his jaw, brushing sweat from his cheekbone. He shivered once, chest rising slower now, and gathered me in so tight I could barely breathe.

He pressed his mouth to my forehead in a tender kiss, and he lingered.

I clung to him, knowing the peace wouldn't last. Soon, we'd have to get dressed, go back, and return to the gathering room with all its tension and decisions that still had to be made. The weight of this brokenness pressed in on us.

But for now, we had this.

He pulled back enough to look at me. A soft smile spread over his lips, softening the sharp lines of his face. "I love you, Briar. More than I thought possible." He cupped my face in his hands, his touch reverent. "No matter what happens, remember that. Even if I had known you were Aureline before we were wed, I still would have chosen you."

Heat flooded my chest, the warmth expanding until I thought I might burst. "When this is all over, we need to find a place where no one can find us. Where we can just *be*. At least for a little while."

A low chuckle rumbled through him, vibrating into my bones. He whispered, "I agree, my love."

He kissed me again, then stepped back and sighed.

I understood that sigh. It was time.

Sliding off the crate, I cleaned up as best I could. One of the nearby chests held waterskins, bandages, and healing salves. A full bath would have been nice, but this would do for now.

"Well." I brushed hair away from my face and wrung out a damp cloth. "Time to return to all our cares and responsibilities, Shadow Vaddy."

Vad froze mid-motion. His head cocked, and his expression twisted between horror and reluctant amusement. "What did you just call me?"

"Shadow Vaddy." I twirled the cloth like a lasso before tossing it into the crate. "It's an Earth thing."

He grunted, unimpressed. "My name is Vad. Not Vaddy."

I waggled my eyebrows. "I'll be certain to remember that the next time we fight."

When I began to gather my wedding dress, it came apart in my hands, separating into multiple garments. A slim, pale lavender slip slid free. Interesting. When I'd first worn it, the fabric had wrapped around me seamlessly, forming a full ensemble, including undergarments, corset, overskirt, and shoes. Now it seemed to have separated into individual garments, as if the magic had begun to unravel.

I held the slip. It resembled a sturdy sundress and was far more practical for movement than a full gown. The outer layers pooled at my feet, still blood-speckled but hauntingly beautiful.

Fate had made this for me. And the shoes were some of my favorites. They still said *Shadow Queen* on the bottom.

Vad pushed his long, dark waves out of his face. A contemplative smile spread as he watched me. "Part of me resents that this is where we finally consummated our marriage. I wanted to spoil you, feed you the finest delicacies of my kingdom, and wrap you in silks and velvets. But here we are."

I tied my hair back with a strip of white cloth from the crate. "So long as I'm with you, I don't care where we are. Though I wouldn't say no to a hot meal that wasn't that broth Vyraetos was making."

"Soldier stew. It's his specialty." He picked up his torn shirt and pulled it on.

I lifted a brow. "Made out of actual soldiers?"

He snorted. "Probably best not to inquire too much on the ingredients. It tastes like shit, but it'll keep you standing when you have nothing else." Vad pressed his lips together. "Our next focus should be clothing. We need armor, at least leather. Anything's better than nothing at all."

"What about the clothing we found in the Healing Hall?" I smoothed the slip down my thighs and glanced at the discarded robes we'd scavenged earlier.

"Better than the wedding dress." He winked

I opened my mouth to reply when a scream tore through the air.

One of terror, not pain.

It came from the gathering room.

Something was wrong.

CHAPTER TEN

Vad and I burst in...and froze.

Pure chaos filled the gathering room. The stench of blood slammed into me, making my stomach twist.

Two of the walls had split open at two points of the chamber, the jagged black gashes pulsing. The openings throbbed like infected wounds seeping straight through the stone. Shadow spilled from them like smoke...and several wolves stalked the room.

Shadow beasts, Vad linked to me, his own panic bleeding into mine as he grabbed a sword.

A hulking beast barreled toward Rhielle, fangs gleaming and eyes burning.

Vad swung his sword in a low circle and cleaved the wolf's throat with a single motion. It collapsed at Rhielle's feet, the shadow mist evaporating around her boots.

But more were pouring through the holes, making this a war zone.

Two wolves already lay dead on the floor, but eight more surged in, their snarls rumbling so deep that my ribs ached. The air burned hot, metallic, and thick with death.

My throat closed. I didn't have a weapon, but I couldn't

stay where I was.

Lips peeled back, a shadow wolf snapped its head toward Quen and Thalira. My stomach knotted, and I bolted toward them, my bare feet slapping stone.

Thalira was sprawled limply on the stone floor with her eyes closed. Blood poured from a wound in her neck and soaked the front of her dark-blue dress. Quen crouched next to her, pressing her hands over Thalira's chest and throat and sobbing, ragged and desperate. Blood leaked through her hands.

"Watch out!" I screamed, launching myself between them and the oncoming wolf.

I slammed into its ribs with my shoulder, making sure that it didn't get anywhere close to the women. We crashed to the floor, the air knocked from my lungs as I landed on top of the snarling monster.

Its breath reeked of rot, and I gagged and drove my forearm into its throat, forcing its snapping jaws away from my face. Its claws tore into my shoulder, and hot, sharp pain flared down to my fingertips.

But I didn't let up.

Instead, I pressed harder, grinding my knee into its ribs. The wolf's eyes glowed brighter, and it opened its mouth wide as if ready to end me. I didn't have anything to stop it from reaching my throat, and I gritted my teeth, knowing I had to fight as long as I could to have a chance to survive.

The shadow wolf jerked, the force of its spasm catching me off guard. My arms weakened as a dark blur flashed in the corner of my eye. The wolf's head fell from its body.

A sickening *crunch* echoed in my ears, and a hand yanked me back to my feet. Vad towered over me, a deep scowl on his face. Shadow mist drifted off his blade, confirming he'd been the one to behead the wolf.

His grip remained urgent. "Stay behind me!"

My arm stung, and blood ran from my new scratch, but there were too many for me to retreat. “I’m not going anywhere,” I snapped, already scanning for the next wolf.

I looked across the room and saw Elias standing over Quen and Thalira with a dented pot gripped in his trembling hands. Broth stained the floor, mixing with Thalira’s blood. His eyes were wide and glassy with terror, but he held his ground, swinging wildly whenever a wolf crept too close. The clang of metal against bone rang out, causing the wolves to hunker back.

To their left, Silus had planted himself like a wall in front of Elara. His sword hissed through the air as he slashed at two wolves closing in. Blood streaked his cheek, but he didn’t flinch. Behind him, Elara clawed at the wall, trying to rise. Her face was pale but furious, and her wings fluttered in sharp, panicked bursts. She clutched a bloodied dagger awkwardly, a sword lying forgotten at her feet.

Vyraetos caught a wolf’s snapping jaws against the edge of his dagger. His muscles bulged as he pushed it back, snarling. “The shadow beasts have gone mad!” He forced the beast off balance and slammed it to the floor.

At the far edge of the chamber, Veralt grappled with one of the wolves, holding it by the throat. It writhed, claws tearing bloody streaks across his forearms, but he squeezed harder until its neck gave way with a brutal *snap*. He hurled the limp corpse into another charging beast and dove toward the pile of discarded weapons.

Rhielle ducked beneath a lunging wolf, her tattered gown fluttering like a flag of war. Her sword flashed clean through a beast’s flank. Her jaw was tight, and her eyes held steady as she spun into her next strike.

Another wolf forced its way through the pulsing gash nearest Quen. It lunged, and with a cry of pure rage, she punched it square in the snout. Bone cracked beneath her fist.

The beast reeled, stunned, and cowered away. Quen collapsed over Thalira's body again, her shoulders shaking as she once more pressed hard against the wound in our friend's neck.

My gaze snapped to Thalira's still form, and I sobbed.

Hands drenched in blood, Quen looked at me. "I can't stop the bleeding. She won't stop bleeding, Briar!"

I rushed to them, slipping in the spreading pool of crimson. A wolf snarled nearby, claws scraping the ground as it circled behind us. I managed to regain my balance and spun around just as Vad linked, *Don't worry. I'll handle the wolves with the others. Just see if you can help Thalira.*

Trusting him, I dropped to my knees and pressed my hands over the wound on Thalira's chest, and my palms were immediately soaked with slick, hot blood. "Hold her steady," I choked out, barely hearing myself over the clash of metal and the howls.

A deep gash was cut across the base of Thalira's throat, the blood no longer pouring but leaking. Her chest wasn't stirring. Her lips were dull grey, and her eyes were tightly shut. My bottom lip quivered.

"No! Keep the pressure on!" Quen screamed. "She'll bleed out. We can't move her until we stop the bleeding." Quen pressed both her hands over mine against Thalira's wounds. The heat of Thalira's blood seeped through our fingers, but her warmth was fading.

She was gone.

"No—no, no, no!" Quen sobbed and shook her head hard. "We can still save her. Just help me—"

A shadow wolf appeared over Thalira's body, looking toward us, fangs bared. I tensed and straightened on my knees.

"He's lunging!" Rhielle shouted.

The shadow wolf dove low, and I took the brunt of its weight on my forearm. Its teeth snapped an inch from my throat a moment before Vad's blade cleaved clean through its skull with a wet crunch. Shadow mist exploded like smoke.

"Stay low," he barked, already spinning to face the next wolf. They collided midair, claws and steel meeting in a brutal crash.

"She'll bleed out," Quen wept. "We have to stop it, we have to—"

Tears burned my eyes, and I had to fight to say the words. "She's gone." My voice cracked under the truth.

Another wolf rammed the wall beside us, dust and pebbles raining down. Veralt's war cry rang out, and the beast flew across the room and smashed like a rag doll into a pile of broken furniture.

I couldn't breathe. The metallic stench of blood, the endless snarls, the screams pressed in on me. Still, I knelt beside Thalira. My hands trembled. My chest cracked open, and a raw, quiet wolf howl ripped out of me, curling into the smoke above us.

The air pulsed like a shockwave through my bones.

Vad linked, *What are you doing?* Panic echoed down the bond.

I lifted my head. All around the chamber, the wolves had frozen in place, ears flattened, their eyes glowing like twin suns locked on me.

The far wall tore open with a gurgling sound. Another gash split the stone, wider this time. Black mist poured out like a tide, curling through the room in skeletal tendrils.

The spell shattered. Every wolf turned and howled in unison, their rage renewed.

Of course, we couldn't have a moment's rest. Fate kept pushing us, and I wasn't certain how much more I could take.

"Grab what you can and go *now*!" Vad's roar cracked the air.

His sword sliced through another beast with terrifying speed, shadow blood spraying across the floor as it collapsed.

I couldn't move. If I did, I had to leave Thalira. I looked at her face, her blood congealing on my hands.

Briar! Vad connected, causing me to jerk my attention to him. "Get to the larder path on the right!" He clawed a wolf off Silus's back.

But I still couldn't get myself to stand. Another friend lost to cruelty and hate.

I jolted as a heavy hand clamped around my upper arm. "Move!" Vad snarled into my ear. "She wouldn't want you to die here!"

He was right. And the longer we stayed, the more lives could be lost. Letting out a shaky breath, I gave Thalira's lifeless body one last look, then tore myself away, grabbing Quen's sleeve and yanking her to her feet.

I clenched my jaw and shoved down the grief threatening to split me open. As I turned, a wolf hurtled at Vad. He snarled and swept up his sword, his long claws gripping the hilt and cutting into his own palms. The blade sliced through the wolf's throat, releasing a hot spray of blood over both of us. The wolf fell to the ground.

Up ahead, Rhielle pivoted, gasping, her sword catching another wolf's shoulder as it lunged. Veralt clubbed the wolf, and Rhielle grabbed two bags and slung them over her shoulders. A wolf seized the third, and she kicked it.

Veralt seized the wolf by the scruff, muscles bulging, and slammed it into the wall. Its neck broke with a sickening snap. He spun, picked up his fallen sword, and hacked at the next, wild-eyed. "We can't hold them off forever!" he barked.

"Don't wait for us," Vad shouted. "Grab the lights and go. Follow Silus."

Silus was already fighting his way toward the door, striking at the wolves and pulling Elara along. He had two bags on one shoulder and the other arm gripping Elara, who was trying to wield the sword, rage and terror in her eyes as she bared her teeth. Elias stumbled along behind them, a sword clutched in one hand.

The crowns lay beyond the wolves near the wall. Elara hesitated as if debating dodging the wolves to grab them, but Silus glared at her. "We'll come back for them!"

Elara set her jaw but complied. "May the beasts rip apart anyone not of our line who takes those crowns!"

Quen scooped up a bag and three lamps. She blew out two and tucked them under her arms while holding the third tight to her chest.

"Where are Thalen and Myantha?" The words screamed out of me.

Vad's gaze snapped up and around; then his jaw tightened. He shoved me toward the door of the gathering room. "Not in here. Go!"

I cupped a hand over my mouth. "Thalen! Myantha!" My voice cracked with terror at the thought of what might have happened to them.

Thalen appeared in the doorway then, eyes wide and tunic rumpled. Myantha was behind him. "What in the scaffing void happened?" he shouted.

"Larder path! We're moving out," Silus shouted back. "Grab whatever you can."

A wolf snarled and barreled toward Thalen. I surged forward, my muscles screaming in protest. I kicked the wolf from the side, knocking it off balance. Vad was there in an instant to finish it with his claws hooking beneath its jaw, ripping its head clean away. The body crumpled with a sickening thud. He adjusted his grip on his sword, growling.

Thalen leaped over the threshold, barefoot, half-dressed,

his silver-white wings flaring wide. He dove for the weapon pile and snatched up a fallen sword. "Well, come on then! You can't expect me to leave you here."

Myantha darted forward on bare feet and grabbed a run bag and a lamp. Her golden-brown locs whipped behind her as she turned back toward the hall.

Three more wolves bounded out from the portals.

I grabbed one of the last remaining run bags and a sword, my shoulder burning as I flung the bag across my back. My breath sawed in and out as more wolves howled and charged.

Vad shoved me through the doorway and seized the handle. He jerked it shut as claws and teeth battered the other side. The thuds echoed, dust trickling from the lintel. "That'll buy us seconds."

The corridor pulsed with noise from our friends already sprinting ahead, Silus half-carrying Elara, Veralt and Rhielle right behind them with blood streaking their arms, Vyraetos clutching the medicine bags and a flickering lamp. Quen trotted beside him, her expression grim and her face tearstained while looking back at Elias.

Then I smelled it—wet fur, sharp and sour, closing in from the side passage. My stomach twisted. *Wolves. There are more of them*, I linked and pointed toward the passage.

Vad's head snapped in the direction as a faint, hollow *toktoktoktok—trrrr* rolled down the stairs beyond the doorway, like wooden beads scattering over stone.

Everyone froze.

Something is coming through the dungeon path, Vad linked. Silus caught his gaze from the front, and Vad lifted one finger and pointed.

My pulse thundered. The echo of that sound—*toktoktoktok—trrrr*—lodged itself in my bones. It wasn't loud. It didn't need to be.

It was a warning.

Vad turned toward the side passage, every muscle in his body pulled taut like a drawn bow. His nostrils flared. My own senses sharpened, honed by instinct and terror.

The scent hit again a second later... wet fur, smoke, and blood. More wolves.

I gripped the sword tighter, my palms slick. The weight of the run bag across my back dragged at my balance. My breath rasped too loudly in my ears.

The door behind us shuddered as the wolves we'd trapped howled and snarled.

Another *toktoktoktok—trrrr* sounded down the corridor, closer this time.

Ahead, Veralt and Rhielle slowed, weapons raised. Silus angled toward the tunnel that veered left, guiding Elara beside him. Her limp was more pronounced now with one wing dragging low, but she didn't utter a sound. Vyraetos flanked them, the medicine bags bouncing against his hip and the lamp in his grip trembling slightly with each step.

We crept forward, each footstep painfully loud in the narrow corridor. My pulse slammed against my ribs, sounding louder than even our steps. The walls narrowed around us, and the ceilings pressed low, as if the passage itself meant to trap us. The hall split both to the right and to the left. Each swing of the lamps cast shadows that jerked and crawled like claws reaching from the darkness.

Behind us, the wolves continued their assault, claws shredding wood and snarls vibrating through the air. The door we'd barricaded was holding, but only barely.

Vad stayed pressed to my shoulder with his sword in his bloody hand. He bristled with tension, each impact behind us twitching through his frame. If the door failed, there'd be nowhere to run. The wolves would have a narrow stone corridor to rip through.

I looked back. There was still nothing visible, but the *tok tok tok* had fallen silent. The quiet before the storm.

Silus reached the door at the end of the larder path and shoved his sword into Elara's hands before fumbling for something in his tunic. The door groaned, and the hinges screamed. The sounds cut through every bone in my body like ice water.

Then came the eyes.

Five sets of yellow eyes emerged around the bend, slinking forward like flames in the dark. One blinked... and then another.

Vad.

I see them, he replied and shifted in front of me.

Snarls rumbled down the corridor like thunder, and the wolves broke into a sprint.

Silus jerked the door open, and a rush of cold air spilled in from the tunnel beyond.

"Go!" Vad commanded.

We surged for the opening. Silus shoved Elara through first, then Vyraetos and Quen dove in next, clutching lamps and supplies. Veralt and Rhielle flanked the door with Rhielle's sword drawn and Veralt's hands bloody but steady.

Thalen and Myantha bolted in next. I turned, but Vad closed in behind me, corralling me through just as the first wolf lunged.

Its claws scraped stones inches behind my heels.

I stumbled into the next tunnel, spinning around in time to see Vad brace himself in the doorway. The nearest wolf launched, but Vad's blade caught it midair.

Another beast dove low. Vad kicked it back and slammed the door with a brutal clang. The lock snapped into place just before claws battered the other side.

The howls rose again. Angrier. Hungrier. Louder.

Dust rained from the stone above as they threw themselves at the door.

"I don't suppose anyone knows what in the fecking void has made the shadow beasts lose their minds?" Rhielle tightened the straps on one of her bags.

Veralt scoffed and rubbed the back of his head.

Quen looked at Vyraetos, her eyes bloodshot from crying. "Well, old man?"

Vyraetos frowned. "They've snapped."

"Thanks." Thalen rolled his eyes. "We hadn't figured that part out."

The tunnel air shifted, feeling cold, thick, and sour. Each breath tasted like spoiled water. My lungs burned while the wolves snarled and tore at the wood behind us, fury undiminished.

"They're going to break through." I tugged at my wolf, who had regained some energy. I might need her strength and could shift shortly. "Where do we go now?"

Vad turned from the door, blood smeared down his arms like war paint, sword still clutched in one clawed hand. His chest heaved with each breath, but his voice came like steel: "We run. Straight through. The southern passage is dry right now. If we move fast, we'll beat the river before it rises and reach the forest before the wolves catch up."

A beat of silence fell between us.

The others surged forward into the tunnel, the heavy banging of the wolves against the door continuing like a drumbeat of doom. Shadows stretched long and crooked in the lamplight, flickering over the uneven walls. My feet scraped on grit, each step jarring my bones.

I felt hollow inside. The memory of Thalira's face wouldn't leave me. Her blood still clung to my hands.

Beside me, Elara stumbled against Silus, her lips white and

eyes sharp with pain.

I swallowed hard, throat raw. If we lost her too... I stopped, unable to finish the thought.

Vad's voice cut through the tension. "Did anyone save her medicine?"

Vyraetos raised the leather satchel. "Got it."

"Good." Vad nodded once, then pushed ahead. "Keep close. No noise."

We moved fast, deeper into the earth. The tunnel dipped lower, the air turning thick and sour. Every creak of leather, every footfall, every strained breath echoed like a scream. No one spoke. Even our grief had gone silent.

Then—howls.

Not behind us. Ahead.

We rounded a bend, and the walls widened into a branching cavern. The lamps cast jagged shadows over the stone, but my stomach turned to ice.

Then something in the wall *tore*. Another slit appeared, black and seething, shadows pulsing inside it like living rot.

The scent hit first. Wet fur. Iron. Decay.

More wolves.

I opened my mouth to warn the others, but pain exploded through my left calf as teeth clamped down, piercing flesh and bone. I let out a bloodcurdling scream.

Chapter Eleven

Sharp teeth crushed my foot, and the ground vanished beneath me. The corridor flipped as I was wrenched backward toward the gaping, writhing wound in the wall.

Pain spread through my ankle, and I thrashed and clawed at the ground, looking for a way to fight my attacker. My nails split on the stone as the shadow wolf tugged me closer.

Briar! Vad's voice crashed through our link, our connection blazing from his anger. The others screamed and shouted.

Shadows pulsed like a heartbeat, the portal yawning wide just feet away, eagerly waiting to devour me. The air churned with rot and static, like wet stone struck by lightning. Claws scraped for purchase behind me. The beast's jaws clamped tighter, crushing leather, tearing through flesh.

This wolf was larger than the others, its eyes crimson like the figure in the tapestry and on the banner. The pressure from its jaw intensified though still not as hard as it could bite me, and I whimpered.

Vad collided with the wolf in a furious storm of wings and claws. His talons punched into the creature's side, and he yanked it off me in one savage motion. The beast shrieked as Vad tore into it, his snarls raw with rage. Blood arced through the air, and he slammed the wolf into the wall with a crunch of bone.

Rhielle dropped beside me. Her arms locked under mine, and she helped me to my feet as Veralt surged past. A flash of steel came from the corner of my eye, and Veralt's blade cleaved through the wolf's skull in one clean stroke.

As soon as I put the slightest pressure on my foot, I gasped. Pain flared, sharp and hot as fire.

"We need—" Rhielle started.

"It's fine," I managed, breath hitching. "Looks worse than it is."

Thalen appeared on my other side, catching me as I swayed. "It's very clearly not fine, Chaos."

"Get some bandages," Elara called out from several feet away where she was leaning on Silus. "Did it crush your foot, Briar? Is it broken?"

Vad whirled away from the crumpled wolf, blood streaking his arms like war paint. His chest heaved, and his eyes burned molten silver as he stormed toward me, shoulders taut, every line of him seeming carved from stone. Relief and fury warred in our bond. "Everyone, hold your position and watch the portal. If another one comes through, kill it."

He crouched in front of me and lifted my bloodied foot.

I bit back a pained cry and gritted my teeth.

"Sorry," he murmured, voice rough with guilt.

Vyraetos knelt beside him with the lamp and the medicine bag, eyes scanning the wound with grim focus. "Deep lacerations, but the bone's whole. You're lucky."

"If I shift, I'll heal. It's not a terrible wound." I hoped I could. I'd been injured horribly and had still managed to shift twice, but there had been times recently that I'd tried to shift, and something had prevented me.

"You shouldn't shift yet." Vad's voice was tight with fury.

"Not until we're somewhere safe." Concern bled through the bond, weighing it down with a dull throb.

Rhielle pressed a scarf to the back of my neck and tied my hair out of my face. "That wolf's eyes weren't the same as the others. Something's changed."

"Doesn't matter what color their eyes are," Veralt muttered, still gripping his blade. "We kill whatever comes through next."

Quen glanced at the tunnel and adjusted her grip on the lamp she was holding. Elias steadied one of the bags slung over her shoulder.

"Does this mean all our beasts have gone mad?" Her words shook. "Are the fire beasts in my kingdom insane as well?"

"Probably best to assume so." Silus scanned the passage.

The portal pulsed before us, its dark purple veins writhing and alive. An uncomfortable ripple of power shot through me, reminding me of the stag's energy but more unsettling. My stomach churned, and my skin crawled. "We need to get moving. Anything could follow."

Vyraetos tied off the bandage on my ankle.

Grunting, Vad rose and stood beside me with a set jaw and one hand pressed to his chest. "What can you give her for the pain?"

"If it'll slow me down or cloud my head, I don't want it." I tugged at Vad's wrist and turned his hand over to find blood welling from four fresh slashes. *You cut yourself on your claws. You need to wrap that. If more wolves come through or come later, they'll be able to track the scent.*

He grumbled and swiped another bandage from the bag. As he bound his palm, a flicker of guilt shot through our bond, chased by anger. *I'm not used to fighting with weapons while having my claws out. Now that our magic is gone, they won't retract.* He lifted his surcoat and tore off some strips of cloth, then wrapped them around his sword handle to make it easier to hold.

Maybe you shouldn't be using a sword.

He raised an eyebrow at me but smiled slightly. *It's not ideal, but I need the reach if I'm going to be fighting shadow beasts.*

Vyraetos placed the items back in the bag. "I'm afraid all the medicines would have side effects. Sleep is the best antidote for pain."

"I prefer intoxication," Quen mumbled. "Works for the body and the mind and, if you drink fast enough, super quick." She drew in a shaky breath and dashed a hand beneath her eyes.

Elias gave her an awkward half-hug. She leaned into him like it was the only thing holding her together.

Up ahead, Myantha had edged toward the corridor we'd come from. She froze and pointed. "Do you hear that?"

The pounding against the cellar doors had shifted to high-pitched squeals and metal shrieking under pressure.

Vad growled. "The hinges are giving way. Move!"

Chaos erupted with bags hoisted and lamps gripped. Silus shifted Elara's weight against his side while Thalen's wings flared. Veralt and Elias flanked the rear, weapons drawn.

Myantha spun to face Vad, keeping close to Thalen. "Which direction?"

"How bad is your foot?" Rhielle's gaze darted to the shadow-drenched portal behind us. "Can you walk?"

Veralt stepped forward, already ready to assist. "I'll carry her. She won't be able to walk fast."

Vad's head turned slowly, the look he gave Veralt nothing short of lethal. "If anyone's carrying her, it's me. Now this way!"

Before I could protest, he had one arm under my knees and the other behind my back. With practiced ease, he lifted me into a bridal carry. *I'll get you clear of the portal. Then you can shift.*

I curled into him, fingers clenched in the front of his tunic. The tunnel blurred past as Vad surged forward, his strides long and merciless. Every step jostled my injured foot, sending hot shards of pain up my leg, but I didn't tell him to stop. Behind us, the others followed, shadows clawing at the walls with every flicker of lamplight.

CLANG-KRAAANG-SKREEEEE-BOOOM!

Metal shrieked against stone, and then the echo of something heavier slamming into place resonated down the corridor. Silence held for a quick breath and was shattered by a chorus of snarls.

"They're coming," I breathed.

A howl split the air, reverberating so deep the walls seemed to tremble. Another answered closer to us but farther left. My blood ran cold.

They're coming from multiple directions, I linked to Vad.

His arms cinched tighter around me, his steps never slowing. *I hear them. I have a plan.* His gaze swept the tunnel, and he took a right fork without hesitation. "Stay close," he snapped to the others. "No splitting off."

The tunnel veered sharply. His chest heaved beneath me, muscles bunching as he ran harder. The grim set of his jaw didn't change, but tension spiked through our bond.

Are they going to cut us off? The path sloped steeply, with new tunnels branching out like veins. I tried to memorize the route's twists, turns, and elevation drops, but the howls were closing in too fast. There had to be at least a dozen, maybe more, and their sounds were feral and frenzied.

They'll try, Vad responded.

The tunnel grew colder, air thinning as he charged deeper into the maze, dodging the occasional stalactites and stalagmites in the cavernous labyrinth. Every time his foot hit the ground, my leg jarred, and pain shot through me until I became nauseated. His grip on me never faltered, but it wasn't going to be enough. Not with the scent of blood trailing us.

Snarls echoed down the passage, closing in all around us. No direction was safe.

I twisted in his hold, eyes searching the dark beyond the flickering lamplight. I called on my wolf vision, eyes sharpening past the glow. Shadows darted along the far wall with their claws scraping stone.

Too close.

I linked to Vad, *More coming. Behind us. At least fifteen now—*

"Vad!" Silus shouted.

"I know." Vad's tone was steel. "We won't outrun them in this corridor. There's a steep drop-off ahead with a ledge above it that we can climb onto."

My heart slammed against my ribs, and tears blurred my vision.

"It's after the next curve in the tunnel, and the opening narrows there. Getting into the elevated access point will be tricky—full wing spans won't make it, and the stalactites are sharp." He sighed. "We go one at a time, focusing on the wounded first. Does anyone have razor wire?"

"Quen!" Silus barked. "It's in the bag with three black bands."

"Quen, as soon as we get to the drop-off, leave the bag at the edge," Vad ordered. "No delays."

The tunnel curved, and as Vad had promised, the ground farther ahead vanished into a pit. A cliff face beyond the pit rose up about ten feet on the far side and then leveled into a narrower ledge and, I assumed, a continuation of the passage. Jagged stalactites hung from the ceiling, and long, sharp rocks resembling teeth framed the opening. It was too narrow for anyone to fly through easily, especially carrying someone.

I judged the trajectory it would take for me to get up there. *Don't fly me. Just throw me.*

Fear shot through our bond, and Vad's jaw tightened even more.

I trust you, I told him. *Now trust me.* I looked over his shoulder in time to see glowing yellow eyes rounding the bend.

I don't like this one bit, he growled, but ran to the edge of the drop-off and launched me into the air.

Wind roared past my ears, and my palms slammed into stone, followed by my body, my fingers curling over the lip to hang on. Pain exploded in my injured foot, but I gritted my teeth, trying like hell to ignore it. I hooked my good leg over the top and dragged myself onto the ledge, then rolled flat against the rock. Breath heaving, I turned fast and braced myself at the edge.

Silus flew toward me, carrying Elara, his face red with strain. His dark, feathered wing hit a stalactite. He hissed but powered upward while bracing his feet against a thick ridge on the wall below the ledge. Elara reached for me, and I grabbed her arms and dragged her onto the ledge with a clumsy yank.

"Your ankle!" Elara exclaimed.

"It's fine," I rasped. Heat flared through my foot, and the bandage warmed like blood was spilling into it.

Briar, what the feck are you doing? You're injured! Vad's horror blew right through me.

Helping our sister. Don't worry about me—focus on setting a trap. I flung myself back toward the edge just as Quen's wings sliced into view. She shoved both oil lamps into my hands. "Take these," she cried.

The glass burned my palms, but I jammed them safely into a nearby crevice. As I ducked back, my head slammed into an outcropping of rock. Stars sparked behind my eyes, but there was no time to react. My pulse thundered in my ears, loud and erratic.

I struggled back to the end of the ledge just as Thalen shoved Myantha through the opening, but her hips and legs remained dangling over the edge. His right wing clipped a stalactite, and a sickening *crunch* echoed. He groaned, blood spilling from the joint of his wing. "Climb over!" he barked through clenched teeth.

Myantha seized the end of the ledge. "Thalen!"

His face twisted and reddened as he fell backward and kicked off the rock. He crashed back onto the path we'd come from on the other side of the abyss, then pushed himself up slowly, grimacing.

Elara grabbed Myantha's arms and tried to drag her up, but she started to slide with the added weight. Myantha yelped and dug her fingers into any crevice she could reach.

I jolted forward, my ankle screaming as I wrapped my arms around Elara's waist, preventing her from sliding further. Tears streamed down my cheeks, but my hold didn't falter. Elara and I leaned back and pulled Myantha to safety while my muscles screamed in protest.

I hate that you're always getting hurt. Vad tore through Quen's bag and pulled out the razor wire and pinchers. He darted back toward the bend in the tunnel and looped one end of the wire around a thick stalagmite. With no anchor on the opposite side, he had to stretch the coil diagonally to another stalagmite farther back. Using his claws, he wove the wire between jagged points, tightening and twisting the line fast with quick, brutal movements.

I feel the same way about you. Be careful with the wire, and get up here. Still, I kept my focus forward, refusing to allow anyone else to die on my watch.

I'll be up there as soon as I set up as many layers of this razor wire as I can.

The wire glinted in the lamplight but blended into the wall. The trap was silent and deadly.

Vyraetos yanked a thick bottle of oil from a pack and hurled it past the wire, the glass shattering in a splash across the stone.

"Catch!" Quen shouted, grabbing a dropped bag and throwing it up to me across the ten-foot gap.

I snagged it and passed it to Elara. Myantha scrambled to sit up just as Quen lobbed another pack. This time, Myantha caught it with a grunt.

Quen turned and nodded sharply at Vyraetos.

Thalen limped toward us, his injured wing dragging behind him. "Come on, Badger Claw." He grabbed Elias by the back of his tunic and began to fly him up. His wings pumped hard, and he managed to get high enough for Elias to slam chest-first into the ledge with a loud grunt. But Elias's hands immediately began slipping.

"I've got him!" Elara yelled, grabbing Elias's shoulder.

I rushed forward and wrapped my hands tightly around one of Elias's wrists. The weight nearly dragged me over, but I held tight, my feet braced on slick stone.

"Hold on!" Myantha cried, leaning over to grab Thalen's arm as he reached up, face pale.

Snarls echoed from the tunnel, and shadows streaked into view.

Quen's red, leathery wings flared wide, and she launched up and snagged Elias's other arm. Her right wing clipped a stalagmite with a sickening *snap*. She screamed and twisted violently as she slammed into the ledge, her injured wing snagging on a jagged rock jutting below the edge.

"Quen!" I shouted, yanking Elias up another inch. "Grab me!"

Warmth exploded and then constricted in my bond with

Vad as his concern and anger swirled together.

Quen's nails bit into my shoulder. "My wing's stuck, and Elias is slipping!"

"Don't fight it." My heart pounded against my ribcage. "Let go of him and put your weight on me."

"I'm all right." Elias strained, sweat sprouting on his forehead. "Don't tear your wing—"

Quen whimpered but released Elias. She leaned her weight onto me, and I nearly collapsed under her, my ankle throbbing. I locked my knees and braced against the ledge.

"Get her off Elias and Thalen!" Rhielle shouted from below. "Quen, you're going to shred your wing if you keep thrashing!"

A *thud* sounded beneath us. Silus had reached them, and he didn't hesitate to shove Thalen up with a groan while still gripping Elias. His talons scraped for purchase on the rock wall, his legs shaking from the strain.

Snarls and the scrabble of claws on stone echoed all around us. A guttural howl reverberated off the walls so fiercely that the ledge itself seemed to shudder.

The first wolf leapt over the oil and smacked the razor wire full-force. A sickening wet *rip* echoed as it was caught mid-air, the wire tearing deep into its shadows. The beast howled, its body jerking as it thrashed against the nearly invisible blades, trying to reach Vad and the rest of our group, who were still on the path below. Blood sprayed across the drop, dark and glistening in the lamplight.

The other beasts slammed to a stop, growling, pacing, too feral to retreat but too wary to follow. Two slipped on the oil.

Myantha and Elara yanked Elias and Thalen to safety, and I caught Quen under the arms and hauled her up with everything I had. Her wing ripped free with a tearing sound that made my stomach turn. She shrieked, but I didn't stop.

Below us, Veralt lifted Rhielle onto his shoulders, and then he leaned forward, tilting her over the pit, and Rhielle gripped Quen's legs and lifted her up. I wrapped my arm around Quen's waist and helped her lift her wing, my ankle screaming in protest. With another scream of pain and a deepening of the tear, we got her wing free. Quen spasmed and flailed as I clutched onto her with all my strength.

Rhielle yelped with surprise as Quen's foot clipped her, and she lurched back. Veralt tried to compensate, but the two slid backward and crashed against the far wall on their side of the pit. Rhielle braced herself against the rocks and leaned forward over Veralt's shoulders as he struggled to gain his balance again.

I skidded forward with Quen's weight but dug my knee into an indentation. Grunting, I dragged her up the rest of the way. She gasped with relief and tucked her torn wing in close.

As soon as she was safe, I leaned out over the edge and saw Silus clinging to the wall below the ledge. His fingers were jammed into a crevice, and his muscles shook while one wing hung limply, dragging him off balance. Blood ran from his palms onto the wall.

The ledge bit into my ribs as I stretched down and reached for him. His arm trembled as he tried to wedge his fingers deeper into the fissure. He glanced up once, sweat slick on his brow, eyes stark with strain.

Briar, Vad linked to me. *Let the others handle it! You're just going to get yourself—* His message cut off, and pain filtered through the link. When I glanced up, I saw that the razor wire had cut his palm.

Why don't you *let someone help you?* I linked back, wincing. "Someone hold my legs," I shouted. "Silus, hold on!"

As I leaned over, I realized how much more precarious Silus's position was. He was too far down to easily jump up and reach us, and with his one wing badly wounded and his position unbalanced, he'd never be able to correct and jump high enough.

Vyraetos ran to the edge of the pit on the lower side and prepared the last items to fling up as Vad finished binding up another layer of razor wire. Concern flashed through Vad's eyes. "Silus?"

Thalen struggled to push himself up, his wing also sagging, and I feared it was actually broken. He panted for breath and ran back to the edge with me. Myantha and Elara grabbed me by the backs of my legs, and I folded over the edge and strained to reach Silus. My heart shredded when Silus's eyes widened, his hands wedged in. "No. Don't let go. Hold on." I shook my head and leaned down. I needed to grab him at a good angle, or else we'd all be dragged over. "Guys, lower me a little farther. Silus, I can almost reach you."

"Don't let go, Silus!" Elara cried out, her voice raw. "Don't you dare let go!"

Chapter Twelve

Grinding his teeth in pain, Silus twisted his body. My fingers brushed his wrist, and he jerked to the side, his hand locking around mine just as the narrow ledge beneath him crumbled.

The sudden weight hit me like a jolt of lightning. My arm went taut, my shoulder nearly wrenched from its socket. The sharp edge of the ledge dug into my ribs, grinding bone and stealing my breath. Silus's full weight dragged me forward. The nails of my other hand scraped the stone, sparks of pain shooting through my fingers as I tried to brace myself, but my body lurched, threatening to topple over the edge with him.

Elara and Myantha strained behind me, heels digging into the rock as they anchored my legs. Quen flung herself across my back, her elbows jamming into my spine to hold me steady.

Silus's grip was slick with blood, his wing dragging him sideways, its feathers bent at twisted angles. His boots scrabbled against the wall, kicking stone chips into the abyss below.

"Hold on!" I choked out, my chest grinding against the ledge so hard I could barely breathe.

A rush of air swept past me—Thalen. He half-stumbled, half-lunged, his injured wing dragging, but his reach still strong. He dropped beside me and caught Silus's other arm, teeth bared, muscles trembling with strain. "Fecking bastard! If you die on me, I'll never forgive you, especially after you were such an ass."

Silus groaned, trying to brace his foot, but the stone beneath him cracked with a hollow snap that echoed through my chest. My muscles screamed as I took more of his weight, but I refused to let go.

Below, Rhielle and Veralt had recovered from their fall against the tunnel wall. Veralt crouched, bracing his legs wide as he gripped Rhielle's thighs and lifted her up again in a surge of brute strength. "Don't kick my woman in the face," he growled.

Rhielle gritted her teeth and grabbed Silus's legs, shoving upward.

With a guttural cry, Silus surged, his body scraping over the edge until he collapsed beside me, chest heaving, blood streaking his face and hands.

I crumpled next to him, gasping, my whole body shaking from the effort. Myantha fell back, panting with strain, before crawling to Thalen, who was clutching his mangled wing. Elara threw her arms around Silus, pressing his head to her chest and kissing his temple like she could anchor him there.

Louder and sharper snarls tore through the tunnel. The scrape of claws became a pounding rhythm, relentless and closing. The smell hit next—wet fur, blood, and that sharp electric tang that bled from the portal.

I scrambled back to the edge with my heart hammering. Rhielle was already reaching down to Vyraetos while Veralt braced her from behind. Vad sprinted beside them with the last of the bags. He thrust the coil of razor wire and the pinchers into Veralt's grip before slinging the remaining packs over his shoulder.

The wolves snarled, pacing back and forth and biting at the air as if testing it. Then the new leader charged forward over the corpses, but it didn't see the razor wire either, and hit full force, the thin blades slicing through its throat. Blood sprayed in a crimson arc as the creature's momentum carried it forward, then bounced it backward and crashed it into the two wolves behind it. They went down in a snarling heap, tangled in the wire, but more poured in behind them.

"Move!" Vad's voice cracked through the chaos.

I leaned farther over the edge as Rhielle and Veralt hauled Vyraetos up between them. The old fae's face contorted as we caught his hands and dragged him higher. Thalen slid in beside me and caught Vyraetos's other arm. Together, we hauled him over the edge, where Myantha and Quen pulled him clear.

I dropped flat to my stomach again, stone biting into my ribs as I reached for Rhielle. Her slick fingers locked around mine. "Hold on!" I gritted. Thalen crouched beside me again, his silver-white wings shaking as he caught her other arm. Together, we pulled, inch by inch, until she, too, scrambled over the ledge, chest heaving, eyes wild.

The tunnel pulsed with snarls and the wet shuffle of limbs.

Vad dropped low, hands laced, and barked, "Veralt!"

Veralt started to scoff, some half-formed snide remark on his lips until he looked back.

The wolves that had survived the first razor wire line were dragging themselves upright. Blood dripped in thick rivulets from slashed flanks and shredded shoulders, but they moved, snarling low and jaws gaping. One limped forward, its ribs exposed, its side peeled nearly to the bone. Another twitched violently, a ragged length of flesh hanging from its haunch like a torn cloak, but its head stayed low, and it kept its eyes locked on Vad and Veralt.

Then it lunged straight into the second line of razor wire. The metal sliced clean through its chest. Blood sprayed, and its body thrashed before it collapsed in a heap.

More wolves barreled around the bend. Four. Six. Eight. Too many.

"Come on, big man!" Thalen motioned with his hands. "Everyone else, get ready to grab!"

I dropped flat, bracing one arm, reaching with the other. My eyes flicked between Veralt and Vad. I knew Vad would be last. I understood why. But I still hated it.

Veralt ran, boots striking hard on stone, then pushed off Vad's hands and launched. He hit the ledge hard, his ribs and forearms colliding with the rock. His legs kicked above the drop, and his fingers clawed for purchase but found nothing.

He slid, and we lunged.

Thalen and I dove first, our bodies snapping forward. His weight yanked me painfully down, my bandaged ankle scraping the jagged rock.

Silus dropped beside us, knees slamming into the stone. He caught Veralt's other arm just as Rhielle flung herself across my back, her hands locking in Veralt's collar. Her gasping grunts matched the panic blazing through the bond.

Vad was still below.

We heaved together, bodies straining, dragging Veralt over the edge so he wouldn't block Vad's path.

Cold tendrils of fear choked me as I linked, *Come on!*

The bond ignited, Vad's fear mixing with mine, sharp as a lightning strike. His focus locked on the wolves spilling over the second razor-wire line. One vaulted cleanly over the wire with its claws shrieking against stone as it landed in a crouch. Another followed, yellow eyes burning bright.

As soon as Veralt was clear, I twisted free and flung myself forward.

"Vad!" I screamed, stretching both arms out. "Now!"

He leapt, wings flaring wide just as a wolf lunged and snapped its jaws around the thick leather of his boot, then slipped with a sharp yelp down into the pit. The jolt knocked Vad sideways, throwing off his flight mid-beat. His wings pumped, strong and desperate, once, but it was too late.

He slammed into the rock face below the ledge with a guttural grunt, his claws raking stone, desperate for a hold. But his boots slipped.

The bond drowned me in rage and terror. His. Mine. One wild, pulsing flood of emotions between us.

I caught his arms, and his hands locked around my shoulders. He pressed his palms flat, keeping his claws from tearing into me, but his weight pulled me down like an avalanche. My ribs ground against the stone. My ankle screamed as it jammed against a jagged rock.

Thalen shot past me in a blur of silver-streaked feathers and caught Vad's shoulder. Silus lunged in, looping an arm under Vad's other side. They braced and lifted, wings trembling, muscles corded tight.

"Pull!" Thalen roared.

I hauled with everything I had. Stone shredded my arms. My body burned with strain. Silus's jaw locked in a grim snarl as we dragged Vad over the edge, one brutal inch at a time.

The wolves barked louder, their howls scraping across the stone walls like a curse. Veralt grabbed my hips and anchored me, grunting from the effort. With one final heave, we yanked Vad up and over.

He collapsed beside me, breath sawing through his chest. I rolled onto my back, gasping, my muscles shaking. Thalen and Silus staggered back, wings half-spread for balance and blood dripping from torn feathers. The shadows from our oil lamp danced across their strained faces, turning them sharp and hollow.

Below us, the wolves growled, pacing and snarling—too many to count, too angry to back down. One edged toward the ledge and sniffed the air, head tossing. Another charged halfway and skidded to a stop just before the wire.

More would come, especially with all the blood here.

Weapons and gear littered the ledge around us, along with two bags and the oil lamps.

I forced myself upright, ignoring the pain flaring in my feet, legs, chest, and back. My body screamed for rest, but I shoved the feeling away and crawled to Vad. My arms wrapped around him tightly. "Don't ever scare me like that again," I breathed into his neck.

That goes for you as well. You need rest. Don't try to tell me otherwise. His jaw flexed. The ghost of a grin, half snarl, half relief, touched his lips before vanishing. "We need to keep moving." He spoke loudly, trying to be heard over the ear-shattering noise below us. "We don't know how many more are coming."

Silus touched his injured wing, grimacing. "We don't even know how they're opening those portals. If they cut us off from the forest—"

Quen whimpered.

Vad cut him off. "Then we find another way. But we tend wounds first. This is as safe as it's going to get for now."

My heart expanded as I watched him take charge and calm the panic. In that moment, he reminded me so much of my sister that it hurt.

Veralt dragged a boulder from farther up in the cave toward the mouth of the tunnel with a grunt. It wouldn't stop a horde, but it'd buy us time.

I hobbled over to check Quen's wing. The damage was worse than Vad's had been from the spear. Skin was shredded, and the leathery membrane punctured in multiple places, with blood drying in streaks. She wouldn't be flying anytime soon. Thalen and Silus were in similar poor condition, but Quen's was the worst.

Vad dug through the bags we'd managed to keep and took out Elara's medicine and the vials containing the hair samples. He laid them beside the bandages.

Vyraetos crouched beside him, inspecting the supplies. His brows pinched as he picked up one vial and held it to the light. "What's this?" He lifted the vial and tilted his head as he studied the one with only half the hairs glowing.

"Physician Morlo was analyzing the samples. He suspected Kaylen had been consuming Elias's magic. Half her hair confirms it. The rest may still be reacting."

Quen leaned into Elias as Vyraetos began cleaning her wing. "Didn't you see who was taking your magic?"

Elias's voice was quiet. "They siphoned it into vials. I was usually blindfolded. Sometimes I heard a woman in the next room. But I never saw her. She needed more blood than just mine... They talked about taking from other prisoners, too."

Quen's jaw tightened. "Kaylen, then. No question."

Myantha raised her hand slightly. "Is the sample from when your bracer got stuck in her hair?" She tugged at her own locks. "Calla Lily was next to you, remember?"

From across the space, Thalen lifted an eyebrow. "I thought you were focusing on other things when Vad got the hair."

She blushed but didn't look away. "I can multitask." She tilted her head, voice softening. "Besides... it was kind of funny. Her face, when her hair got stuck like that."

"If Calla Lily mixed her hair in with Kaylen's..." I bit my lip, piecing it together aloud. "That could explain why some of the strands are glowing while others aren't."

Elias sat on Quen's other side, his hand brushing hers.

I turned to him. "Elias, is there anything else you remember? Anything about who was consuming your magic?"

He shook his head. "No. I'm sorry."

I tried to give him a reassuring smile, but it felt closer to a wince. "Don't be sorry. None of this is your fault. And it's not like any of us have magic, so whatever Kaylen or Calla Lily absorbed won't help her. Not yet, at least."

"That's assuming it even *was* one of the bridal candidates." Silus sighed. "We have no idea how many traitors are embedded in the court. I wouldn't put it past them to use others as cover without Kaylen's knowledge."

Vad's voice sliced through the uncertainty. "We'll figure that out later. Right now, we move. We need to get somewhere secure so that all of us can start healing."

No one argued.

In the dim light, we worked quickly. Wounds were bound with the remaining supplies. Not wanting to use them up, I shifted the most agonizing shift I'd ever done before. My bones cracked, and the skin stretched around my injury like it wasn't going to heal.

I whimpered in pain, but somehow, the skin closed enough not to destroy my leg. However, as soon as I inhaled a breath of relief, my wolf began to retreat from me, and I realized that I could be stuck in this form. Shit! I would need to be able to talk to the others soon.

Before she receded too far, I forced another shift back into human form. My body contorted in ways that it never had before, and I cried out.

What's wrong? Vad appeared beside me, his eyes wide.

I wanted to answer, but I couldn't. My bones broke and reformed brutally, and fur remained on my arms. I shifted into some weird combination of human and wolf, the magic trying to surge and retreat, warring with itself. I'd never experienced pain like this, not even during my first shift as a child.

"Vyratoes!" Vad said loudly just as my body completed the transformation.

I shifted into my wolf form again, long enough to heal, and then returned to human. The slip retained some of the wedding dress's magic and went with me. A small gift from Fate.

I'd have traded it to have Thalira, Yuki, and Velessa back.

"I'm fine," I gasped. "I just need to let my wolf magic recharge." That made sense. Shifting back and forth like I'd just done was dangerous, but we had to keep moving.

Quen blew out one of the oil lamps and poured its contents into the remaining one.

Helping me to my feet, Vad surveyed the area. *Do you need to rest more now?*

I shook my head. *No. We've got to keep moving.* It would take a day or so for me to recharge, and that kind of delay wasn't an option.

Do you need me to carry you? The concerned light in his eyes cut me, and a warmth spread in my chest at the sincerity in his question.

No. I promise, I'm fine, I linked back to him, smiling despite the pain and exhaustion.

He scoffed slightly, narrowing his eyes. But that gentle affection surged through our bond. *We will have to redefine that term.*

Later. We've got to get through this first. I straightened my posture, ready to take on the next challenge despite wishing with all my heart this situation could be done and Vad and I could disappear into one another's arms, someplace cozy and warm.

Down below, the wolves were still making noise, determined to find a way up. My foot was still throbbing, making it clear that it wasn't fully healed. But it wasn't nearly as bad as it had been prior. Luckily, we'd had enough bandages for all of us, and we took off walking.

Darkness swallowed us as we moved forward. After a

bit, I couldn't keep track of time. Hours or ten minutes might have passed, and the twisting path seemed endless, every step stretching into eternity. The glowing hair vials offered faint light in a pinch, but they barely reached a foot ahead. Not enough if the wolves could appear out of nothing.

The howls started up again intermittently, then steadily, as if the wolves were tracking us. We quickened our pace and changed directions several times, Vad choosing the higher ground and narrow stone paths above ravines. I had no idea how he was navigating, but I followed without question.

Elara was lagging, but her expression never wavered. Whether the medicine was helping or she was driven by pure willpower, I didn't know. But she kept walking, just like the rest of us.

It felt like we were clawing through a never-ending nightmare.

Eventually, exhaustion weighed me down, every muscle in my body trembling. My foot throbbed in time with my pulse, and even Vad's steps slowed. He lifted one hand. "Here. We stop. Just for a bit."

Relief crashed over the group like a wave. No one protested.

We slid down against the tunnel wall, our gear hitting the ground with dull, exhausted thuds. My body screamed as I lowered myself, grit grinding into every tear in my slip, but I didn't care. Someone passed me a strip of dried meat that was as hard as stone, dry, nearly flavorless, but I chewed anyway. My lips cracked and bled, the iron tang flooding my mouth, but I ignored it and continued eating.

Our circumstances weren't sustainable. And we all knew it.

The oil lamp was low, barely a third of the fuel remaining. If it burned like Earth oil, we had four, maybe five hours of light left. And that was being generous.

"How much longer until we reach an exit?" The words scraped my throat like sandpaper.

Everyone stilled. Even Thalen and Silus looked to Vad now, their expressions tight.

Vad surveyed the passage, eyes narrowing. "A couple hours, maybe. We'll rest for one. The light should hold."

It wasn't a guarantee. I was haunted by the thought of being lost down here forever while Aureline assassins attacked my sister.

No one argued. Quen lowered the lamp's wick to preserve what oil she could, then curled in close beside Elias, her damaged wing draped over her chest. The rest of us followed suit. There was no room to stretch out, so we pressed in shoulder to shoulder, backs to cold stone, as the shadows swallowed the space around us.

No one talked. The only sound was the occasional shuffle of bandages being changed, the wet rasp of breath pulled through clenched teeth, or a quiet, pained grunt when someone moved wrong.

There was no comfort, no safety. Only silence that seemed to stretch forever.

When Vad roused us, it felt too soon. My body ached, my muscles were stiff, and my wolf was whimpering inside me. We choked down the last bites of our rations and drained the little water we'd brought with us.

Placing a hand on my shoulder, Vad said, "It'll be all right. There's water deeper in this cave."

I believed him, but it was hard to find hope with what surrounded us.

We continued on, time measured by the slow bleed of the lamp oil and the dull echo of our footsteps. The light weakened, casting ever fuzzier, flickering shadows on the damp walls, while fatigue clung to us like a second skin.

Then I caught a sound and a luxurious scent.

Something low and rushing, with clean moisture in the air.

"Water," I breathed.

Everyone stilled, and the sounds filled the air around us again.

Vad's eyes glimmered silver in the lamplight. "That's the river." His voice was low, weight behind every word. "We're close."

Hope stirred like a spark catching dry kindling, fast and fragile. The group surged forward, a little quicker now despite the bone-deep weariness. Our shoulders brushed as we crammed through the narrow passage, drawn forward by thirst. The air grew damper with each step, curling cool against my cheeks. I could taste the river on my tongue.

Vad reached the bend ahead of us and rounded it.

Then stopped short. "Feck!"

CHAPTER THIRTEEN

I stepped around the corner and halted beside Vad. Ice shot down my spine.

A wall of jagged stone, crumbled boulders, and shattered slabs rose like a dam, sealing the tunnel. The floor had already flooded, and a steady stream of water gurgled in from somewhere beyond. But this water wasn't crimson like it should've been. It was a pale milky gray, frothing where it churned against stone.

It looked *wrong.*

Vad's wings flared wide behind him as he stepped to the edge. His hands braced against his belt, jaw clenched tight as he scanned the blockage. Frustration and calculation pulsed hot through the bond. This was it. This was where the path ended. At least, for now.

How bad is it? I linked, not wanting him to have to say it out loud in front of everyone.

He crouched, fingers dipping into the swirling water.

Rhielle knelt beside him, scooping a handful. "It's not crimson... or silver. This is..." Her eyes narrowed as she let it spill through her fingers. "It's *clear.* I've never seen water like this."

"That's what water looks like on Earth." If we weren't so

tired and stressed, I would've laughed at their thinking this water looked strange, but now wasn't the time.

Stepping beside the wall, Vyraetos pressed a palm to the stone as if feeling for a heartbeat. His shoulders slumped. "The magic has bled out of this place. Even the mountain mourns. The water is only water now."

I studied the rest of the cavern, looking for alternative exits. About ten feet away, another slab of rock jutted up and curved back into darkness where the passage continued.

"Can we dig through it? Even a small gap..." Elara swayed slightly, pressing a hand to her ribs. Her right wing lifted an inch—subtle, but promising.

Elias shook his head. "If I had my magic, I could get us out of this situation, but like this?" He glanced at the ceiling, assessing the weight hanging over us. "It'd take hours. Maybe days. And the ceiling could collapse."

I didn't need him to explain further. That mound could fall on us. The water could rise fast. Any mistake would be catastrophic.

Silus took the lamp from Quen and tilted it upward. Veralt snagged it from him so he could lift it higher. The golden light flickered across the rock pile and the ceiling above, revealing the sheer scale of the collapse. Solid. Impassable.

"No one's getting through *that*, friend," Veralt said grimly, the smirk on his lips empty of humor.

"Is this the only way out?" Rhielle's arms were folded tightly, and her hand tapped an anxious rhythm on her opposite elbow.

"At this level?" Thalen winced as he shifted his injured wing. "Yes. Unless the royals have more tricks tucked under their crowns."

Myantha stepped closer to him, pressing her cheek against his shoulder.

Vad's silence stretched. His eyes never left the water, but

the weight of his tension echoed down the bond. His jaw was ticking.

I brushed a hand across the bandage on his wrist. He turned his palm and curled his fingers through mine. The buzz sprang to life between us.

"We can't stay." Vad's voice was low but carried authority. "The water will keep rising. The southern passage curves up. It leads to the vesting chamber. If there's any place left in this gods-forsaken mountain that still has lingering magic... it'll be there."

"And if not?" Elias asked softly.

"Then we secure it. Wait for night. And escape through one of the old shafts near the top. If they haven't caved in."

Thalen moved to the drier side of the rock path. "This water is already two feet deep, and it's freezing. If the flood started after the quake, that means the lower tunnels are filled. We must figure this out because I'm too sexy to die." He met Vad's eyes and arched a brow.

"He is." Myantha agreed.

"Thank you, my love." He smiled, but the humor didn't quite reach his eyes. He was trying to ease the tension, but even his jokes landed flat. He tugged on his injured wing and winced. "If we're avoiding the shadow beasts..." His lips thinned. "Scaffing void. That leaves us *one* path, doesn't it?"

A low sound echoed as the river lapped, creeping inch by inch up the stone.

Silus turned to Veralt and raised a brow like he was sizing up a blockade. "Can the giant even fit?"

Veralt scoffed and folded his arms. "Fit through what?"

"The safest path will be a tight squeeze," Vad admitted. "You can move to higher ground farther in, and we'll come back for—"

"I'm not staying behind," Veralt cut in, passing the lamp

back to Quen and then shaking his hand from the heat. "Not when this place is crawling with shadow beasts. It isn't safe for my woman to stay here, and she won't leave me."

"Of course I won't." Rhielle stroked his arm and curled her fingers around the muscle of his bicep. "If we have to find another way, we will."

Vad's gaze held steady. "As long as he isn't claustrophobic, it'll be fine."

Something cold licked the bottom of my feet, causing me to glance down and confirm my worst fear. The water had advanced, creeping up in steady, silent waves. In the next few minutes, it would claim the stone beneath our feet.

There wasn't time to debate further. "We need to move soon, or we won't have the option." A shudder rippled through me as I imagined crawling through a narrow stone chute with that icy current on our heels.

Attention shifting to Elara, Vad asked, "Are you strong enough to climb?"

Despite her pale face, Elara nodded and lifted her chin in what must have been a quiet resolve. "I am."

"I'll be with you every step." Silus laid a hand gently on her shoulder.

She leaned subtly into the touch, but Vad's voice cut through before either one could continue. "Your wing is still healing."

Silus stiffened, and his mouth parted.

"You tore the muscle, not just the membrane," Vad added, tone firm but not unkind. "That won't hold your weight in the air, and you know it." He went to his sister and held out an arm.

Elara wrapped an arm around Vad's shoulder, accepting the help. She wouldn't want Silus taking the risk either.

"You, Thalen, and Quen won't be flying for at least another day. Maybe longer," Vad added, not unkindly. He pointed toward the island of stone on the other side of the rising river. "Just beyond that point and to the left is a tunnel behind the eastern wall. That's our path. I'll fly the lamps over. Do *not* wade into the water. We don't know what's beneath it, or if the ground will even hold."

He took the lamp and flew across, the golden light bobbing through the darkness with him. Shadows clung to the ceiling like a warning.

"Stupid plan," Quen muttered under her breath. "Hanging up giant, pointed rocks from your ceiling? Honestly. Who does that?"

"Does your wing still hurt?" Elias asked quietly.

Quen's wings fluttered tighter to her back. The bandages over the membrane were stained, but not leaking. She shrugged and lifted the lamp closer to her chest. "Not enough to stop me from debating who I hate more—Kaylen or Calla Lily."

Rhielle scoffed, but her smirk held no humor. "I've got enough hate for both of those scaffing wretches and everyone else involved."

Licking his cracked lips, Elias rocked back on his heels. "Do we have enough oil for light to get to the vesting chamber, or at least another supply stockpile?"

Vad returned, landing beside me. "It'll be close." He exhaled. "But the vesting chamber has ceremonial oil. That should be enough for a refill."

The water sounded like a whisper, growing louder and lapping against my foot. I didn't look. I didn't need to. I could feel its icy hold on me.

With a soft grunt, Vad lifted Elara into his arms and launched back across the gap. His wings flared out, catching the still air in the cavern. As he landed on the far side, a flicker of pain that had to be due to his wing injury pulsed through our bond.

I hated that he had any discomfort at all, but I was able to admire the way he acted with quiet strength and unwavering focus, putting his people first. Even if he wasn't a wolf, he understood what it meant to protect the pack. To lead when everyone else could only follow.

He looked back at me, wings furling tight behind him. His concern tightened through our bond. "Will you be able to jump? I can come back and get you."

"I'm good." I adjusted the bag slung over my shoulder with my jaw tight. Elara didn't need to be left alone for even a second.

He studied me, a wrinkle between his brows. *Seriously, I'm coming back. Just hold on.*

Nope, not waiting, I retorted.

Backing up a few steps, I shook out my arms. The water slid around my ankles, cold and steady, creeping halfway up my foot as I moved. My stomach dropped, and the hairs on my neck rose as I sprinted forward, splashing water with each step. The stone blurred beneath my feet...and then I jumped. Air sliced past my face, and then I landed safely on the other side. The ache in my injured foot flared, stealing my breath.

Vad grabbed my arm and steadied me. *You're so stubborn.* He huffed and kissed my lips.

You knew that coming in. I snorted. *That's on you.*

His fingers laced with mine as he placed a hand on Elara's shoulder, keeping her steady on her feet. The buzz between us was comforting.

One by one, the others crossed. Some jumped; some were carried. Quen nearly lost her grip on the edge of the rock island and had to be pulled up by the sleeve. The rising water had worked against our jumps and ability to maneuver. No one spoke. Not with the water lapping against the stone behind us and the shadows stretching overhead like clinging threads.

The river's edge had claimed the rest of the stone floor, and the air felt thicker by the time the final boots hit dry ground.

My gut twisted.

"This way." Vad led us to what looked like a solid wall, but as we drew closer, I spotted a narrow vertical gap that was barely wide enough for Veralt's shoulders.

Vad turned sideways and slipped through first, his wings pressed tight to his back. Stone scraped as he vanished into the dark. "Come on," he called, voice echoing hollowly from the rock.

I followed, twisting sideways to fit. The passage closed in on me at once, cold and damp. The soft rush of the river sounded far off now, but not far enough. It wouldn't take much to trap us here.

The floor sloped sharply upward. I braced both hands against the walls as I climbed after Vad. My feet scraped against damp stone, the incline steep and slick. One wrong step, and I'd end up knocking the whole line backward.

"Watch your footing." Vad slid farther into the passage and offered a hand to me. I caught it and slid my fingers across his bandaged palm. The ceiling hung low enough that I had to duck my head in several spots. The run bag I carried bumped awkwardly against my hip as I climbed.

"This isn't exactly a comforting tunnel," I muttered, trying to ignore the growing tightness in my chest as the passage narrowed further.

Behind me, Elara and Silus slipped in next, elbows brushing the walls. Their breathing echoed in the narrow space. Quen followed with the lamp, its glow flickering wildly, casting strange, stretched shadows across the stone.

The rest of our group filed in slowly—Elias, Vyraetos, Thalen, and Myantha. Veralt grunted as he began forcing his way in, the stone scraping his back and shoulders. Rhielle followed him, one hand on his arm.

"Everything all right?" Vad called back.

"Delightful." Veralt spat. "If you like crawling through rock coffins."

The passage twisted tighter. At times, I had to duck or press my back to one side, using Vad and my other hand against the stone wall to keep from sliding back. My breath created small puffs of condensation that clung to the rock. *How much farther?* My chest tightened with the thought of getting stuck.

A few hundred feet. He continued forward as discomfort leaked through the bond despite his calm tone. *Then it opens up.*

I checked on Elara beside me. Sweat beaded her forehead, and her jaw was set tight. Silus stayed close behind her, and I caught a glance from Quen behind them, her focus split between keeping the lamp steady and checking on the others.

Elias moved just behind Quen, his face tight and unreadable, like he was reliving his time in the prison. Vyraetos followed, his movements controlled, every breath measured to conserve energy in the narrowing space. Thalen and Myantha came next, whispering quietly to each other as they steadied their steps, hands brushing the rock to stay upright on the slick incline.

A low grunt echoed from the rear as Veralt was wedged in a section so narrow even Vad had struggled. His massive frame pressed against both sides, shoulders scraping stone. Rhielle stayed close, her hand splayed on his back, offering silent reassurance with every step he forced forward.

Above, the path steepened again, and even more rocks bit into my feet.

We climbed hand over foot, shifting sideways when the passage narrowed too much for us to face forward. Our backs dragged against one wall while our palms searched for holds on the other. The air grew thinner, the silence heavier. Only the soft shush of leather boots on stone, ragged breathing, and the occasional scrape of someone's pack reminded me we weren't alone.

The line of us inched upward, breathing labored, the tension thick in the still air. No one was talking now. We were all too focused on climbing, squeezing, not slipping.

A sharp yelp rang out, followed by a loud *thud* and rattling stones. My heart lurched into my throat as I twisted my head around.

"Myantha!" Thalen shouted.

She'd lost her footing and fallen sideways into a tight bend in the wall. It looked like her shoulder and thigh were wedged firmly. Her efforts to free herself shook dust loose from above.

"Don't move!" Quen called from above. "Everyone hold!"

The entire line went still.

The stone groaned above us, a low grinding echo, like the cave was warning us not to push our luck.

Myantha's breath came in quick gasps. "I-I'm stuck."

"I've got her." Thalen braced a shoulder against one side of the rock while reaching for her. "It's just a bad angle. I'll get you out."

"Thalen, be careful." Vad squeezed my hand more tightly. "You could easily fall and get stuck, too."

A lump formed in my throat, and I wondered if we were even going to make it out of this cave alive.

"No one else move!" Elias hissed. "We don't know how stable this area is."

I hated the thought of Elias reliving his time in prison. This tight space was impacting me, too, but I hadn't crawled into such small spaces to hide like he had.

Vad turned slightly, voice tight. "Can she be pulled or pushed?"

Thalen grunted. "Only one side's open. I'll have to wedge

behind and shift her forward."

A beat of silence passed with only the sound of water dripping as dust settled around us and in our eyes and mouths.

Then a soft scrape of boots, Thalen squeezing into place. "You're okay, I've got you. On three, I'll shift, and you push with your leg a little."

He counted down calmly as Myantha closed her eyes. Then they moved together.

Her leg slid free with a pop and a pained gasp, her shoulder following a second later. Another cloud of dust rained from above, but nothing collapsed.

"You're safe," Thalen breathed, catching her with one arm as she slumped forward.

My throat dried so much that I needed water quickly.

Vad exhaled. "Keep moving. Slowly. Carefully. Everyone else, watch your footing there."

The line moved again, quieter than before, the tension building until Veralt made it through the space with a fair amount of grunting and huffing.

We were all too aware now of how narrow this space was, how little room we had if anything went wrong. Every scrape of stone sounded louder. Every heartbeat felt closer to the surface.

Vad's bandage snagged again on an outcrop of stone, and he winced, pain flashing down the bond. I squeezed his hand gently in response. He didn't speak—just pressed forward.

From the back, Veralt cursed while forcing his way through a narrow curve. Dust fell from the ceiling as he pressed forward, his shoulders scraping.

We moved hand over foot, the stone cold and unyielding. My muscles ached. My lungs burned. The farther we climbed, the more the closeness of the space pressed in on me. But stopping wasn't an option. Not when the water was rising behind us. Not when we had no other way forward.

Our breaths echoed off the stone, shallow and strained. The tunnel walls were slick with condensation. Beads of moisture dripped from above, pattering against my arms, but the steady gurgle of the river below chilled me more than the air ever could. Every pause stretched time thin, every breath a reminder we couldn't afford to stop.

Then the air shifted, and something electric brushed my skin, making me freeze.

A prickling sensation started at my ribs and raced down my legs like a warning. The wall in front of me shuddered just enough to make me doubt my senses as shadows pulsed across it, snaking tendrils like living veins. My stomach dropped.

Red eyes blinked open by my thigh.

"No—" I rasped.

A massive shadow wolf lunged through the wall and clamped its jaws on my skirt.

A scream ripped from my throat as the stone vanished beneath my feet. My hands scrabbled for purchase, nails scraping uselessly across the slick wall.

"Briar!" Vad's roar hit the tunnel like a shockwave.

My body slammed down, my skull cracking against the rock as the wolf yanked again. My legs slid forward, and the portal swallowed me, inch by inch.

"Let *go*!" I clawed at the stone, fingers tearing against the unforgiving rock. Blood slicked my palms. My wolf surged inside me, growling and snapping, desperate to fight, but there was nothing to bite.

Vad dove after me, his hand locking around my wrist in an iron grip. Our bond flared hot and frantic, his panic thundering through my chest.

"Hold on!" Elara's voice cracked as she shoved forward, her small frame wedging into the narrow wall beside me.

Elias dropped flat to the stone, reaching out past her. "Grab her—grab her!"

The wolf snarled and pulled steadily, its red eyes glowing brighter as shadows surged around it. The air warped and twisted as the cold void wrapped around me like a current, dragging me inside.

Vad's fingers crushed around mine. "I won't let you go."

My shoulder socket burned with the strain as Vad held tight, his face contorted with effort. The transition through the portal slammed into me like a physical blow, the air pressure shifting, temperature dropping, and the smell of wet fur and old blood overwhelming my senses.

The wolf released my slip, and I scrambled away, gasping, my back hitting something solid.

No. It couldn't be.

Chapter Fourteen

For a moment, I couldn't breathe.

Vad's presence—his weight, his heat, his shield of wings—stole the air from my lungs almost as much as the wolf had. He'd followed me through the portal, and now he was in danger.

Are you hurt? He moved in front of me, blocking me from the beast by flaring his wings wider. He snarled, and his back coiled tightly.

No, it just got my skirt this time.

Everything had gone deathly still.

I stood and prepared to fight. The run bag had fallen off my shoulder, and I didn't have any weapons other than my human hands and teeth since shifting was out of the question. Concern and confusion raced through our bond as Vad remained in front of me. But the sensation of anger wanted to shred me from the inside out. I had no doubt he thought he would lose me.

He moved to block me from the wolf again, but I caught his wrist. The jolt coursed between us, anchoring us to reality. *You shouldn't have come.*

I always will. I protect what's mine until I take my last breath.

He took my hand, and the fight that had built inside me

dissolved just long enough to let me feel everything: the panic, the relief, the ache of still being alive.

Then silence hit.

No snarling. No growling. Still and unnatural.

Something shifted in the air. My wolf raised her hackles, uneasy but on defense, sniffing the currents with a low whine that curled in my throat. Vad tensed again, his concern laced with confusion as his grip on my hand hovered between protective and cautious. The air hummed around us like a taut wire pulled too tight, and I looked around.

We were surrounded.

We stood with our backs to the wall of a circular cavern. Wolves ringed the chamber, all standing with their attention fixed on me like statues carved from shadow and instinct. They weren't attacking, but they weren't retreating either. Every single one had crimson eyes.

A chill ran down my spine.

At the far end of the chamber stood a figure I knew wasn't ordinary. Even in the dim light, it radiated presence. It was massive, silent, and also crimson-eyed.

Its fur was black as a void, the kind of darkness that drank in the light and gave nothing back. It stood motionless, tall as a stag, muscles coiled beneath a pelt that shimmered like shadow and smoke. The weight of its attention hit me like a tidal wave.

My wolf hunkered in my mind.

It's another guardian beast. Vad stayed focused on it, ready to fight if it lunged.

Like the stag. A strange pulse of energy moved through me, stirring in my chest and then moving down my spine. The memory of that moment with the stag flickered to life. I couldn't explain the awe, the fear, the overwhelming certainty that something ancient and powerful was trying to connect with me. That same sensation pooled in my stomach now.

My wrist ached where the frozen butterfly tattoo had once burned. A ripple of cold coiled there, reaching outward, like roots digging into something deeper.

The guardian wolf took a step forward while every wolf in the circle remained still, not a tail nor an ear twitching.

My wolf eased in what I could only explain as recognition. She pressed forward with interest, her attention completely locked on the guardian.

The air between us vibrated as if alive and watching. A sharp realization cut through me. The guardian wolf had been waiting for me. Time slowed around me, each breath dragging as my nerves tightened like violin strings.

Though its paws were massive, they made only the softest sounds, claws whispering over the rough stone.

A strange but irresistible urge to approach curled through my nerves and down into my feet, the pull gentle but as absolute as the tide drawing out the ocean.

Vad moved to block my path, and I realized I'd started forward. The bond between us throbbed with rising alarm. *Don't. Stay behind me. We'll find an exit. If they turn on us in here, we're finished.*

I didn't answer because I wasn't sure he was wrong. Still, I couldn't ignore the pull inside me either.

The guardian's gaze didn't waver. With every step it took closer, I became more certain that it wasn't a threat. Not to me.

Maybe to everyone else. Maybe even to Vad. But not to me.

It's all right. I have to go to it. My throat dried, and my pulse stumbled, but I knew approaching the shadow beast was what I needed, too. It pulled both at me and my wolf.

The guardian wolf's crimson gaze locked with mine, unblinking, as if summoning me forward. With a grace that should be impossible due to its sheer size, it stepped closer, its fur rippling like smoke stirred by a windless current.

Vad's wings flexed as he angled his body in front of mine like a living shield. "Stay behind me," he growled, low and lethal.

The wolf's gigantic head dipped. A deep sound rumbled from its chest, part growl, part breath, part something older than language. The vibration thrummed through the stone, through my bones, until my ribs ached from holding in my breath.

My wolf pressed harder, pacing just under the surface of my skin like a caged storm.

I placed a hand on Vad's arm. "It's all right," I whispered, though I wasn't sure if I meant it for him or myself. Then I took another step forward, but Vad didn't move.

Briar. His voice scraped through the bond like gravel. His claws dug into my arm, not hard enough to break skin but enough to make my pulse jump. *It's not letting me come with you.*

I swallowed, the memory of the stag rising in my mind. It had prevented him from staying with me, too. *I have to do this alone. We have to trust Fate right now. It's calling me.*

Trust Fate? I would rather freeze to death than trust her an inch. Vad's panic choked me, but I couldn't stop the tug toward the animal.

The guardian wolf gave another low growl, steady now. Like an ancient drumbeat counting down.

My wolf answered firmly and resolutely, stating we were equal, not prey. *I have to go. I need you to trust me.*

Vad's grip faltered. His throat bobbed as he swallowed hard. Then, with clear effort, he released me. *I don't like this.*

Neither do I. But the pull inside me wasn't stopping. It had locked on to something deep and hidden... something primal and absolute. I squeezed his arm once, then let go.

The guardian's eyes followed my every movement. It matched me stride for stride, closing the gap until the massive bulk of its shadowed form blocked out everything else. It was over fifteen feet tall at the shoulder, but it moved like a whisper of claws on stone.

The room changed again. Colder now, threading with a static charge. My breath frosted between us while the pulse in my wrist flared sharp and burning cold, like fire forged from ice. The long-frozen butterfly scar blazed to life, no longer dormant but alive with power.

I cradled my wrist against my chest as if I could muffle the magic unraveling beneath my skin. The sensation wasn't just painful. It felt like something was being woken inside me, but I didn't know what.

The guardian stopped inches away, lowering its head until its muzzle hovered at my chest level. Its breath hit my skin like a heavy winter wind tinged with the metallic scent of ozone and ash.

My instincts screamed to run, but my muscles locked. I lifted one trembling hand.

Briar, Vad connected, and even mentally, his voice was strained.

I'll let you know if something goes wrong. My voice was steadier than I felt.

The wolf's wet nose brushed my forehead. The touch was feather-soft, almost reverent, and the heat of its breath sliced through the surrounding cold like a flame in winter.

Something ancient stirred deep inside me...and tightened.

A surge of power slammed into me—first glacial, then molten. My knees nearly buckled, and my vision blurred. The butterfly mark on my wrist ignited, heat searing down to the bone. A scream lodged in my throat but refused to break free.

My wolf whimpered, claws scraping just beneath my skin.

The guardian's gaze held mine, unflinching. Light flickered in its eyes.

I can't get to you. Come back here. Vad's fear crashed into me thunderously. His anger flared in warning, rising like a storm against the walls. He was ready to burn down the world.

My wolf knows it. I forced the thought through the bond, though every cell in my body trembled. Energy pulsed inside me, unfamiliar, yet familiar all at once. The butterfly sigil burrowed deeper with each beat of my heart.

The air thickened with unbearable electricity. My hair lifted at the roots, and the shadow wolf exhaled. Its power rolled through the chamber and made the stone vibrate.

Then the pain struck. Not just in my wrist, but ripping through my chest, clawing up my throat, and burning behind my eyes. The guardian's power wrapped around me like a tether, sinking in deep.

We were locked together now.

Suddenly, the wolf stepped back, like a cord had been cut. The motion broke my trance and nearly sent me stumbling. Around the chamber, the other wolves stirred, muscles twitching, eyes tracking.

Then the guardian tilted its head back and howled, a sound so powerful it shook the air. The others joined, one by one, until the cavern trembled and the stone walls thrummed.

I couldn't move or blink. My muscles had fused to the stone, bound by some force beyond comprehension. The howling didn't sound like an ordinary sound anymore. It became pressure, thick and oppressive, seeping beneath my skin and pushing into my lungs and blood and marrow.

Briar! Vad's desperate voice lashed through the bond. He still couldn't move. Whatever had locked me in place had shackled him, too.

I'm trying— I tried to push to him, but my mind refused to form words. I was drowning in the wolf's gaze. The guardian's crimson eyes pulled me down and deeper still.

My wolf thrashed, snarling inside me. She fought against whatever was happening, fear tearing through her as her instincts howled to run. Adrenaline surged through my system with nowhere to go. I couldn't lift a hand. Couldn't scream.

A broken whimper scraped from my throat.

I'm here. I'm with you. Vad's voice pounded against the barrier between us, fury and helplessness vibrating through the bond. "Let go of her, you fecking beast!" he shouted, raw and ragged.

The pressure in my chest built until every breath felt like shattering glass. Our bond stretched thin, vibrating like an overwound string one breath away from snapping. The butterfly mark on my wrist no longer merely burned; it seared, as if etched anew by a blade forged in shadows and flames.

Agony broke over me as every cell on my body seemed to be lit on fire. Heat collided with cold in a brutal rush, igniting every nerve. Power surged through my limbs, flooding my veins with raw, pulsing energy. Then my knees buckled.

The wolves' howls swallowed the sound of my scream as I collapsed, hitting the stone hard. Pain lanced through me. My back arched, and tears ran down my face, blurring the world into streaks of silver and shadow.

Then the power inside me twisted once...and let go.

I'll find a way to get to you! Vad's ice-cold fear slid into me, adding even more discomfort.

My hands scraped cold stone, and my fingers curled tight. My chest heaved for breaths that wouldn't come fast enough.

The chamber fell silent. Only my ragged breathing echoed off the stone walls.

I forced my head up.

The guardian still stood there, its crimson eyes calm and ancient. Another low growl rumbled from its chest. Slowly, it dipped its head in what felt like recognition before its body unraveled into threads of light that disappeared into thin air.

"Briar!" Vad's voice cracked like a whip through the stillness. Boots slammed against stone, and his wings beat once, slicing through the cold air as he dropped to his knees beside me.

His arms were around me in an instant, pulling me tight to his chest. I could feel his heart pounding—wild, desperate—as he cradled the back of my neck. His smoke-and-myrrh scent engulfed me as his hand cradled the back of my neck.

"What happened?" His voice was hoarse, cracking. "What did it do to you? Talk to me. Please—"

I shook my head, still gasping, my voice barely a whisper. "I-I don't know. Something's wrong with my wolf."

He pulled back just enough to scan my face. Fear was written in every line, tension tight at the corners of his mouth, his eyes wild and searching. He looked like he was about to come undone.

Around us, the circle of wolves began to fade, their forms flickering like dying embers and blinking out of existence, one by one. Like they'd never been there at all.

Vad's hands slid to my shoulders. "What did it do to you? Where does it hurt most?" His voice dropped to a low rasp.

"My wrists." I lifted them with trembling hands. They throbbed like they'd been flayed. The butterfly tattoo on my left wrist had deepened, not just in color but in presence. It was no longer just ink. It glowed faintly, the black almost metallic. A mirror image now marked my right wrist, identical in every line, every winged curve.

Vad's eyes widened. His fingers brushed my skin reverently, as if afraid touching it might hurt me or him. "It's on both now?" His lips parted as he examined the living tattoos, his expression unreadable. "Was this there before? Or did the guardian...?"

"I didn't feel like this after the stag," I rasped. "There was...

discomfort. Nothing else then. This is different. This is from the guardian shadow wolf. My wolf feels...distant now."

He stared at the marks like they were going to bite him. "What do they mean?"

"I don't know," I whispered. "But my wrists still burn."

The pain pulsed like embers buried under my skin. Faint veins spiraled from the tattoos and up my arms beneath the straps of my dress, dark and glinting faintly beneath the surface. "And my back... it itches." I tried to move my wrist and gasped as a sharp pain lanced up my arm.

Vad caught my hands, his grip gentle but unyielding. "Stop moving." His wings flared behind him in a snap, the instinctive reflex of a predator bracing for war. "Is it spreading?" He tugged down the strap of my sundress to examine the veins. His breath hitched. "It stops at your neck."

"I can feel it," I whispered, blinking past the burn in my eyes. "Like something's inside me—pushing... pulling."

He shifted his weight behind me. The air still shimmered faintly where the guardian wolf had vanished, the echo of its presence rippling like aftershocks.

"I'll kill it if I have to," he muttered, low and cold. "The second you're safe, I'll hunt it down." He peeled the back of my dress down carefully and swore under his breath. "It's running straight down your spine." His voice dropped to a growl. "We need to get you out of here. Now."

The last thing I wanted to do was make him more upset and worried. "I'll be fine." My words cut off as another wave of heat surged from the marks. I clenched my jaw. "It called to me, Vad. I don't know what happened, but it changed something."

He moved in front of me and cupped my face, his hands framing me like I might disappear. His gaze burned with panic barely held in check. "I should have stopped it. Kept you from going to it."

"There was no stopping it." My throat tightened. "Whatever that thing was... it *chose* me. I felt it." My wolf whimpered. "She's not gone—my wolf—but she's different. Distant." Another spasm of fear pulsed through me. What if I wasn't going to be able to shift again? Was she all right?

Vad's expression darkened into something raw and dangerous. He pulled me flush against him, bracing his arms around me like he could hold me together by force. "Then we fix it. Whatever this is... whatever it did. We find a way. Do you need me to help you?"

The words should have steadied me, but the heat beneath my skin only deepened. The veins along my forearms pulsed faintly with shadowed light, like ink moving through glass. The burn intensified. "It hurts," I gritted. "Fuck, it hurts so much."

His forehead dropped to mine, the desperation in his expression mirroring the pain in my chest. "I know. Just breathe. I've got you." He wrapped his arms around me tighter.

Then he went rigid.

His attention snapped to something over my shoulder. His claws pricked lightly into my skin as our bond flooded with sudden, sharpened alarm.

The guards found us, he linked.

I tensed, dragging in a shaky breath. My body still throbbed with residual magic, the veins along my arms pulsing like shadowed lightning beneath the skin. *I don't know if I can fight them yet.*

His voice turned to steel. *Then hold on to me, Briar. Because I will end anyone who tries to touch you.*

Chapter Fifteen

I drew Briar behind me and flared my wings in warning. To my right, a narrow crack split the stone wall—just wide enough for one person to fit through. From its shadows, a guard stepped into view. Leather armor clung to his frame, streaked with blood and torn with what looked like bite marks. His gloved hand gripped a lowered sword.

"Your Majesty?" he called, voice cautious. "Do you and the queen require assistance?"

My nostrils flared. He was saying the right things, but I didn't trust him. Not after the betrayals that had driven us into the underground tunnels of the palace, into the waiting jaws of shadow beasts.

This could be a trap, Briar linked, exhaustion and strain weighing on our connection.

My blood warmed to an uncomfortable level without the restraint of my cold shadow magic. The thought of us being attacked with Briar in this situation was worrying, especially if there were more than a few guards.

He might be alone, or he could be bait. I couldn't afford to guess wrong. Not with Briar trembling behind me.

Can you still tell if he's lying? I stood in front of her, ready to rip out his throat.

Briar hesitated. *Lie to me.*

My head jerked so I could look at her over my shoulder. *What?*

My wolf feels distant. She's how I can tell if someone is lying. I need to make sure I can still tell.

It took me a moment to think of what to say as a lie. *You are an Ignis Fae, and your hair is pink. Also, I don't ever want to meet your family.*

Her features twisted, her nose wrinkling. *I can still tell. It's not as strong as usual, but you do stink.* A faint smile touched her lips despite everything. *Ask him whatever you want. I've got your back.* She stepped up beside me, leaning into me for support.

Pride and fear warred in my chest. I could still feel the pain the Guardian Shadow Beast had put her through. But she chose to stand with me. My warrior and mate.

The guard edged farther into the cavern. "Your Majesties?" His voice shook. "I swear—I am no threat to either of you."

I lifted my chin. "Are you in league with anyone who wishes harm on my queen?"

"No, Your Majesty. I swear it." He dropped to one knee. "Captain Finbar has sent scouts like me to find you. He's taken control of one of the lower barracks. He has resources and information about what's happening in the palace. And above all else, he remains loyal to your bloodline and queen." The guard bowed his head. "Whatever proof you require, I'll give it."

He isn't lying. Then Briar spoke aloud. "Do you mean any harm to King Vad?" She nudged my arm lightly, causing her legs to tremble. *You can't just ask if he means to hurt me. Your life matters too.*

I bit back the smile rising to my lips. Even now, bruised and burned, she was fierce.

The guard shook his head. "I give you my solemn word

that I mean no harm to King Vad. I am in service to both of you. There are still a handful of us left."

He's telling...the truth. Briar winced, tucking her burning wrists against her chest while hiding the pain from the man before us.

My frown deepened. The link hadn't faltered before. Either something had shifted, or I was imagining things. Regardless, I couldn't ignore the ache of what the Guardian Shadow Beast had put her through. I braced my hands on my belt. "And Captain Finbar wants us to follow you?"

Briar's hand caught my arm before I could take another step. She linked, *What about the others? Where are they? What if they've run out of oil, or the water keeps rising?*

The sharp weight of her worry pressed into me through the bond, tightening around my chest. Her voice didn't shake, but her fear bled through every word.

I turned to face her and placed my hand over hers. *Elara, Vyraetos, Veralt, and Rhielle can see in the dark. We'd moved through the worst of the narrowing passage, and Elara, Thalen, and Silus know the way. The best we can do now is get supplies and information. If we reach the vesting chamber and they're not there, we act. But believe me when I say that I trust Silas and Thalen to find a way to get them all to safety.*

Her lips trembled, and her fingers curled tighter. *All right. Of course I trust you.*

Stay on guard. This one is telling the truth, but the others could have lied to him.

The guard hesitated at the entrance he'd come through, his hand resting on the wall like he could sense the tension behind him. "Your Majesties?" His voice was careful. "Is anything wrong?"

"No," I said, keeping my tone clipped. "Lead the way. Quickly." I took Briar's hand.

He nodded and turned, accepting the warning without flinching. "This way, Your Majesties. Stay close. The passages aren't secure, and the shadow beasts have gone mad."

I moved after him, ducking low to pass through the narrow split. The ceiling lifted on the other side, the stone walls ascending upward in a sharp incline.

"How far is it?" Briar clutched my hand, her breathing steady despite her condition.

"Not too far, Your Majesty." The guard glanced back. Though his sword stayed at his side, his grip had tightened. "We cleared out the tunnels as we searched, but the area is unstable. The yellow-eyed shadow beasts are attacking everyone. But the red-eyed ones... they are different. They seem to be looking for something." He swallowed and dropped his voice. "They don't even look at us. Just pass by like we're nothing. Terrifying in their own way, but better than the others. The yellow ones will tear you apart before you can scream."

"What's your name, soldier?" Briar spoke in a quiet voice, but it carried easily through the stone corridor. She walked with steady grace despite her exhaustion.

"Brelven, son of Theln." He led us to the right as the tunnel forked and the incline grew steeper with every step. The stone walls shifted from deep jet and charcoal to a softer, cooler slate gray. We were moving into the western side of the palace. If Finbar had formed a rebellion and taken control of one of the lower outposts, the direction made sense because those were located just beneath the palace level, but a couple of levels higher than the vesting chamber. They were isolated and defensible but could be blocked off and turned into a trap by anyone who knew the terrain.

If Finbar's soldiers were stationed here, it meant the primary paths were either secured or laid with traps. I hoped Thalen's caution would serve the rest of our group well. I didn't want us all converging into one place yet, not until I knew the full extent of Finbar's forces and whether their loyalty to Briar matched their loyalty to me.

As we continued upward, the passage widened. The air smelled less stale here, with hints of leather and oil. Brelven slowed his pace and raised a hand in a cautionary gesture.

"We're approaching a checkpoint," he whispered. "Don't be alarmed."

We rounded a sharp corner and came upon two Shadow Fae guards blocking a narrow stone archway. Their armor was better maintained than Brelven's, but their expressions were taut with exhaustion. Their hands hovered near their weapons.

"Halt," the taller one commanded. Then his eyes locked with mine, and his entire stance shifted. "Your Majesty? You're alive."

"So I am." I lifted my chin and gently tugged Briar closer to me.

Brelven stepped between us and the guards. "Captain Finbar requested they be brought directly to him. He's in the war room."

The guards shared a brief glance. The shorter one gave a stiff nod. "He'll want to see them immediately."

I studied them carefully, noting the way their gazes darted between Briar and me.

I narrowed my gaze. "Before we proceed, I want your oaths. Do you swear loyalty to me and to Queen Briar?"

Without hesitation, both men dropped to one knee, fists clenched to their chests.

"Our lives are yours, Your Majesty," the taller one said. "For the crown. For the queen."

Briar linked to me, the bond warm with amusement despite her pain. *Are you going to make every person we meet swear loyalty to me like that?*

Of course, I linked back.

The guards stood and stepped aside.

As we passed through the arch, a large cavern spread before us, roughly carved but well-organized. Torches lined the walls, casting a golden glow over the shadows within.

Roughly fifteen soldiers and a handful of servants moved about with quiet purpose. Five guards crouched at makeshift tables, repairing armor or sharpening blades. Two sat near crates of crossbow bolts, testing the balance before sliding them into quivers. Others organized supplies along the back wall by stacking crates, unrolling maps, tying bundles of cloth and bandages.

The cavern hummed with urgent energy, the soldiers speaking in hushed tones as they worked. Torches lined the walls, casting long shadows across the stone floor. Despite the circumstances, there was order here—purpose.

"This way," Brelven said, cutting through the cavern's center.

I kept Briar close, wrapping one wing slightly around her without drawing attention. Her fingers tightened in mine, but her posture stayed straight, with no hint of weakness.

A few soldiers paused as we passed, some bowing their heads, others dropping to one knee. I didn't trust them. All it took was one traitor.

These were soldiers who'd bled under Colm's attack. Some had likely watched friends die because of him. But loyalty to me didn't guarantee loyalty to Briar, not when propaganda and fear had twisted so many truths.

I didn't like being this exposed. And judging by the twitch of Briar's fingers against my palm, neither did she.

I moved my hand to her elbow, guiding her through the activity. Her gaze swept the cavern, noting exits and soldiers, every movement calculated. Even battered and burned, she was a warrior—sharp, deliberate, alert.

Brelven led us to the far side of the cavern and stopped before a small wooden door, oddly out of place in the rough stone wall. He knocked twice, then opened it without waiting for a response.

"Captain, I've found them," he called, stepping aside and motioning us to enter.

A chill ran down my spine, but there was no turning back now. I entered with my claws ready to be used if needed.

The room beyond was modest but efficient. A heavy wooden table dominated the center, its surface cluttered with hand-drawn maps, half-burnt candles, and a scattering of crimson wax seals. Iron sconces shed a flickering amber light that danced across stone walls lined with weapon racks and scroll holders.

Captain Finbar stood bent over the table, his finger trailing a route across one map. Two lieutenants flanked him, both in marked leathers, alert even before we entered.

Finbar's head snapped up. His lined face registered a flicker of relief before discipline returned. He straightened and bowed deeply. "Your Majesties, thank Fate you're alive. Is the princess safe, or should we continue searching for her?"

Both lieutenants followed suit, dropping to one knee.

I studied Finbar as he rose. His armor bore fresh battle scars with slashed leather and blood spatters. A bandage wrapped his right hand, the fingers bruised, but he stood without wavering.

"She is safe for now. Report, Captain."

"The palace has fallen into chaos," Finbar began. "Over half of our forces defected or fled when the magic failed. The initial attacks overwhelmed those still loyal to the crown. But we've regrouped and established this stronghold and secured two additional outposts in the tunnels, one beneath the Ceremonial Hall and the other under the Ascension Hall. There may still be a few stragglers among the royals and servants who weren't captured and whom we haven't been able to find. I suspect a few are plotting their own vengeance. Fate help them if they haven't escaped yet."

He motioned to the map, pointing to each marked position in turn.

"Colm and his Aurelines control the main halls. But they are fighting the yellow-eyed shadow beasts, and they've suffered losses."

"Colm?" Briar's voice was tight as boiling rage shot through the bond. "*He's* in charge of all this? Not just overseeing some of it?"

A bitter taste filled my mouth. Colm Ainle had tortured my beloved and so many others in Firellan's Spine. Though that had already sealed his fate, I would make sure his end was extra painful since he had also killed Physician Morlo.

Finbar's jaw tensed. "There may have been others involved in the initial uprising, but Colm has assumed full leadership. Anyone who hasn't sworn to him and his would-be queen has been imprisoned. Or executed."

"His queen?" I demanded. "Who?"

"At first, we assumed Siray. She's royal-blooded—Ignis Fae. But it's not her. Colm made a show of taking Calla Lily. The one Councilman Bryn declared as the victor of the trials."

Briar's expression didn't waver, but her energy coiled tighter. A spike of cold hatred echoed through our bond.

"Calla Lily winning was a lie," I growled. "They forced Bryn's hand and threatened his family."

"I believe you, Your Majesty." Finbar raised both hands in surrender. "And Colm's tactics support your claim. He's silencing dissent, executing loyalists, and twisting tradition to serve his ambition. He's demanding full unification of the realms under one ruler, one bride, and one throne."

"And he plans to use Calla Lily to stake his claim?" Briar asked, her voice low with contempt.

"Yes, my queen. He's using her to paint your union with His Majesty as an act of treason and not Fate."

Something akin to sludge pulsed through my body. I would not allow *him* to rewrite our story. "That will *never* happen."

Still, my mind circled on one thing. "Does he truly plan to take over all the kingdoms?" If that was the case, Colm wasn't just seizing power; he was enacting full-scale realm domination.

I opened my mouth to ask how he expected to control the other rulers without a drawn-out war, but the answer settled cold and heavy in my gut.

The coronation and wedding had been a trap.

Every royal who'd attended and refused to bow was likely imprisoned beneath the Shadow Palace. And if any escaped? Colm had their children.

We already knew he'd captured two young royals from the Sylvan and Aquen kingdoms. "Is he torturing them?"

"For now, they're sealed in the old dungeons on the eastern side of the palace." Finbar's jaw tightened. "He plans to starve them. All of them. Men. Women. Children."

Colm was even more of a monster than I'd believed.

Briar's hand gripped mine like a vise. "We have to get them out. Is there... water in the cells?" Her face paled, the question dragging something deep and sharp out of her. *We can't allow that to happen, Vad. All those poor people. They're innocents. They don't deserve this.*

Her heartbreak swelled inside of me. She wanted to protect everyone, especially those facing injury and abuse. It was a rare quality that made her just as lovely on the inside as out. *We'll get them out.*

Finbar braced a hand on the map, pointing toward the east. "There's water. And if we can, we'll get food to them, but time is critical. They're barely guarded—merely locked in and barricaded. Our focus has been on retaking the palace. If we free those prisoners, we'll fracture Colm's narrative. But right now, fear has those who aren't prisoners and aren't working with us listening to him."

Briar straightened. "Fear of what?"

His expression darkened. "He's claiming that the loss of magic is punishment. That your union broke Fate's laws and that you come from a wretched family, starting with your father, who also chose defiance when he claimed your mother. The tipping point came about due to an Aureline marrying into the Shadow Court."

I would kill everyone loyal to the fecking bastard. One by one, with my own hands.

Briar scoffed and shook her head. "So they're blaming me for the collapse of magic... to justify a coup?"

"I'm afraid so." Finbar's sigh was weary. The shadows beneath his eyes told me he hadn't slept since his brother's and my father's murders.

"They've been planning this from the start." I inhaled deeply, trying to stay grounded and not give in to anger. "Rigging the bridal trials. Poisoning alliances. Killing my father. Draining fae to steal their power." My voice dropped. "This didn't begin at my coronation. This was always the plan."

"If we can prove that *they* corrupted Fate's balance, more will turn against him." Finbar rubbed his hands together. "The people fear that magic is gone forever. But if they believe Colm caused the loss... if they see him as the one who brought down Fate's wrath..."

"They'll fight him." Hope and resolve swirled between Briar and me.

"We have one former prisoner who might testify." The thought of the two women who'd tried to kill Briar and take her place made my stomach revolt. "And Physician Morlo's records—he found traces of stolen magic in the hair of either Kaylen or Calla Lily. One of them has been consuming another's gift."

"It's something," Finbar said. "But not enough."

"We'll need more," I agreed. "Whether it's additional witnesses, a confession, or proof that they can't twist or burn away. They've likely destroyed anything from Briar's quarters that bore signs of Fate's favor. Her gown might've once held power, but it's been so stained and shredded, I doubt it will convince anyone."

A thought struck me. "What happened to Kaylen? They were dragging her off before everything collapsed. She looked shocked. Angry." And her shock and indignation had seemed genuine.

Finbar grunted. "Kaylen was imprisoned with the other guests. She was quick to offer fealty at first, but they locked her in the old dungeon, in the southeastern block near the entrance."

Pursing her lips, Briar lifted her chin. "As much as I hate the thought of seeing her again, she may know something." Her voice dropped slightly. "We should get to her before they decide she's not useful."

I calculated the route in my head and set my hands against my belt. *Do you wish to handle the interrogation?*

Something bitter inched through our bond. *Hell, yes, I do.*

Finbar spoke up. "If you wish to divert forces, we can try to breach the main entrance—"

"No," I cut in. He didn't know about the hidden paths, and I had no intention of revealing them. "We'll manage it. Show me the schematics so we can make a plan."

Finbar inclined his head and turned toward the map. "Of course, Your Majesty." He tapped a square labeled *Ceremonial*

Hall. "Colm intends to crown himself king tomorrow. All current loyalists will be present. If we can provide proof that they'd been planning this takeover before the magic was gone, this is the moment to do it."

"Who else will be in attendance?" I raised an eyebrow and tilted my head back. "If the royals are locked away, is he assembling their advisors?"

"He's calling for secondary leadership to swear loyalty. Likely to claim this was a unanimous decision among the courts, not a coup."

"And the excuse?" I leaned forward and tried to wrap my head around how much of a monster this man truly was.

"That you and your Aureline bride violated Fate's laws. That your union caused the collapse of magic. They sent messengers shortly after the attack—so quickly it had to have been coordinated. There are contacts embedded in every realm. It's why nearly every royal line was here to begin with."

I gritted my teeth. "So we have one day."

"Yes." Finbar met my eyes. "What do you require, Your Majesty? This outpost has no sleeping quarters, but we can secure a location for your group to rest if needed."

My instincts screamed *no.* "Splitting up is safer for now. But we'll need supplies."

"I'll arrange everything." Finbar waved his hand. "If you give me a destination, I'll have a soldier and an attendant deliver the items."

Briar's hand brushed mine, and she linked, *He hasn't lied the entire time, and it would save us time.*

I nodded. "As long as we're sure the people you send can be trusted."

"I want to speak with them." Briar released my hand and turned toward the door. *I'll make sure none of them are lying.*

Finbar hesitated then inclined his head. "I vouch for my

men with my life. But if my queen wishes to confirm their loyalty herself, I welcome it."

"Then see it done," I said.

Finbar opened the door. While he gave orders and discussed logistics with me, Briar stepped forward to conduct her assessments, silent but sharp-eyed. I watched her, pride stirring low in my chest. She was a true leader and warrior, because even injured and exhausted, she did what was best for us and the others. And she didn't flinch from what had to be done.

I followed her, watching her move among the soldiers. Pride bloomed within me even more, watching her stop and assess people without showing even a hint of how horrible she felt. After each encounter, she'd link with me and fill me in. So far, everyone had cleared.

But a few looked her way and lingered too long. A low growl curled in my throat, enough to remind them she was claimed. One step out of line, and not even Fate could shield them from me.

When she returned to my side, her brow was furrowed. Concern rippled through our link, the sensations fading in and out, which had never happened before at this strength. It was getting worse.

I reached out for her elbow, my claws grazing her flesh. "What troubles you, my love?"

"It's working, but...I feel even more distant from my wolf. And...it's all fainter." She pressed her lips into a line, trying to hide her discomfort.

My jaw clenched. "Is she in pain?"

"She's restless. Whimpering. I can't reach her properly. It's like trying to grasp fog." Her voice thinned, frustration bleeding through her expression.

I took her wrists gently and examined both tattoos. The

veins around them pulsed dark and slow, the marks looking more like brands than ink. Why had the guardian done this to her?

"We'll find the answer." I pressed a kiss to her temple. Her scent of cinnamon and ginger was a balm to my fury. "Do you want to stay here? You don't have to face Kaylen."

Her spine straightened. "I don't fear Kaylen. You bet your sexy ass, I'm going."

Finbar approached with supplies. He handed Briar a pair of boots that were a little too large but better than her going barefoot, and a long black tunic that hung off her frame but hid the worst of the grime. She pulled them on without comment. He brought me a clawed sword and a reinforced belt, but no armor. Still, it was better than nothing. For Briar, he had another belt with a light sword attached, appropriate for her height.

Once I'd issued final instructions and supplies were en route to the vesting chamber, Briar and I set out.

We moved fast, our steps echoing softly through winding tunnels. The air grew colder as we descended toward the eastern dungeon. At each intersection, I paused, scenting the air and listening, but there was nothing but stone and silence. Briar stayed close behind me, her boots whispering against the floor, discomfort pulsing from her wrists, and the distant ache of her wolf's absence throbbing through our bond.

Then came the cries. They were soft at first, then rose like a chorus of the void from women, men, and children. My stomach twisted. Rage simmered low and hard. I felt Briar flinch, her hand brushing mine before she masked her heartbreak.

The final passage narrowed to a cleft just wide enough to slip through sideways. I pressed my shoulder into it and squeezed forward until we reached a slanted pocket door. I pushed it open a fraction.

Empty.

No patrols. No posted guards.

Only corridors lined with cells, dim lamps guttering against stone slick with moisture. The reek of sweat, filth, and despair hit hard. I swallowed against it, teeth grinding. The cells were not meant to hold so many, and my father had sealed these halls decades ago. At least, it wasn't claustrophobic. The halls themselves were wide enough for two men to walk while hauling a coffin between them with ease.

The cells were little more than chiseled tombs: no windows, no beds, only bare rock and holes for waste. Water dripped from small pipes. It was deliberate suffering, meant to keep a guilty prisoner in darkness and isolation until either madness or starvation claimed them.

Briar's breath hitched, and our bond stuttered with her raw need to help these people. Her hand caught mine as the low wails and murmurs of the imprisoned reached us through narrow viewing slits. *The best way we can help them is to take back the palace,* I reminded her through the bond.

I know... It's just— she started.

A piercing voice echoed, bouncing off the stones. "No, guard! Is there someone out there? Wait! Don't walk away! Let me out! I don't deserve to be here!"

Briar and I exchanged a look and crept forward silently. Two corridors passed before we turned right, following the echo of the voice.

This corridor stretched longer, the stench of piss and feces choking now. Each cell was identical and empty, and there were no guards in sight, just as Finbar had said.

I led the way down the narrow corridor, every instinct on edge. The air stank heavily of rot and something fouler still. Several of the doors were slightly ajar, as if they'd been recently checked. No other prisoners cried out near Kaylen, which was a small mercy, but strange. These cells had been used to hold prisoners before executions in my great-grandfather's time. Had she been set apart for some reason?

With nowhere to hide if someone came this way, we had to move fast.

The hall stretched ahead, maybe five hundred more feet until it joined another corridor in the dungeon's grid. This section was too close to the main entrance for comfort. One wrong step, and any patrol glancing down the line would spot us instantly.

Feck.

Kaylen's voice broke the silence. "Let me out! I don't deserve to die!"

I crept toward her cell, Briar at my back. *Go ahead. I know you want to be the one to talk to her.*

She didn't hesitate, inching in front of me. I moved slightly toward the cross-corridor near the entrance, every muscle taut, half my attention fixed on Briar's voice and the other half on the echo of distant footfalls.

"Kaylen," Briar called, her tone firm but soft. "Keep your voice down. Why did they imprison you?"

"Briar?" Kaylen rasped. Her pale face appeared between the slits in the stone door, barely reaching them on her toes. I stood behind Briar, arms folded, unreadable.

Briar nodded as she looked up at the narrow slits. "Tell us what happened."

"Get me out, and I'll tell you everything," Kaylen said, her voice shaking. "I swear. I will help you defeat them. They can't be trusted—"

"Neither can you," Briar snapped, her tone sharpening like a whip crack. Her nostrils flared. "You were involved."

A dull *thunk* sounded from the other side of the cell, like Kaylen's head hitting the stone. "I don't want to die."

"You'll face justice," Briar said coldly. "But if you want a chance to begin to make things right, then you will talk."

I admired Briar's heart and strength. We both knew she wouldn't leave Kaylen here to die, even though Kaylen deserved death. Her life was the only leverage we had to make her desperate enough to talk.

"You don't understand." Kaylen whimpered. "They lied to me. I swear. I'll tell you everything, but you have to get me out. They're going to execute me!"

I narrowed my eyes, resting one hand on my sword hilt. "Why?"

"They executed Bram," Kaylen blurted. "An Aureline Council member. He helped Colm. He was crucial to their success, according to him—*and they killed him anyway.* I'm next."

I raised an eyebrow at this. Bram was the Aureline Council member who had been in the garden when Briar was framed. A grim satisfaction passed through me. Some of the Aureline traitors had already received their comeuppance, but *why* would they eliminate the young Aureline councilman when he'd been involved, at the very least, in framing Briar and likely my father's murder? Unless they were eliminating everyone who could attest to that act. That definitely didn't bode well for Kaylen.

"Because?" Briar pushed.

Kaylen exhaled in a rush. "Because I tried to smash Calla Lily's perfect little face into a wall and said some things she found distasteful, and maybe set her dress on fire. The scaffing bitch set me up!"

I blinked and had to hold back a laugh.

"She told me to go up there and declare myself queen. She *set me up.*" Kaylen stomped, her foot splashing in something I didn't want to think about.

"You were arrogant enough to believe you could just walk onto the dais and demand to be my queen," I growled. "You deserve worse."

Briar's jaw clenched. "When's your execution scheduled?"

"As soon as they come back." Kaylen's voice cracked. "Please, I will swear *any* vow—"

"Swearing won't help you," I cut in. "Your vows mean nothing now. The magic's gone." I scoffed at her. *She'll say anything to get out of there.*

I know. Briar didn't flinch. "Talk, and we'll consider helping. But not before."

Kaylen's tone sharpened. "We're not friends. But if there's one thing about me that you know, it's that I'm a mean, petty bitch."

I lifted a brow. "You're not wrong."

Briar's arms stayed crossed. "So what?"

A heavy *clang* of metal on stone split the air.

Skkrrraaang!

An axe blade struck the wall. My entire body snapped alert.

The guards were coming, and Briar and I couldn't fight them alone.

Chapter Sixteen

Dread weighed on me as the sharp scrape of metal against stone grew louder. This had to be Colm's doing, using a brutal tradition from the past. He wanted the prisoners to hear the instrument of their execution coming. Let it scream down the hall like a promise. *Feck.*

Briar turned toward me with her shoulders squared and determination tightening the corners of her eyes. But beneath her calm exterior, her pulse thrummed wildly in the hollow of her throat. *If they kill her, we have no chance of learning what she knows.*

I bared my teeth. "Kaylen, swear—"

"Yes! I swear it!" Her voice cracked through the slits in the stone door, ragged and raw. "On my life and my name, I'll help you burn them down. Just get me out!"

Her desperation wasn't what convinced me. It was the sound of that blade dragging closer to us, grinding against the wall like bone against a whetstone.

My claws closed around the iron key still tucked in the torn edge of my surcoat. The scent of blood clung to it. Metal rasped as I shoved it into the lock.

Click.

The tumbler fell.

Footsteps neared the bend in the corridor—slow and deliberate, something dragging behind them.

Skkrrraaang.

Each scrape sent a jolt down my spine, and I couldn't wait to get my revenge on Colm and everyone involved with him.

I threw the door wide. The hinges groaned, but the shriek of the approaching blade swallowed the sound whole.

Kaylen stumbled out, blinking in the dim torchlight. Her sky-blue gown hung in ragged strips, plastered with filth and sweat. Her hair hung limp and greasy, and her face was a mess of bruises, one eye nearly swollen shut.

Briar grabbed her wrist, hard enough to make her flinch. "Move," Briar snapped.

Don't put your back to her, I warned.

Briar huffed. *Don't worry, I won't. I wouldn't trust this woman as far as Elara could throw her.*

The axe grated closer, echoing through the corridor like a death summons.

"Don't slow us down," I snarled, shoving the cell door shut. My claws curled around Kaylen's wrist, forcing her into place on my left before I caught Briar's hand with my right. Briar's steady pulse thudded against my palm. I glanced back at Kaylen and warned, "If I have to choose between you and Briar, you lose every time."

Kaylen didn't argue. That was the first smart thing she'd ever done. Well, second after she'd agreed to cooperate.

Skkrrraaang.

The executioner was almost upon us.

We ran.

The corridor tightened around us as if the dungeon itself wanted to keep us inside, and torches streaked past like dying stars. Sweat slicked the back of my neck as I choked on the putrid air.

The axe blade cried again.

The bare stone walls mocked us, the flames of the oil lamps flickering wildly as shadows stretched long and sharp. "Left," I grunted at the end of the hall.

Skkrrraaang—closer still.

We veered hard left. We had one more bend and one more corridor. If we didn't make it to the hidden passage, we were dead.

The scrape of the axe shrieked again with its sharp, rhythmic, merciless sound. Then it stopped, the pure silence deafening. A single breath passed.

"She's gone!" a deep voice shouted.

"Prisoner escape!" another gravelly voice roared.

"You, check the other cells," a male ordered. "You two, that way. Sound the alarm!" The heavy slamming of doors started as they searched, footsteps scuffing toward us.

I yanked Briar and Kaylen down the final corridor as chaos erupted behind us. My pulse thundered in my ears, too many voices too close to us in all directions. Briar cast a look back over her shoulder, her expression grim but fierce.

The alarm bell rang, low and heavy, vibrating the stone under our feet. Beside me, Briar kept pace, but something felt... off. Distant. Like she was present, but disconnected, her energy muted, like a tether stretched too thin.

We rounded the corner, and although we were less than four hundred feet away from our destination, the distance felt endless. I spotted the hidden pocket door in the wall, concealed by flickering shadows.

Another shout echoed. Then a *thwip***.** The sharp whistle of a bolt hurtling toward us.

I lunged sideways, dragging Briar with me, just as the crossbow bolt slammed into the wall inches from my face. Stone exploded across my cheek in a sting of grit and heat.

"Down!" I shoved Briar and Kaylen against the wall, my body automatically moving to shield Briar.

At the corridor's opposite mouth stood a soldier in worn leather armor, already sliding another bolt into his crossbow.

Behind him, another voice shouted, "They're over here!"

Feck!

The hidden door was about seven feet away, between the dancing flames of the oil lamps, with an armed guard blocking our path. And the bastard was already lining up his next shot. He'd have to be an incompetent fool to miss. A second guard appeared behind him, crossbow at the ready.

I drew my blade, the familiar weight in my hand grounding me to the present. *Briar, get Kaylen down into the passage. I'll deal with the guards. Keep right once you're in. It will lead you to an outpost for—*

Briar shoved up, her own sword singing free. *When will you get it through your head that I'm not leaving you?*

My heart surged. By Fate, I loved this woman, but I also wanted to shove her through the wall to get her to safety.

Kaylen crouched and flattened against the stone wall, eyes wide with panic.

The first crossbowman growled. "One move, and I shoot the redhead between the eyes."

Footsteps sounded behind us, then a third guard rounded the corner at the opposite end of the hall, sword drawn.

Fate must hate us.

Briar tensed, her blade ready and her jaw locked. Even with my wings spread wide to shield her, I knew she'd go down fighting at my side.

And that was about the only option we had left.

We were pinned in the middle of a hall with no cover and enemies in front of and behind us. There wasn't anything to use for protection; not a crate, not a tapestry, not even a damn statue. And now two crossbows were aimed at our skulls. At this range, we wouldn't survive the next shot.

Then an all too familiar voice sliced through the tension. "Well, well. Of all the things I expected tonight, someone breaking out Kaylen wasn't on the list." Calla Lily stepped into view, her silk skirts whispering as she passed between the guards. Her golden hair swayed around her shoulders, an onyx shadow-beast hairpin keeping her hair from falling in her face. She set her hands on her waist.

Her eyes widened, though, when she saw us. "Briar?" Her tone turned disbelieving. "You're rescuing Kaylen? You *hate* her."

A glint of the torchlight hit the onyx hairpin.

Rage twisted inside me, and my claws curled tighter around my sword. That hairpin belonged to Elara and had been passed down from our mother.

We *couldn't* get captured. If they locked us in those cells, the keys wouldn't help. The locks were inaccessible from the inside. I shifted subtly, angling my body toward Calla Lilly with my right shoulder pointed at the pocket door.

Briar's glare fixed on Calla Lily. "Kaylen and I have our differences, but she doesn't deserve to rot to death. None of these people do."

Calla Lily sniffed. "And you don't deserve to be queen."

She then turned her smile on me, syrupy and cruel. "My darling will be *most* pleased to learn about the two of you. I didn't expect this outcome, but that just makes it more entertaining. You'll die, of course. Publicly. Perfect timing for our coronation."

Briar growled, low and feral, and again, the bond between us wavered, like it was fading. For a moment, I couldn't feel her emotions. I experienced only my own rage and tension.

"You've locked up children," Briar spat. "Starved the innocent. If you think I'll let that slide and not tear your throat out with my teeth, you're more of a dumbass than I thought."

"Not if you're drawn and quartered first." Calla Lilly's smile didn't even twitch.

"Touch her," I said flatly, "and I'll raze this castle and everyone in it." Then I linked with Briar. *Angle toward the door. Take Kaylen and head in first to lead the way back to the others. I'll be right behind you.*

Briar didn't answer me through the link, but she did take Kaylen's hand and draw her to her feet. That disconnection wasn't like her. Concern twisted my gut.

But she was moving like I wanted her to, so I focused on the plan. "You know he's using you, right? You weren't good enough to be my bride, and you aren't good enough to be his. Even if Fate hadn't chosen Briar, I would never have chosen you."

Her eyes blazed, and she sucked in a breath. She pressed her lips into a thin line and pointed at me with a trembling hand. "You— You—"

I stepped forward and slightly to the side, wings flaring just enough to block her view of Briar's subtle movements. "Careful, you're shaking. Guilt, perhaps?"

"Halt!" The first guard motioned with his crossbow, glancing at Calla Lily for orders. The second guard mirrored the motion.

Smirking, I turned my head just enough to keep them guessing, then flicked my gaze back to Calla Lily. The swordsman behind us hadn't moved, still holding his position to block what they thought was our escape path. "What's the matter, Calla Lily? Did the shadow beast get your tongue, or is it guilt from stealing jewelry from my sister's room?"

Color drained from her face, and the torchlight caught

the glitter of the numerous rings she wore. Half of them were from the royal quarters. The fury rising inside me iced over into something far colder.

"Sho—" she started.

Briar cut her off with a sharp, wild laugh. "That's right. Go ahead and shoot us! I'd rather die here and now than see Colm's ugly face again." Her voice faintly brushed my mind again. *Laugh and move.*

Oh, clever woman. I forced a deep, mocking laugh, covering my face, and pretended to stagger sideways, moving closer to the pocket door.

Kaylen blinked, half crouched between us. "Are you two insane?"

"What are you laughing at?" Calla Lily hissed. Her face reddened, and her red-brown eyes blazed. "This isn't funny!"

"It is *funny!*" Briar tilted her head and bared her teeth in a feral grin. "You have to spend eternity with Colm. That's the joke, isn't it? You think he actually cares about you, while he locks up children and lets innocents starve?"

"Politics are cruel. I don't need to justify myself to you!" Calla Lily clenched her fists. "Arrest them now!"

A flash of red caught my eye from the corridor to the right of Calla Lily. A small glowing orb sailed through the air, arcing cleanly before it struck the stone floor just behind her with a *crack*. Oil splashed across the floor and then ignited.

The explosion of heat tore through the hallway. I threw my wings wide, shielding Briar as the fire erupted upward, devouring the air and casting molten gold light across the walls. The guards yelled, stumbling backward as the blaze climbed toward the ceiling.

Calla Lily shrieked, slapping at her gown as embers caught the hem. "What in the ashing void?"

A woman strode out of the smoke and flame, long black

hair streaming behind her. A small crossbow gleamed in one hand, a second red orb burning faintly in the other. "Run, Briar! You can take out the main guard at the entrance before reinforcements arrive! There should only be three still there!"

Shock jolted through me. Another bridal candidate was still alive and fighting.

She swung the crossbow toward the swordsman at the far end of the corridor. "You move, and I'll put a bolt through both your precious queen-to-be's faces! Not that I plan to kill you yet, Calla Lily. You deserve to *suffer* first."

"Siray?" Briar's eyes widened, and she took a step forward, lowering her sword slightly. Shock rippled through our bond before dulling once more. "What are you doing here?"

Expression hardening, Siray snarled. "I'm here to save my family. Now *go!* I'll cover you!"

Briar froze.

The blaze behind Calla Lily cracked and surged higher, throwing wild shadows across the corridor. One guard flailed at his smoldering coat, his hair singed and his face streaked with soot. His crossbow lay discarded on the ground beside him.

But the second one, near Calla Lily, held his ground, jaw clenched and crossbow steady, aimed at Briar's chest. He hadn't moved an inch. Sweat streamed down his brow, but he stood like a trained killer waiting for the right command.

Behind us, the swordsman shifted uneasily at the far end of the hall. His blade dipped a fraction as he eyed the growing fire. Smoke curled into the hall, and the scent of scorched silk and burning oil stung my nostrils. He kept glancing toward Calla Lily, waiting for her order—*or a reason to disobey it.*

I had no doubt she was torn between instinct and reason. *We need to go—*

But Briar ignored me and straightened her shoulders. "Do you mean us harm, Siray? Will you betray us later if you get the chance?"

Siray's glare burned. "No. I was only in that fecking competition because Fate chose me and I wanted to survive it. And I wanted to see if I could best the challenges."

This was the candidate who had separated herself from the others, but she had still cussed out the council for not letting Briar's friends reach her.

Briar glanced at me then and gave a small nod. *We can trust her.*

The guard in front of Calla Lily shifted his stance, his finger twitching on the trigger. I caught the subtle readjustment—was he weighing the odds, trying to decide if she was worth dying for?

Calla Lily turned toward him, her expression twisted with fury. "What are you waiting for? *Kill them!*"

But he didn't fire.

The fallen guard coughed, dragging himself toward the wall, shaking uncontrollably. The fire had scorched a trail behind him, blocking off part of the corridor. The hallway was quickly becoming a furnace.

We have to move, and I need you to take the lead. Crossing the final few feet, I pressed the hidden indentation and slid the pocket door open, the mechanism grinding softly.

"Siray, this way!" Briar shouted. "We'll help you free your family, but more alarms have gone up. You'll never get them out now without help."

Clanging metal and thundering footfalls echoed from the end of the hall nearest the main entrance, growing louder by the second. At least a dozen more guards were racing toward us.

"Move! Now!" I grabbed Briar's arm and pulled her toward the hidden door.

Calla Lily's narrowed gaze snapped to the subtle motion. "You think you can just vanish?" Her voice sharpened, venom laced through every word. "Guards!"

Siray hurled the second red orb at a spot next to Calla Lilly, and a loud crack exploded. The orb smashed against the opposite wall, sending up a blinding burst of smoke and fire. The flames whooshed outward, forcing Calla Lily and the guards with her to recoil, their shouts drowned beneath the roaring blaze.

Siray darted in front of Calla Lily with her crossbow raised. Her dark eyes glinted with fury. "Try to follow," she dared. "Let's see how well your fancy shoes hold up against burning oil and broken bones."

Calla Lily cursed and stumbled back, heat shriveling the hem of her gown again. The guard on the ground swatted at her dress, trying to extinguish the sparks while coughing on the thick smoke.

That was our window.

I gestured to the pocket door. *Go, lead them. Down the passage, then left at the first split.*

Briar met my gaze, jaw locked with fierce resolve, and gave a clipped nod. She would hate not being at my side as much as I would hate not being at hers. She grabbed Kaylen's wrist and plunged into the narrow tunnel without hesitation, the darkness swallowing them both.

"It's too dark and tight!" Kaylen's voice echoed from inside.

"Then get through it faster," Briar snapped. "And if you block the path, I swear—"

"Siray!" I barked. "Now!"

Keeping the hand crossbow leveled at Calla Lily, Siray tossed a third orb at her. "Have fun, Your Majesty." Then she pivoted sharply, snatched one of the oil lamps from the wall, and dove into the passage, brushing past me with the scent of ash clinging to her clothes.

Calla Lily lunged, but the wall of heat forced her back. She shrieked in frustration, slamming her hand against the stone as flames licked higher along the walls.

I ducked in last and hauled the stone door shut behind us. The lock clicked into place just as something slammed against it from the other side, followed by screams and pounding.

"Can you block it?" Siray's voice was so high it hurt my ears. "If they break through—"

"Just keep moving," I said gruffly. "We'll lose them in the tunnels."

The air was cold and carried the smell of earth and old stone. Unlike the main palace's defensible escape passages and others with additional security measures, this was a rough-cut tunnel with only one way forward.

Are you all right, Briar? I turned sideways as the passage narrowed. From this angle, I could make out the back of her head as she led our strange group deeper into the mountain surrounding the palace.

I'm fine, she replied, but it seemed to come from far away. *Just... focusing on keeping us moving.*

The bond flickered again, the thread between us stretching thin. My chest tightened. We needed to talk, but not with Kaylen and Siray between us.

Kaylen whimpered. "It's so tight... I hate this!"

"Silence. Whining helps no one." I shook my head.

Siray moved ahead of me with one hand steady on the wall and the other holding the oil lamp high. Her steps were quiet but sure. "They'll regroup. Colm won't let us get far."

"We're not giving him a choice." Briar huffed. "We just have to keep moving."

The pounding on the door behind us dulled with distance, replaced by our own breathing and footfalls. We pressed onward into the dark.

As soon as we reached the branching path, I cut in front of

Kaylen and Siray to reach Briar. Her small smile gave me some comfort, but the strain in her features and the faint, flickering bond between us chilled me far worse than the damp air.

"Stay close," I said, more to the others than her. "The shadow beasts have gone feral."

"I know." Kaylen stomped. "They attacked some of the guards when they brought me to the cell. Everything's going wrong."

"If you know, then shut up and keep your voice down," Siray snapped. She adjusted her grip on the oil lamp, the crossbow slung low but ready in the other. The glow painted her sharp cheekbones in harsh orange light, igniting the fire in her glare. "Otherwise, someone might take off your head."

I was certain she didn't mean the shadow beasts.

"Eyes up. Listen for shifts in the stone or a scent like singed metal," I added. "Portals have a lightning smell when they open."

"What were you doing in the prison, Siray?" Briar glanced over her shoulder as we kept moving. Her voice was even, but I could feel her trying to focus through exhaustion and something heavier she wasn't ready to voice.

"My family was here for the wedding. My aunt and uncle are the queen and king of Ignis. They brought everyone with them." Siray's jaw worked. "My cousin Liya is their middle daughter. She's young and had no obligations at the wedding. We snuck off to see the unicorn foal from the third trial."

Kaylen snorted. "You gave up a front-row view of a royal coronation to play with a stable beast?"

Siray's glare could've frozen lava. "Had I behaved like you, I'd be rotting in a cell."

Flinching, Kaylen fell into sullen silence.

With a deep breath, Siray continued. "We only got away because we weren't where we were supposed to be. But Colm's men spotted us. Liya and I escaped for a while, but they locked down the grounds. We found out our family had been captured. We were going to break them out." Her voice cracked, the mask slipping. "I didn't know Calla Lily was the traitor. That she was working with him all along."

"She could've done so much better than an upstart torturer," Kaylen muttered.

"Yes, clearly, that's the biggest problem," Briar spat as her annoyance flared down our bond and made me bite back a smile.

The tunnel curved left, then twisted hard right, opening into a low chamber where four paths branched outward like points of a compass. The ceiling dripped with damp, and the air here was colder and closer to the deep heart of the mountain.

I stepped forward, smelling the air for any trace of the beasts or guards. I didn't detect anything concerning. I gestured toward the passage on the right. "There."

"Was your cousin captured, Siray?" Briar's voice was firm but quiet.

"No. They murdered her. The rest of my family is imprisoned." Siray's voice tightened. She drew in a sharp breath. "I won't stop until they are safe."

"We'll get them out," Briar said. "We're going to turn the tables on Colm. They're with the other prisoners deeper in the dungeon, right? None are set to be executed."

"No." Siray's voice sounded flat. "And I won't stop until they're free."

Suddenly, there was a faint *crack*. A subtle echo of stone under pressure, magnified in the silence. Then the unmistakable sound of metal scraping stone...*boots.*

My ears twitched toward the tunnel behind us. I lifted my hand. "Quiet."

Briar's spine straightened. She turned toward the sound

with the same grim realization that seized my chest. The others stilled instinctively, even Kaylen going rigid.

Siray dimmed the lamp to a faint blue, plunging us into dark shadows.

The footsteps grew louder, more distinct. There were at least three guards, probably more, and getting close fast.

I gestured toward the tunnel branching to the left, the layout of the old paths unfurling in my mind after decades of studying them. We turned fast and slipped deeper into the mountain. Briar kept pace at my side, her hand on her sword, her steps sure but... off. The bond between us flickered like a flame exposed to wind—lit one moment, snuffed the next.

She glanced at me, her eyes searching for something.

I linked to her. *I'm here. We're going to figure this out.*

I...I know. Her throat bobbed, but she squared her shoulders and pressed on.

Our steps echoed through the narrow space like ghosted heartbeats. The farther we went, the heavier the air became, thick with wet stone, old minerals, and ancient secrets. Shadows clung to the walls, wrapping us in jagged teeth.

Behind us, Kaylen muttered, "I think I just broke my damn toe."

"Be silent," I hissed. "Unless you want the guards to finish the job."

Mercifully, she grumbled under her breath then fell quiet.

We rounded a sharp bend, and I ran my hand across some etched grooves in the stone. Old markers carved for escape routes. We were close now. Two more turns, and we'd reach the vesting chamber.

Briar's breath quickened. She didn't speak, but I could guess what she'd say if pressed. *I'm fine.*

The sounds of pursuit faded, but I didn't trust that. Not with the way Fate liked to twist its claws into us. The slope of the path angled down, the rough stone biting into our boots. Siray adjusted the lamp, the flicker catching the sheen of sweat at her temple.

"Almost there," I murmured, more for Briar than anyone.

The tunnel widened into a small antechamber with a ritual-smoothed floor. Silver inlays shimmered faintly in the flickering light on the floor and walls, old sigils predating Colm and even my father. This was the last threshold before the vesting chamber.

I slowed automatically, the weight of history and tension falling on me.

Kaylen stumbled with a *thud*, catching herself against a wall. "Ow! Why do we have to move so fast? I can't even hear anyone behind us! Can't we slow down?"

"By Fate, be silent!" I turned on her, my temper snapping.

Then Silus exploded around the corner, his face twisted with fury, his teeth bared, his sword already mid-swing.

Chapter Seventeen

Briar blurred into motion, shoving Kaylen behind her as Silus's blade came down.

My heart stopped. What was she doing? I moved forward to shield Briar, but there wasn't time.

Kaylen stumbled, gasping, nearly tripping over the uneven stone floor. The sword missed her by inches, sparking against the ground with a sharp *ring* of steel meeting stone.

"Stop!" I barked, standing between the sword and Briar.

Silus growled, and his nostrils flared. "She doesn't belong here." His sword didn't leave his hand. He turned sharply and spotted Siray stepping from the shadows, the dim glow of the orb lamp outlining her silhouette.

"You brought Kaylen?" His voice turned hard. "And one of the other candidates?"

I gritted my teeth, my heart returning to the regular rhythm now that Briar was out of danger. I didn't like his tone. It was clear he thought I'd once again made a bad decision.

Before I could answer, a familiar voice echoed from behind him. "Well, if you were going to bring back reinforcements, you could've done better," Thalen drawled, poking his head around the corner. The flickering lamplight caught on his silver-white hair, casting a ghostly sheen over his grin. "Though I'm not thrilled Silus wasn't able to kill that one before Briar saved the ungrateful wench."

Briar exhaled, but her grip on Kaylen didn't ease. "She swore she'd tell us everything she knows. If she doesn't, Silus can finish the job, or we can hand her back over to the guards."

Snorting, Kaylen lifted a brow. "You'd never be able to do that. You want to be everyone's savior."

The urge to strike the horrid woman soared through me again. Few people ever made me feel so violent by merely talking. I pivoted around Briar and shoved Kaylen away from her. "Do not speak ill of my queen again. You'd be dead if it weren't for her, and she won't have to be the one to harm you. After everything you did to her, I will enjoy taking your life, and I can ensure that whatever fate Colm and Calla Lily had in store for you looks like a mercy if you ever cross Briar again."

"You'd better be right about this." Silus wrinkled his nose and focused on Siray.

"Whoa!" Siray stepped back. "I'm not here to cause trouble, but I am here to take those pyre pots down."

"Enough." I clapped Silus on the shoulder. "They're with us. For now. Did Finbar's men arrive?"

He nodded, still coiled tight. "They dropped off supplies—blankets, food, oil, and medicine. Nothing fancy, but better than starving. Some decent blades too."

"And the shadow beasts?"

Silus's jaw flexed. "Two attacks by yellow-eyed bastards. We held them off, but they're getting bolder. They were focused on the western entrance, probably smelled the guards trying to leave."

Thalen gave an exaggerated shrug. "Too bad they didn't lose their magic too. Fighting insane shadow beasts wasn't in my plans, but hey, why not? It's just so much fun."

"Is everyone safe?" Briar's voice was steadier than I expected. She kept an eye on Kaylen.

"So far. The palace is old, but the tunnels are holding, and water is flowing. We won't be impacted by the flooding. The good news is we have strong doors. Never thought I'd be so grateful for having working doors."

"If you're commenting on what happened back in the onyx cellar, I'll have you know we kept the doors shut the whole time. But if you want a show, just let me know." Thalen waggled his brows.

Silus glared at him. "Not the time or the place."

Thalen shrugged and winked, his grin coy. "Maybe not now. But you really ought to try—"

"Do not finish that statement." The last thing I wanted to think about was Silus doing anything like that with my sister. "Or I will *kill* you."

"At least I'm not the only one he's threatening," Kaylen muttered.

Thalen looked down his nose at her with a sharp lift of his eyebrow. "Don't even try to put yourself at my level."

Before anyone could respond, Elara's head peeked around the corner. Her dark-blue eyes focused on us, then moved to Kaylen and widened. "What's going on?"

I didn't want to explain multiple times, so I gestured behind her. "Let's get inside, and I'll tell you everything."

Elara stepped aside, though her sharp gaze remained pinned on Kaylen and Siray. "Ladies." She gestured them through.

Kaylen entered first, her chin high despite the bruises. Siray followed close behind with her lamp and bomb still in her hand.

Elara arched a brow. Her posture seemed steadier than before. Though her skin was still pale and bruised, and one wing gave a faint twitch, there was a quiet resilience in her now. An unwavering strength that reminded me of Briar. "I suppose we should go in," she said, voice dry. "Make sure our guests aren't gutted on sight—since I assume their presence isn't without purpose?"

My father always told me that enemies of my enemies could be useful in war. "It's not."

Thalen leaned against the wall with a grin. "Well, Chaos is involved, so that's the answer." He winked at Briar. "You've got a real knack for picking up strays. Just try to keep them from bleeding on the carpet. Oh, wait, we don't have carpet. Go ahead and bleed then."

Briar gave him a half-smile in return, the kind that could pass for confidence to anyone else. But I noticed her lips trembling at the edges. The bond between us stretched thinner than before, fraying like old thread.

Then chaos erupted.

"Why are you two here?" Rhielle's voice cracked through the air like a whip.

Briar stiffened beside me.

"You know these women?" Veralt demanded, his tone edged with concern, as if he were evaluating what he was supposed to do.

Quen's voice followed, sharper and angrier. "What in the fecking forsaken void are *you* doing here?"

"Sounds like we've missed the warm welcome," Thalen muttered.

"We should've been faster," I growled and picked up my pace.

"Please don't worry about making me feel unwanted," Kaylen said from within, voice layered in thorns.

"You *are* unwanted," Quen snapped. "After what you pulled, I'm shocked you'd actually show your face to us. Hold on. Siray? What are you doing here? What's going on? You think I've forgotten what *you* did? I've got fire for both of you!"

"Please stop," Myantha said, her voice soft. "We can't fight among ourselves. Briar must have a reason for bringing them here. We've lost too many friends to lose potential allies now."

We stepped into the vesting chamber just as the argument heightened.

"You need to leave and go jump in the void now!" Quen stood with her arms crossed, feet planted wide, fury radiating off her in waves.

Kaylen tossed her hair back, the motion stiff with pride. "You're acting like I knew I'd be made a fool of! Do you think I wanted to be Colm's pawn?"

"Don't you dare pretend you're a victim," Rhielle snapped. Her jaw ticked, and her eyes flashed. "People *died* because of you."

Myantha pressed trembling hands to Quen's shoulders, trying to hold her back. "We should talk—"

"Stay out of this, peace lover. We can't all get along after what they did!" Quen barked.

I bit back a sigh and took in our resting place. The tension was thick enough to choke on, but the strangeness of the room settled over me. It looked far different from the last time we were here. The chamber's mystical pulse was gone, with no more shimmering walls or swirling shadowlight. It was just cold stone and stale air. The crimson hue of the water had faded, and the only illumination came from the flickering oil lamps scattered throughout. A stark contrast to a couple of days ago, when Vyraetos and those loyal to my family had vested the power of the Shadow Kingdom in me. The column and the orb in the center of the room remained, but the orb now rested on the top of the column instead of floating.

A dark wooden door stood partially ajar on the far side

of the chamber, revealing a narrow closet-like space. Inside, shelves contained the ceremonial cloths, empty oil containers, chipped bowls, and worn linens for ceremonies performed by Vyraetos and the Shadow Council members that required items other than pure magic. The sink in the back corner trickled drops of clear water. Aside from lamp oil and water, the room held little of real use now that the ceremony had given way to survival.

To my right loomed the main entrance, still hidden behind the heavy carved panel that had once required magic to reveal. Now, it was just another door connecting to the primary access points that led to the actual palace. The left exit led back into the caves, toward the narrow river that cut through a small embankment. If we needed to run, there were half a dozen tunnels we could take, assuming they hadn't collapsed or been overrun.

Elara had done what she always did, finding order in chaos. Even with limited supplies and dragging wings, she'd made sure everyone would be as comfortable as possible here. A section of the circular room had been converted into sleeping quarters. Dark-blue wool blankets formed neat sleeping areas, buffering against the cold and rough stone floor. Elias lay curled under one, face hidden in the crook of his arm, chest rising steadily with sleep.

"Enough!" Siray lifted her hand. "We don't have time for this." She stepped forward, a scowl on her face. "You think I want to be here? I came because my family's imprisoned, not to relive a bloody trial."

Quen scoffed. "You expect sympathy from me after the stunt you pulled during the first trial?"

"Careful." Siray narrowed her eyes. "We did what we needed to do in order to survive, and I don't have time for weaklings. I'd have let you back in the circle if you'd proved you were strong enough."

Veralt loomed nearby, his red hair tousled and his hand resting on the hilt of his blade. Rhielle shifted closer to him, her shoulders stiff, while Myantha's wide-eyed gaze darted helplessly between them.

Behind them, Vyraetos was using a mortar and pestle to grind something up. Several bottles of herbs and oils and some of the medicine sat beside him, as well as the vials with the glowing hairs. Near him, the boxes and crates from the closet and Finbar's supply drop-off had been stacked into a makeshift seating area surrounding a cracked basin filled with flickering lamp light. Bottles of salves, dried herbs, and strips of bandages sat nearby.

Briar moved around Myantha and stared Quen and Rhielle down. "We are not doing this. Not here. Not now." Her voice wasn't loud, but it cut through the room like tempered steel.

Anger still simmered behind Quen's glare, and Rhielle's lips were pressed into a bloodless line, but both women hesitated.

"I brought them because we need answers," Briar continued, her voice unwavering. "I understand you don't like it. *Believe me.* Kaylen would've stolen Vad away if given an opportunity, but she isn't a threat to us anymore. Right now, we have to not only survive what's coming but win."

My chest warmed with pride. Briar was such a fierce leader, and these women would listen to her more than they would to me.

Kaylen opened her mouth, but Briar cut her off with a look so sharp it might have well been a dagger. "And you? You'd better prove your loyalty fast. Because if you're not forthcoming with us, I won't stop Silus next time."

And there was that edge that made her fecking sexy.

The room went quiet except for the slow drip of water from the corner sink and the low hiss of burning oil.

"Well said." Elara crossed the room, her limp pronounced but her posture regal. She turned her cool gaze to Kaylen and Siray. "I'll give you one chance to behave as guests. Otherwise, there will be consequences."

It was all the others needed to hear. Quen exhaled through her nose, looking not quite appeased but willing to let it go for now. Rhielle stepped back. Myantha offered Briar a small, grateful smile.

Rhielle rushed to Briar first, throwing her arms around her with a relieved gasp. Quen followed next, muttering something about "Stupid girl" and "Don't ever vanish like that again." Even Veralt offered a nod of respect.

Thalen shut the heavy stone door behind us with a groan of effort. "Well, that was heartwarming. But I, for one, demand answers. You two look far less destroyed than we feared. I was preparing a eulogy."

"It could've been far worse," I muttered, glancing at Briar. Fear still coiled tight within me. Her wolf flickered faintly beneath her skin like a dying ember. Our bond had thinned into just a thread of gold where once it had roared like fire. I wrapped an arm around Briar's shoulders and continued. "Briar needs food, and we have much to discuss."

She gave me a tired smile, one corner of her mouth tilting upward. "You need food too."

It would've been dramatic to say she was all I needed, but my stomach growled, betraying me.

She raised a brow. "I'm not eating unless you eat."

"As you wish, beloved," I murmured.

"You are so whipped." Thalen laughed.

I cut my eyes at him. "Don't think I haven't noticed where your attention's been focused lately. You aren't acting like it's just a fling."

"Never said I couldn't relate," he shot back with a smirk.

"And it definitely isn't a fling. But we do have actual food now. Not just soldier stew."

Over the next few minutes, we settled into the chamber, gathering near the stacked crates that had been turned into makeshift seating around a cracked oil basin. Elara and Vyraetos distributed bread, dried meat, hard cheese, salted nuts, seed cakes, and fortified wine. Vyraetos moved efficiently, checking on wounds and doling out medicine as needed.

I kept my focus on Briar, making sure she had enough food before I took my first bite. Her fingers trembled slightly as she broke off a piece of bread, and the fading strength of our bond echoed in my chest like a distant heartbeat.

Kaylen and Siray lingered in the middle of the room, most likely unsure of their place. Siray finally made an effort, offering to help Elara distribute supplies. Kaylen said nothing and stood there, tense with unease.

Good. She deserved everything that had happened to her for being greedy and power-hungry.

Vyraetos returned to his post, grinding herbs with a mortar and pestle, his expression unreadable.

Briar sat beside me on one crate, Rhielle standing behind her like a silent guard. Quen had taken a seat on Briar's other side, her arms crossed and her foot tapping. Elias sat close to Quen, watching everything with a sleepy wariness.

Veralt stood behind Rhielle and gently rubbed her shoulders, his protective stance impossible to miss. Elara perched on my other side, with Silus beside her, the two of them speaking in low tones about the tunnels and patrols. Thalen and Myantha had wedged together on a crate nearby, Myantha resting her cheek on Thalen's shoulder, his arm loosely wrapped around her waist. Siray paced behind the group, brow furrowed, while Kaylen finally took a seat opposite Briar, her hands plucking at the threads of her torn skirt.

I took another swig of the fortified wine. The aftertaste from the skin couldn't quite hide the sharp tinge of herbs, but the wine settled the tension in my limbs, making me feel a little steadier. "All right. We don't have much time. Captain Finbar is preparing his forces for an attack on the Ceremonial Hall during Colm's coronation. We need to be ready to reveal the truth. And to fight."

Briar leaned forward, her attention on Kaylen. "You said you had information that could help us. Start talking."

Kaylen let out a long breath and raised her chin. "Let me start by saying I never intended to be involved in any coup, and I never really did anything wrong—"

"Fecking shut your mouth if all you're going to do is spew lies," Quen snapped and wrinkled her nose.

"Oh, please." Rhielle rolled her eyes. "Don't pretend you left your viciousness in the arena. You were probably the one who slit my throat." Her hand brushed the scar on her neck.

Veralt tugged Rhielle back gently against him and pressed a kiss to her temple, but his eyes stayed locked on Kaylen.

Groaning, Kaylen pressed her face into her hands. "That wasn't me. I don't cut throats."

"No," Quen said. "You stab people in the back."

Kaylen peeked between her fingers, unapologetic. "Well, yeah. That way, they don't see it coming. It's like a mercy kill."

This woman was a worse person than I'd imagined. "Enough." I raised a hand, letting command bleed into my voice. "Kaylen, you're alive because Briar spared you. You're going to repay that by telling us everything you know. *Now.*"

Briar sat beside me, silent and steady. However, although she was close, her soul felt distant, the bond between us strained and threadbare. I resisted the urge to reach for it and to ask her what she needed. That could wait for later, when we were alone-ish.

Taking a deep breath, Kaylen set her shoulders. "Calla Lily came to me with a member of the Aureline Council, Bram. The one with light blue eyes, freckles, and red hair. They told me I'd won. That the Council had chosen me. They said I had to be ready to make my claim and that they'd support me. But it was a lie."

Her voice cracked, and she looked away, shame flickering across her face.

I watched her, completely unmoved by the tears trailing down her cheeks. No one else rushed to comfort her either. Even Myantha, the kindest among us, lowered her gaze and shifted further into Thalen's side as if to separate herself from the weight of Kaylen's words.

"The guards dragged me off." The skin around Kaylen's eyes tightened. "They locked me in a cell for what felt like forever. Then they brought me to the royal quarters. I thought maybe the Council had changed its mind, but...that's when I met Colm."

She looked up, and her expression twisted with a bitterness that almost masked the tremor in her voice. "He said I'd been useful. That I'd served my purpose. But I wasn't going to be queen of anything."

Briar pursed her lips. "You'd never seen Colm before that moment?"

"No." Kaylen's upper lip curled. "I'd remember someone that ugly. I had seen Bram, though. From the beginning. He helped me a few times. Said I was... beautiful enough that Fate would obviously choose me." Her lower lip wobbled, but she breathed the weakness away with a sharp inhale. "I know it was foolish. But I wanted to believe it. So I did."

She squared her shoulders. "He brought me stronger healing salves than the others. Told me which trial was coming next so I could practice. He even made sure my gowns were lighter, my weights adjusted."

Expression tightening, Rhielle crossed her arms. Veralt stood behind her, protective, his hand resting on her hip, acting as her silent anchor.

"But I didn't cut Rhielle's throat," Kaylen said quickly, her voice rising. "That was Calla Lily. She bragged about it. Said she could do the same to me. Told me I'd never be queen. So... I punched her and set her on fire. All right?"

"You didn't stab her in the back?" Rhielle snorted. "That's more your style."

Kaylen huffed and flicked her hair over her shoulder. "If she'd turned her back, I would've. I'd have come up with a better plan too. But I got mad. It was a spur-of-the-moment decision."

"She's Ignis Fae." Quen scowled. "You know we're fire-resistant. What exactly was your plan?"

"I never said it was a good plan, Quen!" Kaylen snapped. "She said that, and I lost it!"

"So critical thinking is your strong suit." Thalen tapped a finger to his chin. "Got it. A good attribute for becoming a queen."

Silus chuckled quietly.

Kaylen clenched her hands. Her cheeks reddened.

Briar's gaze didn't waver. "Why didn't they kill you on the spot?"

Hanging her head, Kaylen winced. "Because they're dramatic as feck, all right? Calla Lily said I didn't deserve a quick death. She wanted to watch me suffer. She said they'd execute me by axe, make it slow. Draw and quarter me with multiple blows. That they'd been doing that all day to traitors, and I'd be the finale." She swallowed hard. "Afterward, they planned to put my head on display in the Ceremonial Hall."

I shifted my weight. "I didn't smell blood in the dungeons.

I assume they weren't killing anyone there?"

Kaylen shook her head. "No. They blocked off the Ceremonial Hall and some area beyond it. That's where the executions have been happening."

A brief silence followed her words, broken only by the soft scratch of Vyraetos's mortar and pestle.

"But I'll testify," she added quickly. "I'll tell everyone what they did. I'll say anything you want. It's just uh..."

"What?" Briar asked, her voice sharp.

Kaylen didn't answer.

Siray stepped in before she could. "Kaylen's not a great witness. No one likes her. She doesn't come from any noble lineage. She has no political weight or influential allies. And she's burned bridges in every court she's set foot in."

Kaylen scowled but didn't argue.

Vyraetos leaned in then, holding one of the glowing vials near Kaylen's head. The light inside dimmed.

"She's telling the truth about one thing," he murmured. "She hasn't consumed any essence. Hers are the strands that don't glow. Calla Lily's are the ones humming with residual power."

"So," Quen said dryly, "she's incompetent and powerless. Great."

"I mean, who else would it be?" Kaylen muttered, arms crossed tight. "She's so conniving; I didn't even catch a hint."

"That's not much of an observation," Myantha murmured, her tone just shy of scolding.

Thalen arched a brow, smirking. He leaned close and whispered something in Myantha's ear, and color bloomed across her cheeks.

Exhaling through his nose, Vyraetos set the vial aside. "In some ways, it may be a mercy that our magic has been stripped. If it were to return, Colm and Calla Lily would be nearly unstoppable. Elias confirmed they did this to others as well. This wasn't a singular offense, and I doubt they've shared the full extent of their plans with anyone else."

"They haven't." Siray paced in the center of everyone. "Every Aureline Council member— from the joint or High Council—was imprisoned. Many were executed. They've accused Rhielle and Ceana of conspiring with Briar, They've already beheaded Ceana. And it sounded like they were going to claim Liya was a bridal candidate too, even though she wasn't involved. They're making examples of the brides publicly and brutally. If they catch me, my head will be in there as well."

A ripple of revulsion tugged at the bond. Briar's expression didn't falter, but I felt tension in the way her shoulders tightened and her gaze locked on Siray. "Is there anything else?" Her voice was calm... too calm.

Siray shrugged, but her eyes were sharp. "Now that they know you're still in the palace, they'll double their efforts to find you both. You and Vad are the prize. They want a spectacle. Dragging the couple responsible for Fate's silence to the stage, stringing you up as the ones who broke magic—call it justice, vengeance, whatever they need the people to believe. They want the coronation soaked in blood."

I would die to protect Briar. They wouldn't lay a hand on her. "Then they'll be disappointed. Are they keeping the bodies in the Ceremonial Hall?"

"At least the heads are taken there." Siray's face wrinkled in disgust. "They've turned it into some grotesque demonstration."

"If the shadow beasts are like wolves," Briar said, her voice low, "they're opportunistic. Drawn to blood and dead flesh."

"That could explain the attack locations." Silus adjusted his position on the crate with a wooden groan. "They're following the scent and attacking whatever they find."

"Great." Thalen chuckled darkly, running a hand through

his hair. "Blood and death. What more could we ask for?"

"That doesn't explain the portals." Rhielle looked upward like the ceiling might hold answers.

Briar rubbed her wrists beneath the sleeves of her tunic. Her discomfort fluttered through the bond, fragile and fleeting, like trying to grip smoke. "No. But maybe we'll get answers soon."

"At the very least"—I reached over and took her hand—"we know where the beasts will concentrate next."

My thumb traced the back of her knuckles, slow and steady. I didn't know whether she felt it—whether anything I did even reached her now. I had to figure out a way to bring her wolf back to her. She was struggling, and so was I.

But the coronation was closing in, and with it, our window. That ceremony offered our cleanest shot at taking back the kingdom, despite more blood being spilled. Dozens of guards on high alert and loyal to the wrong throne. We wouldn't get a second chance.

A plan sharpened in the back of my mind. "You said they're staying in the royal family quarters now?"

Both Siray and Kaylen nodded.

"They've completely taken over," Siray said, her voice flat. "Liya and I considered striking then and there to cut the head off the snake, but the guards were thick at the entrance. We'd have been torn apart."

"They brought me to Colm." Kaylen shuddered. "It was this huge room with a glass dome overhead—"

"The observatory?" Elara interrupted, her wings giving an agitated flick.

"Sure." Kaylen shrugged. "He had books, potions, stone orbs, some weird light stuff, and piles of jewelry everywhere, like he was hoarding it."

A muscle ticked in my jaw, and a pang shot through my

heart. That had been my sanctuary, where my mother and I had spent so much time together, and I found peace there. He'd better not have destroyed it, but I had little hope of that. Of course Colm would claim that very place and twist it into something of his own. Still... that detail, that space, it was an opening.

I glanced toward Silus and Thalen. They caught my meaning immediately.

"Taking the head off the snake might be our best option after all."

CHAPTER EIGHTEEN

Briar folded her arms and turned toward me. "What are you thinking?"

"It sounds like Colm is planning something else." I frowned, hating the thought of him breathing air in that room. "Calla Lily was wearing the shadow beast hairpin from Elara's room. She had other family pieces too. None of them were enchanted, right?"

Elara stiffened. "My mother's hairpin? That was never magical, just sentimental. Father bought it for her and said it was beautiful, like her." Her voice cracked.

I nodded slowly, thinking back. I hadn't seen Calla Lily with any jewelry that could potentially have residual magic. But if she and Colm had taken over the observatory and gathered the remnants of our family's relics, there was a chance...just enough of one.

"Why would that matter?" Briar's forehead wrinkled. "Magic isn't working right now."

"Some stones," I said carefully, "especially ones tied to enchanted objects, hold fragments of residual power similar to portals. It's usually dormant. But if someone found a way to extract it—"

"Like breaking it down?" Briar bit her bottom lip.

"Exactly." I met Vyraetos's eyes. "Could that restore power to someone like Colm?"

The old fae tilted his head, running a hand over the stubble on his jaw. "Not without magic to manipulate and siphon the essence. But...if he's desperate—and we all know he is—he might be trying anyway. And we have no idea what else he's found and what measures he's willing to take. If he finds a way, he will be unstoppable. It isn't likely, but...it isn't impossible either."

Not the answer I wanted. But it told me one thing—we couldn't wait.

Siray stepped forward. Her mouth was a hard, angry line, but her voice was cold steel. "This affects me now, so let me be clear. I'll help end Colm. I don't care about you or your people, but I care about my family."

She looked straight at Quen. "You were right. I threw you out. I didn't care if you lived or died. If you weren't strong, you were nothing to me. I'm not going to pretend to care now. I don't. I'm not here to make friends. I'm here to end this."

Her hand lifted, swiping at the corner of her eye before the tears could fall. "I love my family. If we break out the prisoners, my aunt and uncle will testify about what has happened. They'll stand against Colm. I swear it. They've been starving in the dark while he rewrites the world."

She paused, then added, "They won't care about Briar or Vad being wed. Hell, they probably won't even flinch at the idea of an Aureline with a Shadow Fae. They'll care about survival. And they'll burn Colm for what he's done."

"We won't let the prisoners die," Briar said. Even with our bond weakened, I felt her resolve like a spark, small but fierce. She looked at me, and I nodded, sealing the silent vow between us.

I turned to Siray. "I know your aunt and uncle. They

are noble rulers. And even if I didn't, I wouldn't allow this to continue. None of us will. We'll get them out."

I scanned the room, weighing options. "With the shadow beasts in the caverns and tunnels and the palace exits under guard, we need a place the children and the vulnerable can hide. Maybe forty could stay here. What about the stables? Are they still accessible?"

Siray's lips pressed into a tight line, her expression grim. "No. Colm's forces blocked them off. Liya and I barely made it out."

Disappointment pulsed in my chest, but not surprise. "How many guards are at the prison itself?"

"Between three and six." Siray closed her eyes like she was trying to pull up the memory. "But a dozen rotate through every few hours and take it in shifts. If an alert goes up, backup swarms within minutes. And now that they know we're in the palace, they'll double the patrols and keep an eye out for hidden passages."

"They already suspected secret passages existed." Kaylen scoffed. "Colm even questioned me about them."

Siray shot her a look. "Clearly, they didn't know about the one we escaped through."

I downed another mouthful of the fortified wine. I needed a clear head, and the sharp edge of the herbs helped me think faster and feel less.

What are you planning? Briar's voice nudged into my mind. I had to focus on it like a sound from another room.

We might have a way in. I'll take—

I'm going with you. Her response cut through like a blade. Her green eyes flashed, unyielding.

Despite the storm churning inside me, her fire made me smile. I pressed her hand to my lips. "All right. Here's the plan. I'll take a small team. If we can reach the observatory, we'll take

Colm prisoner or kill him."

Elara tilted her head. "You think he'll be there?"

"If he's working on what we think he is, yes." I didn't need to question that. He was power hungry. I'd known it the moment I'd stepped into that awful prison. "And if we can strike before he regains magic, we stand a chance."

Elara glanced toward Silus, who gave a slow nod. "Then we'll hold this post," she said. Her voice was firm, but shadows lingered beneath her eyes.

Thalen leaned forward with a low, deliberate cough. "I hate to be predictable, but no way in the forsaken hells are you going without me. I'll pack light. I know you prefer the dark, but I'll bring my own light source in case we get separated. Don't argue. You need me."

I opened my mouth, but Quen beat me to it.

"I can help—"

"No." I lifted a hand, silencing her. "Everyone else stays here. Thalen is the only one to join us."

I turned back to the two girls. "Siray. Kaylen. You will remain in the vesting chamber and follow Elara's orders. If she prefers it, you'll be bound."

"I do prefer it," Elara said coldly.

Kaylen's jaw dropped, and Siray just nodded like she'd expected it. Elara pointed a pale hand at Kaylen. "Go clean yourself up in the storage closet. There's soap and a sink. You reek."

Kaylen scowled. "Is there hot water?"

"No. Why would there be hot water?" Elara didn't even blink. "Quen, escort her. Myantha, grab rope from the supply crates. Vad, do you need anything else before you leave?"

The pride swelling in my chest caught me off guard. I crossed the room to Elara, studying her carefully. "Do *you* need anything before we leave?"

Her wry smile flickered. "Just two things. Come back alive, and take that bastard out."

I placed my hands on her shoulders and pulled her into a brief embrace. "Father and Mother would be proud of you."

A sharp ache bloomed in my chest. I pushed it aside. Not now.

She blinked quickly and lifted her chin. "They'd say the same about you and your bride."

"You're really going?" Rhielle stared at Briar with her arms folded and one brow raised. "You need rest, not another fight."

Briar's soft smile didn't reach her eyes. "I'll rest when we come back."

Rhielle blew out a breath, then hugged her tight. When she stepped back, her expression hardened. "Then take Veralt with you. Please. I'll stay here and make sure those two—" she nodded toward Siray and Kaylen "—don't do anything stupid. But you might need backup, and you know he's better with a blade than I am."

I looked to Veralt, who was already striding over, setting a hand on Rhielle's shoulder.

"It'll be tight," I said. "We can't afford to make noise or draw attention."

"Worse than the passage we were in before you got dragged off by a shadow wolf?" he asked.

I smirked. "Not unless something goes catastrophically wrong. You should have enough room, but your head may scrape the ceiling a few times."

He grunted. "I've dealt with worse. I'm in."

"Good. We leave in five minutes. Make your preparations."

As the others moved, I stepped between Rhielle and Briar, gently guiding Briar toward the shadowed alcove near the door that led to the caves. Her shoulders were drawn tight, every line of her posture coiled with tension.

I cupped her cheek, the coolness of her skin stark against my palm. "Are you all right, Briar? Is your wolf..." I trailed off, not even sure how to finish the question without unraveling her further.

Her lips trembled, and for a moment, pain streaked through her emerald eyes before she locked it away behind a wall of composure.

"She's more distant than ever," she said, voice low. "And our bond... I can't feel you consistently either. It's flickering. I—" Her voice broke. "I don't even know if I can tell anymore when someone's lying."

A quiet rage burned through me at all that had happened to her. More than anything, I wanted to fix it and take the weight from her shoulders.

I kissed her forehead, then leaned in, pressing my lips to hers and wrapping my arms around her. The lack of a buzz at our touch emphasized the dampening of our connection even more. "We'll get through this. Whatever is severing your link to your wolf, we'll find the answer. If that means tracking down the Guardian Shadow Beast or summoning one of the others, I'll do it without hesitation."

"I hate not feeling close to you." Her voice cracked, barely above a whisper.

"I never thought I'd say this, but even when I can't feel you through the bond, you're still everywhere inside me. You are my constant, no matter what. My love for you is just as strong, if not stronger."

Her eyes softened, catching what little light remained in the chamber. "When did you become so sentimental?" she teased, though her voice trembled. "You're such a sweet talker."

"You've turned me soft." I stroked a strand of her copper hair between my fingers. "You arrived swinging, ready to set fire to my entire kingdom, and I told myself I wouldn't fall. But you proved me wrong in every way that matters."

A smile tugged at her lips.

"I cursed Fate," I said softly, "but I owe her everything. Because she brought me you. And once this is over, once we've secured the kingdom and saved our family, I intend to spend every moment reminding you of just how much I adore you."

Blushing, she tilted her head back with a glimmer of mischief in her eyes. "I still don't understand Fate, but I'm grateful too. You're everything to me, Vad. I can't fathom not having you in my life. I just wish I could've found you faster."

That was all it took to undo me.

I kissed her, pulling her close, pouring every fear, every vow, every raw thread of devotion into her. Her breath hitched as my hands slid into her hair, cradling her like something precious, because she was that to me. She tasted of fortified wine and something that was all her own, wild and sweet and wholly mine. In that kiss, I gave her everything I couldn't speak aloud—my terror of losing her and my desperate hope for the future we deserved together.

When we finally broke apart, she was breathless. Her lips were parted, her eyes wide and shining with desire. For one fleeting moment, the bond between us sparked bright and hot, pulsing like a second heartbeat in my chest.

I leaned in once more, pressing my forehead to hers. "That is a promise of everything waiting for us on the other side of this."

Her lips brushed mine. "I love you, Vad."

The words echoed through me, warming me despite the chill of the chamber. "And I love you, Briar. Always."

I reluctantly released her and turned to face the others.

Thalen waited nearby, a smug grin tugging at his mouth with one brow arched like he'd caught us doing something scandalous. Veralt, in contrast, checked the edge of his new sword with quiet focus and tested its weight with a slow arc through the air. Elara had already resumed giving instructions, her voice strong despite the lingering edge of weariness in her posture.

"Are we ready?" I scanned them.

Thalen patted the satchel at his hip and folded his bandaged silver-white wings behind his back with more care than usual. "Only if you're done whispering sweet nothings and don't need another minute or two."

Rhielle approached Veralt and tugged him down for a quick kiss. Her grip tightened on his tunic. "You take care of my girl and come back alive, you hear?"

"Of course." He dipped his head and brushed his lips to her forehead, his voice softer than I'd ever heard it. "Anything for you, my heart."

Thalen cast a playful glance over his shoulder toward Myantha, who was currently elbow-deep in a storage crate, hunting for rope. "I'll see you again soon."

She flushed, dropped the rope, and surged forward to kiss him fully. "Come back in one piece, please."

"Returning with all limbs attached is officially a priority." He winked.

I gave them a beat longer, then turned toward Briar and inclined my head toward the heavy stone door. "Let's move. Time is not on our side."

With a shove, I pushed open the slab, its weight grinding over the uneven floor. The sound echoed ominously into the cavern beyond. I paused, letting the stillness settle. No noise, so I gave the signal to proceed.

The passage was short, barely a dozen steps, before it opened into the massive, jagged cavern. The air was colder here, sharper. Fragments of rock littered the path, courtesy of the most recent quakes that had cracked the foundations of the palace.

"Vad, I can't see as clearly." Briar's voice rose in panic. "I can make out a little, but it's dim."

I stepped around a particularly large boulder. "Watch your step." I reached back for her.

She slipped her hand into mine. Her touch was steady, though I could still feel the fatigue and fear humming beneath her skin. Thalen followed, one hand resting lightly on her shoulder to help guide her over a loose patch of stone.

"Do you need me to get the lamp out?" Thalen asked. "We can light it here."

"No," Briar said, her voice tight. "I can see enough with Vad guiding me."

We moved in silence, the only sound the soft crunch of gravel and the faint, rhythmic scuff of boots on stone. Veralt brought up the rear, his blade out and held low, his eyes flicking constantly across the shadows.

The structure, though battered, had held. There were no cave-ins and no sudden drops, just the rubble and the weight of silence.

"The tunnel's holding," I whispered. "We're fortunate."

Thalen scoffed under his breath. "If this is what counts as fortunate, I dread what disaster looks like."

I didn't answer. The farther we descended, the more the air thickened. The scent of damp stone and old blood still clung faintly to the walls, as if the tunnels remembered too much.

The beasts would be drawn to the Ceremonial Hall where blood, death, and desecration summoned them. With the royal quarters in the opposite direction, we had a narrow window to move undetected.

I hoped Fate wouldn't play games this time.

After over an hour of cautious progress and switchbacks to mask our trail, we reached the narrow tunnel that would lead us to the royal observatory. The change in the stone was subtle, the rock becoming more polished and intentionally carved. The walls here were smoother, and the ceiling overhead was reinforced. Above, the faint outline of a drop-door was etched into the stone, concealed unless you knew what to look for.

I raised a hand and gestured for the others to stay back.

Stepping forward, I scanned the threshold for signs of tampering or traps. Nothing stood out in the entire fifty-foot corridor leading to the stairs. It was as quiet and pristine as the day it was carved.

It didn't look as if they'd found this route yet. Good.

I motioned for the others, and we moved again. Each step sent a beat of tension through my spine. My pulse thudded, loud in my ears, as we reached the top of the staircase.

At the final door, I removed my keys, unlocked it slowly so as not to make noise, and then pressed a hand against the cold metal handle. A dull cracking sound came from the other side of the door. Someone was in there.

I turned the handle slowly. A warm, golden glow poured in through the growing gap, but so did an acidic stench. It hit the back of my throat like vinegar and rotting meat as if dead magic was being expelled.

I froze.

My grip faltered, and my jaw locked tight as something unspeakable twisted in my gut. The door trembled beneath my palm, and I felt like I'd been punched in the gut.

Chapter Nineteen

VAD

My claws curled inward until their stinging sharpness cut into my palms, grounding me.

The fecking bastard scum.

He had desecrated my observatory.

My precious books, logs, and records lay scattered across the floor and under the table and desk, spines broken and pages torn or bent. The shelves were empty of all their former treasures and were now haphazardly stacked with crushed gems, broken figurines, and shattered jewelry.

And my telescope, a masterpiece of craftsmanship and a representation of the precious bond between my mother and me, was dismantled. Every single piece had been taken apart and strewn across the nearest table beneath the domed window.

He hadn't just taken over the room. He'd tried to erase me from it.

Every oil lamp had been lit, from the ones on the walls to the hand lamps on the table and desk. The glow caught in the shards of fractured jewelry and cracked crystal, sending glints ricocheting off the ceiling and the domed window above. Some of the light even caught on the telescope lenses and beamed upward. Enchanted objects littered every surface, most of them split open or melted down, as if he had been clawing through them for some hidden truth.

The night brandy was gone and the decanter overturned and thrust against a pile of gold and silver jewelry, the two matching cups next to it. The couches had been kicked askew. Pillows tossed aside. Not even the rug had escaped unscathed, with blood or ink streaked across it.

At the center of it all, like a parasite nesting inside a hollowed-out host, stood Colm.

He wore one of my black, embroidered robes. The fine silk swam over his frame, and the sleeves dragged near his wrists as he hunched over a shadow beast sculpture at my desk. He worked the chisel with an obsessive calm. A low hum vibrated from his throat, tuneless and hollow. His filigree silver claw tips gleamed in the lamplight, clicking against the tools.

I gripped the doorframe so tightly that the stone grated beneath my fingers. Rage pulsed through me, molten and merciless. He had violated everything sacred. This room had been my sanctuary. It was here I'd first kissed Briar. Where I'd realized how much I loved her. Where I had retreated when I needed peace.

And now? Now it reeked of him. That sharp vinegar scent burned my nostrils.

My wings flexed tightly against my spine, readying to attack.

He had to die.

Briar's hand pressed against my shoulder. *Vad, what's wrong?*

Briar's voice bled into my mind, frayed and fading through our weakened bond, but clear enough. She grounded me and pulled me back from doing something reckless.

I straightened, aligning my spine and wings with sharp control. *It's fine.* Not the truth, but enough for now.

I'm sorry, she linked back.

There was nothing to apologize for. She understood. She *always* understood.

I gave her a sharp nod, then slowly unsheathed my sword. The whisper of metal against scabbard was a promise—one I intended to keep.

I pushed the door wider, and Colm didn't look up.

The crack of stone rang through the room as his chisel struck again, splintering the sculpture's neck. He hissed, sounding displeased with the result. He adjusted one of his claw tips, then dragged it along the fracture, testing the resistance.

"Worthless thing," Colm muttered, flinging the chisel over his shoulder. It clanged against a shelf, sending a small avalanche of broken jewelry clattering to the floor. He reached for another figurine, this one a merlinite stallion etched with silver veins. "Perhaps you'll prove more useful."

I moved farther into the room, careful not to disturb the fallen books any more than I had to. Briar followed close behind, her steps silent and her sword lowered. Thalen slid out to the right, his sword drawn as well. Veralt brought up the rear, ducking to avoid striking his head, his sword sheathed at his side and his hand resting near the hilt.

Colm set the stallion on the desk, picked up the chisel and mallet, and broke it apart. The neck snapped, and a faint puff of dust rose up. The vinegar scent intensified as the remnants of whatever magic had once existed within it vanished. He growled.

I lifted the blade of my sword, preparing to chop his head off.

The shadow of my raising arm slid across the desk, and I realized too late that my usual ability to keep my shadows contained had vanished.

Feck.

Colm froze, and with maddening calm, he set down the broken stallion and turned, squaring his shoulders. "I wouldn't recommend that." He cut his gaze to me, his dull green gaze looking unbearably smug. "Killing me wouldn't end well for you or your little family, especially the prisoners. If anything happens to me, they all die."

"I don't need to let you speak to end you." I stepped forward, letting the edge of my blade cut the side of his neck, drawing a thin line of blood. "You won't have time to give any orders, and even if you scream, they won't get here in time."

He flinched slightly but didn't retreat. Blood welled at his neck, and yet his smile never wavered. "Are you *sure* about that? Willing to gamble with innocent lives?" His voice dripped with poisonous amusement. "Children, you know. Helpless little ones who've never done anything wrong."

Veralt moved closer, stepping through the wreckage of paper and ink-stained pages. "What in the void are you talking about?"

"That's not a funny joke," Thalen growled from the side. "Say another word like that, and I'll show you exactly what pain feels like while you're *begging* to die."

Colm chuckled with a sly grin that curled his hatchet-shaped face into a sneer. "You think I don't know? Not that it matters. Children will know what that's like if you kill me or make me disappear."

Briar stepped beside me with her sword pointed at his heart. Her stance was lethal and still, and she kept her eyes locked on him, unblinking. But something punched through our bond. The pressure of unease and concern.

I scowled, acid pooling in the pit of my stomach. He was far too calm. *Is he lying, Briar?*

I...I don't know. Her voice flickered in my mind, taut and conflicted. She adjusted her grip on her sword but kept it aimed at Colm, maintaining a mask of calm and confidence. *The vinegar smell—it's too strong. It's masking everything. I can't tell.*

Damn it. I kept my blade at his throat, even as my instincts warred inside me. *It's all right. We'll take him prisoner and get our answers.*

Colm beamed. "Are you frightened, *Briar*? You should be." He chuckled.

Briar's shoulders locked, her breathing tightening.

Enough.

I struck him in the mouth with my fist and the hilt of my sword. He stumbled back into the desk with a choking cough, still clutching the broken figurine in one hand. Blood gushed from his lips and down his chin, but even as he clutched his jaw, his grin widened grotesquely.

"You can't kill me, Vad," he croaked with red staining his teeth. "And you *really* shouldn't take me prisoner." He tapped his silver claw tips together, the metallic clicks echoing through the ravaged room. "This was your mistake. You've already lost."

He turned his gaze toward Briar. "If you all surrender now, I'll give you a mercy none of you deserve. A swift death. Even for your wretched little *mutated mate*."

"You do not speak of her that way. Don't even *look* at her." A growl rumbled from deep within my chest as I pressed the flat of my blade against his shoulder, the edge aligned with his throat. I pushed just enough to break skin, sting, and make a mark. His eyelids fluttered, but he didn't protest or flinch... just stared.

I spat out, "Thalen, get rope. Veralt, check the door."

Colm's smile never faltered. "While you're scuttling about, go ahead and take this off my hands." He flung the fractured shadow beast sculpture toward Veralt with a flick of his wrist. "It's as worthless as everything else in this place."

The back of my neck burned as fury surged through me.

My grip tightened, blade ready to drive straight through him if this was an attempt at escape or distraction.

Veralt's eye widened in surprise. He lurched to the side, catching the two broken pieces just before they could strike the floor. His thigh slammed into the table, sending everything atop it into motion. Crushed gems and fractured lenses clinked and jostled. The oil lamp rocked precariously, its red liquid sloshing just shy of spilling over the rim. The beam of reflected light fractured and disappeared.

Nothing had fallen, but it had come damn close.

"Fecking void." Veralt's shoulders slumped. He cradled the pieces for a moment, then carefully placed them on a clear stretch of the table. Adjusting his eyepatch, he shot Colm a glare. "Destructive sort, aren't you?"

Thalen let out a low whistle. "Clutter's never been my style, but this?" He gestured to the chaos. "You've taken junkyard chic to a whole new level. You prefer trash dens over actual research?"

Briar's breath eased slightly, but her sword never lowered. Her upper lip curled. "You're the most vile man I've ever met. And I've met murderers. I won't let you hurt any of those children."

Colm turned toward her and smirked.

A snarl ripped from my throat, and I used the flat of my blade to force his face back toward me. The edge sliced a shallow line into his cheek. "Try that again, and I *will* silence you. Your guards won't save you. Don't even think about screaming for help."

He rolled his eyes. "Please. The guards are stationed at the front of the royal quarters, not here. And even if they *did* hear something, they'd assume it was me dismantling more of your precious trinkets."

He gestured vaguely at the destruction around him. "It's

been exhausting, sorting through your family's pretty little secrets, peeling back the layers of enchantment. Most of them don't even hum anymore. Magic long since faded. Some were crafted well, I'll admit. But everything breaks eventually."

"As will you." My voice dropped into a lethal rasp.

He grinned through the blood trailing down his chin. "You don't have enough time left to break me."

Veralt reached out and steadied one of the large glass lenses still rocking on the table. "That was almost a disaster," he muttered, then winced as he realized he'd stepped on a pile of scattered books. "Sorry. He's flung everything everywhere! I can't take a step without messing something up." Another spine split beneath his heel, the sound sharp in the tense silence.

Colm watched us like he was watching a comedy, not bleeding and pinned at swordpoint. That smug, patient calm chilled me deeper than any threat. He wasn't worried at all.

There were no visible traps and no warning alarms activated. The door itself wasn't especially secure, but it would take a few blows to bring it down. Still, that didn't mean he didn't have other means of protection. I narrowed my eyes. "Take off the claw tips and remove every weapon you have."

Thalen moved through the mess of the observatory carefully, using his boots to nudge aside books without stepping on them directly. Pages rustled underfoot, whispering reminders of what had been lost.

Across from him, Colm removed the claw tips from his fingers, one at a time. Each metallic click echoed too loudly. "You're wasting your time. None of this will play out the way you think. At best, you'll tie me up and go skittering off into the ruins of your former life, hoping to delay the inevitable."

"You keep talking like we can't just kill you." Thalen snapped the rope taut between his hands with a dry *crack*. Dust plumed upward. "Honestly, I'm still not clear on why we shouldn't."

"Veralt, search him," I ordered, keeping my blade steady at Colm's shoulder. "Make sure he doesn't have any other weapons."

Colm slid off the final claw tip and dropped it with a delicate *clink*. "Go ahead. Kill me or take me prisoner. Pretend you have control, but if I fail to give an order to a specific individual in a specified location within a specified time, things will unravel quickly."

He shrugged off the black silk robe, revealing bare arms laced with scars. Some were fine as spiderwebs, while others were thick and jagged, like shattered glass was hidden beneath the skin. The raised lines crisscrossed his forearms and disappeared beneath the sleeves of a gray tunic riddled with reinforced seams and narrow pockets. His trousers matched in utilitarian dullness, both shades able to vanish in shadow.

"Even without magic, pain is a remarkably easy thing to create. And poisons..." He smiled thinly. "Poisons do not discriminate, especially the choking kind." He folded the robe with unsettling precision."

Briar went rigid beside me.

Colm's voice lowered, almost reverent. "Your dungeons were brimming with delightful relics such as war room blueprints and all sorts of torture implements. It didn't take much effort to rig them up and establish crude mechanisms for their delivery into the water supply, and it doesn't take much time to create that choking gas. If I vanish or fail to check in, my men will release it."

My claws dug into my palms. The blade at his shoulder wavered ever so slightly.

After folding his robe, Colm set it aside. "My men check on me every three hours. Let's be generous and say the last round was recent, so we'll pretend you have nearly three hours. If everything goes flawlessly, you might save some of the adults. But the children?" His smile curved wider, crueler. "The infants? Even a small exposure can be fatal to bodies so small. Horribly. They will die. Can you live with that?"

Briar's breath caught. Her fingers clenched tighter around her sword hilt until her knuckles bleached. Her fear pulsed through our bond, quiet and raw beneath the rage in her eyes. If it wasn't for that, I never would've known and would've assumed it was only rage.

"What kind of poison?" she bit out.

Colm blinked slowly. "Now, why would I tell you that? You don't have enough time to break me, sweetheart."

Veralt moved in, silent and grim. He patted Colm down with calculated force, retrieving a dagger, two vials of viscous green liquid, a silk-wrapped sliver of a blade with no hilt, a set of bone-handled lockpicks, a pouch of black powder, and several tight packets of dried herbs that smelled faintly metallic.

He lined the items up on the closest table, beside the rubble of broken crystal and scorched metal. The display looked like an assassin's kit.

The cold weight in my chest deepened. My instincts screamed this wasn't a bluff. Every word he'd said had been delivered with the quiet, bone-deep confidence of someone who believed he'd already won.

"Bind him," I ordered. My voice was low. Final. "To the chair. *Now.*"

I shoved Colm forward with a hand between his shoulder blades, and Thalen stepped in without hesitation. He bound Colm's wrists behind him tightly, securing them with a series of rough, practiced knots. Then he dragged him toward the velvet black chair in the corner and forced him down into it.

With no back spindles to anchor to, Thalen looped the rope around the carved legs and tied off the slack with sharp jerks, making sure Colm couldn't shift an inch.

Colm exhaled, unbothered. "Hope you have a plan, Vad. Because the clock is ticking."

"We're just going to tie him up and leave?" Veralt spread his arms wide.

Colm answered before I could. "Unless you'd prefer to be the reason a few dozen children die choking on their own blood, then yes." He grinned, a wild glint in his eyes as he turned toward Thalen. "Go on and pull it tighter. I don't mind pain."

"Tell us how to deactivate the traps in the prison." I struck him across the cheek with the hilt of my sword. His head snapped to the side, blood spraying from a split in his lip, but when the bastard recovered, he just smirked.

How much time did we really have?

Briar stepped forward with fury flickering in her eyes. She stopped beside me, her hand flexing at her thigh like she wanted to reach for something sharp.

"We already have Calla Lily," she whispered with each word honed with venom. She leaned down so that she was near his face, her hand pressed against her thigh, and her fingers tensed. "You either tell Vad what he needs to know, or... when we get back, we'll kill her. And if we don't make it back, we left instructions for someone else to finish the job. So. Your move, Douchewaffle."

Colm's grin faltered. "No... You're bluffing. I know you, Briar. You wouldn't—"

"Wouldn't I?" Her voice dropped to a dangerous whisper as she set her hand on her hip and pointed her sword at his chest. "You think you know me? You tortured me. You *almost* broke me. But even then, you knew one thing—there's *nothing* I won't do for the people I love."

Her voice cracked, but she didn't waver.

"Calla Lily is responsible for so many deaths. Yuki. Thalira. She cut Rhielle's throat, didn't she? She threatened Vad. My grandfather. She helped you kill King Merrick." Her blade trembled, not with fear but with restraint. "She's a monster. And I'll end her myself."

Desire grew deep within me, but I fought it off. I'd take care of that problem later. Right now, Briar didn't need saving. She *was* the reckoning.

Colm's throat bobbed. A breath caught in his chest. "You can't kill her. She's only in this because she *loves* me."

Briar's jaw clenched. "Then she can die with you."

His mask cracked. An angry hiss tore from his throat. "You fecking *brat*—"

Briar grabbed him by the collar and yanked him forward. "Tell us *now*—"

A thunderous *boom* cut through her words, shaking the observatory door in its frame.

My blood turned to ice, and I spun, sword raised.

"Colm!" Calla Lily's voice rang out, high and shrill. "I saw the light shift! Are you all right?"

Thalen blinked. "Well... that's bad timing."

Colm stiffened beneath Briar's grip. The fear in his face vanished, replaced by a slow, triumphant smile. "Oh, *well played*, Briar. You almost had me. I'm impressed." He tilted his head mockingly. "What a vindictive little bitch you've become."

Briar paled. Her lips mashed into a tight line.

I struck him hard across the face with the back of my hand. "*Back to the passage!* Now!"

Another crash splintered the thick wood of the door. They were using something heavy. Probably one of the axes we'd seen in the armory. Based on the speed, two were chopping at once.

"Go!" I pushed Briar toward the hidden door.

Veralt grabbed a chair and hurled it toward the entrance.

The frame cracked as it slammed against the wood, buying us a second at best.

"You're too late," Colm choked out, laughing through bloodied teeth. "You've *lost*, Vad! Hurry, Calla Lily! The former king is here!"

Briar snarled, and her gaze flicked to the door, then back to Colm. Her sword trembled in her grip.

"Come on, Chaos!" Thalen yelled, already at the table. He ripped an oil lamp from its wall sconce, securing the casing so it could be carried.

I grabbed Briar's arm. She didn't resist as I dragged her toward the hidden entrance. We'd been *so* close.

Veralt vanished into the tunnel, Thalen right behind him. Briar darted in after, her hair whipping behind her. The main door to the observatory burst open with a final, bone-shaking crash.

"Colm!" Calla Lily's voice rang out. "Hold on. I'm here!" Her gaze snapped to me then, and she shouted, "Guards, get them!"

I turned just long enough to see her rush in first with a dagger already in her hand and several guards at her back. She fell to her knees beside Colm and began slicing through his bonds.

I slammed the hidden door shut and yanked out the key. With one quick turn, I locked the mechanism. Something struck the door from the other side and shattered.

Thalen was halfway down the passage with his lamp held high. Its glow cast long shadows and warped them against the narrow stone walls.

Briar pressed a hand to her temple, her voice raw. "We can't let them kill those children... all those people."

"He won't succeed." I forced certainty into every syllable and shoved my sword into its sheath. "We'll regroup. Stick to the plan. Hit them fast, hit them hard."

Veralt gave a sharp nod and turned toward the exit. "Then let's *move*."

But before we took more than a few steps, a deep grinding sound echoed through the stone.

The wall at the far end of the passage shifted, then *slammed* down like a guillotine.

Veralt bellowed and punched the door. "It's sealed! Feck—*we're trapped!*"

I locked in place, gripping my sword as Colm's laughter rang out from the other side of the door. We were trapped.

Chapter Twenty

My pulse thundered in my ears, syncing with the pounding on the other side of the wall. Heat crawled beneath my skin, the instinct to fight clawing its way to the surface even when there was nothing left to strike but stone.

Think.

There had to be a way out. There always was. The air thickened, smelling sour with smoke, sweat, and the sharp, metallic tang of fear.

"Open the door, Vad," Colm said, his tone muffled yet smug.

Calla Lily giggled, the sound high and manic. "It was so thoughtful of you to have that second door installed. Very helpful."

The lock clicked, and I jammed the key back in and twisted it hard. *Click.* The door was locked again. I kept my hand there twisted in place, not wanting to chance them unlocking it and coming through the door. "My key overrides the mechanism. I can do this all day."

"As can I," Colm sang back, amusement dripping from his voice. "It's not as if you can go anywhere. Might as well surrender now and save yourself from a slow death."

Four rubber tubes wriggled under the bottom of the door. My stomach dropped, knowing that they were the ones for poisonous gas. I stepped on them to block anything from getting in, but I knew it wouldn't stop everything if he released the gas.

"I've heard being unable to breathe is a big problem." Calla Lilly snorted.

Veralt slammed his shoulder into the stone wall at the far end of the tunnel. A frustrated roar tore from him. "Trapped like rats," he growled, breath labored. "I can't punch through this."

He backed up and rammed his shoulder into the stone again, but the wall didn't even flinch. Dust fell in a lazy waterfall.

Thalen held the lamp higher, his sharp eyes scanning the walls. "There's got to be a seam or... something. Come on, these places were built with *fail-safes.*" He paused, then dug into his pack and pulled out a knife with a thick, reinforced spine. "I'll try wedging it under the edge. If I can loosen the seam, maybe Veralt can lift it."

The metal scraped stone as he worked. Veralt stepped in beside him, gripping the edge with both hands and straining. His arms bulged, veins standing out beneath sweat-slick skin, but the door didn't move.

"This place was built to survive a siege," I muttered.

Briar's cinnamon-and-smoke scent cut through the choking tension and anchored me. She stood at the center of the tunnel, palm pressed flat against the sealed door. Her knuckles were white, her whole body trembling just slightly, like a wire stretched too tight. Her eyes locked on mine. *What are we going to do?*

Her voice was so distant in my thoughts now that she might as well have been on the other side of the door and on the far side of the room. *We'll figure something out.* I told her, forcing confidence I didn't feel.

I kept the key in the lock to keep Colm from deploying the locking mechanism again, but my thoughts were in turmoil.

Behind the wall, Colm's voice rang out again. "Oh, this is going to be so incredibly satisfying." His tone was soft, almost reverent. "To know that I'll have the privilege of slaying the father, the mother, the son, and the mate. Maybe even your sister, too, if we find her before the shadow beasts do."

A stillness fell over me. It wasn't calm or fear. It was something colder. "What did you just say?" My wings flared wide, slamming the stone walls on either side of the narrow corridor. Heat exploded down my spine like a lightning strike, and every muscle in my body went taut.

"You were involved in my father's death," I said through clenched teeth. "But my *mother's* too?"

A strangled breath escaped Briar. "He's trying to torment you. Don't believe anything he says."

On the other side of the wall, Calla Lily giggled. Colm's voice sounded elated as he said, "I'm fairly certain your ears still work, Vad. Yes, I killed your mother and father. Now I'm going to kill you, Briar, and Elara too."

"You bastard!" Briar lunged toward the wall, striking it with her palm.

"What did my mother have to do with this?" The rage inside me had turned *glacial.* "You were planning this for that long? Since before my father's death?"

"Of course we were planning before your father's death." Colm scoffed. "You think revolutions happen overnight? It takes years. Decades. Your mother got in the way and influenced your father to do the same. Idealists are always the first to bleed."

Briar's eyes were wide with shock. "Vad, think about it. Why would he be telling you this now?"

She was right. It had to be a stall tactic...which meant he

probably had guards coming to the other side of the stone door. "Fecking void! We have to find a way out of here," I whispered, hoping that Colm couldn't hear.

"We're working as hard as we can," Thalen murmured as he chipped away at the stone next to Veralt.

If Colm was willing to talk, I would let him. Mother's death had never made sense to me. "My father never employed you. You were never a part of this court."

A thin, delighted laugh rasped through the wood. "I trained interrogators and performed *demonstrations* to remind rulers what happens when they grow soft. Your mother called my methods 'barbaric' and said they produced false confessions." He scoffed, a brittle sound crackling with hatred.

"I *swear,*" I snarled, voice low and shaking, "when we get out of this, I will tear him apart with my bare hands, with or without magic." And I would enjoy every second. The metal of the key warmed under my touch as I kept it turned.

Colm continued, not seeming to have heard me. "One opinion from a beloved queen, and suddenly other kingdoms found it *fashionable* to agree. Rulers who once welcomed me began shutting their doors. The Aureline saw me as a liability, and I had to claw my way back to relevance."

He struck his fist against the stone. "So I adapted. Because, unlike your mother, I understood the truth. Fear is the strongest weapon a crown can wield, but she made them believe they didn't need weapons. That they could be *good* and still be obeyed. Self-righteous little saint. Thanks to her, I nearly lost everything."

My head jerked back. He was worse than I'd ever expected. He truly had planned this for decades.

Briar scurried to the other door and began hacking at it with her sword.

"It took years to regain footing. Years of reminding the

weak that the world does not spare them just because they wish it to. But your parents doomed themselves. They were too beloved and too foolish. That kind of legacy had to be broken. Permanently. And now I see it in you."

The dull thuds of Veralt, Thalen, and Briar smashing stone sounded like a battle cry. I searched for anything they might have overlooked that we could use to get out.

"Yes." Colm exhaled. "It took planning, but your precious mother offered me the perfect opportunity. The Crimson Wanderer, that rare comet she adored. She took you to that little overlook near the Umbral Range, so trusting and happy to make a memory with her sweet boy while your father was away." He laughed softly. "She had wards, guards, and spells, but none of them protected her."

Briar moved back to my side and threaded her fingers through mine. "Don't listen to him. He's trying to get inside your head. It's what he does, and he enjoys it."

I leaned into her instinctively, but his words pulled me in. I remembered the smells of pine needles and damp moss, and the crackle of distant thunder. A chill of mist coiled around us, and Mother laughed.

"I couldn't decide which of you I wanted to kill first. But killing you both would have been too...sudden. There is *so much more power* in grief than there is in death."

Something inside me twisted.

"Then you wandered off to find those button mushrooms for your sister. Such a sweet gesture that cost you dearly. Was it your idea, or hers?"

I didn't move. "Mine." It had been my idea. Elara had wanted to come with us, but she had been ill. It was the first time she'd shown symptoms of the illness that had devastated her, though we hadn't known that yet. Mother had promised to do something special with just her later, and when I'd seen the mushrooms, I'd wanted to bring some to her.

Briar sucked in a breath beside me, as if my pain had bled through the rift between us. She placed her hands on both sides of my face and said, "Do not react. Don't let him get inside your head like that." She glanced back at Thalen and Veralt.

"I gave her a choice. Herself, or you. And she chose by sending you away. You were old enough to notice something was wrong. Old enough not to obey her without question. You loved her, didn't you?" Colm's voice softened mockingly. "So why didn't you *save* her?"

The thrust landed with surgical cruelty.

"How did you miss it, little prince? Why did you not care enough to stay?"

The metallic taste of blood filled my mouth, and my breaths shortened. I focused on Briar's presence and touch, but I couldn't kick out the words. "There were no outsiders." That was the part that never made sense to me, but everyone had insisted it was true.

"Well, I can't tell you all my secrets, and I never will. I just want you to know that her death was your fault. Just like Briar's and Elara's will be."

He paused, letting the silence dig in.

"She died so much faster than I intended. The venom on that blade was supposed to cause a slow, painful death, and my skills tortured her without leaving marks initially. When I realized how fast she was fading, I plunged the dagger into her back to finish the job. But it was satisfying to kill your father with the same blade and a perfected version of that venom. I'll plunge it into your heart as well. If I'm feeling merciful, I'll make it swift. We both know you're out of options, but I'm going to give you the same choice I gave your mother, Vad."

Briar shook her head and tugged on my arm. "Don't listen to him, Vad. He's trying to make you give up."

But he was right. When the guards got here and the door opened, we'd be cut off from retreat, and Colm wouldn't hesitate to kill Briar. I had to protect her. I'd failed to protect my mother, and I'd failed to protect Briar several times already. "And what is this choice exactly, Colm?"

Briar shook her head, staring up at me with wide, pleading eyes. "Whatever you're thinking. Don't. We're going to get out of here together."

Colm paused a breath longer. Something light and sharp scraped the door again as if tracing a pattern. "You surrender willingly and allow yourself to be bound, and I will open the second door and let your beloved and your friends run free. Or we will break the door down and capture you, or fill the room with poison, killing you all. I'm not sure which I prefer. I swear to you that, if we do break down the door, I will cut Briar to pieces in front of you. I will skin her alive and take her apart, muscle by muscle."

I curled my hand, the claws biting into my flesh. "Do you swear that, if you let Briar go, you won't harm her?" He would lie. Of course he would, but I had to ask.

"Nothing's working." Veralt panted while Thalen lunged at the door with his shoulder.

"Of course I swear it. I already vowed it." That low, cold laugh sliced through me. We both knew that no magic held him to that vow. "And because I'm feeling generous, I'll give you thirty seconds to decide."

"No, it's a trap," Briar hissed. She tugged on my arm. "Don't give up, Vad. Don't listen to him. This isn't your fault. We will figure something else out!"

Her desperation cut me, but I hugged her close. Our bond was so weak; I couldn't even feel her anymore. Even if part of her wolf magic still worked, we all smelled of that vinegar scent. She couldn't tell if I was lying, but I chose my words with care as I whispered in her ear. "Get ready to run. I'm going to play him. But I need you by the other door so I can get through as fast as I can."

She trembled in my arms but nodded. Her arms clutched me tightly, and I breathed her in, closing my eyes and savoring this moment... the last time I would ever hold her. I didn't dare kiss her, or she might guess what I was going to do.

Veralt and Thalen had stopped beating on the door. Veralt stood with his arms crossed over his broad chest. Thalen still held the lamp in one hand, his bandaged wings drooping. As soon as I pressed Briar forward and she started running down the tunnel, I looked at Thalen. His amber eyes dimmed, but he squared his shoulders.

I mouthed at him *Take care of her* as she ran past him to the stone door. She was between him and Veralt now as she spun back to face me.

I placed my hand once more on the key still in the lock. "I'll surrender on three. You open the second door, and I'll open this one."

"You're so like your mother," Colm said, scorn dripping from his voice. "Very well. One.... Two.... *Three*."

The stone door ground up as the mechanism sprang to life, and I unlocked the door, pulled out the keys, tossed them to Thalen, and then pushed the door open.

The door slid open, revealing Colm standing with Calla Lily at his side. Guards flanked them, swords and crossbows at the ready. Behind me, Briar screamed, and I stepped across the threshold.

Briar

The scream burst from me like a storm, so sharp and ragged it tore at the back of my throat. My body jolted forward, instincts shredding logic to pieces.

"Vad!"

I had to get to him. I had to stop him! He'd lied to me!

He stepped over the threshold and into the light as gloved hands seized him roughly.

I launched myself forward with a desperate snarl. "Vad, no! We do this together!"

Thalen's arms closed around my waist as my body hit his like a battering ram, but he held tight. "No, Chaos. Come on! We've got to go."

I bucked, kicked, screamed. My vision blurred with rage and terror, the hallway tilting as I slid sideways. I clawed at Thalen, not caring that he was my friend. I'd rip the world apart to reach Vad.

"*Let me go*!" I demanded.

"Briar, stop!" Thalen's voice was ragged, strained with effort and something close to grief. He dragged me back with both arms banded around me. Guards appeared in the doorway, swords raised, ready for a fight. They started down the narrow staircase into the corridor.

"Come on, Trouble." Veralt swept me into his arms as Thalen released me and snatched up the lamp. My feet left the ground as I kicked and struggled.

I screamed again, rage blooming so violently in my chest it nearly choked me. I struck Veralt with my elbow, knees, and fists. I lashed out, bit, and clawed with everything I had. I'd rip those guards' throats out! But we were already racing through the passage.

I twisted in Veralt's arms, kicking hard enough that my shins screamed in protest. My nails scraped the stone wall, but it was no use. Veralt only grunted when I bit him.

Another howl of rage and grief rose in my throat, wild and wounded and primal. My body arched, spine bowing. I had to get to Vad.

I had to get to my mate.

The walls and ceiling could fall around me, and I'd still fight. "Put me *down*!" I thrashed in Veralt's hold, spitting and clawing. "I'll kill you if you don't put me down!" I tugged at the link, but Vad felt so far away; it was as if he barely existed. We were hardly connected. A yawning hollowness expanded in my chest.

Thalen ran in front of us, holding the lamp and then gesturing toward a branching path on the right. He glanced over his shoulder, his mouth pinching. "Chaos, we've got to lose them, or else they're gonna track us all the way back."

"I'll fight them. I'll fight them all!" I twisted again, finally breaking an arm free. I slammed my fist into Veralt's chest, once, twice, the heel of my palm bruising. I didn't stop until his grip shifted, and he crushed me tight, still running.

"Stop." He growled. "We can't help him if we're dead."

"I don't care," I spat, voice shaking. "Let me go. I'll tear them apart myself—I'll—"

Veralt growled as he adjusted his grip on me. "We've got to keep her quiet, or she's gonna draw the guards right to us."

Thalen pointed to a passage on our left. The ground angled upward now. "Briar, we'll rescue him, I swear. But I promised him I was going to get you out of here. Remember what you said to the girls before? We don't have to just survive. We have to win."

A horrible, searing pain cut into me. I went rigid, suddenly unable to breathe.

What was that?

Vad.

Our bond had snapped.

My words dissolved as I stared at Thalen, my vision blurring. Ice spread through my body. I couldn't feel him. He was gone. Just...gone.

"You're gonna be all right." Thalen squeezed my shoulder,

his voice tense. "I promise, Chaos. We're going to figure this out together." Grief twisted his expression as well.

Everything in me went numb, my body trembling. My wolf was gone, and my keen sight had vanished. Despair and terror swallowed me.

My pack links were gone, just like the night my entire pack had been slaughtered. The hollowness consumed everything.

"She's not looking so good," Veralt said, his voice sounding far away.

"What?" Alarm spiked in Thalen's voice. "Is she hurt?

The lamp's golden glow swung over my face, but it was dull now. "We don't have much time," Veralt said, his voice heavy.

A droning sound filled my ears. My head lolled against Veralt's arm.

"Briar?" Thalen leaned over me, his hand against my cheek and feeling for my pulse. "Briar, you have to..."

Sounds of metal hit me just as everything went dark.

CHAPTER TWENTY-ONE

Numbness engulfed me, even in sleep. It clung to me like wet wool, heavy and choking, weaving itself into my bones, threading grief into every breath. I drowned in the darkness, fighting to wake up.

The harder I fought, the more the air changed. It became too thin and sharp, circling around me.

Coldness gripped my ankles, and I looked down to find mist curled around them. Darkness surrounded me above and below. I realized I was dreaming, but if it somehow led me to Vad, I didn't give a damn.

As the cold seeped into my skin in slow, pulsing waves, the darkness transformed. The sky above became the color of ash, and the palace appeared in a valley, looming ahead, cracked and hunched like a beast nursing old wounds. I'd never seen the castle from the outside, but I recognized it anyway.

In the night sky above, a red-tailed comet crept across the horizon. Then the ground shook underneath my feet.

The palace shook too, dust rising so thick it blocked out the moon and comet. I glanced to the left and saw a thick mass of hawthorns and oaks, but they weren't swaying, and the mountains to my right weren't shaking. The concentration of the violent tremors centered under the palace. It groaned, then collapsed inward, stone and shadow folding like wet paper.

My heart lurched.

What the fuck was going on?

I'd hoped this dream would show me saving Vad, but instead it showed that we were all going to fail. I had to wake up from this nightmare. I pinched myself hard, but instead of waking up, I could only watch as silver light glowed from within the destruction.

Warmth bloomed and pulled in my chest, as if the silver light were tugging at me. It brightened like the north star and pulsed like a beacon. Out of the rubble emerged a silver stag like the one from the Ceremonial Hall.

Its antlers stretched skyward, catching light from no visible source. Power shimmered in the air around it, both wrong and beautiful. Blood streamed from the broken walls and shattered stones all around it, thick and dark, dripping down columns like rain turned red.

Inside me, a tendril of fear mixed with a clawing urge to fight and overcome.

A low growl rumbled behind me. I spun, my heart pounding against my ribs, to find a shadow wolf stepping into view. Its shadowy fur rippled in the wind, and its crimson eyes burned bright.

I glanced around for a weapon, but the trees were too far away to offer any branches, and the mountains would slow me down. It could easily catch me.

But it wasn't looking at me. Its eyes were locked on the stag.

It threw back its head and howled. Not a sound of anger or fear, but rather one of wanting to be noticed.

The stag lifted its chin and barked, followed by three coughs. Then it repeated the same pattern over and over.

The sound wrenched something deep inside me, like strings being yanked taut. A sharp ache pressed behind my eyes.

The ground trembled again, and more guardians emerged.

The brown bear I'd seen in the first trial lumbered from the trees, each pawfall heavy against fractured stone. The crimson dragon descended from the sky, wings stretched wide, firelight gleaming along its scaled back. The golden eagle screamed and dove, talons bared. From the blood-soaked ruins, the sea serpent rose, coils slicing through water with rippling grace.

They charged and collided with one another, and the crack of sound seemed to shatter the air. Light burst around them in a violent, blinding explosion. The night sky erupted with new stars, twinkling bright and bold.

Grief surged through me so suddenly that it knocked the breath from my lungs. My knees struck the ground. I pressed one palm to the earth, gasping, pain sitting like a blade beneath my ribs.

A broken raw sound escaped me, and I pressed the heel of my other hand to my chest, as if I could shove the feeling back down.

But I couldn't. The ache twisted, sharp and impossible to deny. I bent forward, curling around it.

Vad.

His absence slammed into me, and the pain was somehow even worse than when my pack had been slaughtered. Images flashed into my mind... the way he'd looked at me, protected me, the love that had made him lie to me in order to save me. He'd risked his life so that I might breathe longer.

I couldn't go on without him. I didn't want to. I would rather die by his side. My heart shattered into millions of pieces, the pain so intense I couldn't breathe.

"Briar!" a familiar voice whispered in my head.

But I ignored it, curling my body into the ground. My

fingers dug into the soil as if I could become one with it. I wasn't sure what was beyond this life, but if there was a chance I could be with Vad somewhere else, I'd willingly die to be there with him.

"Dammit, Briar! Don't make me do this," the voice called again, a little louder.

My body shook like the ground was trembling again. I wanted it to open up and swallow me whole. Anything to get away from the crushing agony.

"If you don't wake up, I'm going to have to do something." This time, the voice sank in.

Ember? No! My sister couldn't be here. She'd die. After everything she'd done to protect me, the last thing I wanted was to lose her on top of Vad. I flinched away from the voice and whimpered, "Go away. Don't come here. I need you to be safe."

Pure terror strangled me as my heart disintegrated. This had to be Colm's doing. Had he found a way to get into my mind again? "You bastard! Stay away. You've done enough!" My body shook hard, jarring my bones. "You took everything from me."

Something hard slapped my face, jolting me awake.

"You gotta pull yourself out of this!" Ember screamed, her emerald eyes glistening with tears as she raised her hand to smack me again.

"Babe! Chill." Ryker reached across me, catching Ember's hand. "She's awake." The golden flecks in his brown eyes stood out from his alarm.

I blinked as shock filtered through me. Ember and Ryker were *here*. This couldn't be happening. Maybe I hadn't woken from the nightmare after all. "No... no... this has to be a bad dream."

Tears trailed down Ember's face. "You don't want to see me?"

My head spun, but then the stone pressed against my back, cold and unforgiving, and my fingers clutched at rough wool—a heavy blue blanket tangled around my legs. The air smelled damp and stale, tinged with something earthy and old. The soft hum of conversation drifted to me.

I blinked, trying to orient myself. The dim light was coming from somewhere to my left, flickering and uncertain, and the vesting chamber came into view. Rhielle, Quen, and Myantha surrounded my head with Ember on one of my sides and Ryker on the other.

Reality crashed into me. My sister and Ryker were here, and the first thing I'd said to her since I'd been kidnapped had been cruel. "That's not what I meant. I just... It's dangerous here. I don't want you two to get sucked into the chaos. You have enough to fix back on Earth."

"Briar Sinclair! That's exactly why we're here." Ember narrowed her eyes and pointed a finger at me. Her darker copper hair fell over her shoulders. "Did you think I wouldn't find a way here once I knew you were in danger? What kind of sister do you think I am?"

For a moment, I felt like the Earth version of myself, wanting to support my sister. "The best kind." I smiled tenderly.

Somewhere across the room, Kaylen snorted. "Good to know smacking you in the face and shaking you like a doll is what you consider the best way to treat you. I'll make a note."

"You even think about harming her, and I will rip out your throat!" Ember jumped to her feet and bared her teeth.

"I suspect that Ember and Ryker can turn into the strange shadow beast like Briar can, so I'd be careful." Rhielle scowled.

Hoping to calm things down, I pushed myself up into a seated position. The world tilted, and I pressed one hand against my temple and the other to my cheek, which still stung. My body felt heavy, disconnected, like I was moving through water.

I noted the rest of the group clustered near the entrance to the vesting chamber. Elara was gesturing with one hand while the other rested against her side.

Everyone was here and safe... except Vad. A sob broke through before I could tamp it down.

Briar didn't hesitate, kneeling on the ground and pulling me into her arms. I buried my face in her shoulder, my fingers curling into her shirt. Her warmth and her scent of vanilla and home anchored me.

"Breathe." Her hand stroked my back. "I've got you. I'm here."

Another sob tore from my throat, raw and broken, and my tears soaked her shoulder. Everything I'd been holding back came flooding out at once.

"He's gone," I choked out. "Ember, he's—Colm took him, and I couldn't—I couldn't stop it. I tried, I tried so hard, but—"

"I know." Her voice was steady, gentle, her hand pressed against the back of my head. "Thalen told us everything. I've been talking with your friends. You've been through hell, and I'm so sorry."

"We're going to help you take care of everything." Ryker patted my back. "Those bastards will pay for hurting you."

I pulled back and smiled at my brother-in-law, the alpha of our pack. He stayed in control even when things were difficult.

Someone else stepped from the shadows, followed by the scent of lilacs, roses, and wet soil. Many-Greats observed me from a few feet away, his hands folded like he wasn't certain what to do. His golden-brown skin seemed paler than usual, but his liquid-gold eyes glowed bright and sharp. "I hope you'll forgive my disappearance. And the fact that, yet again, I have returned to an area where you are sleeping."

"You could have told us you were going." I gestured him

over and hugged him, and then whispered into his ear, "You've got to stop disappearing on me."

He huffed a quiet laugh, his tone stern even as his gaze softened. "All I've ever wanted is for my granddaughters to be safe. I promised Ember that, if your life was threatened, I'd inform her, and I had to follow through on my word. I didn't want to argue with you about bringing them back here. I do apologize that it took so long—finding a portal with lingering residual magic and then stabilizing it long enough to function was no small feat."

"It nearly caused a riot when Gage, Kendric, and Xavier realized they couldn't join us because there wasn't enough magic." Ryker smiled. "Although I have to admit, this may be the most elaborate distraction anyone's ever come up with to avoid talking about fae magic."

A faint smile tugged at my lips. It felt like lifetimes had passed since I'd gotten the butterfly tattoo. Ember had wanted to talk about it right away, but I'd put her off. Then Many-Greats had tried to whisk me away before the guards could kidnap me, but they'd grabbed me and brought me to the bridal competition. As frightened and confused as I'd been that night, none of it compared to now.

Elara squatted by Ember. "Why don't we all gather in our makeshift sitting area to discuss our plans? We don't have much time."

"Sounds good." I took a deep breath and stood.

Ember moved to help me, but I shook my head. "Thanks, but I'm fine."

She bit her bottom lip like she was taken aback, but I gave her a tender smile. If I had to lead without Vad, I couldn't show weakness. He deserved that from me.

Rhielle and Quen flanked me, and Myantha took the spot next to Thalen.

"We're going to get him back." Rhielle squeezed my arm. "We won't let anything happen to him."

Quen snarled. "I'm going to enjoy killing each one of these traitors and calling them cowards and pyre pots!"

I forced a smile, though I knew their words were merely for comfort. I couldn't feel Vad anymore, but I couldn't feel Ember or Ryker either, so I was trying to hold on to hope that he wasn't dead.

I chose a crate in the center of the seating area. Ember took the spot next to me, and Ryker crouched on her other side. Many-Greats sat opposite me, his expression severe but his gaze unusually gentle.

Quen sat cross-legged on a nearby crate, her crimson eyes looking at me with concern before she returned to murmuring with Elias. Vyraetos knelt beside her, holding fresh bandages and salve, gently motioning toward her wing.

Rhielle stood with her arms folded tight, though her usual glare had dulled to quiet observation. Veralt rubbed her shoulders, jaw tight and brow furrowed. Myantha hovered protectively near Thalen, who stood rigid and on high alert.

Elara sat on the other side of me with Silus taking his usual spot at her side. Siray had dozed off upright, arms folded over her chest like she was on guard even in sleep. Kaylen sat against the stone wall, her posture stiff and her knuckles pale as her hands rested on her knees.

It should've comforted me to see them all alive, to know we'd survived for now, but that comfort couldn't reach past the missing presence that ripped out my heart.

I focused on the first thing I wanted to address. "I can't feel my wolf at all. Can you two still sense me?"

"Not really." Ember shook her head, her hands on her waist. "Your link is there, but so faint and cold it's almost nonexistent. That's one reason I had to see you."

"I don't understand what happened to my wolf." I fought back tears. If I had my wolf, maybe we could've gotten out of the trap, and Vad would be here with me now.

Elara stood and quickly walked toward the supplies.

"I have no answers." Many-Greats shook his head. "Your wolf shouldn't have been impacted by the loss of fae magic, since it's from Earth."

I bowed my head, struggling to wrap my mind around all these things. All that genuinely mattered to me right now was Vad. If he was still alive, every second counted to get to him.

A gentle hand pressed against my shoulder. I looked up to see Elara had come up behind Ember and me. She knelt and offered me a small bowl of dried fruit and nuts. Tears had stained her face, and she looked as if she had aged years. "You should eat."

Here I was, being selfish. Of course, Elara was impacted by the loss of Vad as well, and here she was, taking care of me. I turned and hugged her, and my arms wrapped all the way around her narrow frame. I could feel the bones in her back and shoulders.

Neither of us spoke. The sadness between us was too raw for words. She was my sister, too, though we weren't blood. Ember knew what to say to soothe me and remind me that I wasn't alone, but Elara understood far better what made Vad special, and I knew we would both give all we had to get him back and stop Colm.

We pulled apart, both wiping at our eyes. I cleared my throat and took the bowl from her hands, nodding in thanks, even though I wasn't sure I could eat. My stomach felt like a hollowed-out cavern, but not from hunger.

Elara took her seat again with a tear running down her cheek.

"You should definitely eat, Briar," Ember said. "And then,

when you're feeling up to it, we're going to leave. Many-Greats thinks he can get us through the portal one more time—"

"No." The word cracked through the air, firm and final, and more like a growl.

Ryker blinked in surprise. Ember lifted her brows, clearly not expecting the resistance.

"I'm not leaving Vad, or any of my family and friends here."

Ember brushed her hair behind her ear. "Briar, they told us what you've been through, and it sounds like hell."

"So what?" She always tried to protect me, but she couldn't anymore. Everything had changed. "I'm—"

Eyes glowing, Ember glanced at Ryker.

Oh *hell* no. She'd better not try to get him to alpha-will me home. "Don't you dare," I seethed. "I won't be forced to go back to Earth."

A low voice cut through the conversation. "You're not taking her anywhere." Thalen now stood near the shadows behind the crates, eyes bloodshot but hard. "Not after everything she's done for us. She nearly died here, yes, and now that it's convenient, you think you can just *whisk her away*?"

"Don't you dare talk to my mate like that." Ryker leaped to his feet.

Touching his arm, Ember tilted her head. "It's not about convenience. She's my sister, and—"

"She's our *queen*." Thalen's voice cracked like stone splitting. "She's the reason most of us are still alive, and I made a promise to my king and best friend that I would protect her. If she wishes to remain here, then I will fight to keep her here."

"She is part of our pack." Ryker clenched his hands.

Thalen came and stood right in front of me and glared at Ryker and Ember. "She *chose* Vad and everyone here. This is her battle too, and we need her."

"Even if you try to alpha-will me, it won't work." I needed

her to understand, and I realized, no one here besides Vad and me understood what we were to each other. "I can't feel my wolf, but there's something even more important than that."

"And what is that?" Ember pursed her lips, trying to fight back her frustration with me.

"He's my mate," I said sharply. "I won't abandon him. What would you do if it was Ryker?"

Ember inhaled and looked away, shoulders stiffening. For a moment, she didn't respond.

Ryker's hands loosened. "Honey, she's right. I can't even try to do that to her."

Many-Greats let out a weary sigh. "As I've said before, Briar is every bit as stubborn as you are, Ember. Now do you understand why dragging her back wasn't an option?"

I squeezed Ember's hand. "I love you. I love all of you. And I miss Earth more than I can explain. But this... this is my home now. Vad is my family. And if there's any chance of getting him back, I have to take it."

Ember's expression cracked, her eyes shining. "Briar, I... I didn't know. I mean, I *knew* he was important, but not—"

"No one does," I said gently. "Not really. They don't have fated mates here."

"What's a fated mate?" Elara placed her hands in her lap.

"Some people call them soulmates." I smiled sadly as a fresh wave of pain crested inside me. "It's when your souls merge and you can talk to each other through your mind, and feel your partner's emotions. They're the piece of you that was missing, and when you find them, you're both whole."

Myantha exhaled. "That's so beautiful."

Thalen looked at her and smiled.

Even though I hated ruining their moment, my priority was Vad. "I'd rather die than leave him here. And I won't abandon our kingdom while Colm tears it apart."

Ember met my gaze again, and this time, it was with understanding. "You're right. I would do the same. No matter what anyone said. So... I'm staying too."

"And of course that means I am too. You're my sister too, and we don't abandon our pack." Ryker nodded, his eyes burning with determination.

Tears pricked my eyes again, but this time, they didn't fall. "I love you both. But let's get the plan together." I swallowed hard, forcing breath into lungs that still felt half-caved in. The hollowness inside me pulled like an undertow, but I pushed through it and rose to my feet. I stepped into the center of everyone.

"I don't know how long I was asleep." No matter the answer, it was too long. Every second that we didn't save Vad, the closer he was to death, if he hadn't already been k— I stopped myself, unable to consider the option. "Do we know anything about Vad? How much time before the coronation?"

Elara gestured toward the exit to the palace corridors. "Finbar sent word. It's confirmed that, as of now, Vad is alive and being held in the Ceremonial Hall."

"Do we know if he's injured or..." Myantha trailed off.

"He's with Colm." Anger roiled through me. "He will have injuries."

Siray frowned, concern flashing in her dark eyes. "Do you think he's died since the last update?"

Rhielle shot her a glare. "Don't."

The question struck like a dagger. Memories of our last moment together and the finality of the snapped tether of our bond lurked beneath my skin like a wound unstitched. I forced myself to stand straighter. "No." My voice was steady. "He's alive. And we *are* going to get him back."

Yes," Elara said. "There are numerous guards and traps set around the main entrance to the hall. They've restored the servant access points and the bride and groom's doors on either side of the dais. Those are made of lighter wood than the older doors, and they have basic locks with simple tumblers. Finbar's man left us with lockpicks. But he warned that Colm is anticipating an attack on the Ceremonial Hall."

"Ryker and I can pick locks," Ember said, nudging Ryker with her elbow. "He showed me how, and I've been practicing."

"So can I." Thalen lifted a hand.

"You didn't tell Finbar which route we're taking, right?" My stomach twisted, bile souring in the back of my throat. Though I'd been able to test the individuals present at Finbar's outpost for loyalty, it hadn't been even half of his forces. Someone was feeding Finbar information, and it would be all too easy for them to be a traitor. I was glad Vad had insisted that only someone I had vetted be allowed to bring us supplies.

"No." Elara's mouth tightened, and she crossed her arms. "It didn't seem wise. Vad didn't tell him everything either. It's not that I distrust Finbar personally, but this is war. And war breeds betrayal."

It did. I set my hands on my hips, grounding myself. "We have a tough job ahead of us, but we're going to give it our all. We also need to release the prisoners and get them to safety. If Colm's forces are focused around the Ceremonial Hall and dealing with Captain Finbar's men, then maybe the other exits will be more accessible, and we can get people out."

Silus rubbed the back of his neck. "It's possible, but it's risky."

"That's the point," Quen muttered under her breath. "Everything worth doing is."

"While we enter the prison, someone can scout ahead to see if the exits are open or easy to break through," Elara suggested. "The rest of us will focus on rescuing the prisoners. It'll take a while to get them out."

Thalen held up a small ring of keys. "Vad gave me these." He tossed them to Elara. "They'll open the cells and might shave off some time, but there are still a lot of prisoners to move."

My skull throbbed, and the ache in my chest pulsed harder than before. I wanted to say *We'll get them all*, but I couldn't lie that much, even to myself. We'd do everything we could, but my main focus was saving the man I loved with everything in me.

We broke down the rest of the plan.

If the palace exits were sealed or swarmed, the most vulnerable prisoners—the children, the elderly, and the wounded—would be brought here to the vesting chamber. It was large enough to shelter them while the rest held the line. The adults would be stationed just outside in the cavern, close enough to the vesting chamber to have some defenses, even if it wasn't much, far enough to avoid being trapped with the gas in the prisons.

Elara, Silus, and Ryker would lead the prison rescue team, with Silus scouting once they were closer. Finbar's information gave them some good details on what to expect. Ryker would keep mental contact with Ember to time everything perfectly. Quen, Vyraetos, Many-Greats, Siray, and Elias would accompany them and explain to the kings and queens what had happened and gain their support. When we reclaimed the Ceremonial Hall, we'd need witnesses for proof of Colm's and his allies' treachery.

The rest of us would breach the Ceremonial Hall directly. Thalen, Veralt, and Rhielle would approach from the bride's side. Kaylen, much to her annoyance, would be tied up and staged in a smaller waiting room off that corridor. Myantha would stay there to guard her, while the others continued toward the dais and would bring Kaylen in if we got that desperate for help.

Ember and I would take the groom's side.

Finbar's men would attack after Colm finished his speech but before he could crown himself king, so long as it didn't look like he was going to execute Vad first. While that attack was happening, both my group and Thalen's would rush the dais, free Vad, and then get him to safety and treatment.

It was a strategic plan, but no plan ever went perfectly. And Colm had proved time and again that he didn't fight fair.

Still, it was our best shot.

I rose, forcing strength into my spine. "All right. Let's move."

My group and Thalen's traveled together until we reached the split in the tunnels. The air grew colder as we advanced, the scent of blood and iron thickening with every step.

Thalen pulled me aside just before we parted ways. "At the hallway past the statues, turn right after the broken alcove. Groom's entrance is the second arch. Repeat it."

And I did twice, knowing that we couldn't afford to get lost.

He nodded. "Good. See you at the dais." He turned and disappeared into the shadows with Rhielle, Veralt, and Myantha close behind. Myantha cast one last look over her shoulder before following.

Ember and I continued down the right passage. The corridor narrowed, and the air smelled of rust and rot. Bile rose in my throat.

Ember's nostrils flared. "It reeks," she whispered grimly.

"What do you smell?" I asked.

"Aside from a lot of corpses, it smells like smoky wolves." Ember looked behind us. Her breath hissed through her teeth.

"Shadow wolves. They're all over the place." I cradled a lamp in my right hand. Despite its heat, it couldn't warm me. "They're like our wolves but bigger, with very strong jaws, and their fur looks like it's made of smoke."

We moved quickly, making the necessary turns into narrow passages lined with blood-soaked rugs and torn paintings. Not long ago, Vad and I had been racing through here with our friends, desperate to escape. My heart clenched.

Soon. You'll be with him again soon.

But the closer we got to the Ceremonial Hall, the more my skin prickled.

We reached the final hallway leading to the groom's preparation room. The outer door had been ripped off, its hinges twisted and mangled. Scraps of artwork and broken frames had been shoved to the sides. Inside, the room was just as we'd left it, except the barricade had been pushed over and the furniture smashed and splintered, like someone had torn through it in a rage. An uncomfortable twinge passed through me, hinting that this access point appeared to only be guarded by the lone door. There would definitely be guards in the Ceremonial Hall around the dais. Was it possible that Colm had decided to concentrate his forces at the main entrance and then the access points Finbar intended to take? My stomach twisted.

Colm's voice filtered through the door, muffled but unmistakable.

Ember dropped to her knees and pulled her lockpicks from her boot. I pressed my ear to the door, tensing as I listened, one eye fixed on the doorway behind us.

Colm's voice sent prickles of dread down my spine. "The kings and queens of our realm have proven themselves unfaithful and incapable of leading. Why have multiple rulers when their interests so often conflict with one another? Multiple crowns only bring division."

Dread coiled in my stomach. The darkness beyond the lamp's soft halo felt suffocating.

Ember slid the pick and lever in, the golden lamplight making her copper hair glow like fire. She bit the tip of her tongue as she focused. The pick and lever clinked ever so faintly. "There," she whispered.

I seized the handle and opened the door.

The Ceremonial Hall had been cleared of debris, and in its place, a far more horrifying display had taken shape.

Knee-high blackwood shelves now lined the back wall near the twin thrones. Upon them sat dozens of severed heads of men and women, their faces frozen in agony, dried blood crusting the wood and marble. I spotted Ceana's pale face front and center, her vacant eyes wide open.

But not Vad's. I released a choked breath, even as Ember gasped softly beside me.

Where is he?

Surely Colm wouldn't waste the opportunity to make a spectacle of him.

Eight wingless helmeted guards stood behind Colm, each clad in full plate and holding spears, their attention locked forward. Colm wore long black and silver robes and had his silver hair bound back, as usual. Calla Lily stood beside him in a feathered, blush-pink gown, her hands folded demurely in her lap.

Between them, in the center of the dais, stood a fluted pedestal bearing two crowns. Not the ones Elara had hidden in the onyx cellar, but new ones formed by twisted silver vines adorned with dark gems.

"You can take this as one such example," Colm declared, his voice rising. "Prince Vad sought to manipulate the trials for personal gain. He chose a bride not appointed by Fate. He murdered his own father to seize his power. How fitting that we have now come here full circle."

His hand swept toward the base of the dais, toward a block of black stone positioned just below the stairs. My gaze followed...and I froze.

Vad.

He was shackled to the stone, his body forced into a kneeling position atop the cold slab. Iron cuffs bound his wrists and ankles, and his wings sagged behind him, one of them twisted at a wrong angle. Blood streaked his waxy skin, and his pale face was bruised, one eye swollen nearly shut.

A dagger was buried deep in his chest.

Blood was pooling underneath him in a dark, slowly spreading lake. His bared chest was covered in freshly bleeding lashes, and the hilt of the dagger jutted from the center, glistening obsidian beneath the ceremonial light.

His head hung forward, unmoving.

I couldn't breathe.

Chapter Twenty-Two

BRIAR

My feet locked in place, and my hands froze against the door frame. I couldn't draw a breath.

I knew that dagger.

It was the same one Colm had used to kill Vad's father and frame me for the murder. And now it was lodged in Vad's heart.

That must have been the horrible pain that had sliced straight through me and broken our sacred connection.

My fingers tightened around the door frame.

Colm's voice echoed through the Ceremonial Hall, ringing with false grandeur and venom. "This traitor prince—this *false* king—sought to destroy the unity of our realms by defying Fate herself. It is only fitting that he be executed here, before your eyes, as my bride and I take our rightful place."

I clenched my jaw, the world spinning. Where was Finbar and his fucking army?

Ember edged closer to me, her voice low and her hand tight over my arm. "I smell wolves."

I finally drew in a breath, slow and quiet, but all I caught was the scent of blood and death...until I glanced back and saw three sets of crimson eyes glowing from the far shadows in the doorway behind us.

Shadow wolves.

They crept silently into the groom's chamber, their massive bodies barely visible in the darkness. Behind them, more eyes appeared.

My mouth went dry. We were pinned, and there was still no sign of Thalen and Finbar.

Colm approached the dais, his robes trailing behind him, and stopped beside Vad. "When I remove this blade, I remove the curse that every single one of these kings and queens has placed upon our realm."

He turned to the nearest servant. "Bring me the ceremonial wine."

No. This couldn't be happening. I couldn't lose him, and especially not like this.

Ember leaned in, her voice a breath of panic. "We have to go. We can't fight off this many. Is there any other way out?"

I shook my head.

Colm was twenty feet away. The guards would see us and attack before we took more than a few steps, but Vad would bleed out the moment the blade was pulled. We didn't have time to delay, but getting caught right away wouldn't save him either.

I scanned the chamber for an answer. We wouldn't make it far if we ran, not with the guards and the shadow wolves both watching for threats. I bit my lip and looked toward the shelves near the thrones. They were tall enough, and the crowd's eyes were fixed on Colm and Calla Lily.

"We crawl toward the back and use the shelves and the thrones as cover. Then..." I stopped myself. I couldn't say the rest out loud, but I unsheathed my sword. Ember would object to me making a death run.

If I could get directly behind Colm, I could charge him and take him down with my own blade. Maybe the wolves would follow us and create a distraction, or maybe they'd rip us to pieces. I didn't give a fuck.

Ember nodded, her jaw set.

I slid to the ground, heart thundering, and began to move on all fours along the edge of the wall. Ember followed, quiet as a mouse. She remained in human form so we could communicate since I couldn't pack link with her anymore.

The low growl of a wolf reached my ears. I glanced back to find more than a dozen of them were halfway into the groom's chamber now. Most had glowing red eyes, but there were a few orange-eyed and yellow-eyed ones in the back. Their massive bodies moved forward on silent paws, smoke curling off their flanks like mist in the dark. One snapped its jaws with a sickening *clack* of bone meeting bone. Another growled low, the sound vibrating through the stone beneath us.

On the dais, a servant in dark gray robes stepped forward, head bowed, and presented a jeweled goblet to Colm.

The scent of spiced wine drifted through the chamber, tainted with something bitter.

Colm turned to face Calla Lily and said, "To the one person who has never faltered in the face of adversity. The one who has proven herself, time and again, worthy of queenship. The one who has never failed me and whom I'll never fail."

He brought the goblet to Calla Lily's lips, and she lifted her chin, eyes shining, and placed her hands around his, parting her lips to drink.

Ember and I crept forward, inch by agonizing inch, the cold stone seeping through my tunic. My elbows scraped the floor as I dragged myself along, ignoring the sting. The dread inside me pressed against my ribs like a stone slab, but I didn't stop.

Running would trigger the shadow wolves' predatory instincts. We couldn't draw their attention. We'd never reach Vad.

We made it to the open floor just in front of the dais, where we were barely hidden behind a low, decorative railing. Still about twenty feet from Colm and the opportunity to stab him to death.

Ember glanced over her shoulder and tensed.

I followed her gaze.

The shadow wolves were coming. Hunting us. The largest of them stepped from the groom's room into the Ceremonial Hall, head lowered, a low growl rolling up its throat, accompanied by the faint *click, click, click* of claws on stone.

The hairs on the back of my neck rose.

Metal slammed against metal, and shouts rang out, echoing through the hall. Startled gasps rippled through the assembled guests, and several surged to their feet. A woman in midnight blue screamed and clutched her companion's arm.

I flattened myself against the marble floor, bile rising in my throat.

Colm turned sharply toward the double doors. His smile tightened, no longer serene. "Honored guests, please," he said, lifting his voice above the rising noise. "Do not be alarmed. This... *disturbance* was anticipated. The odious Captain Finbar and his band of traitors have chosen this moment to reveal themselves. But rest assured, they will be dealt with swiftly and without mercy."

He looked over the crowd, smooth as ever. "We know each of Finbar's points of attack."

"You're so clever," Calla Lily purred, staring at him like he'd hung the stars and promised to make her a gift of them.

She lifted the goblet toward him. "To the one person who has never faltered in the face of adversity. The one who has proven himself, time and again, worthy of kingship. The one who has never failed me and whom I will never fail."

Colm smiled, placed his hands over hers, and drank.

My focus snapped back to Vad.

The dagger in his chest gleamed under the flickering light, a sick reminder of what Colm had already stolen from me. Ember and I crawled faster, using the chaos of the crashing doors and distant battle cries to our advantage. The cold stone bit into my palms with every drag forward, but I barely felt it over the pounding of my heart.

A soft *click* from across the dais made me pause. My gaze darted toward the bride's side door, where Thalen's silver-white head poked through. When he spotted us, relief softened his expression... until his gaze locked on something behind me. Horror twisted his face.

I whipped my head around to see that shadow wolves had moved onto the dais with their teeth bared and their hackles raised.

Something massive slammed into the Ceremonial Hall's main doors again, stone cracking and metal shrieking, followed by another *crash* of metal colliding with the door.

The wolves snapped their heads toward the noise like they'd been triggered. The yellow-eyed ones in the back began pacing and snarling, froth building at their jaws.

Then, as if some unheard command set them free, the wolves attacked. The one nearest to me raced forward.

I ripped my sword free of its sheath, muscles coiled to strike, but the wolf didn't slow. As I prepared to swing, it leapt clean over me and crashed into Colm full force. He staggered backward into Calla Lily, sending the goblet soaring from his hands. Blood-red wine arced through the air, splattering the dais like spilled blood.

Screams exploded from the audience, and panic rippled outward.

Guards shouted orders, and weapons were drawn. Shadow wolves tore through them with wild fury, jaws snapping, limbs thrashing, and snarls echoing off the marble walls.

Calla Lily shrieked as she tumbled backward with her gown tangling in her legs. Colm stumbled but didn't go down. With a snarl, he pulled an onyx-and-silver dagger from its sheath and drove it into the wolf's side.

Thalen, Veralt, and Rhielle burst through the bride's door, weapons flashing as they charged, cutting a path toward us through the chaos.

I bolted upright and ran to my mate.

"Vad!" My hands trembled as I cupped his face, then flew to the chains binding his wrists and ankles. Blood smeared my fingers.

He'd been beaten brutally. One eye was swollen shut, his lips were cracked, and cuts littered his throat and arms.

His eyes fluttered open with a hazy glaze. "Briar?" His voice was barely a rasp, wet and broken.

"I'm here," I choked, brushing blood from his cheek. "I'm right here."

His right hand twitched in its bonds, trying to reach for me. "You shouldn't be here, beloved. Get out while you can."

"No." My voice broke. "I'm not leaving you." My gaze dropped to the dagger still embedded in his chest.

The same blade that had killed his father.

My breath caught, and my chest locked. What if pulling it out finished him? "It's going to be okay. You're going to be fine."

Vad gave me a half-laugh, half-wince. "We need to talk about what *fine* means."

Tears slid down my cheeks. "You live through this, and I'll give you an entire essay with citations and footnotes." But my hands kept shaking.

I couldn't pull the blade, not without a plan. Too much blood had already pooled beneath him.

All around us, the room had descended into chaos.

Shadow wolves attacked the guards and guests without pause, painting the polished stone red. Ember hacked at a yellow-eyed wolf, her blade slick. Veralt grabbed a snarling beast by the scruff and flung it into a guard. Thalen and Rhielle carved their way forward, steel clashing as they took down anything between them and us.

Colm threw the dead wolf aside and yanked Calla Lily to her feet. "Guards!" he bellowed. "End this now!"

Calla Lily's face twisted in terror. She screeched, "How did they get in?"

A red-eyed wolf and an orange-eyed wolf flanked the altar. I hesitated, questioning whether they were about to attack. They crouched low and snarled at the chaos, but not at me.

Wait. Were they *helping* me?

I didn't care. All that mattered was saving Vad. Except... "Ember!" I cried out.

She ripped her sword free from a wolf's corpse, eyes flicking to the two wolves flanking the altar before she sprinted to me. "What?"

"Briar," Vad breathed, his eyelids slipping. "You have to go. Get out of here while you still can."

"No." I cradled his face, my palm sliding to his muscular chest. "I'm not leaving you." I looked at my sister. "Can you heal him?" My voice wavered. "Maybe you have your magic from Earth."

Before Ember could answer, the orange-eyed wolf pivoted toward us, baring its teeth as its eyes turned yellow. As soon as it took one step toward us, the red-eyed wolf lunged sideways and slammed into it with a snarl, knocking it back. Protecting us. Was it just the yellow-eyed ones that had gone mad? The red-eyed wolves were keeping the yellow-eyed away from my friends too.

Ember pressed a hand over the one I held against Vad's

chest, her brows pinched in grief. "I tried healing Elara earlier. Nothing happened. I..." She looked at him, and her voice softened. "Hi, Vad."

Nothing was happening.

He blinked groggily, voice wet and fragile. "Your sister... Ember... do me a favor—take Briar and go—"

"I'd rather die than leave you." My throat burned.

Then something warm flickered in my chest. A spark of energy, near my heart like a coal that had waited too long to be set ablaze. My focus snapped to Ember.

Her breath caught, and her eyes lifted to mine, then dropped to where our hands were touching Vad.

I sucked in a breath as the sensation spread outward and curled through my ribs as if it had been there all along, buried under grief.

I looked at Vad again and gasped.

His bruised eye, the one nearly swollen shut, had started to open. The cuts across his cheek and neck were no longer leaking blood, and the wound down his jaw was knitting closed.

"Ember," I whispered, shaking. It was too good to be true, but it had to be. *Please, Fate, let it be true.* "He's healing!"

Her hand pressed harder against mine, and her fingertips touched Vad. "Something's changing—I can feel it."

A guard sprinted toward us with his spear raised.

No! We couldn't let him reach us. I tried to remove my hand so I could fight him off, but it wouldn't budge, like something was holding it there.

The red-eyed wolf homed in on the guard just as the man hit an invisible wall with a crash like shattering glass. Silver light flared. He flew backward and slammed into the far wall, then crumpled in a heap. The red-eyed wolf pounced on him.

The entire hall shook.

The marble floor groaned beneath us. Columns cracked

overhead. More dust and stone fragments fell from the ceiling in a choking cloud.

The warmth in my chest expanded, and a heavy droning sound filled my ears. It vibrated through my teeth and down my spine, the hum deeper than anything I had ever experienced.

Vad blinked again, dazed, staring at Ember and me. "Your eyes, they're glowing... both of you..."

I didn't know what was happening, but I didn't give a damn. All that mattered was that he was healing.

I glanced at Ember, noting her eyes were indeed glowing gold with hints of green. Warmth flooded me, building and building. The butterfly tattoos on my wrists fluttered, driving away the ache and the chill.

"Your magic is back," I breathed. "We can save him."

Warmth swelled until it felt like it would split me apart. Tears streamed down my cheeks.

"You're healing him! Your magic really is back!" A knot formed in my throat, tears still spilling from my eyes as I looked up at him. "I love you, Vad. You hold on and show me just how fine you are."

Then I wrapped my hand around the hilt of the dagger and ripped it free.

Chapter Twenty-Three

Vad jerked against the chains, and an agonized cry escaped his lips. Blood gushed from the wound, hot and slick. Ember thrust her other hand over the source.

I set the dagger aside and focused on the hand I'd kept on his chest underneath Ember's. The cuts were healing, the skin mending back into place. The heat inside me expanded and intensified. Then, all at once, golden light exploded outward like lightning crackling through my veins.

It poured from my chest and shot down my arms, scorching through my wrists with a burning, blinding force. The stone altar beneath us lit up.

The room shook harder. Then the heat in my wrists surged and whipped up my arms and down my spine from the tattoos and along the dark veins in my arms. I arched forward, then bowed backward with a shaking scream as agony tore through me.

White-hot fire burst between my shoulders and raced down my spine like something alive had just ripped its way out. A scream tore from my throat, and my hand fell from Vad's chest. I dropped to my knees beside the altar, panting. Breathing hurt, like the air itself was made of fire.

Golden light engulfed me, turning hotter and brighter. The shaking continued beneath me as a heavy buzzing sound started and grew so loud I thought my eardrums would burst. Something howled, seeming far away but also near at the same time.

I fought to open my eyes and reach out to Vad. I needed to feel him and know he was with me, but the weight of the energy blazing through me crushed me down.

Heat pooled at the base of my spine and erupted as if my spine had ripped in two. Fluttering pulses moved from my wrists up my arms and down my spine, flowing outward. My back muscles stretched, and flames engulfed me. Something was wrong. Maybe I had to take Vad's place in death, which I was perfectly fine with as long as he got to live.

Another wolf howl pierced my mind like a storm surge. Not distant this time. Not muted. My wolf's presence slammed into me full force, so familiar and yet different. She whimpered like she'd missed me as much as I'd missed her.

The pain finally receded, but the fire didn't leave me. It entwined deep inside me, threading through my veins like it belonged there, and it curled over me without moving and without hurting me. Silver streaks shimmered within the gold light still beaming around me, dancing over my skin. My fingertips tingled, and my ears were still ringing, but I could breathe again.

Metal clanged like chains falling free.

You've always been beautiful, but you're even more beautiful with wings. Vad's voice seeped into my consciousness, and the bond surged between us, making me feel whole once more.

But then one of the words he said repeated in my head.

Wings.

What was he talking about? I blinked and tried to look over my shoulder, but my vision swam with red, gold, and silver light. The buzzing in my ears dulled to a hum as my wolf settled within me, curling into place like she'd never left, her presence warm and steady.

A hand pressed against a strange part of me that I'd never felt before, and I jolted. Shock rippled through me as I moved unfamiliar muscles in my back. The red and gold fire drew away from my face.

And there was Vad.

He towered over me, shirtless, unchained, completely healed. His silver-gray eyes shimmered with something deeper than magic.

Taking my hand, he helped me to my feet. "How can you keep getting more and more perfect?"

At the sound of his voice, my heart cracked open.

"The same way you do," I whispered, the bond between us thrumming so intensely I could hardly stand. I barely knew what to think. How had I gotten wings? Was this a sign of the guardians' favor? Or had their convergence on us, and those prior encounters, all led to this activating my true fae magic?

"Guys," Ember said from behind Vad. "I'm thrilled to see you both doing well, but we're in the middle of a battle. Good news, our magic is back. Bad news, so is everyone else's."

Maniacal laughter came from outside the silver barrier from both Colm and Calla Lily. I'd recognize those horrible voices anywhere.

I watched as the two of them spread their wings and flew about the wolves. Colm's smoky gray leather wings had shades of red, blue, and green. But what really stood out was Calla Lily's. Her former pink leather wings were now dull pink, brick red, pale blue, and garbage green.

Colm removed two of the dark orbs from his jacket. "I brought your family's soulshard orbs with me to bash your skull in after ripping the dagger from your chest. But I only need one for that." Light reflected off his silver claw tips as he tossed one to Calla Lily. "In case you need to strengthen your powers again, my love."

Hot and cold spiraled within our link from both our rage and fear. The merlinite orb was given to him by Vad in exchange for my freedom. He must have located the other one while he'd taken over the palace.

What all can they do? I asked, though fearing the answer.

Given what he's doing with magic and how their wings are now different, nothing good. This is likely some abomination that comes from siphoning off the essence and magic of other people combined with his constant push to advance his skills, Vad replied with his shadows whirling around him.

"We've got to help them." Ember snatched up her sword.

My attention snapped to the chaos beyond our protective shield. Shadow wolves were tearing into guards, snarling and snapping. Fireballs streaked across the hall as magic returned like a tidal wave. A noblewoman levitated a guard into the air and slammed him into a column. Two others conjured lightning. It was a battlefield of color and blood.

Ember charged forward, and Vad and I started to follow, but the silver barrier flashed up. We were trapped.

Vad put his arms around me, scowling. "What in the scaffing void?"

I put my hand out. "We have to get out there!" My wolf howled in response. Not in fear, but in warning.

Ember sprinted back toward us, her expression tight with urgency. "Briar! Vad!" She slammed a fist against the barrier. The shield flared and hurled her backward in a blast wave. She collided with a wooden display shelf, sending severed heads to the ground with dull thuds. "It won't let me back in!"

The earth groaned.

Cracks split the marble floor in jagged lines, spiderwebbing outward from the altar. The wolves stopped attacking, ears flat, eyes wary. One by one, they backed away from the dais, tails low.

"Vad, what's happening?" I grabbed his arm, and the pulse of magic built under my skin. The silver shield around us brightened with every tremor. "Is this because of Colm?"

He couldn't answer because the roar that followed stole every word. It wasn't human. It wasn't animal. It was raw power and judgment, echoing from the deepest bones of the world.

The massive stag appeared at the entrance to the Ceremonial Hall in front of the double doors. Light radiated from its antlers, casting shadows across the room as it moved forward. The ground trembled beneath its hooves, which cracked the broken tile with each step.

The room hushed. Even the wolves bowed their heads.

The stag's eyes glowed ancient gold as they locked on mine.

My breath caught in my throat. Vad's arms tightened around me.

In the far-right corner, the giant shadow wolf emerged, its hulking form swirling like smoke made flesh. Crimson eyes met mine, and my own wolf surged forward in my mind.

From the left corner of the hall strode the bear. Each lumbering step shook the hall to its foundations. Its footprints left traces of grass before it faded, and it shook its heavy head.

A hissing sound came from behind us. The sea serpent slid down the wall, its blue scales glistening and its eyes burning like gems.

The eagle screeched above, the rustle of wings making me tip my head back. The air stirred as the massive golden eagle passed us. The crimson dragon appeared as well with a roar. The two circled us as the other four moved toward us with powerful intensity. A humming vibration built around us, one that moved through my core. The rubble and debris began to shake again.

The hairs on my neck and arms lifted. "They're here for us." My wolf shook her head and surged forward, barking and howling as if she had been waiting for this all along. She paced, urging me to shift.

Vad adjusted his grip on me, keeping me flush against him as the guardian beasts converged on us from all sides.

My dream, I linked to him. *This is just like my dream.*

Yeah? he linked back, his unease tightening our bond. *And how did your dream end? With us dying?*

Fear and excitement swept through me. *No! It was—*

The guardian beasts reached us in an explosion of light, color, and heat that burst in every direction like a shattered prism. The force knocked the breath from my lungs.

A strange, resonating pulse surged through my veins. The sound of it echoed in my bones. I blinked against the blinding glow, shielding my eyes.

When the light receded, the world looked sharper. Clearer. Reborn.

I slowly pulled back from Vad's embrace and stopped short.

The shadows of his wings had darkened dramatically, no longer wisps of ink but solid obsidian etched with silver veins, as if starlight had been forged directly into them. They moved with a life of their own, absorbing light instead of reflecting it.

"Vad..." I breathed.

He turned to me, his silver eyes burning bright, his gaze scanning every inch of me. Reverence softened his features as he lifted one hand to my shoulder and trailed his fingers to my wing.

"Briar." His eyes widened. "Your wings... they're beautiful." His voice cracked with wonder. "It's like... they became what they were always supposed to be."

A tingle ran along my feathers, and I looked over my

shoulder.

They weren't the faint glowing lines they'd been before. Now they were fully formed, shimmering with fire and shadow swirled together, like the wings of my butterfly tattoos.

A series of metallic clangs echoed through the hall as several gray-armored guards dropped their weapons. The sound rippled like a wave across the marble floor. A few guards fell to their knees. The guests cowered in the center of the room, arms raised in surrender, heads bowed low.

I looked up at Vad, the pulsing light between us casting him in an ethereal glow. Our bond thrummed, no longer fragile but alive and unbreakable.

To our left, Colm and Calla Lily hovered midair, their wings keeping them aloft. Both stared at the scene below, their expressions twisted in disbelief.

Ryker pack-linked to Ember and me. *We've dealt with the gas, and there weren't many guards down here. We took most of them out. But they were ready for us and set traps to keep us in here. The main door is shut, and the other passages are blocked due to the earthquake. We need someone to open the door from the other side.*

Ember's concern radiated through the pack link. She looked at me.

I motioned to the groom's door. *Go. We've got this taken care of here. Can you find your way?*

I'll trace my steps back to where we split off and then follow Ryker's scent. Ryker, you guys did go through the main entrance, right? Ember swept her hair back over her shoulder.

Yes. Thought we'd handled them all, too, but some of them were sneaky bastards, Ryker responded. *Be careful.*

Make sure you have your sword, I linked back to her. I stepped forward and found that the barrier that had kept us there briefly was no longer present. It had vanished with the guardians. *Contact me immediately if you need backup.*

"What are you doing?" Colm roared, his voice cracking with fury. "Pick up your weapons! That's an order!"

One of the soldiers near him stepped forward and removed his helmet, revealing a weathered face and piercing blue eyes. "You said this was Fate's will. That you were purging corruption," the guard called, his voice carrying across the suddenly still hall. "But Fate just spoke through the Guardian Beasts. They've blessed King Vad and Queen Briar. We all saw it. The stag even approached her before at King Vad's coronation. Now it has returned with the other guardians to show its favor. No such thing has happened with you or Calla Lily."

His words hung in the air like a spark over oil. Murmurs rippled through the remaining soldiers.

Colm's face twisted with rage. He shoved the merlinite orb into his robes, shot downward like a streak of shadow with his wings tight, and seized the man by the throat. With a violent thrust of his wings, he rocketed up and slammed the guard against a marble column.

His claws tore through flesh. Blood poured down the man's neck, soaking the dark-gray collar of his armor.

"It is not your place to question," Colm snarled. "Only to obey. And if you cannot obey, then you'll serve in other ways."

The man choked, struggling in Colm's grasp. "No... please—"

Colm ignored him. With his free hand, he drew the orb from his robe. Cracks webbed across its surface glowed with dark blue light. With a vicious sneer, he jammed it against the man's forehead.

The guard stiffened, and a guttural scream tore from his throat as his skin blistered and blackened.

"No!" Vad shouted. Shadows snapped from him like whips, lashing toward Colm—

Calla Lily threw up a barrier far smaller than the one the guardians had put over us. But even though it was small, it was efficient, catching Vad's shadow magic mid-strike. Vad's power recoiled, flickering out.

"Stop!" I yelled, scanning the debris for something—*anything*—I could use to break through the shield.

The orb sank deeper. Flesh hissed and bubbled. The man's eyes rolled back as a hole burned through his skull, the scent of scorched flesh drifting in the air. The guard's screams weakened as his body began to shrivel within his armor, his skin turning ashen.

Colm's wings darkened before my eyes, the smoky gray shifting to a slick, oily black threaded with pulsing crimson veins. His aura thickened, turning so dense it seemed to choke the air. Nausea twisted in my gut.

He flung the charred body aside, and it crumpled to the marble floor with a sickening *crunch*. He turned to Vad, a cruel smirk stretching across his narrow face. Smoke blades formed around him. "It used to take so long to siphon magic from others, but thanks to your little gift, it's so much easier now."

His gaze swept down to his guards. "Now then, insolent wretches, pick up your weapons and fight, or I'll give you a fate far worse. Fight well, and maybe I'll forgive this act of cowardice."

Several guards scrambled for their blades, desperation on their faces.

The wolves growled low and crouched.

"Don't do this, Colm," Vad warned, stepping in front of me and pushing me gently behind him. "Release them and surrender. You've lost their trust. Everyone sees you for the liar and fraud you are."

Calla Lily glided toward Colm and laughed. She laid a many-ringed hand on his shoulder and tilted her head mockingly. "There's nothing fraudulent about the pain we can deliver."

"If anyone should surrender," Colm purred, "it's you. I've just consumed another fae's full life force and magic, the entirety of his essence. Can you even begin to understand just how powerful that makes me right now?"

Without warning, he lifted a single clawed finger toward Calla Lily. She gave a barely perceptible nod, and I realized too late that she was dropping the barrier.

Colm clenched his fist.

A concussive blast erupted, the force slamming Vad backward into me.

I screamed as we crashed to the floor. My wings cushioned some of the impact, but pain lanced down my spine as benches toppled and the shockwave rattled the hall.

Colm and Calla Lily laughed, the sound echoing through the hall like a warning.

"Maybe I should offer you a chance to surrender again, but I no longer feel generous." Colm flew toward the bride's door, leering down at us. "Now, attack."

When no one moved, his eyes narrowed at the guards below. Many of them gripped their weapons, but they glanced between us and Colm again.

"I said, *attack*!"

Colm's guards stiffened, and then two dozen of them surged forward with weapons drawn, moving mechanically, eyes glassy, as if their bodies weren't entirely their own. Some charged with eagerness, others with visible reluctance, but none stopped.

Veralt swung a bench like a club, cracking it across the nearest attacker's helmeted head with a brutal crunch.

Thalen stepped forward, hands sweeping wide as glowing wind blades shimmered to life around him. "You really shouldn't bet against us," he shouted.

I shoved myself up, and pain rippled through my side. My wings flared wide, casting long shadows. "You fucking bastards, we'll end you once and for all." Magic pulsed hot in my veins.

Colm sneered. "Handle her, Calla Lily."

He slashed his hand through the air. A streak of gray light exploded from his palm, forming a magical smoke rope that wrapped around Vad and flung him like a rag doll across the chamber. He crashed into the double doors with a thunderous crack.

A jolt of pain seared through the bond.

"Vad!" I shoved myself up, my wings flaring out behind me.

Calla Lily dove toward me, her wings blazing with fire and her eyes full of bloodlust. "With pleasure," she snarled.

Flames danced between her fingers, and she hurled a fireball at me. I rolled aside, my back muscles shifting instinctively to move with the wings I didn't know how to control. The fire struck the marble behind me, charring it black.

I've got her, I linked to Vad. *You handle Colm.*

My wolf howled within me, no longer distant but vibrant and ready. Power surged through my veins, ready to break this bitch apart. I'd shift soon, but this fight needed to happen in my human form.

"I've been waiting for this," I growled, planting my feet and raising my blade.

If you need me— Vad started, but I cut him off. *I will, but don't worry. I'm fine.*

Annoyance flared through our bond. *Not funny, but I'm counting on your word.*

Calla Lily hurled another fireball at me, the heat blistering the air. I rolled aside, my wings flexing on instinct. They beat once, lifting me off the ground. The sensation was disorienting but exhilarating—my wings simply obeyed my thoughts.

I launched myself at Calla Lily, sword raised.

"Pathetic." She twisted in midair, easily dodging my swing.

Below us, Colm's soldiers fought the wolves and my friends. Vad's shadows boiled as he lashed out against Colm, and Colm struck back with smoke blades. Vad's hooked shadows pierced stone walls and pillars, but didn't fully strike Colm or land on him as he was too quick. Frustration flared through our bond, and I guessed that Colm was faster now.

Calla Lily's fire scorched past my cheek as I swerved in midair. The heat singed my skin, but I barely registered the pain. My new wings responded to my instincts faster than my thoughts.

"All you had to do was return to your little human life," Calla Lily spat, flames curling around her hands. "If you'd gone home to Earth and returned to your pathetic family, none of this would've happened."

I twisted and flew higher. "This *is* my home," I snarled. "And I'll burn before I let someone like you take it."

She sneered. "It could have been so simple. Prince Vad dying peacefully in his sleep. Elara too. Such a tragedy, but she was always such a weak, simpering little thing." She lifted her hands and sent out a broad blast of hot air.

It slammed into me like a freight train, sending me spiraling backward. My wings flailed, and I crashed against the groom's door wall, the impact jarring every bone in my body. My head snapped back, striking the stone.

I'm coming, Vad linked.

I slid to the floor, gasping. Stars burst across my vision. My limbs refused to obey my order to move, becoming dead weight, dragging me down.

"Fuck," I gasped. She was stronger than I'd thought. My wings hung limply behind me, muscles trembling. My wolf snarled, furious, pushing me to move. *Focus on your fight. I can take her.*

Above, Calla Lily hovered, smirking victoriously. "You see? You're nothing. You're already dead, Briar. You just haven't realized it yet."

I fought to get up, but she was already descending, her hands cupped together. Flames licked between her fingers, illuminating her face with an eerie glow.

"It can take hours to burn a body completely," she purred. "Consuming essence gives us strength—gifts beyond our kind. And fire..." She grinned. "Fire is my favorite. I love slow-roasting my enemies and watching them scream—"

Suddenly, the fire between her palms sputtered and shrank to half its size. The brilliant light in her wings dimmed, the flames that had been dancing along their edges flickering weakly.

She stared at her hands in shock. "What—? How is it used up already?" Snarling, she shot into the air above the crowd and snatched a young nobleman by the collar. He screamed, fire flickering from his fingertips in a feeble attempt to defend himself. She slammed his head against the wall with a sickening crack, then jammed the orb against his skull.

He convulsed violently. Magic fizzled and died on his skin as he shrieked, his body arching in agony.

I forced myself upright, my fingers fumbling for my fallen sword.

A concussive blast ripped through the hall, but this one was from Colm.

The shockwave sent rubble and bodies flying. A second blast followed, even stronger, tossing me backward and ripping chunks from the ceiling and hurling them across the chamber. Screams echoed off the walls.

Colm cackled as I slammed into the wall and cracked my

head. Blood streamed down my forehead and into my eyes, my ears ringing.

Vad linked to me, disoriented and in pain, just like me. *Briar, you're hurt?*

So are you; just stay focused on your own fight. I partially closed the bond so he couldn't feel me as intensely, and I focused on the bitch in front of me. I froze when I spotted Colm flying toward the bride's side of the dais.

Thalen was hunched on the staircase, clutching his bloodied head. Colm landed beside him and seized him by the front of his tunic. Colm slammed him back against the staircase and then struck him with the merlinite orb.

"Thalen!" I screamed. Pain lanced through my skull as I pushed to my feet, but I ignored it. Blood blurred my vision, hot and sticky, but I wiped it away and staggered forward. The floor lurched beneath me, and my stomach roiled.

I barreled toward them, looking for Vad. He was surrounded, but his magic and sword handled his attackers with ease.

Thalen was in more trouble.

Colm ground the orb against Thalen's forehead. His silver-white hair was soaked with blood, his face twisted in agony.

"Let him *go*!" I roared, my voice drowned out by the ringing in my ears.

Like a lightning bolt of fury, Myantha burst from behind a pillar, her face contorted with a feral rage I'd never seen in her. She leapt onto Colm's back and choked him with surprising force, one arm locked around his throat, the other tangled in his hair.

Colm stumbled, his grip on Thalen faltering. Before he could recover, Myantha bared her teeth and bit off his ear with savage precision. Blood spurted as she tore through cartilage and flesh.

His scream carried through the hall, high and piercing. He thrashed, trying to throw Myantha off, the merlinite orb slipping from his grasp and clattering down the steps.

Myantha spat out his ear, her face twisted in disgust as blood dripped from her lips. She leaned in and whispered something that made Colm freeze, his eyes widening in shock.

Seizing the opening, Thalen shoved free and kicked Colm square in the chest, his boot connecting with a satisfying thud. Colm staggered, flailing his arms as he tried to maintain his balance.

His face contorted in rage and agony. "You beastly little wench!" he shrieked, clutching the ragged, bleeding stump where his ear had been.

Then he threw himself backward into a wall hard, right against Myantha.

Her shout rent the air as she was crushed between his weight and the stone. Her arms fell limp.

I'd nearly reached the dais when something slammed into me from behind.

Calla Lily.

She stood on my back, her heel grinding into my neck like she meant to snap it.

"I'm freshly powered now, Briar," she cooed, voice dripping with malice. "The real question is, how creative do I want to get with making you suffer?" She pressed down harder, until pain flared sharp and hot as her heel bit into my skin.

Footsteps approached fast.

For a heartbeat, I thought it was Rhielle—but no. I looked up into Kaylen's icy eyes as she stopped beside us, hands perched on her hips and a smirk curling her lips.

Chapter Twenty-Four

"Oh, Calla Lily," Kaylen drawled. "This is it? Standing on her neck and giving some overdone villain monologue? How disappointingly predictable."

What in the hell was Kaylen doing?

She wrinkled her nose in mock disgust. "I still remember seeing you at the Ascension Hall. I thought, 'Who let that frizzed-out, fake-smiling, bland wench in?' I almost killed you the same way I did that purple-haired brat."

I groaned beneath Calla Lily's weight. Even with the shadow wolves, we were outnumbered at least five to one. The ringing in my ears dulled the chaos, but not the pain.

Calla Lily flicked her hair and sneered. "And what exactly is your point?"

A bloodcurdling scream came from Kaylen, and she sprang forward.

The moment the weight lifted, I rolled, lungs heaving, and lunged toward the dais, my fingers fumbling for the dagger that had been plunged into Vad's chest. My head spun, blood dripping down my face, blinding me.

Had Kaylen lost her mind?

A thunderclap cracked overhead, and lightning forked

down into the center of the chamber. Thalen shielded Myantha, pushing her toward the bride's door as three guards closed in. He parried their attacks with his wind daggers, spinning them in tight, efficient movements.

Veralt and Rhielle fought back-to-back on the east side of the hall, fending off Colm's soldiers. And Vad held the front line before the double entryway doors, battling Colm again, his shadows tearing through Colm's smoke like blades through fog.

I wiped blood from my eyes. If we could take out Colm and Calla Lily, the others would stop fighting. But with those cursed orbs, that was damn near impossible.

Calla Lily turned on Kaylen, fire blazing in her palms. "You wretched little creature!"

Kaylen sidestepped easily and summoned another air blade. "You lied to me, manipulated me, and cheated harder than I ever did. You don't deserve to be queen. If I could set your mangy ass on fire again, I would!"

"I'm fire resistant, *you're* not, you stupid cow!" Calla Lily shrieked. Flames erupted around Kaylen's feet.

Kaylen launched herself into the air like a damn comet, her magic swirling around her like an inferno. "If there's one thing you should've learned by now, it's that I'm a *petty* bitch. I could've lived with Fate choosing someone better, but to even think that some half-baked, mangy-fleshed, rat-blood of a person who thinks wearing fifteen different rings and six shades of pink is elegant could be queen?" She landed in a crouch, lips curling in a cold smile. "I'd rather die."

Baring her teeth, Calla Lily lunged, a venom-coated dagger flashing in her hand. "Then die."

Instead of dodging, Kaylen *slammed* herself into the blade, driving Calla Lily backward into the altar. She grabbed a fistful of golden curls and yanked hard.

Kaylen trembled, blood already soaking her side, but her

sneer stayed razor-sharp. "Only if you come with me." She jammed her hand into Calla Lily's pocket, yanked out the soulshard orb, and hurled it into the air.

Calla Lily's eyes went wide. She tried to shove Kaylen off, but Kaylen held on even when Calla Lily started twisting the blade in Kaylen's side.

My mouth dried, and I tried to get to Kaylen. After what she'd just done, even she didn't deserve a death like that.

The orb spun through the air until a massive wolf leapt up and snatched it mid-flight like a chew toy. It landed and padded away with its tail held high.

Blood bubbled from Kaylen's side, but she collapsed, smirking.

Hot rage exploded in my chest, and I lunged, grabbing Calla Lily by the hair and slamming her face-first into the altar Vad had been chained to.

She shrieked. "You bitch!" She writhed beneath me, but I pinned her down. "Let me go!"

"Kaylen and I didn't agree on much." I allowed every ounce of hate to drip into my words as I pressed the blade to her throat. "But I'll grant her final wish. This is for everyone you've hurt." A thin line of blood bloomed beneath the dagger's edge. "For every innocent you tortured. And *my* face will be the last thing you ever see."

"No!" Calla Lily shrieked, kicking and thrashing. Her nails raked down my shoulder, but I leaned in harder. "Colm! *Colm!* Help me!"

Across the Ceremonial Hall, Colm's attention snapped to us, and his face drained of color as his sneer vanished.

"Isn't this poetic, *Douchewaffle?*" I growled and then *slashed.*

The dagger tore across her throat. Her scream died in a wet gurgle as warm blood sprayed across my face.

Colm's roar shattered the air with primal fury. His face contorted with rage as he abandoned his fight with Vad and shot toward me like a missile, too rageful for words.

Vad's voice slammed into my mind. *Move right!*

I launched sideways, and Colm crashed into the altar behind me. Stone shattered beneath the impact, shards flying like shrapnel. I tumbled across the dais with my wings flaring to slow my momentum.

Colm had barely risen before Vad slammed into him. Shadows coiled around Colm like chains as Vad drove him back into the altar with bone-cracking force. The stone groaned and splintered again. Smoke blades lashed out, one slicing Vad's shoulder, another cutting a red line across his shoulder and cheek.

My wolf surged inside me. She did not ask; she *demanded.* The shift yanked at me with feral urgency, but instead of bone-snapping pain, the transformation poured through me like a flood. In a heartbeat, I was on four paws.

I shook out my fur, blinking in surprise. It shimmered silver in the firelight, my paws and tail edged in the same deep crimson as my wings.

Around me, every shadow wolf froze. One by one, they turned and locked their crimson eyes on me. Something inside me *clicked* like a door thrown open, and hundreds of new bonds flared to life.

The largest wolf, scarred and hulking, stepped forward and lowered its head in reverence. *What would you have us do, High Queen?*

High Queen? The title startled me, and I ignored it. There were too many other important things to be handled right now. I looked toward Vad, who was still locked in combat with Colm. Shadows and smoke continued to billow around them as they grappled on the altar.

Veralt and Rhielle were surrounded by a tighter circle of guards now, and Veralt's arm bled from a large gash. One of Rhielle's shadows pressed deep into the wound to serve as a working bandage and to keep him from bleeding as badly as she slashed and battled the guards coming after them. Several cuts on her arms and torso were bleeding, her gown shredded.

Thalen and Myantha were cornered under an overhang on the bride-side door, with Thalen sending wind blades and parrying with all his strength while Myantha levitated rocks and struck their attackers. But there were still too many of Colm's people.

Focus on Vad and my friends, and take down Colm's followers.

The shadow wolves howled and surged forward at my command, their crimson eyes blazing as they leapt into battle. They tore through Colm's guards, attacking the ones harming my friends and cornering the ones who dropped their weapons. The massive pack leader launched itself at three guards that were attacking Rhielle with spears, its jaws closing around one soldier's arm and dragging him backward.

A painful spasm shot through the mate bond. I spun back to Vad and Colm. Vad bled from the chest, blood arcing in a spray from Colm's smoke blades. Vad snarled in response, straining to reach the merlinite orb as Colm tried to press it against his forehead.

I shot forward, claws clicking across the marble. This asshole would learn the consequences of harming my mate! *I'm coming. Just get his hand over the edge of the altar.*

Vad twisted, his shadows boiling and dropping. Something in Colm's magic was draining or suppressing his power, but he gritted his teeth. One of his shadows hooked around Colm's hand as two other tendrils fought off the gray smoke blades and another nicked Colm on the cheek.

I leaped the last few feet as Vad shoved Colm's hand out. My jaws parted, and I lunged for Colm's outstretched fingers. My jaws clamped on the merlinite orb, and my teeth pierced his hand, tearing through flesh and bone. The sickening crunch was followed by a warm flood of blood that filled my mouth with its metallic tang. Three of his fingers came away in my jaws.

Colm's agonized scream pierced the Ceremonial Hall. The sound was almost inhuman, echoing off the marble walls as he clutched his mangled hand to his chest.

Vad didn't wait a heartbeat. With Colm distracted by pain, Vad surged forward, his shadows coiling around him like living weapons. He slammed Colm down on the altar, deepening the crack in the fractured stone.

I spat out the orb and fingers by the throne and spun around to see how else I could protect my mate.

Vad pressed his forearm against Colm's throat. If I could be human right now... Something exploded through me, and before I even realized it, I was back in human form. I looked down and gasped.

Instead of my bloodstained gray tunic and trousers, I wore an iridescent purple gown that shimmered with each movement, the fabric flowing around me like liquid starlight. My hands were clean of blood despite what I'd just done.

Bond-curdling hatred seared through me as Vad wrapped his shadows around Colm's throat. "You killed my father and my mother, and you would have killed my mate."

"Do you think I will beg for mercy? I will not," Colm growled, his face twisted in anger.

The dagger!

I searched for it and saw it glistening on the dais floor only a few feet away. *I've got the perfect end for him.*

Vad tensed, his gaze cutting to me. *What?*

This. I snatched it up, enjoying its weight in my palm, then turned to face Colm's remaining guards, who were standing frozen in shock with their weapons lowered, cowering from the wolves.

"Surrender now, and you may be shown mercy!" My voice rang through the halls. "Your false king is defeated. Drop your weapons!" *Wolves, spare anyone who surrenders.*

Several guards immediately dropped their swords, the clatter of metal against marble rippling across the hall. Others hesitated, looking between me and the pinned Colm, uncertainty written across their faces.

I rushed to Vad and pressed the dagger into his hand. His fingers closed around the hilt, our skin touching for just a moment, creating the buzz on contact between us again.

Strength and resolve flowed between us, and Vad linked, *Thank you, beloved.*

He adjusted his grip on the dagger, then looked down at Colm. A muscle worked in his jaw as Colm stared back at him, unrepentant and defiant. "Now it's full circle." Vad plunged the dagger into Colm's heart and then ripped it out.

Colm went limp as his blood spurted.

Vad remained leaning over him, his own chest rising and falling, the dagger gripped in his hand. Relief and rage warred down the bond.

I moved closer to my mate, reaching for him. "Vad?"

He stepped back from the altar, dropped the dagger, and pulled me into his arms, his wings folding around us both in a protective cocoon. I melted against him, feeling the heart that had only minutes before been beating so weakly thundering against mine. Our bond hummed with relief, grief, and triumph all tangled together.

"It's over," he whispered against my hair. "It's finally over, my beloved."

I nodded against his chest, unable to find words as my adrenaline began to ebb, leaving me shaky and drained and incredibly happy. My wings settled against my back, and I pressed closer to him, breathing in his scent. The scent of home.

Then my heart dropped. I wasn't sure if the others were safe. *Ember and Ryker, the fight is over up here. Are you two all right?*

We've freed all the prisoners, Ryker responded.

We're almost there. Quen and Elias are staying with the children, Ember replied, her connection warm and familiar in my mind. *The children and babies are safe.*

I hadn't been too concerned since I could feel both their links in my chest once more, but hearing them brought me relief.

In the main seating area, the remaining guards dropped to their knees and laid down their weapons with metallic clatters that echoed through the hall. The shadow wolves prowled around them, crimson eyes watchful but no longer threatening. Some of the guards pressed their foreheads to the cold marble floor, while others simply knelt with their heads bowed, awaiting judgment.

Rhielle was already binding Veralt's arm while he fussed over her. Thalen held Myantha close, his eyes closed.

Do you require anything else from us? The crimson-eyed wolf who had spoken to me before linked with me now.

No, you can return to your home or wherever you wish. But I would like to know two things. Why did one of yours bite me and why did so many attack us? I linked back, frowning slightly.

The wolf dropped its head. *When the Shadow magic was disrupted, some of our pack went mad. Those with the yellow eyes became as feral beasts, disconnected from the Guardian and unable to heed Fate's call. We knew that we had to get you to the Guardian as swiftly as possible, but without words, we were forced to use what we had. We did not intend to harm you, but some injuries resulted in our attempts.*

My frown deepened but I shook my head, unable to blame them. It did make sense now, but it had still hurt. *I see.*

If you have need of us ever again, you have only to send for us, and we will come, the wolf said.

The great doors at the far end of the Ceremonial Hall suddenly lurched open with a grinding creak. The wolves nearest the entrance tensed, hackles rising.

Wait, I linked to them.

Captain Finbar staggered through the doorway, blood matting his hair and streaking his face. His uniform hung in tatters, and he leaned heavily on his sword. Behind him, a small contingent of loyal guards followed, equally battered and grim-faced.

"Your Majesties," he called, his voice rough with exhaustion. "I apologize for the delay. We were ambushed at every access point." He winced as he tried to straighten, his hand pressing against his side. "The traitorous bastards knew our route. We had a mole, but we've dealt with him."

Vad turned toward Finbar, one arm still wrapped protectively around my waist. "Captain, your timing is..." He glanced at Colm's body, then back to Finbar with the ghost of a smile. "Well, we managed. I'm glad you dealt with the mole."

Thalen limped over to us, one arm draped around Myantha's shoulders for support. Despite the blood caked in his silver-white hair and the deep gash across his forehead, his amber eyes sparkled with their usual mischief. "Barely. But we're glad you could join us. As you can see, we've been having a wonderful celebration. It's almost time for dancing and refreshments. I hope you remembered to bring an appropriate gift for your host."

Captain Finbar laughed and dipped his head forward. "I

have brought him the blood of his enemies." He spread his arms and then bowed more formally.

"And it is a greatly appreciated gift." The fact that we were having a conversation like this in the midst of all the death and destruction was surreal. And yet, a smile spread across my face. "Take Colm's soldiers into custody. We will determine what is to be done with them on a case-by-case basis. The prisoners will be here soon."

Vad nodded and raised a brow. "As for the rest of you, please remain for a short time longer. The hospitality of the Shadow Kingdom will be at your service. It's time to put the venom Colm spewed to rest for good."

I picked up the merlinite orb and slid it into Vad's hand. The smile he gave me warmed me through.

My heart sank when I saw Kaylen's still form sprawled across the marble floor, her body bloody and motionless. Despite everything she'd done, in that final moment, she'd chosen to fight for us rather than save herself.

"She was a horrible person throughout the trials," I said softly. "But in the end, she did something amazing and selfless."

Vad squeezed my hand, his expression solemn. "Yes. And we will honor her sacrifice properly."

We just got here, Ember linked.

I wanted to cry with relief, and I nearly did when my sister and Ryker entered the Ceremonial Hall, followed by Silus, Vyraetos, Many-Greats, Siray, and the kings and queens and various council members. They limped in, most looking like ghosts.

But where was Elara?

Surprise filtered through our bond, and Vad's eyes widened. "Elara?"

Following his gaze, I realized that I hadn't recognized her. She looked the same, but exceedingly more vibrant. She walked down the center aisle toward us, hand resting in the crook of Silus's arm with all dignity, as if this were a grand ball. She looked completely healed, her dark hair full and rich, her dark-blue eyes bright and aware, her wings dark with shadows.

"It's not a glamour." She beamed. "When the magic came back, I became well in a moment."

Vad released me and pulled her into a hug. Refusing to be left behind, I wrapped my arms around both of them. Each snaked an arm around me in return. Tears pricked my eyes, the moment better than I'd ever dared to imagine. There was so much we needed to talk about as a family once we'd sorted things out with the royals and dealt with Colm's attempt to remake Nytheria.

It took several minutes to explain all that had happened and what Colm's actual purpose had been, as well as his lies. The guests whom Colm had brought to serve as his new court and legitimize his rule were horrified at the revelations, especially in learning of his cruelty to the royal families. The corruption of the Aureline Council troubled all. As they spoke, Ember moved through the crowd and healed the worst of the injuries. Each time, her shoulders drooped a little more, her magic drained by every encounter.

"Something must be done to prevent this from happening again," the Ignis Fae king said, arms folded over his broad chest and fingers drumming on his arm. His square jaw tensed. Despite his red silk robe being tattered and filthy, the crimson dragon woven into its fabric glistened in the light of the oil lamps. "Having oversight into the entirety of Nytheria is non-negotiable. Someone must look at the greater picture, including those who are outsiders as well. We cannot move forward with the Aureline Council as it was."

The Ignis Fae queen nodded in agreement as she fidgeted with her equally tattered dress. "I agree. This can never be permitted to happen again."

Siray placed a hand on her uncle's arm. "I agree, and I have a proposal to make.

"What I have seen in my time here is that the care of the realm must be managed. Some of us are far too concerned only with things that affect ourselves, and there are a great many evils that we can perform in the interests of those we love.

"We need rulers who can understand the larger matters and influence the kingdoms to settle disputes. In my time here, I have come to know Queen Briar, and while she and I did not always see eye to eye, she showed me that she is a person of compassion, wisdom, and discernment. King Vad has likewise proven himself.

"I propose that they be named High King and High Queen of Nytheria, to serve in place of the Aureline Council. They may work with the Aurelines and root out those whose intentions are bad. But in the end, they will serve as the final decision makers and protectors of our realm. I trust both of them in that. They could have taken advantage of this situation to claim that they should rule all our kingdoms, but instead, they risked their lives to protect us all."

The royals exchanged looks, their soft whispers rising as they spoke among themselves.

A chill ran down my spine. I didn't want a position like that. I wasn't worthy.

Vad's hand found mine, and he pushed his confidence into me. "We did what was right. The Shadow Kingdom has no desire to take the territory of any other kingdom, or to harm any of the royals or their people."

A man in midnight blue with the Terran insignia on his sleeves stepped forward. "Fate herself sent her guardians. They blessed the king and queen already, and then they defeated the man who intended to destroy our rulers and reshape our world in his image. All of our Guardian Beasts came to favor them. Surely that means something."

Vyraetos cleared his throat from his position next to Many-Greats. "I would certainly agree that it does. Fate is often difficult to interpret until acts are concluded and we look back on them. But it seems that the warning against the union of an Aureline Fae and a Shadow Fae was simply a statement of what would happen. Fate determined Briar's arrival and her success from the very beginning, and I do not think anything could keep these two apart."

Many-Greats tilted his head forward. "Though I am biased, I also agree that this is the best course. Fate has dealt with the rot within our realm and the corruption within our Council. As painful as it has been, it has also revealed our need for different leadership and better oversight."

A woman, whom I assumed to be the Aquen Queen, based on her blue robes and sea serpent markings, cleared her throat. "Perhaps. But the Shadow Kingdom must have its own king and queen. If these two become High King and High Queen, who will look to the needs of the Shadow Kingdom?"

Vad's wings flexed. His shadows curled around his legs and mine, and a faint smile tugged at his lips. Affection radiated through our bond. "When I thought there was the possibility that I could not be with Briar and that I might have to set aside the crown, I knew there was only one choice. She has served this kingdom faithfully from the first day she was able." He extended his hand then to Elara.

Elara's eyes widened. She pressed a hand over her heart. "I would be honored to serve." Her throat bobbed as her eyes misted. "But...I would not wish to rule alone."

"We could host another trial," a freed council member said.

Vad shot him a glare.

Elara ducked her head, a smile spreading over her face. "No. If we are doing things in a new fashion, then I would learn from the excellent example of my father and my brother, and not determine my partner by trial. There is no need for tests of strength and cunning if there is someone worthy who desires me, and I see no point in continuing that tradition." She cut her gaze to Silus.

Silus held her gaze for a moment. Then he dipped his head forward and moved to stand directly in front of us, his boots crunching on the rubble. His gaze homed in on me. "When Briar first arrived and I realized how swiftly and deeply Vad was coming to care for her, I advised him to choose anyone else. I feared she would bring about the downfall of our kingdom. Instead, Briar brought about its transformation and healing. I was wrong in every respect, and I cannot, in good conscience, ask for your permission to request Elara's hand in marriage until I address that matter. Can you forgive me?"

Vad's hand on my waist tightened, subtle and grounding. Pride rippled along our bond, thick with history and pain. *Do you accept this apology?* he asked me.

Yes. The warmth intensified, and even my wolf whined with happiness.

"Yes," Vad said, his voice low but steady. "Even when we have had our differences, I have always known that you are a man of conscience and conviction, and that you love my sister. You have our blessing."

Silus's throat bobbed. His jaw flexed once before he turned back to Elara.

Everyone had fallen silent, the air rich with tension. The Ignis Fae queen pressed her hand to her lips, already smiling. Rhielle folded her arms as she leaned back against Veralt.

His gaze fixed on Elara, Silus dropped to one knee and offered his hand, palm up. "I do not know the day I first realized

I loved you. You have been a part of my life for as long as I can remember, and you have made it better in every way. You said that you desire someone worthy, and that is not me. But I will strive to be worthy of you, and I will love you until my bones are dust and the stars fall from the sky. Will you do me the honor of giving me your hand in marriage?"

Elara's lips parted. Her hands lowered to her sides, fingers curling once before she reached out and touched his cheek. "Yes." Her voice broke. "Of course. And you *are* worthy. You've been worthy since the day I met you."

Silus rose and cupped one hand under her chin while his other moved to the small of her back. Her cheeks flushed as one of her hands slid to his shoulder and anchored her against him. He leaned in slowly and brushed his lips to hers, so gently at first it looked as if he'd barely touched her. Then she leaned in, her hands sliding up his shoulders and her fingers threading into his hair. Their kiss deepened, his hands bracing her tighter against him.

The Aquen King pressed a hand to his chest, his shoulders trembling as if holding back something too moving for words. One of the elder Shadow Council members, her arm wrapped in a bloodstained sling, nodded, her lips parting in a silent exhale. She whispered something to another surviving councilmember that sounded like, "I wondered how long it would take before he asked."

Thalen's applause broke the reverent silence, loud and enthusiastic as he whistled. "About time!" His eyes sparkled under the blood still matting his silver-white hair.

The crowd joined in, their applause echoing through the Ceremonial Hall. Myantha clapped beside Thalen, her smile radiant despite her exhaustion. Rhielle simply smiled while Veralt's deep laugh rumbled behind her. Even the royals and councilmembers added their approval, the sound swelling until it filled every corner of the vast space.

Silus pulled Elara closer, claiming her lips once more in a kiss that made her wings flutter. When Thalen whistled, Silus turned and shot him a glare, then hugged Elara closer as she blushed.

I leaned against Vad, warmth spreading through my chest as I watched them. His arm tightened around my waist, and his thumb traced slow circles along the inside of my wrist. Through our bond, his happiness and pride mingled with my own. His sister was finally getting the love she deserved after so much suffering, and with the man she had loved for so long, even if neither of them had admitted it until now.

As the applause died down, Vyraetos stepped into the fractured circle of stone in the middle of the hall, the tap of his boot against marble drawing every eye. "We have representatives from the leadership councils and the royals of all the kingdoms present in this room. As this is an unorthodox situation, we are pursuing an unorthodox solution. Your Majesties." He fixed us with his calm and weary gaze. "Are you willing to accept this charge?"

Vad linked to me. *Briar?*

Yes. With you, I can do anything, I linked back.

Ember linked to me as well, her green eyes shining with delight as she stood with Ryker. *I should've known that day when I tried to alpha-will you to leave our wolf pack for your own safety, and you stood up to me, that you were meant to be a far better alpha than I can ever be. I'm so proud of you, my sister, Queen Briar!*

My bottom lip trembled. *I love you.*

She smiled, placing a hand on her chest like her heart hurt. *I love you too, little sister.*

Vad's fingers twitched in mine before he dipped his head forward. "It would be our honor to serve."

"Good." Vyraetos turned his hands palm up to face the assembled royals and councilmembers. "And are we in agreement to crown a High King and High Queen to oversee the Realm of Nytheria?"

High Queen. That was what the shadow beast had called me.

Silence held.

Then the Aquen Queen stepped forward. "Yes. Let those who stood up for all of us and fought to save us and our children from death oversee the matters of our world."

One by one, the others answered in the positive. Some with brief nods, others with quiet words of assent. A few raised questions, asking for clarity. No one said no.

Many-Greats beamed at me.

Vad exhaled, low and steady.

My hand slipped into his.

Vyraetos gave one final nod.

And then, across the ruined hall, they knelt. Every last one of them—kings and queens, councilmembers, nobles, and guards. Some lowered their heads. Others rested their hands over their hearts. The sound of knees striking stone echoed like thunder.

And with one voice, they cried, "Long live High King Vad and High Queen Briar!"

Chapter Twenty-Five

BRIAR

A few days after accepting the role of High Queen, I stepped beneath an arched trellis, the vines brushing my shoulders like a welcome. My wings brushed the tops of my shoulders and then caressed Vad's as we followed the black and gold mosaic path through his mother's garden. After all the darkness, terror, and pain of the past weeks, this garden was a beautiful reprieve.

Thalen had asked us to meet him in the Night Butterfly Circle, and Vad and I had agreed we wanted a few minutes alone, for ourselves, before we met with him. The past days had been full. After ensuring that all who were injured were tended, we set about the process of repairing the palace and setting everything to right. Many had died. We held a memorial for those whose lives had been lost, with special honor given to our friends and even Kaylen for her sacrifice. Vad and I agreed that we would build a special garden for them as well, with a memorial to Velessa, Yuki, Thalira, Physician Morlo, and Aelir. If Vad and I had our way, these bridal trials would never be held again. We would have the formal funeral for King Merrick at the end of the moon cycle and lay him to rest with Queen Valora.

Moonlight spilled over the stone tiles, turning the white

flowers silver. The crimson water of the fountain shimmered like spilled wine. Every breath I drew carried the scent of crushed petals and wet earth, heavy with memory. Even without knowing the significance of it, I could sense that this was a sacred place. Vad and I needed to reclaim this sanctuary since the many days ahead of us would be full of so many decisions, compromises, and considerations. It was a small act of strength and defiance in the face of what had been lost, just like cleansing the two soulshard orbs when both were found and placed in their holder, and the crowns that were retrieved from the onyx cellar with my Shadow Queen sneakers.

Vad glanced at me and sighed. "My mother loved this place. She often weeded and tended the flowers herself. Especially her moon lilies. She loved the way their blossoms transformed with the moon. They open for only about an hour, around midnight."

"That's quite specific." I smiled. It amused me how flowers like dandelions could grow through concrete while others like roses could be such divas. "Do you like moon lilies too?"

"Only because they remind me of her." His smile curved a little higher, though there was sadness in it. "I've always been neutral about flowers."

The white marble fountain rose ahead of us, veined with time and hints of silver. Water spilled in slow, rippling streams from the fluted spouts, the sound soft and endless. The red shimmered like garnet in the moonlight, rich and strange and oddly peaceful, a sharp contrast to the black lilies, lavender peonies, and silver roses. Numerous paper-barked trees stretched toward the sky, their thin leaves rustling in the gentle wind.

His father had been murdered on the other side of the fountain. The blood had been scrubbed away, but the memory hung heavy over us. That day, our entire world had changed.

Vad stopped at the edge of the fountain and peered beyond

it to that place. His silhouette was tall and still, his wings slightly unfurled behind him. The breeze stirred the dark strands of his hair.

I frowned as I studied him. Something was bothering him, and it went deeper than the memory.

"The one thing that still troubles me is his final word. You're certain that it was lilies, and not lily?" He tilted his head as his shadows pooled around us. One tendril wrapped around my calf and stroked down to my ankle.

"I'm certain." I folded my arms as I studied him through the link. Something really had him unsettled.

"Hmm." He hummed. "Part of me wondered if perhaps he was saying it was Calla Lily. But it was Colm. And...well, her name was Calla Lily. Not lilies. That isn't the sort of mistake he would make even while dying."

Since it *had* been plural, maybe he'd meant the lilies themselves. I moved to the other side of the fountain and examined the lilies growing there. It might be foolish, but if there was a chance of discovering something, I'd take it. "Since he did say lilies, plural, we can try to figure out the meaning."

My fingers brushed one of the lilies. Its petals were slick but soft, its scent undercut with something similar to jasmine and so delicate I had missed it the last time I was here. My throat tightened. "These are so beautiful. Your mother took great pride in this place."

"She did," he said softly as he joined me.

I turned toward him, taking in the way the moonlight touched his face. It highlighted the faint shadows beneath his eyes and the tension still held in his jaw. He was whole, but not untouched. None of us were.

I focused back on the lilies because, even though we'd survived, something still haunted him.

I spotted something different... a small shape glinting

in the midst of a thick section of the flowers. "What's this?" Leaning forward, I picked it up. It was a fancy button.

Vad's brow creased as he studied the button. He took it from me, and sadness washed over him.

A memory hit me, one I'd forgotten. "Wait. Your father's coat was missing a button that night. I noticed one had been ripped off when I woke from being knocked out."

"It is from his formal surcoat." Vad tilted his head. "He never would've worn it if it had been missing one when he put it on. He'd have been embarrassed."

"Could he have yanked it from his jacket and tossed it into the lilies when he was facing down Colm?"

Vad flipped it over and looked at the back, which was made of leather. A simple three-lined mark marred it.

Confusion swirled between us as Vad's brows pinched together. "This is...it's not a message about his killer at all. This is the mark my family has used for generations to indicate love and the importance of family. For so many years, I was certain Father blamed me for Mother's death."

"It wasn't your fault, and I can't believe he blamed you. It was obvious to me that he loved you." I put a hand on his arm, wishing I could erase his pain.

His hand covered mine, his fingers warm against my skin. "He never said it in so many words. And the silence felt like condemnation. Especially when...I should have known. How could he not blame me? She was out there because of me."

I'd started to respond when Vyraetos appeared on the other side of the fountain. "Of course he didn't blame you, Your Majesty. He was quite protective of you both. He never wanted us to ever say anything that might make you believe your mother's death was your fault because it wasn't. I suppose he hoped that, if it wasn't discussed, you wouldn't feel that way. What you saw was a grief so deep and so profound that it was difficult for him to even function. But you should know he loved you and your sister dearly, even if he did not speak of it."

Vad's grip on my hand tightened, his shadows rippling outward like disturbed water. A wave of emotion coursed through our bond—shock, grief, and relief all tangled together in a knot so tight my chest ached in sympathy. "I—"

The soft strains of stringed instruments filtered through the paper-barked trees. Vad raised an eyebrow.

Vyraetos cleared his throat. "Well, I suspect that is the reason young Thalen has invited us here."

"Who all did he invite?" I asked. What was he up to?

"A fair number of us, I'd guess," Rhielle said from behind me.

I glanced over my shoulder in time to see Rhielle and Veralt walking toward us with Quen, Elias, and Myantha. Quen wore a grin that suggested she knew something I didn't, and Elias looked quietly pleased, while Myantha just studied everything with calm curiosity.

"What exactly is Thalen planning?" I glanced back at Vad.

He shook his head, but I caught the faintest hint of amusement threading through our bond. "With Thalen, it could be anything from a full theatrical production to a simple gathering. He has a flair for the dramatic."

"That might be an understatement," Rhielle said.

Veralt chuckled, his voice a low rumble. He patted her hand, the height difference between them making the tender gesture all the more striking. "You love dramatics."

She clicked her tongue at him. "I suppose that might explain why I love you." Reaching up, she lifted onto her tiptoes and adjusted his eye patch.

The Night Butterfly Circle had been set up with small tables bearing delicate pastries and fresh fruit, as well as trifle, crystal glasses of dark wine, and a variety of small treats and sugar cubes. A string quartet played on one side by a couple of the slender trees.

Silus and Elara were already there, sitting at one of the small tables with Many-Greats, Ember, and Ryker, chatting. When we arrived, they smiled at us. Ember waved us over. "Your friend insisted that we be here. Apparently, you being my family makes us his family too...or something like that."

Thalen appeared from behind one of the larger trees, his silver curls catching the moonlight as he swept forward with his arms wide. He wore a shiny silver robe that was embroidered with all the Guardian Beasts, neatly pressed, fitted trousers, and black leather boots. "There you are! I was beginning to think you'd gotten lost in romantic contemplation."

"We were investigating," Vad said dryly, though warmth pulsed through our bond.

"Investigating, brooding, same thing with you. The only reason you do less of it now is you have someone far better to focus on." Thalen winked at me and clapped his hands together. "Right then. I know we've all been through absolute hell these past few weeks. Murder accusations, betrayals, battles, near-death experiences... You know, the usual royal court entertainment."

Quen snorted. "You have a twisted sense of humor, as usual." Elias pulled a chair out for her, and she sat, then patted the cushion next to hers. Myantha sat on the other side, directly in the center where a name card had been placed indicating it was hers.

"Which is why you adore me." Thalen grinned at her before his expression softened. "But truly, I thought we could all use a moment to simply breathe. And to remember that, when it comes to dramatic declarations, I am, in fact, the actual winner. No one can outdo me, even if some decided to propose in the Ceremonial Hall.

Silus raised an eyebrow mid-sip and lowered his goblet. "Are you telling me you're doing this to try to show me up?"

"Oh, not trying. I'm succeeding." Thalen lifted a hand. "One of my goals in life is to show you and Vad up. Don't think it makes one bit of difference to me that you're both kings now, or will be after the formalities are concluded. You see, Fate granted me all the charm and grace, but did not make me a king because she knew it would be too devastating for others to handle. But I am grateful to you both for providing the necessary challenge to encourage me to improve my game. Now then. Let's get started."

Myantha watched him with wide eyes as Quen leaned in and whispered something to her. She shook her head in response but didn't look away from Thalen. Quen's smile went crooked.

He placed two fingers in his mouth and whistled three high notes and one lower one. The string quartet began a gentle song, rich with emotion and yet soft enough not to overpower conversation. A gentle rustling and *clip-clops* sounded from the path we'd taken here.

I leaned to the side, wondering what the hell he was up to. My eyes widened when I saw a unicorn foal trot forward, holding a small bouquet of flowers wrapped in pink silk in its mouth.

Myantha beamed as it approached.

I covered my mouth, my heart swelling. How had Thalen managed this?

Vad shook his head, a smile tugging at his lips. The unicorn foal dropped the bouquet in Myantha's lap. She picked it up and looked at Thalen with questioning eyes.

Bowing, Thalen gestured to her. "You can open it, my darling."

Myantha's fingers trembled as she unwrapped the pink

silk. The fabric fell away to reveal a small cluster of white moon lilies. Nestled among them, catching the moonlight like captured starfire, was a ring.

The musicians swelled into a fuller, more dramatic melody as Thalen moved forward and dropped to one knee in front of her chair. His amber eyes gleamed with mischief and genuine affection both.

"Myantha." His voice carried over the garden with theatrical precision.

She squirmed as he spoke, her cheeks reddening.

"From the moment I met you, I knew you were extraordinary. You, who hate being the center of attention, prefer quiet corners, wear comfortable clothes, and enjoy honest conversation over pageantry. Who saw through every bit of charm I threw your way and made me work for every single smile. You made me realize what I wanted in my own life and what I needed if I was ever to have any hope of happiness. And I wanted to know if you—"

"Yes!" Myantha launched herself forward and wrapped her arms around him.

I pressed a hand to my mouth, trying not to laugh too loudly as Thalen toppled backward slightly from the force of her embrace. He caught himself on the table, and the garden erupted in laughter.

"Ah!" Thalen caught his balance and gently but firmly placed her back in her seat. His expression was mock-stern, though his eyes danced with delight. "Absolutely not. No jumping to the end just because you know the right answer. I've prepared an entire speech, and you will sit there and listen to every word of it. I've been working on this for hours. Do you know how many drafts I went through? Seventeen. Seventeen drafts! And I promise you, this is the best and the shortest one."

Myantha covered her face with her hands, shaking her

head. Quen openly cackled beside Elias, who looked thoroughly entertained.

Rhielle patted Myantha on the shoulder. "Let him say his piece, hon."

"Thank you." Thalen cleared his throat dramatically and resumed his position on one knee. "Now then. Where was I? Ah yes. I wanted to know if you would like to...spend more time with me." His eyes flashed with delight as she scrunched her face at him. She lifted one eyebrow as if asking whether that was all he was asking her.

His face split with a crooked grin. "Because I want to spend all the time in the world with you." His voice softened then. "I fell for you faster than I knew was possible. You are so shy and quiet, and I know you just want to disappear. I can't imagine wanting that, but what I do know is that, if you need someone to shield you or hide you from the world, I want to be that person. And if you want to go on adventures, I want to go with you. I never knew someone so gentle and so sweet and especially so quiet could burrow so deep into my heart, but you did. I want to marry you. I want to build a life with you. I want to wake up beside you every morning and fall asleep holding you every night. I want to hear your laugh and know that I'm the one who brought it out. I want to be the person you trust with all your secrets, all your fears, all your dreams. I want to be with someone who is willing to risk her life for mine, lil' ear biter." He reached up and took the ring from among the moon lilies, holding it up so it caught the light. "So, Myantha, I am formally asking...will you marry me?"

Myantha practically glowed. "Yes." Her voice trembled, and tears slid down her face. She then leaned forward and twined her arms around his neck once more. He stood, lifting her into his arms and kissing her fiercely.

The garden erupted in cheers and applause. I found myself

clapping along with everyone else, my heart full. Through our bond, I felt Vad's quiet contentment mixing with my own joy. His hand found mine, our fingers intertwining.

Thalen finally set Myantha down, though he kept one arm around her waist as he slipped the ring onto her finger. She studied it with wide eyes, then buried her face against his shoulder as if trying to hide from all the attention. He laughed and pressed a kiss to the top of her head. "Thank you all for coming to join us in celebration tonight. There is plenty of food and drink. Let's make tonight one we'll always remember."

I clapped again.

We joked and laughed and ate well into the night, taking turns petting the unicorn foal while the string musicians played in the background. Eventually, Many-Greats, Ryker, Ember, Vad, and I were the only ones left at the round table.

Ember took a sip of her wine while Ryker twiddled his glass's stem between his fingers.

"All right, you two." Ember pointed at Vad and me. "Now that the show is over, do you think you could slip away to one of those portals and come back to our home for a bit? We'd love to have you over to share some special baking time and a particular tasty treat from a super special family recipe."

My heart warmed, thinking about the red velvet hazelnut cake Ember had created that had become the family's legacy.

"And the rest of the pack would love to see Briar and meet you, Vad," Ryker added.

"I can't wait." The thought of going home and seeing the other pack members made me miss them even more.

Vad smiled, his posture relaxed. He squeezed my hand. "It would be my honor. I've been looking forward to meeting Briar's family." He cut his eyes then to Many-Greats. "But in light of all that has happened, I do hope you understand we don't want any surprise visitors, especially at night."

"Yes!" I pointed at Many-Greats with a mock serious look. "No showing up in our bedrooms, *ever.* You can knock on the door from the outside like everyone else."

Ryker sighed heavily. "Is he still doing that?"

Many-Greats lifted his chin with the sort of severe icy sternness that only an ancient fae could muster, but even so, the faintest twinkle of amusement danced in his eyes. "I go where I am needed and where I choose. None will ever control me."

We all laughed at that, but then Ember stood. "Well, let's get going while we can. I know you two have a lot to do, being High King and High Queen."

I stood as well and held my hand out to Vad. "It's true."

He drew me closer and brushed his lips against mine. "There will never be a shortage of things to do when I am with you."

I smiled against his mouth, warmth flooding through me. Even after everything—the accusations, the trials, the bloodshed—we had found our way here. To this moment of peace and promise. Together. And together, we would face whatever new challenges came our way.

Also by Jen L. Grey

Of Fae and Wolf Trilogy
Bonded to the Fallen Shadow King
Claimed by Shadow and Blood
Forged by Heart and Claws

Rejected Fate Trilogy
Betrayed Mate

Fated To Darkness
The King of Frost and Shadows
The Court of Thorns and Wings
The Kingdom of Flames and Ash

The Forbidden Mate Trilogy
Wolf Mate
Wolf Bitten
Wolf Touched

Standalone Romantasy
Of Shadows and Fae

Twisted Fate Trilogy
Destined Mate
Eclipsed Heart
Chosen Destiny

The Marked Dragon Prince Trilogy
Ruthless Mate
Marked Dragon
Hidden Fate

Shadow City: Silver Wolf Trilogy
Broken Mate
Rising Darkness
Silver Moon

Shadow City: Royal Vampire Trilogy
Cursed Mate
Shadow Bitten
Demon Blood

Shadow City: Demon Wolf Trilogy
Ruined Mate
Shattered Curse
Fated Souls

Shadow City: Dark Angel Trilogy
Fallen Mate
Demon Marked
Dark Prince
Fatal Secrets

Shadow City: Silver Mate
Shattered Wolf
Fated Hearts
Ruthless Moon

The Wolf Born Trilogy
Hidden Mate
Blood Secrets
Awakened Magic

The Hidden King Trilogy
Dragon Mate
Dragon Heir
Dragon Queen

The Marked Wolf Trilogy
Moon Kissed
Chosen Wolf
Broken Curse

Wolf Moon Academy Trilogy
Shadow Mate
Blood Legacy
Rising Fate

The Royal Heir Trilogy
Wolves' Queen
Wolf Unleashed
Wolf's Claim

Bloodshed Academy Trilogy
Year One
Year Two
Year Three

The Half-Breed Prison Duology
(Same World As Bloodshed Academy)
Hunted
Cursed

The Artifact Reaper Series
Reaper: The Beginning
Reaper of Earth
Reaper of Wings
Reaper of Flames
Reaper of Water

Stones of Amaria (Shared World)
Kingdom of Storms
Kingdom of Shadows
Kingdom of Ruins
Kingdom of Fire

The Pearson Prophecy
Dawning Ascent
Enlightened Ascent
Reigning Ascent

Stand Alones
Death's Angel
Rising Alpha

ABOUT THE AUTHOR

Jen L. Grey is an *USA Today* Bestselling Author of romantasy and paranormal romance. In her stories, you'll find angsty fated mate stories with tons of action.

Jen lives in Tennessee with her husband, two daughters, and three Australian Shepherds. When she isn't writing, you'll find her with a nitro cold brew in hand while chauffeuring her children around town or watching television.

Learn more at: jenlgrey.com

ANYA

PAGEANDVINE.COM